MW00353271

CAPRI

DIEM

CAPRI DIEM CAPRI DIEM CAPRI DIEM CAPRI DIEM CAPRI DIEM

CAPRI DIEM

LOVE AND DEATH ON CAPRI

A NOVEL

Cecilia Storhaug

CAPRI DIEM CAPRI DIEM CAPRI DIEM CAPRI DIEM CAPRI DIEM

ILLUSTRATIONS BY
UGO DI MARTINO

AN ARTIST FROM THE ISLAND OF CAPRI

UGO di MARTINO has graciously granted Cecilia Storhaug
permission to use images of his art in her books and on her website
WWW.CAPRIDIEM.NET

The art is showcased in color in the eBook version of CAPRI DIEM
on devices supporting color, and in the limited print color edition.

ACKNOWLEDGMENTS

My deepest gratitude to the people and habitués of Capri, who inspired me in my quest to write a novel that captures the mystery, passion, and beauty of this mythical island.

I wish to give credit to Professor Renato Esposito, the writer and historian from Capri who coined the phrase "Capri Diem," a play on the Latin aphorism *Carpe Diem*, which became the inspiration for the title and theme of my book.

By chance, I read an old newspaper article about Capri, "The Visible Life (Det synlige liv)," written by the Norwegian journalist, writer, and Knight of the Italian Republic, Jan E. Hansen. His article inspired me to create a story of love and death set on Capri. Thank you, Jan!

I am humbled by the generosity of my friend Ugo di Martino, a notable artist from the Island of Capri, who has graciously given me permission to display images of his art on my website www.capridiem.net and in my book *CAPRI DIEM*.

Connecting with my excellent editor Kendra Langeteig was a stroke of luck! Thank you, Kendra, for your patient guidance, enthusiastic encouragement, and insightful critiques!

A special thanks to my brother Erik Storhaug for providing the perfect photo for the book cover and to my friend Pietro Belli for designing the front cover graphics.

I could not have written this book without the support of my brilliant husband Gabriel, a million thanks for his loving encouragement throughout the process of becoming a published writer.

And last, but most important, a heartfelt thanks to Liv, my wonderful mother, who marveled at my desire to become a writer, who always believed in me, and whose support I feel even though she's no longer in this world.

COVER PHOTO
BY ERIK STORHAUG
The eastern cliffs of Capri.

With love and gratitude,
I dedicate this book to

The Island and People of Capri

Live every day
as if it was the last day of your life,
with joy in search of beauty.
When you find beauty,
you desire to be part of it forever

Map of The Island of Capri

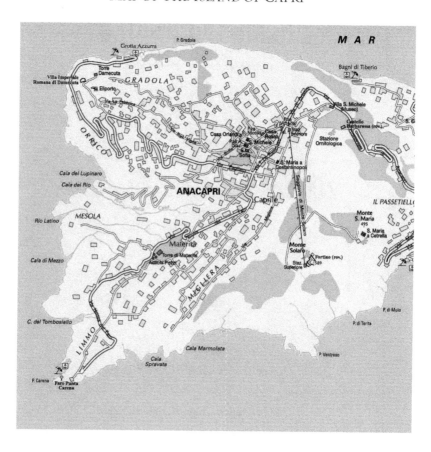

MAP OF THE ISLAND OF CAPRI

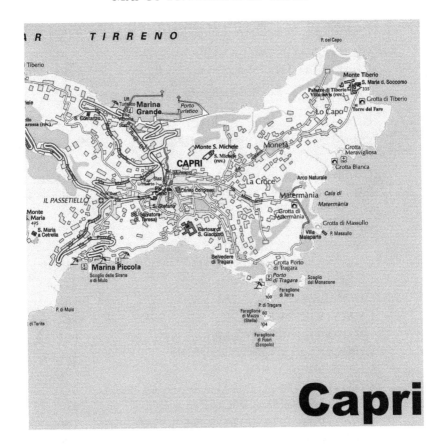

CONTENTS

CHAPTER 1 - PIAZZETTA

T he white coffin carried on the shoulders of six strong men made a dramatic entrance into the Piazzetta, the diminutive central square of the island of Capri. From where Max was sitting, among a handful of other locals in the last row of tables at café Piccolo Bar, he had an excellent view of the procession.

The Piazzetta was tranquil at that hour. Morning sun cast pale light on the tables at the four scarcely populated cafés, whose giant umbrellas were still in storage from the previous night. Towering above the square was the ancient stone-gray campanile with its distinctive blue, yellow, and white clock. The hands of the dial showed twenty minutes to ten.

The funeral procession entered the Piazzetta from Via Vittorio Emanuele and came to a halt at the foot of the broad stairway to the Catholic church dedicated to Santo Stefano. Many of the Caprese, the local islanders, crisscrossing the square on their way to work or running errands, stopped to watch. The owner of the newspaper stall beneath the bell tower looked up; as did his dog. Scattered among the tables of the cafés were a dozen or so summer residents who stared in surprise at the unusual spectacle.

Max had just sat down for a much-needed double espresso after attending a funeral service at the Evangelical Church on Via Tragara, a ten-minute walk away. The sight of the coffin filled him with a nagging feeling of shame. Less than thirty minutes ago, he had reluctantly knelt beside that coffin while placing a white camellia on the deceased woman's chest.

Swallowing the last drops of his bittersweet espresso, he spotted his old friend Mario gesturing to join him in the middle of the square. Mario worked as a waiter at Gran Caffè R. Vuotto across from Piccolo Bar.

"*Buongiorno,* Max. What are you still doing on Capri?" he asked. "Wasn't it just yesterday you told me your vacation was over and you were leaving by the first hydrofoil this morning to get back to San Francisco?"

"True, but the strangest thing happened. Last night my boss called me with an assignment to investigate an insurance claim here on Capri. Can you believe it? The woman lying in that coffin is Camilla Kallberg; she took out a two-million-dollar life insurance policy with my company."

2

Mario raised his eyebrows. "Really! So that's why you're still on the island. Did you know Camilla?" he asked.

Max shook his head.

Enrico, a waiter at Piccolo Bar, walked up to them when he overheard Mario's question.

"Morning guys, I knew Camilla quite well," he said, looking at the halted procession. "The rumor is she killed herself, but I can't fathom it. No way would Camilla have done such a ghastly thing."

"I've known her since she bought her home here, it must be close to twenty years ago," Mario said. "I agree, she wouldn't have killed herself. It can't possibly be murder, it must have been an accident."

Enrico pushed his bright blue CliC reading glasses on top of his balding head. "Murder, here on Capri? That's highly doubtful."

"Look, there's Micheli!" Mario exclaimed. "He's talking to the pallbearers. You may not have met him, Max. Captain Michele Arcuzzi is new on the island. He came over from Naples a couple of years ago; he's now the chief assistant to the commissioner of police on Capri."

Max scrutinized the policeman his friend affectionately called Micheli. Captain Arcuzzi was in his early forties; he was short and stocky with a clean-shaven, olive complexion. He was immaculately dressed: the grayish-blue pants, decorated with a crimson sideband, were stiffly creased; a polished Beretta pistol in a holster hung from his white belt. Despite the summer heat, he wore his blue police uniform jacket, with gold buttons and red-striped *baffi* (insignia) on the epaulets. Constant hand movements accompanied whatever he was telling the pallbearers. Finished gesturing, he joined the three men standing in the Piazzetta.

"Damn hearse had a motor problem," the captain said. "Wouldn't you know it would happen today." He threw his arms up in the air. "It should be here in a few minutes. It will take the coffin to the cemetery."

"Good morning, Captain," Mario said. "So how is the investigation into the death of Camilla going? We were just talking about it. Ah, this is our friend Max De Angelis; he left the island for a career abroad." Mario made the introductions and explained

3

Max's assignment on Capri as an insurance investigator regarding Camilla Kallberg's life insurance policy.

"Really!" the captain raised his eyebrows. "The woman took out a two-million-dollar life insurance policy. And who is the lucky beneficiary?"

"The sister, Katarina Kallberg," Max said.

"Aha, the sister—that's interesting." The captain's eyes lingered on the attractive blonde woman standing directly behind the coffin.

Max debated whether to tell the captain he had attended the funeral service that morning, with the purpose of investigating the insurance claim, but decided against it. The service had put him in a bad mood and the sight of the coffin on the shoulders of the pallbearers in the Piazzetta didn't help. Five years ago, together with three other men, he had carried his father in a wood coffin from the church of Santo Stefano down the stairs to the square. The coffin on his shoulder had felt weightless during the long sorrowful walk to the Catholic cemetery. One year later, he had borne the coffin of his mother with an even heavier heart.

Max noticed that the stairs from the Piazzetta up to the church square were no longer flanked by red geraniums as they had been three years ago, when he and his former wife Tara were last on Capri. Now they were lined with bushy non-blooming plants.

"What do you make of it, Micheli?" Enrico asked. "It was a horrible accident, right, falling to her death down those treacherous cliffs? What the heck was Camilla doing up there anyway? You guys know there is only one reason anyone goes up to Belvedere delle Noci at that hour of the night. And she wasn't exactly a spring chicken, was she?"

Captain Arcuzzi grinned. "You may have a point. These days not even the spring chickens make it up to Belvedere delle Noci for a bit of fooling around. They prefer to stick around the Piazzetta, parading back and forth on their ridiculous high heels all night long." He shook his head. "They can barely make it up and down Via Vittorio Emanuele, for goodness sake. Or they hang out at the nightclubs. Frankly, I don't think young people even *do* it anymore, not like when we were young. Heck, we would climb to the moon, if necessary, for *that*."

4

"If you don't mind me asking, Captain," Max said, "I have a few questions. Did you say the woman fell to her death at Belvedere delle Noci? How did the police find out about it? When did it happen? And do you agree with Enrico that it was an accident?"

"You don't want to know much, do you De Angelis?" the captain said sarcastically. "Well, it is a rather unusual situation. Mind you, this is all off the record, nothing is official yet. At this moment, we have found nothing to indicate it was an accident, but it is a possibility.

Max listened intently as Captain Arcuzzi told them the story.

Camilla Kallberg was last seen at Le Grottelle restaurant on the evening of August 15th but was not reported missing until the morning of the 17th by her sister Katarina. Two police officers with their trained dogs were sent over from Naples; the dogs tracked the woman's scent from the restaurant to the Belvedere delle Noci, the most remote of three lookout points above Via Dentecala.

Together with the police officers and their dogs, the captain walked back from the belvedere to Le Grottelle restaurant, where they waited for a small fire truck designed for the narrow footpaths of Capri to arrive with two firefighters. Then they all walked down four hundred steps to reach Via Pizzolungo, the winding footpath on the eastern coast of the island. From there, they made their way upwards through the jungle-like thicket; but not even the dogs were able to find the body. When the dogs started barking at the foot of a high cliff, the captain called the Italian State Police headquarters, and they sent their latest toy, an AgustaWestland AW139 twin-engine helicopter. The helicopter crew spotted the corpse lying in a crevice, and the body was airlifted to the morgue at Cardarelli Hospital in Naples. That same evening, Captain Arcuzzi accompanied Camilla Kallberg's sister to Naples to identify the body.

The next day, the captain went back to Belvedere delle Noci and spent hours examining every millimeter of it, but he could not find a single clue. The railing was undamaged, and there were no broken branches or bits of clothing or personal belongings of the victim; nor did any eye witnesses come forward.

After an external forensic autopsy, including the use of ultraviolet lights and radiographic imaging, nothing unusual was revealed, and the body had been released and returned to Capri.

The captain finished telling his story and then again raised his arms into the air: "When the hell is the hearse going to get here?"

The speed of the local police investigation impressed Max. He counted in his head: four days ago, the body was found; six days ago, Camilla Kallberg fell to her death. Willingly or unwillingly? he wondered.

"Those two in front must be her relatives," Enrico said. "What do you think, Mario?"

Max realized Enrico was referring to two tall Nordic-looking men carrying the front of the coffin on their shoulders. Both wore blue blazers, white shirts without a tie, and sports shoes—not exactly Italian attire for a funeral, Max thought.

"Yeah, they're Camilla's cousins, and that's Misha carrying the rear end, the Ukrainian gardener who worked for Camilla," Mario said.

"Lorenzo was a friend of hers?" the captain asked. He was referring to the man who stood shoulder to shoulder with Misha at the rear of the casket.

"I've no idea if Lorenzo and Camilla were friends," Enrico said, "but I imagine so. I know Camilla hired him when she wanted to go somewhere by sea."

The captain nodded. "By the way, have you seen Lorenzo's brand-new boat? It's a Gozzo 7.50 Open Cruiser from the Aprea brothers of Sorrento."

"Camilla did have good taste in boats, eh, Micheli?" Enrico teased.

Max knew Lorenzo from his soccer-playing days, and he had recognized him in church at the funeral service. Why would the captain mention Lorenzo's motorboat? Was he envious? The 7.50 was expensive and out of reach for someone on a policeman's salary. Lorenzo was a well-known boatman from Marina Grande, the main port of Capri. Before he started his own business taking tourists on private boat trips, he had worked for the Gruppo

Motoscafisti, the cooperative that takes groups by motor launch to see La Grotta Azzurra, the famous Blue Grotto.

Max thought Lorenzo looked uncomfortable in his tight black jacket; he had never seen him in a suit. The muscular arm holding up the coffin threatened to burst the seams at any moment. Lorenzo was big. Everything about him was big—not fat, just big; his hands were twice the size of any man's, and his thighs were as thick as Capri columns. His mahogany-tanned face looked glum; his green eyes were cool as a glacier.

"I guess Sergio and Peppino were given the morning off. Can you guys believe they're wearing matching purple ties?" Mario was referring to the two coffin bearers in the middle.

Max knew them. They were working as waiters at Da Luigi, the restaurant down on the beach by the Faraglioni rocks. Both were immaculately dressed in traditional black suits, white shirts, and shiny black dress shoes; only the bright lilac color of their ties was unusual.

"I venture to guess that the waiters wore lilac ties at the Faraglioni evening parties Camilla liked to frequent," Enrico said with a grin, proud of his theory.

"You always think you know everything, don´t you Enrì," said Mario.

"What I know for sure is that Camilla would never have killed herself," Enrico insisted, shaking his head. "Impossible."

Captain Arcuzzi shrugged his shoulders. "*Boh,*" he said (a local expression that could mean just about anything). "You know how unpredictable women can be. I'm not saying she did kill herself, but well, she might have had her reasons. This Kallberg woman was a foreigner, you know, a Scandinavian, and she was a widow, so it is possible that—"

The loud clanging of the bell in the campanile interrupted the captain's speculations.

A black vehicle drove into the square and backed up parallel to the campanile while the bell tolled ten times. It was a short limo, half the width of a regular hearse, designed for the pedestrian paths of Capri. Everyone in the Piazzetta watched as the six men eased the coffin into the back of the narrow vehicle. Many of the faces in the procession lining up behind the hearse were familiar to Max; some were locals, others were Neapolitans, the *habitué*s or *i regolari* as they were called, most of whom owned second homes on the island.

"Well, De Angelis," the captain said as the bells fell silent. "May I presume you will pay a visit to my boss, the chief commissioner of police?"

"*Ma certamente.* I will present myself to the commissioner this afternoon," Max said, bowing his head slightly.

"*Ciao ragazzi*, gotta' go, duty calls." The captain saluted, his hand touching the visor of the stiff blue police cap. "Ah, by the way, De Angelis, does the insurance have a nonpayment clause in the case of suicide?"

"*Certamente*," Max nodded.

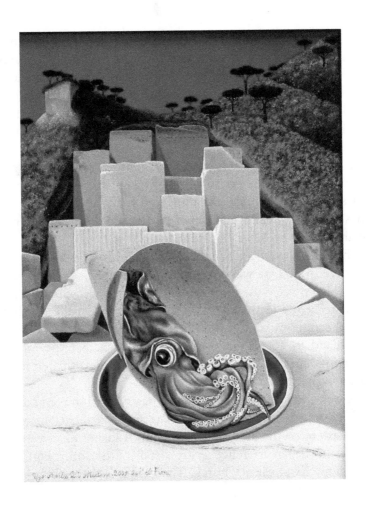

CHAPTER 2 - A PROPHETIC DREAM

SATURDAY, AUGUST 21

Max returned to his table in the last row of Piccolo Bar. Enrico brought him another espresso and a *cornetto integrale*, the café´s popular horn-shaped pastry. He was still feeling strangely unsettled after having attended the funeral service of Camilla Kallberg that morning.

Much about the service at the little Evangelical Church had puzzled him. It certainly had been odd—more than odd; he searched for the right word. Surreal? Yes, that was it. Everything had felt surreal from the moment he walked up the front steps and entered the building until he was back outside, half dazed. He had cleverly avoided the funeral procession by taking the back streets to the Piazzetta.

Had the woman in the white casket jumped to her death? Max wondered. Camilla Kallberg's stunningly prophetic dream recounted by her sister at the service had unnerved him; he shuddered in the warm sunlight, touching his *curniciello*, the amulet hanging from a chain around his neck.

With great reluctance, Max had removed his wedding ring when the divorce from Tara was final; but he refused to stop wearing her wedding day present to him, a platinum necklace with a pendant made of red coral in the shape of a little horn. On the day before their civil ceremony on Capri, Tara had gone to Torre del Greco on the mainland to acquire it. She promised Max that the red coral would bring him luck. Since that day, Max had never taken it off— not even in the shower.

Max was about to take a bite of the pastry when he felt a sudden wave of nausea; he pushed away his plate and leaned back in the cane chair, unaware of the sounds around him. Closing his eyes against the light, he began to relive every detail of the morning funeral service in the Evangelical Church. There must be something—some clue, he insisted to himself.

◆ ◆ ◆

The alluring sound of a lone flute drifted through the open door as Max ascended the church steps. He recognized the piece at once; it was Claude Debussy's "*Syrinx*," composed for Gabriel Mourey's play *Psyché*. The last time he had listened to it was with Tara, who loved the myth that inspired the melody. In Greek mythology, Pan was the god of the wild who fell in love with Syrinx, a lovely wood nymph who turned herself into a water reed to hide from him in the river. Unknowingly, Pan plucked the water reeds to make a pipe to entice her with a tune—and sadly killed his beloved nymph. Pan named his musical instrument "Syrinx" in her memory and was seldom seen without it afterwards.

Hearing this tragic song again, so unexpectedly, renewed the pain in Max's heart.

He entered the church quietly and slid into a wooden pew in the last row. With a crowd of around forty people, the little church was almost full. Max recognized the flute player standing in front of the church beside the altar and blowing into a carved bamboo flute. The long-haired man, clad in a white tunic and loose pants, was a well-known musician from the island. Odd music for a funeral, Max thought, as the haunting melody surged into an impassioned climax and then slowly died away. In the silence that followed, he felt even more miserable than when the flutist was playing; pressure built up in his chest as if he were about to cry. No tears came.

Silver vases filled with white camellias lined the steps to the chancel. The sweet scent of the flowers reminded Max of something; it angered him that he couldn't recall what it was. Camilla Kallberg's white open coffin stood in front of the altar. Max wasn't familiar with Scandinavian funeral customs, but he thought it must be rare to see an open casket in any church these days. He had never seen a white one used for an adult; on Capri, white coffins were reserved for children. He wasn't particularly surprised, as foreigners did all kinds of things that locals would never do.

In all his years growing up on Capri, he had never had the occasion to enter the Evangelical Church, the only non-Catholic house of worship on the island. In contrast to the Catholic churches of his childhood, there were no paintings or statues. The simple interior walls were painted a warm, buttery yellow, and the marble floor pattern was a geometric white, gray, and black. On the arch above the nave was an inscription in black letters; it bothered Max that his German wasn't good enough to translate the words.

Max fixed his eyes on the simple wooden crucifix sitting on the white marble altar. As a child, he had disliked this symbol of his religion. He had found the cross to be rigid and not at all beautiful. How could anything that stood for suffering and death be beautiful? he had reasoned. Max had long since grown indifferent to religion;

now he felt irritated at the sight of the cross, and he swore silently under his breath.

A chaplain appeared at the side door and walked over to the wooden lectern. He seemed a jovial fellow. Speaking Italian, he explained that he had been sent over from the Evangelic-Lutheran parish in Naples and apologized for not knowing the deceased. Max was thankful that the pastor's sermon was much shorter than the ones given at his parents' funerals.

Then a woman in the front row arose from her seat and gracefully walked up the three steps to stand beside the coffin. She turned to face the audience. "I'm Katarina, Camilla's sister," she said softly.

Max was taken with Katarina's natural, unassuming manner. Her blonde curls fell freely to her shoulders, framing a beautiful face. A cream-colored cardigan over a matching dress hugged the slender contours of her body. She took a deep breath, smiled slightly, and proceeded to speak. Max wondered if it was customary in Scandinavian culture for family members to give a memorial speech. He was impressed by how skillfully she managed to alternate between the English and Italian languages, speaking first in English, then in Italian. Her Italian was good with a melodic Scandinavian accent; her English appeared to be the so-called Oxford English he was familiar with from the years he had worked for UGI, United Global Insurance, in London before being transferred to the United States.

Max learned from Katarina's speech that Camilla, who was born and raised in Norway, had been a seasonal resident of Capri for nineteen years; she had divided her time between Oslo, San Francisco, and Capri. Five years earlier, she had lost her beloved husband.

Katarina paused for a moment, overcome with emotion; she stood in silence, looking down at her sister in the coffin by her side. Then she apologized to the Italian speakers, explaining that she would prefer to continue in English without translating.

"We are here in this lovely church because it was my sister's wish," Katarina said, wiping her eyes with the crumpled handkerchief she held in her hand. "Camilla chose this special place for her memorial because it has been an integral part of the international culture of Capri for over a century."

Max was impressed that Katarina pronounced the name of his island correctly as KAH-pree, not like most English speakers, who pronounced it as ka-PREE.

Katarina's soft voice grew stronger. "This is a beautiful place to honor the memory of Camilla. Look around you at the Mediterranean light reflected through the stained-glass windows. These Art Deco windows were donated by Queen Victoria of Sweden, who was the crown princess of Sweden and Norway for twenty-four years, until 1905, when Norway became an independent state. And as some of you know, Queen Victoria maintained a residence here on Capri for many years."

"All of this was planned by my sister, every detail—because Camilla had a dream—" Katarina paused and looked intently at her sister.

"Because—" She choked up and turned her back to the audience.

Katarina raised her face to the morning light streaming through the colorful arched windows above the altar. A moment of silence passed, then she turned and quietly scanned the faces of the audience.

Katarina's sorrowful eyes suddenly focused directly on Max. He got the uncomfortable sensation that she could see straight into his suffering soul and shifted his position on the wooden bench. Did she suspect he had no business being there? That he had never even met her deceased sister?

"It was because of my sister's unusual dream—" Katarina paused again. Max leaned forward, straining to hear her next words. "Because of Camilla's dream you were invited here to delight in the exquisite flowers around you that bear her name—and to listen to the beautiful flute music played by her favorite musician on Capri."

Max sighed with relief when Katarina turned her eyes away from him and looked down at her sister.

Standing up taller and raising her chin, Katarina continued. "Eight days ago, I arrived on Capri from Norway to visit my sister; it was on Friday, August the 13th. On that very first night, a night of a spectacular full moon, Camilla told me about a strange dream she'd

13

had a few weeks ago. It concerned another Camilla, the mythical character in Virgil's *Aeneid*"

Katarina picked up a sheet of paper from the lectern and began to read:

"Camilla's namesake—the Amazon warrior Princess Camilla—charges forward on her horse, her bow pressed against her soft, naked breast and her sharpened arrow aimed high. The virgin Amazon princess is recklessly pursuing the splendid Trojan spoils of the priest Chloreus. Momentarily distracted by her enemy's glorious gear, she is felled by Arrun's spear—and Camilla falls dying to the earth."

Katarina paused and looked up at the audience, wiping tears from her eyes. "My sister told me that when she awoke from the dream, she was horror-stricken—because the face of the Amazon warrior princess lying dead on the ground—was her very own face; it was as if she was looking into a mirror."

Katarina's voice broke and her mouth quivered as she spoke the last words. After wiping her eyes with the handkerchief, she continued: "The night when I arrived on Capri and Camilla told me about her dream, she recited a few lines from Virgil's poem, *"The Aeneid."*

> *She sank to earth undone,*
> *her cold eyes closed in death,*
> *and from her cheeks, the roses fled.*   (Book 11, line 847)

The silence in the church was palpable, as if the audience hardly dared to breathe.

Katarina paused a moment to regain her composure and then talked about her sister's love of life and beauty and her passion for Capri and its people.

Two tall men with curly blond hair got up from the front pew and joined Katarina; she introduced her cousins Leif and Kristian who presented a moving speech together about the joy of growing up with Camilla.

Afterward, Katarina collected an armful of white camellias from a vase and invited the guests to come up and give their last farewells to Camilla by placing a camellia in her coffin. To Max's surprise,

14

everyone accepted the invitation and a line formed in the center aisle. Max realized he would look conspicuous in the tiny church if he remained seated; he got to his feet and was the last person to join the line. A few of the guests ahead of him leaned over and kissed Camilla on the cheek.

The flutist started playing another piece by Debussy, *"Prelude to the Afternoon of a Faun."*

It was Max's turn.

Katarina's unusual eyes—they were almost the color of jade, he thought—blinked back the tears as she handed him a flower and looked searchingly into his eyes. Max sensed that Katarina was wondering just who he was. Had she guessed he was an impostor? Perhaps she had mistaken his own private suffering for grief over her deceased sister.

Taking the flower by the stem, he kneeled beside the coffin to place the camellia on the dead woman's chest. She was beautiful, he thought. Then the sweet fragrance from the many flowers strewn across her long, white gown wafted to his nostrils, nauseating him. Suddenly, he felt dizzy and Camilla's face blurred and faded into Tara's on their wedding day, wearing a crown of camellias in her hair. He lowered his head towards the ashen countenance and kissed her lips. Realizing his mistake, he all but ran out of the church and hurried down the steps.

◆ ◆ ◆

"Max, Max, are you all right?"

Max opened his eyes to see the worried face of his friend Enrico looking at him. He sat up straight in his chair, amazed at how far he had drifted away while reliving the weird events of the morning funeral service. The shock of kissing the dead woman's cold lips in the coffin was still alive in him.

"I see you haven't touched your cornetto, and the espresso has gotten cold; shall I bring you a fresh one?" Enrico asked.

"Yes, please bring me another *doppio*, Enrì, and a glass of water, would you?"

15

Thankfully, the bout of nausea that had overcome Max earlier, on recalling the details of the morning service, had subsided and he was suddenly hungry. He alternated between nibbling on the pastry and dunking it in the hot double espresso that Enrico brought him, while pondering the question foremost in his mind. Was it likely that Camilla had committed suicide?

In Max's professional experience as an insurance fraud investigator, he had never come across anyone who had killed themselves because of a dream. Capri was known as "The Island of Dreams," but he had always imagined those dreams to be about passionate love—not death.

Something else was still puzzling him. The name of the deceased woman seemed strangely familiar: *Camilla Kallberg*. Where had he heard it before? Then it came to him. Of course. The woman who had been a good friend of his father, living in a villa on Castiglione, the castle hill. His father had worked as a custodian there, the last eleven years of his life. Despite his father's wish to introduce him to Camilla, somehow he had never found the opportunity.

How strange, he thought, to find himself on the island of Capri investigating the death of this woman who had been a friend of his father. How strange that Camilla, like himself, had lived on Capri and in San Francisco, and had lost her beloved husband five years ago, the same year he lost his father. What a coincidence to have been assigned to a case that would lead him to Camilla. It was typical that his father had ended up getting his own way. Then he remembered what Tara used to say: There are no coincidences. Better not think about Tara, Max cautioned himself; it only depressed him.

His thoughts returned to the investigation. If, and that was of course a very big if, the beautiful woman in the white casket had not committed suicide, and Captain Arcuzzi had stated that an accident was unlikely, then could she have been murdered?

Speculation was useless in his field of work, as Max well knew; he shifted his attention to the unexpected telephone call from his boss in San Francisco the previous night.

CHAPTER 3 - AN ASSIGNMENT

FRIDAY, AUGUST 20

I t was the blue hour, as Max liked to call it, so named for the intense luminescent color of the sky; the perfect time for an aperitif in the Piazzetta before dinner. Enjoying the privilege of sitting alone at a table in the last row of Gran Caffè with a glass of single malt scotch, Max watched the frenetic activity in *a' chiazz* (as the square is called in dialect) with detached amusement. He had claimed a table early to wait for his childhood friend Raffaele, due to arrive from San Diego; it was their only chance to meet as Max was scheduled to return to San Francisco the next morning.

Every fifteen minutes, the funicular, the cable railway that runs between Marina Grande and the town of Capri, brought dozens of people to the square. Some of the crowd went at once to their lodgings; some stopped in the Piazzetta to meet friends for a drink; others were locals returning home from a day of work on the island or the mainland.

Most of the weekend visitors were from Naples. Many of them were standing on the volcanic stone pavement in the middle of the Piazzetta talking with friends, while keeping an eye on the café tables, oblivious to the people struggling to navigate around them. You couldn't blame them, since the tables of the four cafés in the minuscule square, only twenty-four by twenty-eight meters,[1] were fully occupied. They watched eagerly for any little movement indicating a bill was about to be paid, and as soon as a table was vacated, they pounced on it.

Porters driving electric trolleys carrying luggage and supplies weaved skillfully through the milling crowds. No regular vehicles were permitted to enter the Piazzetta, the gateway to the town of Capri and the surrounding areas. From here all the roads were pedestrian. Even bicycles were not allowed but had to be walked. On occasion, a small emergency vehicle specifically built for Capri's narrow pedestrian walkways would approach the square with its siren blaring, and the waiters would rush to move the chairs and tables blocking its way.

With the constant change of scene from late morning to the wee hours of the next morning, the Piazzetta was like the stage of a theater. It was especially so in July and August, and, barring

---

[1] 79 feet by 92 feet

inclement weather, even more so on weekends from June through September.

The locals tolerated the crowds, since most of the Caprese made their living from serving the summer residents and visitors. A busy time on Capri was a good time for Capri; with luck, it would be busy until the end of September when the islanders could reclaim the island for themselves.

The bell in the campanile started tolling. Out of habit, Max counted . . . seven bells; it was seven o'clock. He was eager to see Raffaele again; they hadn't seen each other since they were both on Capri three years ago.

The Gran Caffè R. Vuotto where Max was sitting had an aura of glamour from its glory days as a venue for celebrities. Raffaele Vuotto, nicknamed *Lattaiolo* (dairyman), bought buildings in the Piazzetta in 1936 and established his café with outside tables. Before that time, the square was used mainly as a fish and fruit market. Vuotto's coffee bar was a tremendous success, becoming the place to see and be seen for international celebrities and the jet set crowd.

Many of the locals preferred, like Max, to sit in the last row at one of the four cafés in the square, leaving the front-row tables for the tourists and newcomers. The *habitués*, the regular returning visitors, and people with second homes on Capri, often choose a table somewhere in the middle. Everyone has their habit and, given the choice, would usually go to the same table at the same café at about the same hour. Out of politeness to his local friends, Max frequented all the cafes.

Watching the ever-changing drama in the Piazzetta had always been one of Max's favorite pastimes, although he would be hard-pressed to admit it to his family. His sisters and their families who lived on the island would rarely sit down in the Piazzetta, and as far as he knew, his parents had not sat at any of the cafés in their entire lives.

For Max, the pleasure of sitting in the square enjoying *la dolce vita di far niente* (the sweet life of doing nothing) was mixed with apprehension that day. The prospect of leaving the island the next morning to return to his humdrum life in America had put him in a melancholy mood. Soon he would have to put up with the demands of a grumpy boss and competitive colleagues. He would have to return to his lonely existence in an expensive apartment without family or friends nearby—worst of all, was having to face the reality of a life without Tara. And he missed Principessa, their beautiful cat, whom Tara had kept after the divorce, since he travelled too much to look after her.

It was the first time that Max dreaded leaving Capri to return to his life in the States. After all these years since he had emigrated to the U.S., a question surfaced in his mind. Who was he? He was Italian, of course—a Caprese, first and foremost. But now that he was divorced, and his parents were no longer alive, he had no place to call home, either on the island or in San Francisco. He felt like he belonged nowhere. It hadn't been easy coming back to Capri without Tara; that was why he hadn't been back since their divorce three years ago. Naturally, his friends and family had asked him about the divorce, since he and Tara had seemed so happy together. But Max was unwilling to talk about it.

Max sipped the last of his scotch, debating whether to refresh his drink or wait until Raffaele showed up. The scotch had done little to improve his mood. The yellow two-story building on the north side of the Piazzetta caught his eye; this was the town hall where he and Tara had been married. Looking up at the sky, as if for an answer, Max saw hundreds of seagulls circling in the air and riding the currents, a phenomenon he had never seen from the square. He wondered what it meant.

The pearl-white dome of Santo Stefano glowed like alabaster against the cobalt-blue sky; the sight lifted his spirits.

Once the cathedral of Capri, this splendid baroque church dedicated to Saint Stephen was situated on top of a broad stairway on the southern side of the Piazzetta. It was built sideways to the square, thereby showing off its magnificent profile. The church had been a prominent part of Max's life while growing up. Every Sunday morning, after Max had polished his best shoes, his mother would slick back his dark unruly hair and hand him a starched white shirt. The whole family would walk to mass together to the sound of clanging bells. The church, *a' chiesa,* as they called it, was built on the site of a Benedictine convent. The twelfth-century campanile and the town hall, *Il Municipio,* were the only traces left of the convent.

"Massimì, Massimì!" At the sound of Raffaele shouting his name above the din of the square, Max cheered up; suddenly he felt like a boy again. Elegant and smooth, as always, Raffaele navigated his way over to Max's table, with a big smile on his face.

Massimì was the name his mother had called Max, and his childhood friends still used it affectionately. On his birth certificate, it said, "Massimiliano," the name of his paternal grandfather, a name used only by his teachers. His father had called him Max, and so had his companions, unless they used his nickname—*Falconcì,* Little Falcon.

"*Benvenuto a casa* (Welcome home), Raffi. If you had arrived any later, I would be waving to you from the plane on my way back to San Francisco," Max joked, knowing Raffaele preferred to be called by his American nickname.

Raffi carefully placed his professional-looking camera on the table and settled into the cushioned cane armchair opposite Max. Grinning from ear to ear, he took off his sunglasses and polished them. Max thought his childhood friend looked good, despite the long trip and the jet lag. Raffi was tall and broad shouldered, and daily runs on the beach in Southern California had kept him in great shape. The combination of pale freckled skin, a perfect Roman nose, cropped curly, light-brown hair—and most important, excellent manners, gave him an aristocratic air. He was quite popular with women but had so far managed to remain single. In their younger and wilder days, the two friends would play the shameful game of competing for the attention of a beautiful woman, usually a foreigner. Eleven years ago, when he was twenty-seven, Raffi had immigrated with his siblings and parents to the United States, and the two school friends had kept in touch.

Mario, the always impeccably groomed waiter at Gran Caffè, approached their table. "Welcome back, great to see you again," he said with a warm smile, shaking hands with Raffi. "What are you guys up to tonight? Sure, you don't want to work here in my place? I could do with a day off," he joked.

When he learned that Max was leaving the next day for San Francisco and Raffi had just arrived from San Diego, he said, "Nah, one day off will not do. I'll take a month off in California and stay at your places, and you guys can divide my job between you; otherwise, you wouldn't be able to handle it."

Mario had just brought Raffi a glass of scotch, and a second round for Max, when Max´s cell phone rang; it was his boss at UGI. Bob was calling from his office on the twelfth floor of a brand-new office building in San Francisco. Max imagined him with his feet propped up on his desk, sitting in front of the floor-to-ceiling windows with a fabulous view of the Bay Bridge, an office Max secretly hoped to take over one day, as Bob was nearing retirement. Max covered the other ear with his hand to block out the noise from the square.

"Maxi boy, I know you're supposed to leave Italy tomorrow, but something has come up—just minutes ago, actually. You know our computer system, any news at all regarding any of our clients and we're automatically warned. What's that noise, Max? Are you in a nightclub?"

Bob didn't wait for an answer before he continued. "Here it is, pay attention. The policyholder is a widowed female, forty-four, the name is Camilla Kallberg, a Norwegian citizen, U.S. legal resident, with a home in San Francisco, and one on Capri. She has been found dead on Capri, can you believe it? She died the night of the fifteenth but wasn't found until the seventeenth, off some cliff somewhere. The funeral is tomorrow. Six months ago, Camilla Kallberg took out a life insurance policy at our San Francisco office for two million dollars. Her sister, Katarina Kallberg, is the sole beneficiary. The policy has a clause specifying nonpayment in the case of suicide within two years."

Bob paused. Max could hear his heavy breathing over the phone. Bob's heart was not happy about Bob's ever-increasing waistline. Max knew that drinking ten diet drinks a day wouldn't exactly help, but he never had the guts to give Bob advice.

"Here's what I want you to do, Max." Bob had managed to catch his breath and his voice boomed even louder. Max adjusted the sound level on his cell phone.

"Stay on Capri and find out everything you can about this woman and her death. From over here it smells like suicide, but you'll have to do the research. Just in case the determination of the cause of death is disputed, we'll likely need the unequivocal death analysis. Gather as much background on the case as possible—and I mean, right away. You'll respect the local law officers, of course, but get all the information you can, any way you can. You know your job, you know how it all works. And you know the place and the lingo better than anyone. I'm counting on you to get the police to reach the right verdict. Nobody on Capri wants a homicide, do they, let alone smack in the middle of the summer tourist season."

"I'm pretty sure nobody here wants a murder on the island, you're right about that Bob." Max finally got in a word.

"Then I can count on you. Two million dollars are on the line. The office is e-mailing you all we got on the case as we speak. I'll rely on you to take care of this as fast as possible, so you can get your butt back here to San Francisco. We need you; we're swamped."

The line went dead; Bob had hung up.

"What was that about?" Raffi looked up from the zoom lens of his camera; he had been taking pictures of the clock on the campanile. The sapphire-blue evening sky made a stunning background for the large square clock at the top of the bell tower. An iconic symbol of Capri, the clock is adorned with Roman numerals and 144 polychrome majolica tiles in black, yellow, and peacock blue.

"Looks like I won't be leaving Capri for a few days. My boss just assigned me to a case right here on the island, would you believe it?" Max's face flushed with excitement as he told Raffi all about the assignment—well almost all. He'd left out the part about his boss's wish—or had it been a demand? —for a particular outcome of the case.

After toasting to Max's lucky break, they parted ways. Raffi went to sleep off his jet lag at his aunt's place, where he usually stayed now that his family no longer had any property on the island. Raffi's father had lost the family fortune through a bad investment. Max headed for Hotel Gatto Bianco to look for his friend Antonio, one of the owners of the hotel, to see if they had a room available.

Max was in luck; the hotel had just received a cancellation for the luxurious Kennedy suite, so named for Jacqueline Kennedy, who frequented Gatto Bianco. Antonio gave him a good price—good, that is, for a suite at the renowned hotel. What the heck, Max thought, his office would cover the expenses; after all, it wasn't easy to get a decent hotel room, let alone any hotel room, on Capri in August.

Max was glad he wouldn't have to sleep on the couch at his sister Mona's any longer. He walked over to her home, just up the road from the square, to pick up his luggage, and returned directly to the hotel.

After checking e-mail on his laptop and doing some research on the case, he left the hotel and slipped past his sister's home on Via Posterula; a road named for the small gates set into the fifteenth-century walls enclosing the houses along the road in the southern part of town. He soon found himself in front of the counter at his favorite *pizzeria*.

Silvio, the *pizzaiolo*, was expertly sliding the long handle of *la pala di pizza* into the wood-fired oven. When he turned and saw Max, he came to give him a hug. Max had grown up just around the corner, and although Silvio was much older, they were like brothers. They chatted heartily about old times, while Silvio rolled out the pizza dough until it was as thin as he knew Max liked it, and then spread on a base of fresh tomato sauce and topped it with pieces of mozzarella made from buffalo milk, and local cherry tomatoes. After it had been properly rotated a few times in the fiery hot oven until it was done, Silvio sprinkled pungent basil leaves on top of the golden-crusted pizza; it was true perfection.

Balancing the familiar pizza box with one hand, while holding a bottle of red wine in the other, it occurred to Max to ask Silvio a question: "By the way, did you know Camilla Kallberg, the lady that was found down the cliffs at—" Max didn't get to finish the sentence.

24

"Of course, I did. Camilla passed the *pizzeria* every day; she lived up at the Castiglione hill. Sometimes she would come in to get a pizza and we would talk."

"What was she like?"

"Just like you Max, a connoisseur of food and life. She liked her pizza prepared—just like yours."

After saying goodbye to his old friend, Max ducked under the arcade of the pizzeria and stepped out into the medieval street of Via Madre Serafina. How strange, he thought, that my old friend Silvio had known Camilla.

Max sat down on the terrace of his hotel suite and ate the pizza with his fingers, folding it into wedges, Neapolitan style. He finished most of the bottle of Aglianico, a wine harvested from black grapes grown in volcanic soil on the slopes of Mount Vesuvius. These grapes, Max well knew, were the principal component of the world's earliest first-growth wine, Falernian, one of the most highly prized wines in Roman times, some two thousand years ago.

Was it true what Silvio had said? Max asked himself, as he left the terrace to turn in for the night. Do I know how to enjoy life? It was true that he had loved his life back in the days when he was growing up on Capri, but he could hardly say that he loved his life now. Max laid down crosswise on the king-sized bed of the cool dark bedroom. How can I get the joy of life back in my heart? he wondered, as he drifted off to sleep.

Chapter 4 - The Investigation Begins

SATURDAY, AUGUST 21

IN THE CELLAR OF THE CHURCH

The loud clanging of bells from the campanile in the Piazzetta interrupted Max´s review of the previous day´s events. Counting the bells, he realized it was eleven o'clock. What an extraordinary bit of luck that I was still on vacation when Bob called yesterday, he thought, grinning. How lucky I am to get a work assignment here on Capri. One day later, and I would have been on a return flight to San Francisco. He swallowed the last dregs of his tepid espresso and gestured to Enrico, the waiter at Piccolo Bar, to bring his bill; it was time to start his investigation into the death of Camilla Kallberg.

Max decided the best place to start would be the Evangelical Church where the funeral service had been held earlier that day, in hope of questioning his friend Ruggiero, the custodian, whom he had seen at the service. Since Camilla apparently had made her own funeral arrangements, Max thought she might have been in contact with Ruggiero.

At the end of Via Camerelle, the road curved sharply, and the ocher-colored stone church came into view, surrounded by a brilliant display of blooming plants. The Evangelical Church, with its tapering tile roof, was situated high above street level at the beginning of Via Tragara, the enchanting street famous for its posh hotels and luxury villas.

The small cellar door underneath the main steps to the church was open; Max peered inside. The long narrow church cellar looked like a scene from a fairytale; it was piled with masses of fragrant colorful flowers. Leaning over a wood table in a shaft of light, a lanky man with sinewy hands was busy bundling the flowers into bouquets. It was Domenico Ruggiero, known as "Mimmo." He and his family owned the flower shop next to the church, as well as the colorful nursery garden behind it. Domenico and his brother Raffaele were the great grandchildren of the legendary Mimì Ruggiero, who was the most sought-after gardener among Capri's more illustrious residents during his lifetime.

Ruggiero looked up. "*Uè* (hi), Max. *Come stai* (How are you)? Come in, come in, I spotted you in the church this morning. You were a friend of Signora Kallberg?"

"Not really, Mimmo…"

Max sat down on a wooden crate in the cool cellar and proceeded to explain that he was a life insurance investigator in the Kallberg case. "I came here to find out if you knew Camilla personally."

"Yeh, sure. I met her years ago when she first came to Capri. Camilla bought her plants from me, you know."

"Is there anything you can tell me about her funeral arrangements?"

"Well, since you ask, some weeks ago she showed up at the shop and had a couple of unusual questions for me. I didn't think much of it at the time. But now, I can't help wondering if she was thinking about—you know—doing away with herself. May she rest in peace." Ruggiero crossed his heart and then continued bundling the flowers.

"Tell me about it if you can, please."

"Well, she wanted to know if funeral services were held at the Evangelical Church, and if so, who would one contact for permission and who would one hire as a pastor. I gave her the telephone number in Naples for the person in charge of events at the church. The Evangelic-Lutheran Parish in Naples is the owner of this church; they send over a pastor to officiate at the services. As you heard yourself this morning, she must have made all of the arrangements for her own funeral."

"Anything else, Mimmo? What was your impression of her? Do you think she could have committed suicide?"

Ruggiero hesitated for a moment. "Well, I must say, the idea of suicide doesn't seem likely. She always had a bright smile for me whenever she came into the shop." His face lit up with a lopsided grin: "You should see her garden! She had such a passion for flowers."

Ruggiero looked down sadly. "Her death took me completely by surprise. I guess that shows you how little we know about what goes on inside a person when we judge only by appearances."

Max got up from the crate; the intensely sweet fragrance of the flowers was beginning to nauseate him—as it had earlier that day at the funeral service. He grimaced and attempted a weak smile. "True enough, Mimmo. Thanks, I'd better go. I'm expected at the chief inspector's office. Let me know if you happen to think of anything else."

COMMISSARIATO P.S. CAPRI

On the way to the police station, Max decided to stop at Bar Due Golfi, so named for the view of the Gulf of Naples to the north and the Gulf of Salerno to the south. The cafe was located at the busiest intersection on the island, between the slopes of Torina and the town of Capri.

Max waved a greeting to his old friend Giovanna, an officer with the Municipal Police, the *Vigili Urbani*. Dressed in her blue uniform, with the smart jacket, tight skirt, and cap, over a head of curly brown hair, she was a lovely sight. She was directing traffic at the roundabout outside the café, where Capri's four major roads intersect: the northern road, leading down to the main port of Marina Grande; the southern road, leading to the little port of Marina Piccola; the western road, which climbs uphill to the town of Anacapri; and Via Roma, the shortest carriage road, leading east to the Piazzetta, the entrance to the town of Capri.

Max exchanged some gossip with Riccardo, the owner of the bar, as he downed a glass of freshly squeezed orange juice. Then he headed for the police station located practically next door at Via Roma n. 68/b. He walked underneath a white wooden arch, with "Commissariato P.S. Capri" painted in black letters, and entered the building. Even though Max often passed the police station, this was the first time he had gone inside. Less than ten minutes after presenting his credentials at the front desk, he was informed that the head of the state police on Capri, Vice Questore Aggiunto, Dottoressa Maria Maddalena Monti, would see him.

Max was surprised and impressed when he stepped into her office. Not only was the head of state police on Capri a woman with a doctorate, she was also young for her position. Max guessed she was around thirty-five. The black epaulets on her blue uniform jacket had the police insignia: two gold stars over a golden castle with three turrets. She was also attractive. Her straight black hair was cut short and tucked behind her small ears, adorned with grey pearls in a silver setting.

The head of police stayed seated, her spine so straight she didn't touch the back of the chair. Her delicate manicured hand gestured to a chair in front of her desk. Max noted she wasn't wearing a wedding ring. Under her desk lay a chocolate brown dachshund with his face next to her feet, clad in black pumps. Captain Michele Arcuzzi stood at the side of the desk, holding his cap in his hand; he was still wearing his jacket despite the mid-day heat; he nodded to Max.

"Good morning, Signor De Angelis. I'm Chief Inspector Monti. I'm in charge of the investigation into the death of Signora Kallberg. I understand you have met Deputy Chief of Police, Captain Michele Arcuzzi. The captain reports directly to me in this investigation. He has told me that your company has a major life insurance policy on Signora Kallberg. Interesting."

The chief inspector looked straight up at Max, her black eyebrows ever so slightly raised. Max felt as if her penetrating cold gray eyes had the ability to see right through him.

"Please sit down and tell us everything you know about Signora Kallberg, but first explain your role in the case."

"I'm an insurance fraud investigator at United Global Insurance in San Francisco—in California," he said. "Camilla Kallberg is our client; six months ago, she took out a two-million-dollar life insurance policy. I'm investigating the cause of her death."

"I do know that San Francisco is in California, De Angelis." Chief Inspector Monti didn't smile. "Please proceed."

Max went on to explain all—or rather, the little, he knew about Camilla Kallberg. Then he explained his background, adding that he was born and raised on Capri.

"Ah, you are Caprese," the chief inspector said.

Max thought he detected a note of disapproval in the way she pronounced the word "Caprese."

She continued, "Now let's sum up what we know about the possible cause of Kallberg's death. First, we must consider the possibility of homicide. According to the coroner's report, there is no sign of a struggle, and there is no evidence of foul play, such as poison or drugs in the body; but we are continuing our investigation. Considering this latest information about the insurance policy, it now appears that the sister, Katarina Kallberg, may have a motive. We will contact Camilla Kallberg's solicitor regarding her will."

Chief Inspector Monti pushed her chair away from the desk. The little dachshund got up on all fours, after a yawn and a long stretch of his hind legs; he looked expectantly up at his mistress with liquid brown eyes.

"Second, we have to consider whether the death was caused by an accident. Barring any new information, we are ruling it out. If it had been an accident, one would think someone would have reported it; after all, why would this woman be alone at that remote and uninhabited place close to midnight?"

"Third—" the chief inspector bent over to pick up the dachshund and put him in her lap.

"Thirdly, we must consider the possibility of suicide. I expect that would be your assumption, De Angelis," she said, with a half-smile that didn't reach her eyes.

She turned towards her deputy. "Captain Arcuzzi, why don't you tell us what we have so far on that?"

Captain Arcuzzi took out a small notebook from the inside pocket of his police jacket and began to read aloud:

"Camilla Kallberg – Items indicating the possibility of suicide.

1. Coroner's report confirms the cause of death was subdural hematoma; head injury due to the height of the fall. Blood tests were all normal, no drugs or medicines, and only traces of alcohol. No signs of a struggle. Trauma to Kallberg's body corresponds with impact of fall, not wounds inflicted by a weapon or bruising typical of strangulation.
2. No torn clothing at the scene of the incident at Belvedere delle Noci.
3. Death of husband five years ago; possibly still grieving her loss.
4. Death of her cat one year ago, according to lawyer.

5. According to sister, possibility of a past love affair gone wrong.
6. Kallberg recently made detailed arrangements for her own funeral on Capri.
7. According to her lawyer, Kallberg recently changed her will; details to be provided soon.
8. Suicide by jumping off a cliff is the preferred method on Capri. Statistically, falls from heights are rarely due to homicide, but to accident or suicide. So far, there is no evidence to confirm an accident or a homicide."

Arcuzzi looked up from his notebook. "And now this: Recent substantial life insurance policy with the sister Katarina Kallberg named as beneficiary," Captain Arcuzzi said, as he wrote down item number 9.

"Do you have a time of death?" Max asked.

"The coroner estimates her death to have occurred sometime between 11 pm on August 15th and 3 am on August 16th."

"Thank you, Chief Inspector. Would it be possible to have copies of the reports as well as copies of any photos taken of the place where the body was found?"

The chief inspector looked miffed. "It is not customary to share such information De Angelis; it's out of the question," she said curtly. The tone of her voice matched her steely eyes.

Max didn't press his case; he knew it would be better to wait for a future opportunity. He noticed the adoring brown eyes of the dachshund looking up at his master. There might just be a tender person hidden behind the inspector's flinty demeanor, Max thought.

"So, De Angelis, before you received your present assignment, I understand you were vacationing here on Capri. Were you alone?" Chief Inspector Monti asked casually, interrupting Max's thoughts.

"Yes."

"No wife, no travelling companion?"

"No." Max said coldly, annoyed by this personal question; he was damned if he was going to tell the inspector that his wife had left him for another man.

"Tell me, Signor De Angelis, did you know Camilla Kallberg?" the inspector continued, while caressing the ears of the dachshund in her lap.

"No."

"Did you go to her funeral this morning?"

"Yes."

"Why?"

Max shifted uncomfortably in his seat. "I felt it important to learn as much as possible about Signora Camilla Kallberg and I wanted to see who attended the service."

"A bit unethical, don't you think, encroaching on the family under such sad circumstances. Is that the way you do it in America?"

Max took his time answering; the chief inspector was right of course, it wasn't ethical. "My father was a good friend of hers," he said. "He worked as a custodian at her villa before he passed away."

"If your father was such a good friend of hers, why didn't he introduce you to her?"

Max didn't answer.

"Were you on Capri the night Signora Camilla Kallberg died?" Chief Inspector Monti continued.

"Yes, I was here on vacation."

"And what were you doing on the night of the 15th?" she asked.

"I was staying at my sister's apartment on Via Posterula. My sister had decided to stay at the home of her companion after the fireworks, so I was alone that night."

Inspector Monti raised her thin eyebrows in disbelief. "How unusual for a Caprese to be alone on August 15th, the evening of holy Ferragosto,[2] perhaps the most important day of the year for a family celebration. And you were not with your family on the island—nor with your friends."

---

[2] The Catholic feast of the Assumption of Mary is celebrated on August the 15th in Italy and is a public holiday known a Ferragosto. It coincides with the Italian summer vacation period around mid-August, which may be a long weekend (*ponte di ferragosto*) or up to three weeks.

Monti sounded increasingly skeptical as she continued, "And apparently you don't have an alibi for the time of Kallberg's death. Are you sure you hadn't become acquainted with Camilla Kallberg before she died? If not on Capri, then maybe in San Francisco? We understand that Camilla owned a home in San Francisco."

Max didn't answer. He wasn't going to lower himself to explain why he hadn't been with his family on Ferragosto; his two sisters didn't get along, and if he had picked one of them, the other would have been insulted. Nor was he going to tell the chief inspector that he was too proud to tell any of his friends that he had no plans that night, or that being alone on Ferragosto wasn't a big deal for him. He didn't give a damn about the holiness of Ferragosto.

"Well, Signor De Angelis, let's help each other get to the bottom of this mystery, shall we?" Monti's voice had suddenly turned sugary sweet. She placed the dachshund gently on the floor and stood up.

"Let's all hope that a murder was not committed here on Capri. And please do not take it amiss, but we kindly request that for now, you do not leave the island without our permission."

The audience was over.

DA GREGORIO

By the time Max was back outside the police station; he was fuming with anger. Cursing Chief Inspector Monti under his breath, he absentmindedly ducked into the underpass on Via Roma, then walked slowly down Via Mulo, the footpath towards Marina Piccola on the southern side of the island.

The insinuations of Inspector Monti were insulting. "Bloody ridiculous!" he said loudly, boiling with rage. To imagine that he had anything to do with the death of the woman he was professionally investigating, or that he needed an alibi for the time of her death seemed utterly absurd. The questions of the police were clearly meant to intimidate him. He knew the nasty interrogation methods used by the police, and admittedly, he had sometimes resorted to using them himself.

Why were they trying to make it seem as if he had something to hide? Max wondered, as if he were lying about not knowing Camilla. He realized that the police must resent him as an outsider, especially an outsider sent over from the U.S.; former local boy, now meddling in their affairs. No, they weren't going to tolerate that. "It's all a bloody power game," he muttered under his breath. "Damn the police!" He was determined to find out the truth. He wasn't nicknamed "bloodhound" at the office for nothing.

"*Buongiorno,*" Max said, greeting an old woman on Via Mulo who was feeding leftover pasta to a couple of stray cats. He suddenly became aware that he was starving, and his feet, following orders from his stomach, led him down the path toward Gregorio's restaurant in Marina Piccola.

The Piazzetta of Marina Piccola, for which Gregorio's restaurant was named, was dedicated to Totò, the beloved actor Prince Antonio de Curtis. Close to the square were five of the lidos, or bathing establishments, on Capri, as well as a small pebbled public beach.

Gregorio beamed with pleasure when Max walked in the door to greet him. He accompanied him up the stairs to the wide shady terrace overlooking the minuscule square, with its picturesque little fishermen's church named in honor of Saint Andrew. From the terrace where he sat, the views of the famed Faraglioni rocks rising from the blue Tyrrhenian Sea were magnificent.

Alfonso, the faithful waiter, served him a mouthwatering meal of baby calamari and linguini with fresh seafood accompanied by ice-cold Falanghina wine. After he had eaten a few delicious bites and had drunk some wine, all thoughts of the unpleasant encounter at the police station vanished from Max's mind.

Soon everything that troubled him from the past began to fade away as well, and he felt better than he could remember feeling for a long time. If this job took a bit longer than expected, that wouldn't be bad at all; he felt as though he could stay on his island forever. So what if the police don't want me to leave the island? Fine by me, he thought. I'm getting paid a salary plus expenses. And what better excuse could he have to avoid seeing the face of his obnoxious boss

Bob for a while; still better, not having to see the face of his colleague and nemesis Sebastian, whom Max had nicknamed *il ciuccio* for his donkey face. By the time he had finished the bottle of wine, he was almost grateful to the haughty Chief Inspector Monti for forcing him to stay on the island.

"Espresso, Max?" Alfonso grinned.

Max had known Alfonso and Gregorio for as long as he could remember; he had been at the restaurant countless times, memorable times with delicious food, wine, and friends. Every time he and his former classmates had a school reunion, they would choose this place to celebrate.

"Thanks, Alfò, better make it a doppio. Ah, wait a minute Alfò, may I ask you a question? Did you know that woman Camilla Kallberg, the one who fell to her death at Belvedere delle Noci?"

"Ahh, what a horrible and sad story. Yes, Camilla was a regular, a lady who knew how to enjoy life. I was very fond of her, you know. She and her husband came here often. After he passed away, she continued to come, sometimes alone."

"So Alfò, when she wasn't alone, who was she with—recently, I mean?"

"Bah—different people—sometimes with family, sometimes with a friend. I'll get the espresso, doppio you said?"

Max nodded. He knew better than to push Alfonso. On Capri, there were many unwritten rules. One of those rules was never to reveal the whereabouts or personal details of clients if you wanted to stay in business. The Caprese had learned it was preferable to pretend to be both deaf and blind on occasion. Through the centuries, they had successfully cultivated discretion and a high level of tolerance for nonconformist behavior.

Gregorio, the owner of Ristorante La Piazzetta, was standing by the cash register at the level of the square when Max walked down from the terrace to pay his bill. "We haven't seen you for some years, Max. How's life in California?"

There weren't many locals, or *habitués*, who didn't appreciate Gregorio's generous and hospitable manners. Although a native-born Caprese, his bright red hair and multitude of freckles gave him the look of a northerner. Max thought he might be an offspring of the Vikings, who had a history of rape and plunder in the Mediterranean, and he liked to tease him about it.

"Working in America is hard work, Gregorio," Max sighed. "I know you work hard here, too, especially during summer, but people on Capri don't work all the time, do they? In America, it never lets up. Vacations are short, a week at the most, with the occasional long weekend. I go mountain climbing whenever I get a chance, you know how much I love climbing; mostly I make do with a climbing gym. Right now, I'm working here on Capri. I got an assignment to investigate a life insurance claim. Can you believe it? You probably knew the woman, Camilla Kallberg; my late father was the custodian at the villa where she lived on the Castiglione hill."

"Yes, certainly I knew Camilla. Too sad to think about it, Max; she was too young to die. She celebrated life to the fullest, and saw the beauty and joy in everything. Camilla knew how to live in the moment." Gregorio's eyes grew moist.

"Do you recall seeing her with anybody special—a romantic companion?"

Gregorio took his time answering while polishing the already spotless bar counter. "I often saw her pass outside the restaurant after a day at the beach near the Faraglioni rocks. Sometimes she took a taxi or a bus up to town, and sometimes she walked up. At other times, she came to swim in the bay of Marina Piccola, and often she had her lunch or dinner here. She had many friends, Max— some might have been more intimate friends."

"Thanks, Gregorio. If there is anything else that you can remember, let me know, please. I think I'll go for a swim. May I leave my wallet and cell with you?"

"Do you need to ask! And swimming trunks, Max?"

"Always wear them under my pants when I'm on Capri."

After a long swim in the transparent waters along the coast, Max decided to pay a visit to his other sister, Mimì, and her family, who lived in Anacapri, the other town on the island of Capri. After all, there was no need to rush the investigation. It was clear the police would much prefer that he leave the case to them. Tomorrow was another day. His boss in San Francisco could wait. He felt like a schoolboy playing hooky as he got in line for the direct bus from Marina Piccola to Anacapri.

Hanging onto a strap, while the small packed bus made its way up the narrow winding road towards Due Golfi, he enjoyed the exuberance and bright chatter of children returning from a day playing in the sea. The distance between two small buses passing each other from opposite directions on the road was, at times, no more than a couple of centimeters. Sometimes a bus or taxi was forced to back up to a place on the road wide enough for the other vehicle to pass. Luckily, only a few private cars travelled this road, as there was no public parking in Marina Piccola. He marveled at the diverse horn and hand signal communications between the bus and taxi drivers. One of the things he missed in America was the sense of cooperation and camaraderie that existed between the islanders to smooth out the inconveniences of everyday life, an essential quality that they had perfected to coexist amicably on a small rocky island four square miles large.

It wasn't until the bus was winding up the hairpin turns on the spectacular scenic road between Due Golfi and Anacapri that Max remembered the insinuations of the commissioner of police. His boss would not be pleased if he were to learn that one of his top insurance fraud investigators was under suspicion of murdering the woman whose death he was hired to investigate. More than likely, his colleague, that *ciuccio* (donkey) Sebastian, would be promoted ahead of him. Max shuddered; his sense of satisfaction from playing hooky vanished in the stifling air of the crowded bus. He decided he had better pay a visit to Katarina Kallberg at Villa Ciano the next morning, even if it was a Sunday and only one day after the funeral.

CHAPTER 5 ~ REMEMBERING MAMA

SUNDAY, AUGUST 22

H is mother was in the kitchen stirring a big pot on the stove. She had her back to him as he walked in the door, a checkered apron tied around her ample belly. Then she turned, and he watched her stern wrinkled face as she waved a spoon at him and said, "*A capa, 'a capa Massimì, addó sta, che te si scurdato?* (Where is your head, Massimì, what have you forgotten?)"

Max woke with a start from his dream. The scene with his mother had been so true to life that he felt a longing for her physical presence.

It was two o'clock in the morning. He grabbed the bottle of mineral water on his nightstand and went to sit on the couch in the *salotto* (living room). The luxurious Kennedy suite at Hotel Gatto Bianco had two bedrooms and two bathrooms, a large living room, and a terrace. He felt almost ridiculous being the only occupant. His childhood home had been less than forty square meters.[3] Two rooms and an attic bedroom had housed his parents, his two sisters, and himself, the last to be born.

What did Mama mean by those words in the dream? What the hell had he forgotten? Struggling to recall a time when she had said anything like this, nothing came to him. Then he remembered something she had often said when he acted rashly, without thinking:

"*Tiene 'a capa sulo per spartere 'e rrecchie*. (The only thing your head is good for is to keep your ears apart.)" The memory of his wise mother was so vivid, when he closed his eyes, he could see her as clearly as if she were still alive.

Max believed that Mama was the smartest one in the family. Although she was raised by nuns at an orphanage in the province of Naples, where the children received only elementary schooling, she had impeccable manners and carried herself with dignity. How intelligent and capable Mama was, and yet how vulnerable; many times, as a child, Max had watched her suffer the torment of a mysterious illness.

Nerves, they said it was—unexpectedly, an attack would come on, and with it, the awful screams. Usually one of the neighbors in their building would call the police, as Papa was so often away at the hotel where he worked. Little Max and his sisters Mona and Mimì watched helplessly as they forcibly dragged Mama out of the house and escorted her to a mental institution on the outskirts of Naples.

On rare occasions, Papa would take Max on the long trip by ferry and bus to visit Mama in that dark miserable place. During those visits, Mama would hold onto Max's small hand and talk with him quietly, refusing to let go of him when Papa said it was time to leave. Max had to pry her fingers from his wrist, all the while feeling as if he had a heavy stone in his heart. He never once cried. He would go home and wait patiently for the day when Mama would come back. And she always did.

---

[3]431 square feet

Max soon learned from his experience not to show emotions or talk about his feelings; instead, he would escape. Whenever Mama was taken to the asylum, Max would run down the road until he felt his lungs would burst. There was a special place on an isolated stretch of rock overlooking the sea where he liked to hide and be alone. He would lay down and listen to the birds and the sound of the waves and wind, until he no longer heard his mother's cries echoing in his head. Once revived, he would return to their modest home and go about his life as he always did, doing everything his father and teachers expected of him, and more. Nobody ever demanded more from Max than Max himself.

With Mama away at unexpected times, and Papa working long hours as a porter at Quisisana Hotel, Max and his two sisters learned to fend for themselves from a very young age. Mama had taught them how to cook their own meals, as well as how to do the cleaning, ironing, and other housework. For all that, they were diligent students.

As soon as they were old enough, the children started doing odd jobs after school, on weekends, and during summer vacation. Max helped his father carry luggage at the hotel as a boy, and then he was hired as a dishwasher, and graduated to the position of a waiter; later he served as a bartender at Quisisana. During high school, he served as the manager of a nightclub.

Neither of his sisters ended up with a higher education, even though they had performed better in most subjects than Max. His oldest sister Mona married an artist named Roberto at sixteen and had three children with him. Roberto was recognized as a rising star among his generation of painters on Capri. But when their children were still quite small, Roberto died of cirrhosis of the liver. After his death, Mona raised them alone in a tiny apartment she rented from the Catholic church and earned her living by making sandals on an old sewing machine. She continued to support herself that way and lived in the same apartment after her children had left home, now paying rent to her son, a construction worker, who had bought the property from the church.

Max's older sister Mimì married Andrea at eighteen; he was a hard-working plumber from Anacapri with his own business and a lovely home. They had a daughter and Mimì worked part-time in her husband's business.

The De Angelis family was poor by most standards, but Max and his family had never thought of themselves as poor. Although money was scarce, Papa made sure there was a roof over their heads and food on the table. Mama would often run up tabs at the stores; to spare herself the embarrassment of being asked to pay the bill, she would sometimes ask Max to go shopping in her place. His mother, *Mammina* he called her, made sure that her children's few items of clothing were always clean and pressed. Max had two pairs of shoes, one for school and one for church, and he often wore hand-me-down clothes; but he never felt deprived, not even among his more affluent school mates, such as his friend Raffi, who lived in a villa on Via Tragara.

Max's father was set against him getting a higher education; he didn't see the point, as Capri offered little work that required book learning. Another wage earner was sorely needed in the family. Papa's work as a porter was hard for a man with a slight build, and his body was getting worn out. He hoped that his son would take a position at the hotel, but Max had firmly decided that he was going to study mathematics and computer science. To please his father, Max made him a deal; he would work nights and weekends while going to school to help the family.

Max never complained about his situation. He had learned from his mother's example. Whenever Mama returned from one of her stays at the mental institution, she would never talk about her time there. If anything bothered Max, he would find a way to talk about something else, often retreating into silence.

Tara used to say that not talking about something important was the same as escaping from yourself. She believed in talking things out, but he had never learned how to do it.

Max forced his thoughts away from Tara and returned to bed; sometime after three o'clock he drifted back to sleep.

Max woke up to the sound of birds; daylight was streaming through the blinds of his hotel room. Why had his mother appeared to him in that dream? He was still puzzled by her words. What had he forgotten? He missed his incredibly wise and wonderful *mammina*. It seemed as if he thought about her even more as time passed. Max let go of his memories while he shaved and got dressed for the day; after a quick inspection in the mirror, he went down to the breakfast room.

Breakfast at Hotel Gatto Bianco was a lavish affair. Max didn't take advantage of it; a glass of water and an espresso was all he needed to fortify himself. It was time to get down to business and officially meet Katarina Kallberg. He had decided to take a chance and walk up to Villa Ciano with the hope of finding Katarina at home and willing to talk to him.

Striding up the stairway from the Piazzetta, Max went past the ex-cathedral of Santo Stefano and walked under an arch into the narrow tunnel-like passageway of Via Madre Serafina. Out of habit, he quickly scanned the old walls plastered with funeral notices. Camilla Kallberg's obituary was dutifully posted among a handful of notices of Caprese family members. The tradition of posting funeral notices close to the church was still essential to the islanders. One of Max's daily chores as a boy had been to memorize the names of the recently deceased to recite to his mother.

Via Madre Serafina, one of the oldest pedestrian walkways on Capri, was constructed inside the medieval protective walls of the town of Capri; the series of Moorish arches and gray plaster walls gave the narrow road a mystique.

This part of Capri was sacred ground to Max; the ancient quarter of Santa Teresa was where he had grown up. He was suddenly overcome with an irresistible desire to see the place where he had been born and raised. Taking a few steps down Via L'Abate, the alley named for the abbot's residence built there in the seventeenth century, Max glanced up at the kitchen window of his modest childhood home on the third floor of the old stone building. He wondered who lived there now. After the death of his mother, the rental residence had come up for sale, but he hadn't the funds to buy it.

Opening the faded yet familiar green wooden door, he smiled when he saw the steep, narrow staircase; it was still tiled with a mismatched mix of old majolica tile that his father had salvaged from demolitions. How many times, after working at the night club, had he tiptoed up those well-worn steps in the dark so as not to wake anybody? It seemed like only yesterday when he was living in this place where he truly belonged, and his parents were alive. Max gently closed the door behind him.

Via Madre Serafina opened onto a little square dominated by a compound with the baroque church of SS. Salvatore and the adjacent convent of Santa Teresa. Max had served as an altar boy at this church. As he passed by, Max smiled, recalling the times when he and his friends played soccer on the old majolica tile floor after Sunday service until the kindly priest chased them out.

Madre Serafina was a local Capri girl born in that quarter, who became a Carmelite nun. She founded the Santa Teresa convent in the seventeenth century and went on to establish another six convents in her lifetime. *Suor Serafina di Dio*, as she was called, was a charismatic mystic and writer accused of being a witch by the holy office of the Catholic Church; she was confined in prison for six years before she was exonerated.

Many of Max's schoolmates grew up in the convent and cloister buildings, which had been converted to private homes for Caprese families. The children were convinced that the spirit of Madre Serafina protected them from evil.

From Santa Teresa, Max walked uphill on the footpath of Via Castello, turning off at the shortcut of stairs that connected him to the winding road, Via Castiglione and Villa Ciano, Camilla Kallberg's residence.

CHAPTER 6 - THE GARDEN OF VILLA CIANO

SUNDAY, AUGUST 22

A blue Alfa Romeo 159 police car was parked in front of the gate at Villa Ciano. Max hid behind a pillar of the archway at the top of the pedestrian shortcut to Via Castiglione. With the memory of his unpleasant visit to the police station still fresh in his mind, he wasn't in the mood for another encounter with the police.

At once, two police officers appeared at the gate of the villa and got into the car. Max recognized one of them as Captain Michele Arcuzzi, the officer handling the investigation into Camilla Kallberg's death. He was surprised to see the captain working on a Sunday, but then again, it wasn't a common event for a foreigner to be found dead on the cliffs of Capri.

As soon as the Alfa Romeo disappeared around the curve of Via Castiglione, Max crossed the street and entered the gate, which was slightly ajar, onto the grounds of Villa Ciano. Closing the gate behind him, he was lured into the maze of the garden, where he wandered down the paths, lost in memories of his father.

When home on Capri for vacations, Max had sometimes gone with his father to the villa on the castle hill—*'ncopp o' castiello,* as his

Papa had called the place. Only occasionally did he refer to it as "Villa Ciano," and he would always whisper the words, since the name had associations with fascist Italy and Mussolini, whose daughter and son-in-law had built the villa.

Under the influence of his father's magical green thumb, the villa's park grounds were transformed from an arid desert of a *pezz 'i terren* (plot of land) into an abundant paradise. His father had reasoned with the condominium owners that since he had to water the garden every day, he might as well water edible plants at the same time. Within the beds of colorful flowers and shrubs, he had cultivated every species of vegetable that grows on the island. A row of flowering purple artichoke plants bordered one of the walkways; sunflowers lined another; there were olive and fruit trees, pomegranates, prickly pears, and his father's beloved fig trees.

Papa collected seeds from the sunflowers, made olive oil, and pressed grapes to make wine. The vegetables he harvested from the garden were cooked by Mama and covered with olive oil in glass containers, and the fruit picked from the trees was dried and stored. All this bounty sustained the De Angelis family during the winter. Papa kept a dozen chickens on the grounds; he drank a raw egg every single day. "Good for the libido," he would say with a wink.

Max noted with sadness that the garden was no longer the Eden of his father's time. The abundant oleander trees and agave plants were still there, and the tall pine trees, and the imported giant palm. But the vegetables and many of the fruit trees were gone, as were the sunflowers, artichoke plants, and chickens.

A statue of Benito Mussolini on horseback was said to have once stood in this garden. *Il Duce*, as Mussolini was called, had often visited the villa built by his daughter Edda and her husband Count Galeazzo Ciano; ambassador of Italy to China and minister of foreign affairs during the twenty years of fascism. After the fall of the fascist regime, Mussolini set up a puppet government in the area of northern Italy still under German occupation, called the Italian Social Republic. Ciano was considered a traitor by Mussolini, for having voted against him on July 25, 1943. Under pressure from the Nazis and Italian fascists, Mussolini sentenced Ciano to death in January 1944 and he was executed by a firing squad. Max recalled this history from the book by Count Ciano's oldest son Fabrizio: *Quando il nonno fece fucilare papa* (*When Grandpa Had Daddy Shot*).

After the German forces withdrew from Capri in September 1943, British Rear Admiral Sir Anthony Morse was appointed governor of Capri and took up residence in Villa Ciano. The British rule was short; only three weeks later, U.S. Army Air Force Colonel Carl E. Woodward was named governor and Capri served as a rest camp for American airmen for the rest of the war.

Edda Ciano, Mussolini's eccentric and favorite daughter, continued to come to her villa for many years after the war. Eventually, she sold it, and the villa was converted into condominiums, one of which was owned by Camilla Kallberg.

The views from the garden of Villa Ciano, set on a plateau high above the town of Capri, were magnificent. Max walked to the semicircular viewing point on the northern edge of the garden to admire the bright blue bay of Naples; from there, his father used to enjoy watching the arrivals and departures of the ferries and hydrofoils at Marina Grande. Mount Vesuvius, with its smoldering active volcano, rose like a gray pyramid from the sea; the densely populated towns at the base of the volcano were masked by the morning haze.

Max's eyes followed the outline of the town of Capri below him. The houses, stacked one on top of the other like building blocks, climbed the hill to the peak of Monte San Michele. Looking all the way to the northeast, he could see Monte Tiberio. Further east was the fertile valley of Matermania and the verdant Monte Tuoro. To the south, and above Villa Ciano, the turrets of the medieval castle on Castiglione Hill rose above the forest.

Max walked along the stone wall on the perimeter of the garden; down the western slope, he could see the saddle of Due Golfi and the police station. Rising above Due Golfi were the green slopes of Torina capped by the majestic Monte Solaro. To the southwest was a bird's-eye view of the jewel-like cove of Marina Piccola. Max suddenly froze. This was the spot where he had last seen his father alive.

Pain welled up in Max's heart when he recalled that day. Every detail was etched in his memory. He had walked up from town to Villa Ciano to say farewell to his father at the end of a short summer vacation with Tara. That was five years ago.

◆ ◆ ◆

"You've come to say goodbye?" Papa said; it wasn't so much a question as a statement.

He sat down wearily on a tree stump with his shoulders hunched over; his face reflected the sadness in his voice. As usual, Papa wore his black-rimmed glasses and a sun hat with the brim turned up. It seemed to Max that he had shrunk; he looked so frail. Lately, he was harder to get along with than ever. It pained Max to look at his father and he couldn't speak; he only nodded.

"When will I see you again?"

"I just don't know right now, Papa; it depends on work, you know." Max tried to sound cheerful. "As soon as I can get away, I will come and visit; you know that."

"Are you happy, Max, with your life in America—and with your wife?"

Before Max had time to formulate an answer, his father asked another question: "What about children—are you and Tara thinking about it?"

Max didn't know what to say. He couldn't confess to his father that Tara had tried in vain to become pregnant, and that she had even wanted them to try in vitro fertilization, though he had been dead set against it. His marriage wasn't going very well; perhaps his father had guessed it.

"We are working on it, Papa." Max sat down on the ground next to his father.

"Good."

Max fell silent.

"Will you promise me one thing, Max?"

His father's voice was barely audible, and he seemed bitter and dejected.

48

"Will you—bring your son back here to Capri one day, will you teach him what I taught you, will you tell him about his *nonno* (grandfather)?" His father spoke these words quietly, almost solemnly.

Max promised. But he hadn't fulfilled that promise; in fact, he had been a total failure. What would his father have said about his divorce?

Chapter 7 - Tea on the Roof

C oming out of the garden of Villa Ciano, still lost in thought, Max jumped when a short, stocky man suddenly blocked his path with a wheelbarrow. Spade in hand, the scruffy man scrutinized Max with a menacing look. A cigarette was dangling from the side of his mouth, his unshaved face and unkempt hair reminding Max of the Beagle Boys bandits in his childhood Donald Duck magazines.

Then he recognized him; it had been years since he last saw him. Zi' Bacco, that was his *sopranome* (nickname); what his actual name was, Max couldn't remember. Apparently, he was the custodian of the villa now.

"Zi' Bacco, how are you, old guy?"

He gave Max a blank look.

"Remember me? I'm Max—De Angelis. When I was a kid, you used to chase me out of Lo Scoglio delle Sirene when you worked there as a *bagnino* (beach attendant)."

Zi' Bacco removed the cigarette, and his face broke into a million wrinkles. "Yeh, now I do; you always were a *mascalzone* (rascal), that you were, showing up in places you had no business being. What the hell are you doing here? I thought you were an intruder. The police were just here, you know, asking me lots of questions."

"I've come to visit the sister of Camilla Kallberg," Max said.

Good old grumpy Zi' Bacco; it was hard to imagine that in his youth he was known as the Don Juan of Marina Piccola.

"You know the sisters, then? You heard about the awful thing that happened to Signora Camilla?"

"Mm," Max mumbled. "Why do you think she killed herself?"

"I ain't got the foggiest idea. I mean, she owned this place and had plenty of dough and everything, and I'm sure you would agree she was a looker. So why the hell would she do it?"

"Then do you think she killed herself?" Max asked.

Zi' Bacco lit himself another cigarette from the stub. "It ain't right, of all the days to pick, holy Ferragosto; it's a sacred day, you know."

The custodian's righteous anger amused Max. He doubted whether someone about to kill herself would care what day of the year it was, and besides, Camilla was not Catholic.

"Strange, yes," Max said. "She had lots of friends, right? Was she seeing anyone special here at the villa—any regular visitors?"

"You're just as nosey as those idiot police officers," Zi' Bacco snapped. "I mean, what do they think I do here? I ain't no bloody spy, you know."

"Of course, you're not a spy," Max laughed, and hoping to calm Zi' Bacco, he added in a conciliatory tone, "The garden looks great; it must take a lot of work. I don't know if you're aware that my father Bruno De Angelis used to work his butt off here in this garden during the last eleven years of his life."

"I remember Bruno, yes, he knew his stuff. It does take a lot of work, that it does, the work never ends," Zi' Bacco said with a sigh.

"Ah, there is *il fico* (fig tree). I see I came here at the perfect time." Max reached up and grabbed a ripe, luscious green fig from a branch of the tree; he ate it on the spot without bothering to peel it, just as he used to do as a boy.

"You like figs, do you?" Zi' Bacco grinned. "So did Camilla. She ate them every day, you know, when they were ripe. Come to think of it, I used to put the figs in an old wicker basket; she told me it was woven by your father."

"How did you and Camilla get along, were you friends?" Max was fishing anew.

"Yeh, we were friends. Signora Camilla was the only one at the villa who cared about the garden—and cared about me—" Zi' Bacco sighed heavily. "I miss her, you know, and I won't be the only one, the sister, of course—and no shortage of friends."

"Then she didn't kill herself because she was lonely?"

"Oh no, I don't think she was lonely, not at all. Signora Camilla was as happy as a clam I would say—and —" Zi' Bacco lowered his voice to a whisper. "Between us," he winked, "well, you know— she was a widow, not only a beautiful widow, but also a well-to-do widow—she had suitors."

"And who were the suitors?" Max asked.

Zi' Bacco didn't bother to answer. Instead, he walked ahead, leading Max into the courtyard of the villa, where flowering vines climbed the trellises and dozens of terra-cotta urns overflowed with hibiscus, geraniums, and hydrangeas. At the far end of the courtyard was a tall rock wall covered with night jasmine; blooming plants in terracotta pots cascaded from the ledges cut into the rock.

Zi' Bacco pointed a tobacco-stained finger toward an open doorway opposite the colorful terraced rock—it was the entrance door, flanked by flowering trellises and terra cotta urns. Perched above the louvered double doors was a Romeo and Juliet style balcony with purple bougainvillea climbing the railing.

The prospect of meeting with the sister of Camilla in this romantic setting had an exhilarating effect on Max.

"Catarì, Catarì!" cried Zi' Bacco, as if on cue.

A melodic voice called out, "Here, up here on the roof!"

Straining their necks to look up to the roof terrace, they saw the lovely face and wild blond curls of Katarina, peeping between purple bougainvillea.

"I'll be right down," she said.

"Do you take care of the plants in the courtyard as well?" Max asked Zi' Bacco.

"Thank heavens, no, Misha does that—he's Camilla's gardener. Well, I better get back to work. She's beautiful, too, the younger sister, don't you think? I suppose you know she is divorced." Zi' Bacco winked. "Camilla told me all about it, you know. See you around."

"I don't believe we have met, have we? though I saw you at the funeral. I'm Katarina."

The sight of the beautiful woman standing at the open door, framed by flowering vines, was intoxicating. The shorts and tank top revealed her slim and perfectly formed athletic body, but it was her smile that took his breath away; it lit up her whole face and showed off the dimples in her cheeks.

"Max De Angelis, please call me Max."

"Come in, Max. I'm having breakfast on the roof. Care to join me for a cup of coffee or tea?"

"Whatever you're having is fine."

Max was a little astonished by Katarina's carefree show of hospitality so soon after her sister's death; though he reasoned that a woman adept at the social graces would turn on her charm for anyone who came to call, and regardless of circumstances. Yet nothing seemed artificial about her.

He followed her into the kitchen and watched as she placed a small handful of green tea leaves into a warmed teapot and added a scoop of matcha green-tea powder from a tin can. She poured a kettle of boiling mineral water into the teapot, and then placed the pot and two Japanese stoneware teacups on a bamboo tray. Max was impressed; only in San Francisco's Japantown had he seen a better tea preparation.

Max carried the tray as he and Katarina climbed up three flights of narrow stairs to the roof terrace. The views were magnificent, even more enchanting than from the garden; it was like being on top of the world. Katarina took the tray from Max and set it on a table beneath a gigantic blue and white canvas umbrella that provided shade from the bright morning sun. They sat down beside the table on comfortable lounge chairs.

Katarina filled their teacups in silence. The only sound was the chirping of birds and seagulls squawking in the distance. Max enjoyed a few sips of the delicate tea, noting its lingering sweetness; the tea reminded him of fresh grass. He braced himself to ask Katarina about her sister.

"If you feel like telling me about what happened to Camilla—"

"My sister was murdered," she said, looking straight at him.

The moment her fiery jade-green eyes met his, they both felt a jolt, and it had nothing to do with the words she had just uttered. Katarina busied herself refilling the teacups and Max shifted in his chair, both pretending not to have noticed their mutual attraction.

"But what about the dream and the funeral arrangements and so on, wasn't that an indication of—well—you know—a plan to end her life?" Max said.

"Nonsense!" exclaimed Katarina. "In the scene from Virgil's *Aeneid* in my sister's dream, the heroine Camilla was killed in battle. She was a warrior, and so was my sister. Camilla loved life passionately; she would never have killed herself. How do you like the tea?"

"Eh—the tea is excellent, thank you," Max said, noting how abruptly Katarina's indignant tone had vanished. "But why? I mean—why would anyone want to murder her?"

"I've no idea why, but I intend to find out who the murderer is if it is the last thing I do, I swear to it." Katarina's green eyes flashed with anger as she sought out his eyes.

Max was the first to look away. "So, do you have any suspects?" he asked.

"Not yet, do you?" Without waiting for a response, she stood up and said, "I saw you kiss Camilla in the coffin; were you close friends?"

"I don't have any suspects," he said, evading the second question. The kiss—the bloody stupid kiss in the church, he thought, cursing himself, that was a dumb thing to do.

"And where were you the night of Ferragosto, do you have an alibi?" she asked, standing in front of him with her arms folded over her chest.

Bloody hell, Max thought, not only do the police think I'm a suspect; now the sister is suspicious of me as well. Max tried to remember where Katarina had been standing when he knelt by Camilla's coffin. What exactly had she seen? The accusatory look in her eyes was disturbing. Did she suspect that he hadn't told her the whole truth? Would it help if he told Katarina that he had kissed her sister—on the lips—because he had momentarily confused her with his ex-wife? And of course, he would have to explain what he was doing in the church in the first place. He decided against telling the truth; he would sound like an idiot.

"No—" he paused to take another sip of his tea. "No—actually— I don't have an alibi." Then he looked boldly into her eyes. "And do *you* have an alibi?"

Her eyes, with their unusual shade, like jade, flashed at him again. Then a wave of emotion suddenly arose from deep inside of her and she exploded into laughter; it was a contagious belly laugh. Max barely managed to keep himself from laughing as well, even though he had no idea what was so funny.

"You know, the police were here, just before you showed up. They asked me the same question—absolutely ridiculous. Ha, ha, ha. . ." She couldn't stop herself from laughing.

"No, I don't have an alibi, not really," she finally said.

Collapsing onto the chair, she covered her face with her hands. When she looked up again, her eyes were wet with tears.

They finished drinking the last of the tea in silence.

Afterwards, Katarina offered to show Max the house. "You've never been here before?" she asked, as they left the roof terrace and stepped into her bedroom.

"No."

She looked at him as if she didn't believe him.

Max memorized every detail as he walked through the home. In Camilla's luxurious bedroom, located a flight of stairs below Katarina's, he had to restrain the urge to peep into the French armoires or open the books stacked on her antique nightstands. Tall double doors with embroidered blue and white drapes opened onto a balcony with a splendid view of Monte Solaro. The large en-suite bathroom was tiled with handmade turquoise ceramic tile from Vietri; it had fancy English fixtures, a double glassed-in shower, and a tub under a large window that opened to another stunning view of the mountain.

"If we're going to find the murderer," Max said, as they walked down another flight of stairs to the living room, "we need all the clues we can get."

She stopped on the stairs and looked up at him with a mocking expression in her eyes. "What do you mean by, *we*?"

"Well, don't you think two heads work better than one?"

"Maybe."

"OK then, why don't you tell me everything you can remember about the circumstances of your sister's death?"

They entered the high-ceilinged living room; it was filled with antique French furniture. Old Italian mirrors and prints of Capri in ornately carved frames fought for space on the walls with Neapolitan School gouache paintings. Max recognized a few paintings by local artists as well. They sat down across from each other on a pair of blue satin sofas.

Max smiled encouragingly at Katarina. "Tell me if there is anything that struck you as strange or unusual about the night of Camilla's death?"

"Well, for starts, she made plans to have dinner without me that evening. She said I would be bored by the company. But I enjoy all of Camilla's friends. So, I can only think of one reason she wouldn't want to take me with her that night—she was having a secret rendezvous with someone after dinner, although I have no idea why Camilla would want to keep me out of her private life," Katarina said, sounding hurt. "Maybe something bad happened during that rendezvous."

Max didn't interrupt with speculations of his own, but simply nodded encouragingly.

"If it wasn't a rendezvous with a lover, then maybe it was a robbery," she continued. "But that doesn't make any sense to me. Why would someone kill her just to get a diamond necklace? And why take her to such an out of the way place? I can't see how—"

"Hey, wait a minute, what did you just say?" Max interrupted. "What diamond necklace?"

"Well, Camilla always wore a diamond necklace when she was on Capri. She called it her 'Cleopatra necklace.' It was a family heirloom from her mother-in-law. But when I went to the morgue to identify Camilla, the necklace wasn't around her neck. I asked everywhere for it. The police were kind enough to check with the helicopter crew and the people at the morgue, but nobody came forward to say they had seen it; in fact, they all said she wasn't wearing a necklace when they found her."

"And are you entirely sure she was wearing it that night?"

Katarina hesitated, "To tell you the truth, I don't remember if she was wearing it. I'm so used to seeing her wear the necklace that I just assumed she had it on, but I couldn't swear to it. The police asked me the same question. I have looked for it here in the villa, but I haven't been able to find it."

"Could the necklace have broken when she fell down the cliff?" Max wondered aloud.

"I guess it is possible; even if the chain has a safety latch."

"Can you think of anything else that might have been stolen from your sister that night?"

"Yes, in fact Camilla's purse is missing; a purple evening bag. I reported it to the police, but so far no one has found it."

Max gave her a blank look, and she explained: "I'm talking about the purse Camilla had with her when she went to have dinner with her friends at the restaurant Le Grottelle—after we had a drink together in the Piazzetta. I thought the color of the purse was just the right shade for the outrageous dress she was wearing."

"So, a missing purse, hmm... Might Camilla have had something valuable in the purse, something she would want to protect?" Max was doing his best not to sound as skeptical as he felt.

Katarina shook her head. "I can't think of anything at the moment."

"Well, for argument's sake, let's consider the case of suicide, if you don't mind. What would you do with your purse if you were about to jump to your death?"

"I don't know. Maybe I would leave it at the top of the cliff; but the police didn't find a purse at Belvedere delle Noci, did they? I certainly can't imagine jumping off the cliff holding a silly purse in my hand. It doesn't make any sense, does it? —unless of course she didn't jump, but was pushed. Or maybe she hid it somewhere...before she was pushed."

Max didn't know what to say, and he seriously doubted that the purse had any significance. He imagined what his boss Bob would say if he told him he had reached the conclusion that the woman hadn't committed suicide because her purse hadn't been found.

"Did your sister have a cell phone?" Max asked.

"Yes, but she didn't take it that night. The police found it here in her bedroom. They confiscated it, along with her laptop. Camilla told me she was writing a book about her life. I haven't found a manuscript in the house, maybe it's on the laptop."

"Anything else?" Max got up. He couldn't resist examining the contents of the bookcase in the living room.

Katarina waited to speak until he had finished leafing through some of the books.

"The police asked me this morning if I knew anything about Camilla's private life. They wanted to know if she had a love interest and if there were any spurned lovers or quarrels or anything like that."

"What did you tell them?"

Katarina looked into his eyes again, as if searching for an answer to something. "Camilla was at times secretive about her private life; for the past year or so she never talked to me about anyone in particular. Then, of course, it's possible that I was so preoccupied with my own personal life that I didn't pay much attention to what she was going through. When I arrived on Capri, though, I found out that something had changed."

"What changed?" Max had to admit to himself that it was possible that his interest in this case was no longer entirely professional. His curiosity about the cause of Camilla's death was already piqued, but the presence of the lovely sister didn't hurt to make him take a special interest in the case.

"Yes, it was rather strange. Camilla practically apologized for keeping me in the dark about a foolish affair she had been having. She said that it wouldn't have been wise to reveal her secret. She said her affair with that man was over. She promised to explain everything to me the next day. And then—"

Katarina's eyes filled with tears. "The last thing Camilla told me— she said—she was in love—again."

CHAPTER 8 - BELVEDERE DELLE NOCI

Z i' Bacco was busy watering the garden as Max waved goodbye before skipping down Via Castello to the Piazzetta in less than seven minutes. He felt almost giddy after his meeting with Katarina, who had agreed to meet him for dinner the following night. He crossed the Funicular square and walked past the tables and chairs outside Bar Funicolare, occupied by a bunch of gossiping old-timers. Around the corner from the funicular building, he found the person he was looking for.

"*Che bello vederti, Raffi!* (Nice to see you, Raffi!)"

At hearing Max's cheerful voice, Raffi looked up from his iPad. He was sitting at a table in his "office" on the little-known back terrace of Bar Funicolare.

"Morning, Max. Sounds like your day is going well."

"Yeh," Max smiled. "Are you up for a walk? I'm heading towards Belvedere delle Noci, then how about having lunch at Le Grottelle?"

"Since when have you become a tourist?" Raffi joked as he packed away his iPad in his backpack. "Hey, I thought your vacation was over. Aren't you supposed to be working on the case, even on a Sunday?"

"Believe me, I'm working as hard as I possibly can," Max grinned.

Walking up Via Longano, Max told Raffi everything that had happened since they last saw each other. He talked about his suite at Hotel Gatto Bianco and seeing his friend Silvio, the *pizzaiolo* on Friday night. Then he went on to describe Saturday´s events: Camilla Kallberg´s odd funeral, questioning the church custodian Domenico Ruggiero, and meeting with the Chief Inspector of Police. Lastly, he talked excitedly about just returning from Villa Ciano where he had met the custodian Zi' Bacco and had tea with Katarina, the beautiful sister of Camilla Kallberg.

"Sounds like this sister is quite enchanting. You say it's in her best interests that the death is not a suicide? Looks like two million dollars in her interests. You have a bit of a conflict of interests, don't you?" Raffi said teasingly.

"Mm, maybe," Max couldn't hide a smile. "If it's not suicide, then Katarina is a suspect; she doesn't have an alibi. And if she knew about her sister's insurance policy, that would give her a definite motive; she may not have known about the nonpayment clause for suicide."

"And you don't know if she is in her sister's will, right? Seems like Katarina would inherit some of her sister's estate, even if there are other family members."

"You're right. I've no idea what's in the will; the police said they're checking into it. From UGI's records, Camilla Kallberg's parents are deceased, so is her husband and the only sibling is Katarina. There are no children."

After a twenty-five-minute walk uphill, Max and Raffi decided to take a break and walked onto Piazzetta delle Noci, the most well-known of three belvederes in the Dentecala area. There in front of them, the Sorrentine Peninsula and the Amalfi Coast spread out along the Mediterranean Sea; the hazy gray outline of Monte Faito, named for the many beech trees, was barely visible as it rose above the Gulf of Salerno.

"Look, Li Galli!" Raffi exclaimed, pointing to the famous little islets close to Positano. "Did you know that the sea around the archipelago is now a national underwater park?"

"I think that's great. What are the odds that parts of the sea around Capri will be made into a protected national park as well? It would be a bloody miracle if that ever happened," Max said flippantly.

Raffi shook his head; he had pulled out his camera from the backpack and was positioning it on a pullout tripod. "No chance in hell, with all the commercial interests competing for tourist money on the island."

In the middle of Piazzetta delle Noci was a miniature votive temple with an exquisite figure of the Madonna set into a niche carved in a rock below a gnarled ancient tree. Votive temples with the little figure of the Madonna were all over Capri; the locals called it a *Madonnina*, frequently honored by fresh flowers placed at her feet. After Raffi had taken a few dozen photos of the Madonnina and the surrounding views, the two friends climbed up a broad incline with intermittent steps. Passing cackling hens and parading roosters behind fenced-in plots of land along the way, they soon came to a plateau of pine trees named Piano delle Noci.

From the plateau, Max and Raffi descended a narrow path and arrived at Belvedere delle Noci.

They were rewarded with a mesmerizing view of the jagged eastern coastline of Capri, where sheer cliffs and spires plunged into the dazzling turquoise waters of the Mediterranean.

Standing by the railing shoulder to shoulder, they fell silent; this was the place where Camilla had plunged to her death, whether voluntarily or not.

The belvedere was built right on the edge of the cliff. It was both an intimate viewing terrace and a precipitous balcony. A series of protective railings prevented visitors from falling down the steep, treacherous cliffs; only the foolish would test the railings by leaning on them. This spectacular setting was ideal for watching the rising of the moon; it was also known among insiders as the best place to go after dark to watch *le stelle cadente*, the falling stars. Max had seen these magical light shows many times in his youth.

While Raffi was busy adjusting the lens of his camera, Max sat down on a stone bench. Shutting his eyes against the blinding sunlight reflected off the sea, he had a vision of Tara sitting there beside him on the night of San Lorenzo, said to be the time when one can see the most falling stars. My God, she was beautiful! As they watched the stars streaming down from the sky, one after another, they each made a secret wish. Max's wish hadn't come true. He didn't know about Tara's. Max touched the horn-shaped charm on the chain around his neck and raised it to his lips.

"Are you OK?" Raffi's concerned voice interrupted his melancholy thoughts.

Max opened his eyes. "In all your travels around the world, have you ever seen a place more beautiful?" he asked, ignoring his friend's question.

Raffi shook his head. "Nothing beats this."

Max and Raffi didn't find any clues at Belvedere delle Noci, despite examining every millimeter of the terrace, the railings, the path, and the surrounding vegetation. Apart from old cigarette butts and pieces of debris—nothing. Just in case they had missed anything hidden in plain sight, Max photographed the grounds and railings with his cell phone, while Raffi photographed the panoramic scenery.

Max suddenly came to the realization that Raffi preferred taking pictures without any people in them. It was as if he wanted his photos of Capri to be timeless—like memories from the past. Max could not remember seeing a single photo with people in it that Raffi had taken on Capri.

He wondered about Raffi's obsessive need to record the scenery on Capri with his camera. Whenever he visited Raffi in San Diego, scenic photos from Capri were running non-stop on his 60-inch TV screen. Raffi was justifiably a bit nostalgic; he had been practically forced out of Capri by his father's bankruptcy and subsequent decision to leave the island for good and move his family to America. Perhaps when Raffi was visiting, he could only bear to look at beautiful images of Capri through the camera lens to keep himself at a safe distance from his lost island. Max knew better than to ask his friend this question.

She Was Not Alone

Max and Raffi were walking back on Via Dentecala when they heard a voice calling, "Max, Max!" They looked around.

"Here, I'm up here!"

Just above their heads, a round face, beaming with joy, leaned over a stone fence of Da Tonino restaurant. "Max, it's been ages!"

Domenico, an old classmate of Max from their *Liceo scientifico* [4] (secondary school), came rushing down the stone stairs of the restaurant to greet Max and Raffi; he insisted they all share a glass of bubbly with some aged Tuscan pecorino cheese.

"Please, both of you, come for dinner one night, will you?" Domenico said, brimming with enthusiasm. "And bring your friends, you will be my guests."

After some pleasantries, Domenico asked Max what he was doing on Capri, and when Max told him about the case he was investigating, Domenico got excited.

"Yes, yes, of course I knew Camilla; I knew her very well. She was an old friend of mine; she loved coming here. I was incredibly sad to hear of her tragic death."

"So, what do you think, Domenico, since you knew her so well, do you think she would have killed herself?"

Domenico's round amiable face grew serious. "It is my experience that nobody knows for sure what goes on inside another person's head, especially here on this island. Capri is like many small places where everyone knows everything about everyone, and people often hide their true feelings. Capri can make a gentle soul feel melancholy, you know."

Max nodded.

"Do you know the time of her death?" asked Domenico.

---

[4] Liceo scientifico (literally *scientific lyceum*) is a type of secondary school in Italy. It is designed to give students the skills to progress to any university or higher educational institution. Students can attend the *liceo scientifico* after successfully completing middle school (*scuola media*).

"According to the coroner, it was sometime between 11 pm and 3 am on the night of Ferragosto,"[5] Max said.

Domenico shook his head sadly. "She passed by Da Tonino just before eleven; it's so strange to think of that now."

"What do you mean, Domenico?" Max was flabbergasted.

"Well, actually she passed by on the street below the restaurant—just where I saw you today—and she wasn't alone. She was talking with someone."

"Did you see them?"

"No, no, I didn't see them, I was terribly busy with the restaurant. But I recognized the voice of Camilla, she had a distinctive accent when she spoke Italian, you know. Yes, it was her, there is no question. I was surprised to hear them on the street at that hour. I almost expected them to walk into the restaurant."

"Did you recognize the voice of the other person?" Max asked.

"Mm, nah, I don't know who it was."

"Did you see her with anyone lately? What about here at the restaurant?"

"Well, Max, I saw her around Capri with a lot of people. She often came here with friends, but she hadn't visited for a while."

"Do you recall anyone who seemed to be a special friend?"

Domenico shook his head, and then he smiled, "To tell you the truth, it seemed that everyone was special to her. She even made me feel special."

---

[5] August 15th

CHAPTER 9 - LE GROTTELLE

A fter leaving Domenico, it took Max and Raffi less than ten minutes to reach Le Grottelle, a picturesque restaurant set into a series of natural caves. It was here that Camilla ate her last meal in the company of friends on the fifteenth of August, the night of Ferragosto.

The two friends found a table on the terrace with a spectacular view of the blue-green sea and the Amalfi Coast. While Raffi answered a couple of emails on his iPad, Max went to greet his old soccer friend, Gregorio. The tall, handsome *pizzaiolo* was putting logs into the restaurant's pizza oven, built into a little cave on a terrace a few steps above the restaurant. When he heard Max call his name, he turned around. "Max, old rascal, it's been forever, what a surprise!" he cried enthusiastically and gave him a big bear hug.

They chatted for a few minutes while Gregorio turned the focaccias in the glowing hot oven. "Go and sit down, my friend. I will bring one to you," he offered.

Minutes later, Gregorio skipped down the stairs on his long legs, carrying a hot, fragrant focaccia with rosemary and garlic to their table. Giovanni, the charming waiter who had worked at the restaurant for more years than Max could remember, brought them a chilled bottle of Greco del Tufo wine, and several platters of delicious appetizers. Then came *i primi* (the pasta course): plates of *mezzi paccheri con gamberi e zucchine*, tube-shaped pasta with shrimp and zucchini. This was followed by *il secondo* (the main course): a whole grilled *pezzogna*, sea bream, fished that very morning from the deep waters between the islands of Capri and Ischia.

Raffi scooped up the last of his grilled fish with a piece of focaccia. "*Allora* (So), Max, is this a suicide case or not? What do you think about this mystery person Domenico said Camilla was with?"

"Impossible to say, Raffi, we need more information."

Max excused himself for a moment; he had just seen Luigi, his old rock-climbing friend, and the owner of the restaurant, walk into one of the larger interior caves of the restaurant.

Luigi looked up from behind the cash register, his head almost touching the roof of the cave.

"Hey Max, I haven't seen you for ages! What are you up to? Are you rock climbing on Capri?"

"No, not this time. Right now, I'm here on business."

"Too bad," Luigi said. "By the way, did you know old Francesco passed away in the spring? Ironically, he died of natural causes. We know from experience that he could have died dozens of times from his reckless climbing on Capri."

"That old fox. No, I didn't hear about it." Max's face saddened. Francesco was his mentor; he had taught Max everything he knew about mountain climbing.

"What are you working on, Max?"

"I'm investigating an insurance claim regarding Camilla Kallberg. Strange case. I think you knew her, she was here the night of—"

"Of course, of course. I knew Camilla and her late husband Daniel very well. Can you believe it? She comes here to eat and then dies! What kind of advertising is that for my restaurant? You tell me."

Max shook his head. "If the police arrest you, I'll be glad to testify that it certainly wasn't the food that caused her death. I just had one of the most memorable meals ever, and coming from me, you know that says a lot."

"Yeh, I thank God every day that Mama is still with us. Can you believe that she's still cooking every single dish on our menu every day? Although it hasn't been easy for her since Papa passed away. Of course, my sister Costanza is invaluable in the kitchen as well. Ahh, I see you are with Raffi. Why don't we join you for espresso?"

The Sunday lunch crowd had all departed by the time Luigi's sister Costanza came out of the kitchen, built into yet another small cave, carrying her signature dessert on a large platter.

"You're not leaving without having a slice of my *Torta di Ricotta*, are you?" she said with a smile.

Costanza, wearing the traditional white chef's costume, complete with white kerchief, was as cheerful and sweet as Max remembered. Mama, the queen of the kitchen, followed, wearing an apron and a red kerchief, and carrying a bottle of chilled limoncello. Her piercing dark eyes had the ability to sum up anyone's character in an instant; not much escaped her in life.

The eight of them—Mama, Luigi and Costanza, the two waiters, Gregorio the pizzaiolo, Max, and Raffi, gathered around a large table under the shade of a pergola made of *pagliarelle di canna* (reed twigs).

They chatted while eating slices of Costanza's freshly made ricotta cake, followed by glasses of limoncello and espresso.

They soon produced their own theories as to why Camilla would kill herself; then they discussed the reasons for the opposite case.

"Nah, I don't believe it, I just don't think she killed herself," Mama said, shaking her head, the dark curls escaping the kerchief bobbing from side to side.

"Neither do I!" Roberta exclaimed with passion as she joined them at the table. She was Luigi's other sister, the delicate pale-skinned sister who looked much like her deceased father.

"OK, OK everyone," Max laughed. "So, let's reconstruct the evening, shall we? Let's start with you Luigi. Do you remember who Camilla was with that night?"

"They were a party of nine, all *habitués*. The lawyer, *Avvocato* Giordano, had made the reservation for nine o'clock. I seated them at a large table on the main terrace. Giordano was sitting at the head of the table, and his wife sat somewhere in the middle. I remember Camilla sat at the far end, close to the railing; she was the only single woman."

"The bill was divided in four," the waiter Giovanni volunteered, "and they all paid cash. I remember the Aragones and the Imperatores were there—"

Roberta broke in: "*Dottoressa*[6] Maria Rosaria Troisi and her companion were there. I chatted with them about how hot it had been on the day of Ferragosto, though nothing compared to the heat and humidity in July."

"All right, so what can you tell me about these four couples? Does anybody know where they reside on Capri?" Max asked.

Luigi, the owner of Le Grottelle, spoke up. "The Giordano's have a residence on Capri, but they told me they were returning to Padova the next morning. I'll give you his telephone number, Max."

It was the waiter Giovanni's turn. "The Imperatores have a villa somewhere at the very bottom of Via Occhio Marino; they are Neapolitans."

---

[6] A woman with a doctorate. A female physician..

"The Aragones live on Via Tiberio near my place. They own Villa Moneta, and they are from Naples," said Gregorio, the pizza maker.

"And I believe *Dottoressa* Maria Rosario Troisi bought and renovated the villa high up on Via Tuoro," Roberta said. "You know, the one that used to belong to the *armatore*, the ship-owner. She and her companion are also from Naples."

"Thanks, everyone, that helps a lot," Max chuckled. "Now can anyone tell me if you saw Camilla wearing a diamond necklace that night?"

He looked around the table at each of them, and one after another, they shook their heads; nobody recalled seeing a necklace.

"What about a purse? Do any of you recall seeing Camilla carrying a purse?"

No one spoke up.

"Well then, do any of you remember anything different about Camilla that evening, or anything unusual that happened while she was at the restaurant?" Max inquired.

"She was very quiet," Giovanni said. "I would say she was not at all like her usual cheerful self. And she left early, before the dinner was over. I have never seen her do that before. Also, she passed by me without saying good night."

"Yes, I remember it now," Roberta added. "She didn't talk to me at all the whole evening. That was definitely unusual for Camilla."

"She didn't stop in the kitchen to say goodbye to Costanza and me," Mama said. "She usually did."

"Either something bad had happened, or she was very depressed," concluded Luigi.

CHAPTER 10 - VIA TUORO

Max glanced at his cell phone as he and Raffi left Le Grottelle; it was almost five o'clock. "What do you say we go for a walk to digest our lunch? Let's see if we can find Doctor Maria Rosaria Troisi at her villa on Via Tuoro on a Sunday afternoon."

"Excellent idea," Raffi answered.

From Via Matermania, they took a shortcut that only locals would know about. By jumping over private gates, trespassing through colorful manicured gardens, and walking down a steep switch-back path, they arrived on Via Tuoro, which ran parallel to Via Tragara, but higher up. This was one of Max's favorite pedestrian pathways on Capri; it had kept the character and charm of bygone days. Behind the ornate gates set into the masonry walls, stairways led to stately old villas on the Tuoro Hill. Out of season, when the villas with few exceptions were empty, this was the road Max would come to as a boy whenever he wished to pick flowers for his mother to make her happy. He would scale the stone wall of one of the villas and climb into the beautiful gardens after the gardeners had finished their workday.

At the end of Via Tuoro, Max and Raffi climbed a steep path of stairs until they arrived at the gate of the last villa on the hill.

"I saw you at the funeral service for Camilla," Maria Rosaria said to Max as she came to open the gate; she seemed pleasantly surprised by the visit of these two handsome men.

Maria Rosaria Troisi was a tall, attractive woman in her mid-forties, with a sun-bronzed, freckled face; her long, wavy auburn hair was streaked with gold highlights.

Max introduced Raffi and himself and explained why they were paying her a visit.

The Signora led her guests out to the villa's terrace and then excused herself. Max and Raffi settled into comfortable white-cushioned arm chairs to admire the bird's-eye view of the milky white town of Capri, stretching in a wide arc along a saddle of land between the hills of Castiglione and San Michele.

Signora Troisi returned carrying a silver tray with a pitcher of lemonade topped with sprigs of mint, tall crystal glasses, and a plate of bite-sized pieces of *frittata di maccheroni*. She sat down beside Max and Raffi and poured lemonade into their glasses.

"Compliments on the lemonade; are the lemons local?" Max asked, after he had taken a sip from his glass.

"Thank you. You guessed it—quite local; the lemons and mint are from my garden."

"And compliments to the beauty of your home and its setting, only matched by the beauty of the maker of the lemonade," added Raffi.

Maria Rosaria smiled; she wasn't immune to gallantry. After passing around the plate of frittata, she looked at them and said, "I shall miss Camilla very much. We were quite alike in certain respects. Is there any way I can help you?"

"Yes, perhaps you can. Since you were a close friend of Camilla, do you think it possible that she committed suicide, and if so, why?" Max asked.

"I hesitate to answer that question since, in my profession as a psychotherapist, we continually come across unexplainable aberrant behavior. What I can say is this, I never would have expected it. I have no idea as to why Camilla would commit such an act. She was so full of life! Camilla didn't leave a suicide note, did she?"

Max shook his head. "Not that we know about, unless someone took it," he said.

"Camilla did say something that stuck in my mind when she was here at the villa for a dinner party a couple of weeks ago." Maria Rosaria paused and searched Max's eyes.

"Please go on," Max said, more than a little curious to hear what she had to say. Was he about to learn something that would confirm that Camilla had indeed committed suicide?

"We were sitting here in my garden together after dinner. The view that evening was too beautiful for words, almost unreal. Camilla said to me: 'I understand why Capri is sometimes called 'lotus land,' or the land of the 'lotus-eaters'. This island is a magical place where the outside world can be forgotten, and that is why sensitive souls who venture here have an aversion to returning to the ordinary world.' And then she said: 'Living an illusion can be a dangerous state of mind.'"

Maria Rosaria looked over the treetops at the dark silhouette of Monte Solaro as the sun cast its last golden rays from the ridge.

"That is what Camilla said, as I recall, and her tone was serious when she spoke those words. I thought at the time that she was just being philosophical. But after what happened to her, I wondered if she had been alluding to something in her personal life. Perhaps she had become disillusioned by someone or something."

"Do you think she had any enemies—anyone who may have wanted to murder her?" Raffi asked.

"I very much doubt that she had any enemies, and the idea of anyone wanting to kill her seems farfetched to me."

"Did she have a special friend, or maybe a lover?" Raffi asked, wiping his mouth with a linen cocktail napkin after swallowing a bite of the *frittata*.

"Let's just say, I would be surprised if she didn't. Camilla was a beautiful and vibrant woman. Many men were attracted to her."

"Do you know of anyone special that she was seeing?" Max asked.

Maria Rosaria took her time answering, slowly refilling their glasses before she spoke.

"I think it's not particularly useful to speculate about something one doesn't have concrete knowledge about. It could have grave consequences, don't you agree?"

So, Max thought, she may know something about a lover, but she isn't going to tell.

"Do you remember anything that seemed unusual when you last saw Camilla on the night of Ferragosto?" he asked.

"I sat next to her that night, and she looked splendid. I remember she was wearing a beautiful long silk dress, multicolored like a parrot, with blue suede sandals. She was quiet and thoughtful, but she didn't appear distraught. However, it was not like her to leave before we had finished dinner, and by herself. To be frank, I had assumed she was leaving early because she had a date with someone."

"Do you remember if she was wearing a diamond necklace? And was she carrying a purse, a purple purse?" Max asked, as he helped himself to another tasty morsel of the homemade *frittata*.

"Sorry, I don't remember seeing a purse, though I assume she brought one; but yes, she was wearing her outrageous diamond necklace," Maria Rosaria said with a smile.

"Are you absolutely sure she was wearing the necklace on that particular night?" Max asked.

"Yes—I'm sure. I remember noting that her dress had such a high neckline that it didn't do justice to the dazzling necklace; in fact, it almost hid the large diamond." Maria Rosaria's brows were knit together in a frown of disapproval.

Max marveled that someone other than himself noticed these minute details. "Compliments on your observational skills," he said. Then he asked, "Your companion, is he on Capri?"

"Fabrizio? No, he left for Naples about an hour ago. His vacation is over; he must return to his law practice tomorrow, and I, alas, must go back to work in Naples next week."

"And you were together the night of Ferragosto between 11 pm and 3 am?"

"Absolutely, I can swear that is the truth," Maria Rosaria nodded.

After some pleasantries, Max and Raffi thanked Maria Rosaria and reluctantly took their leave.

"By the way," Raffi said as he closed the gate behind them. "I like your line of work, Max. You get to spend your days socializing, eating, and drinking with beautiful women and friends, and you get in shape by taking long walks and climbing stairs—not to mention staying in fancy hotels free of charge. Not bad, not bad at all."

Max laughed, "True, I do like it well enough; but you know, this Capri assignment is not quite like anything else I've worked on. I'd like nothing more than to stay in 'lotus land' and continue investigating this insurance claim for another month or two. However, I have a feeling the office won't be that patient. I doubt my boss will pay me to stay on Capri for very much longer."

"You said the police thought that accidental death was unlikely, so from what you learned today, do you think it was suicide or murder?" Raffi asked, as they walked back to town in the early twilight.

"Let's just say, there are a few missing pieces to this puzzle. Who was Camilla walking with on the way to the belvedere? And where are the missing items—the diamond necklace and the purse. As far as motive and opportunity for foul play, the only suspect so far, apart from myself, is the sister. The police have a lengthy list of arguments for suicide, and I can't say I have found any evidence to refute it. So, the police might very well call it a suicide, which would make the office happy and move me up in line for a promotion, a promotion I've been waiting for way too long, I can tell you."

"I know how hard you've worked for it," Raffi said sympathetically. "How are things working out for you in San Francisco?"

"Not too bad, the job keeps me busy, but the rent for my apartment is sky-high, which makes it almost impossible to put any money aside—not that I could afford to buy anything in San Francisco anyway."

"Where is Tara living?" Raffi asked. "Do you ever see her?"

"Well, she kept the house in San Francisco, fair enough; it was money from her grandmother that helped us to buy it. I hardly ever see Tara, but she dropped off the cat with me before she left for a trip to India. I took the cat to Tara's neighbor before leaving for Capri, since Tara is still in India. How is life in San Diego, are you seeing anyone special?"

"Nah, you know me, I don't want to commit, not yet."

They walked in silence for a while, contemplating their lives back in the States. Max sensed that Raffi, the jet-set bachelor, was lonely in his life, too.

At the end of Via Tuoro, they turned left at Ruggiero's nursery above the Evangelical Church and arrived at Via Camerelle, a pedestrian road dating back to Roman times.

"Back to civilization," Raffi said humorously.

"More like the *lack* of civilization," Max quipped.

On the uphill side of Via Camerelle, the Romans had built about forty *camerelle*, little rooms, each with a massive brick arch. The rooms were originally designed to serve as cisterns along this road that connected Castiglione, the Imperial villa on the castle hill, with the Imperial villa of Tragara. Restaurants and fancy brand-name boutiques occupied the cisterns now, their chic awnings offering shade under the Roman arches. Max and Raffi passed by the most iconic building on Via Camerelle—the blood red Villa Pompeiana high above the street; when it was built on top of the arches in 1879 this road was nothing but a dirt path.

The trendy Via Camerelle was bustling with dressed-up vacationers on their way out for the evening. Some of the *habitués* were still dressed in beach attire; the women wearing flowing caftans or simple linen outfits, the men wearing shorts and polo shirts or t-shirts. They were on their way back to their residences to change, after a day spent at the beach or on a boat, perhaps after having stopped for a drink in the Piazzetta.

At this hour, *i giornalieri*, the day-trippers, were gone. Most of the weekend crowd had left as well. This Sunday's departure from the island was particularly busy, as it was the final day of the Ferragosto holiday week.

As Max and Raffi came to the end of Via Camerelle, the imposing peach-colored Grand Hotel Quisisana came into view, its terrace tables filled with well-dressed patrons taking their aperitifs. This was the hotel where Max had learned to mix drinks while working behind the bar one summer.

The Quisisana has been favored by wealthy Americans since the days when it served as headquarters for American airmen on R&R from 1943 to 1945. The American Officers Club had been in the hotel and Colonel Woodward, the governor of Capri during those war years, "commuted" by jeep on the pedestrian roads between his office in the Hotel Quisisana and his lodging in Villa Vismara at Punta Tragara.

A few steps up the street from Hotel Quisisana, the two friends stopped outside the arcade leading to Max's hotel, Gatto Bianco.

"Do you feel like joining me tomorrow morning?" Max asked. "I want to walk up to Villa Moneta to speak to the Aragones, who were present at the dinner with Camilla Kallberg that night."

"I wouldn't miss it for the world," Raffi grinned. "I almost forgot, my aunt invited you for dinner tomorrow night, want to come?"

"Sorry, I have other plans. I'm meeting Katarina Kallberg."

"You rascal. This beautiful Katarina, she isn't available by any chance, is she?" Raffi joked.

"Yes, she's divorced. But this meeting is strictly business."

"I'll bet." Raffi raised his eyebrows.

CHAPTER 11 - TWO SISTERS

ALL ALONE - MONDAY, AUGUST 23

Opening the bedroom shutters wide, Katarina took a deep breath of fresh air while marveling at the stark beauty of Monte Solaro, colored pink in the early morning sun.

Finally, she had slept through the night, after nights of anguish and restlessness from the shock of Camilla's death.

Eight days had passed since Ferragosto, the night when her sister fell to her death on the cliffs of Belvedere delle Noci, only two days after Katarina had arrived on Capri for her vacation with Camilla.

The week had been an emotional rollercoaster for Katarina. Her joyous time with Camilla abruptly collapsed into long hours of terrifying suspense when her sister was discovered missing, followed by the horror of finding out she was dead and then having to identify her body. The days that followed were a nightmarish mixture of grieving and hectic preparations for the funeral.

Leif and Kristian, her cousins, arrived on Capri the night before the funeral and left for Norway soon after the burial. Emilio Ascione, Camilla's lawyer, returned to Naples with them that afternoon on the same hydrofoil. Taking advantage of his opportunity at the cemetery to stand shoulder to shoulder with Katarina, Emilio had whispered in her ear that he would be happy to spend the night with her, so she wouldn't have to be alone. She was touched by his solicitude but had declined the invitation; somehow it felt like an untimely flirtation.

Then there was Lorenzo, the boatman—faithful Lorenzo, big and strong and dependable. Camilla had always relied on him to solve any problems, as if he had been her own brother. After Camilla's burial, he had persuaded Katarina to have dinner with his family, so she wouldn't have to spend the evening by herself. The dinner with Lorenzo and his wife and children was a bit awkward since she had never met his family before; afterwards, he drove her home to the villa. There they had a couple of glasses of grappa, while sitting sadly on the blue couches of the living room. If Lorenzo had offered to stay the night, she might have accepted; she desperately needed someone to snuggle up to, but after giving her a warm embrace, Lorenzo went home.

Then Katarina was all alone. She crept into bed and cried until exhaustion overtook her and she fell into a restless sleep.

The terrible grief continued in the days that followed, and it seemed as though her heartache would never end.

Katarina prepared a thermos of coffee and a basket of breakfast items to take up to the roof terrace, just as she had always done with Camilla. She reclined in her chair under the shade of the giant white and blue umbrella. While sipping her coffee, she tried to remember everything that had happened since her arrival on Capri.

ARRIVAL - A FULL MOON - FRIDAY, AUGUST 13

"Kati, Kati! Over here!" It was Camilla, shouting and waving from the pier. Katarina waved excitedly to her sister. The first person off the hydrofoil, she ran to hug her sister, who was standing at the side of the impatient crowd waiting to embark. "Kati, finally you are here. I'm so happy to see you!"

Camilla looked radiant, sun-bronzed, and elegantly dressed in a short white silk dress with a parrot-green scarf slung casually over her shoulders.

Arm in arm, they walked the short distance to one of Camilla's favorite restaurants, Approdo, the Italian word for "landing." This was the place where Camilla would take guests for dinner when they arrived on the main port of Capri, before riding up to the villa in a taxi.

Camilla ordered a bottle of Greco di Tufo by Benito Ferraro with the dinner. They ate slowly, enjoying the fresh *impepata di cozze* (steamed mussels with ground pepper), fresh grilled scampi, and a simple salad of rucola while they chatted non-stop. There was so much they wanted to share during Katarina's visit.

Marina Grande was exceptionally beautiful that night. The sky over the sea was indigo blue, and the warm, velvety air caressed the skin. The brilliant orange rays of the sun, setting behind the island of Procida, reflected on the rippling water of the harbor and turned everything to gold. Katarina loved the sight of the little boats drawn up on shore, and the row of ancient multicolored houses along the waterfront. The huge brightly lit car ferry docked at the pier dwarfed everything else in the harbor. She drank it all in—the beauty of Capri, the joy of her newfound freedom after her painful divorce, and the love she felt as she watched her sister's radiant smile.

When they had finished their delicious dinner, and were sipping the last of the chilled wine, Camilla looked at Katarina with unexpected seriousness.

"There is something I want to talk to you about, Kati."

"Shoot."

"I've had an intuition—or a premonition, you might call it, and it has made me decide to put my house in order, so to speak."

"Whoa! What are you referring to—exactly." Katarina was startled.

"I had a dream a few weeks ago, and it reminded me of this scene from Virgil's *Aeneid:*

> *She sank to earth undone,*
> *her cold eyes closed in death,*
> *and from her cheeks, the roses fled.*   —Book 11, Line 847

Katarina felt a chill go down her spine while listening to her sister recite the lines of the poem.

Camilla went on to describe the dream about her namesake, the Amazon warrior who was killed in battle. "In the dream, I recognized the face of the virgin warrior as my very own, as if I was looking into a mirror!"

Katarina felt a desperate need to joke. "A virgin?"

"Fortunately not, Kati, I wouldn't want to die a virgin." Camilla suddenly laughed, the big open laugh Katarina knew and loved.

"You think you're going to die—just because of a silly dream?"

"I hope that it was only a dream and not a premonition, but I've made a list of instructions for my funeral just in case. And I have made provisions for you in my will."

Katarina was speechless.

Camilla continued. "Here it is, with all the instructions in case something happens to me. Too few people think about all the hassle they will create for their relatives when they pass away if they don't leave clear instructions. My will is with Emilio, you know, my lawyer in Naples. I'm leaving my home on Capri to you. Please, Kati, don't look at me like that. Let's toast, shall we? To us!"

After dinner, when they took a cabriolet taxi up to Camilla's villa, the full moon shone brightly over the illuminated town of Capri.

A BEAUTIFUL DAY - SATURDAY, AUGUST 14

The following day, they didn't talk about Camilla's dream or her will. The sisters spent a glorious day on the beach at Da Luigi by the Faraglioni rocks. The beach club was crowded, as on most Saturdays in the summer. Katarina chatted with several of Camilla's Neapolitan friends; many of them had become her friends as well. Then they put on snorkels and fins and went for a long swim before lunch.

Their lunch at the beach restaurant was divine, with fresh grilled anchovies, grilled vegetables, and chilled Fiano di Avellino, followed by espresso for Camilla and the usual café Americano for Katarina.

While Camilla relaxed on her sun lounger after lunch, Katarina dove into the sea. When she climbed back up the ladder to the beach, a charming man complimented her on her diving skills. He introduced himself as Giovanni Tempesta, a lawyer from Naples. He invited her to join him for coffee in the late afternoon, and she accepted, enjoying the attention. He talked excitedly about a public Ferragosto party at Gradola on Anacapri the following night. The food was expected to be fabulous, and he seemed extremely excited about going to the event. She got the distinct feeling he desired to see her again.

Later that day, Camilla and Katarina walked straight up the steep path from Faraglioni to Belvedere Punta Tragara and arrived dripping with sweat. Camilla had brought hand towels for them to dry off before enjoying a leisurely walk along Via Tragara into town. Once in the Piazzetta, they crowded around a table with animated friends from the beach, chatting and drinking Bellinis.

When they returned to the villa, they cooked dinner together, as Camilla preferred dining at home on crowded Saturday nights. They prepared one of Katarina's favorite pasta dishes, made with fresh garlic, pepperoncino, and sliced baby zucchini cooked in extra virgin olive oil from the local Brunetti Brothers. Chopped zucchini flowers, basil, and mint were added towards the end and served over *spaghetti alla chitarra*. The dish was sprinkled with freshly grated cheese from a nice chunk of Parmigiano Reggiano.

"This is a very special present from my dear friends Grazia and Albino; they know I'm crazy about Taurasi," Camilla said, as she opened a bottle of aged Mastroberardino Radici Taurasi Riserva DOCG. "I think tonight is the perfect occasion to taste this wine." Camilla poured the deep ruby-red wine into their wine goblets. "Try it and see what you think. The grapes come from the volcanic soil of the Avellino province."

When Katarina tasted the velvety wine, she was impressed by the intensity and complexity of the elegant wine. It brought back memories of picking wild blueberries in the forests of Norway with Camilla, and picking black mulberries in their grandmother's garden.

"Don't laugh Kati—would you believe it? I've decided to write a book about my life on Capri," Camilla said after finishing her plate of pasta. "Do you think it's a silly idea?"

"What a fantastic idea! You would never write a silly book; I can't wait to read it." Katarina got up from her chair to hug her sister.

"Shall we walk to the Belvedere Punta Cannone to digest the pasta?" Camilla suggested while they were putting the dirty dishes in the dishwasher.

It took them less than ten minutes to reach the half-moon shaped belvedere on the other side of the Castiglione hill. The belvedere was named Punta Cannone because the French, who controlled the mainland at that time, had strategically placed a cannon on this plateau in 1808 to defend the island's southern sector against the British. In the twentieth century, it became known as "Mahler Platte," or Painters Square, for the many artists who came to paint the dramatic landscape from there.

They had the splendid place all to themselves. Katarina walked over to the edge of the terrace and leaned over the cement railing to view the sea, 220 meters[7] below; she felt a sudden wave of vertigo and held onto the railing, then slowly stepped back while fixing her eyes on the ground.

---

[7] 722 feet

"Be careful, Kati!" Camilla hurried over from the other side of the belvedere and put her arm around her sister's shoulder.

"Why do you think the crowds in the Piazzetta don't come here to see this?" Katarina asked. The bustling, noisy scene in the square a couple of hours ago sharply contrasted with the quiet splendor of this natural setting.

"Mostly out of disinterest or laziness; I guess they don't want to walk uphill for twenty minutes. But I gave up searching for an answer to that question a long time ago. I'm just so happy we can share this moment together— Look, Kati, look!"

An enormous red fireball appeared between the Faraglioni rocks and the promontory of Tragara. Katarina and Camilla watched as if spellbound. A day past being full, the red moon cut a swath of rippling gold in the bay. Against a sky as blue as a peacock's feather, the moon rose higher; its color changed from red to ochre and then to white, and moonlight gleamed silver in the midnight blue water of the bay.

Speechless, they watched the spectacle of nature unfold. Far below them, they could see the beaches of Marina Piccola and the houses stacked up on the hillside as clear as daylight. They could see every rock and crevice of the Arsenale shoreline, and through the transparent turquoise waters close to shore, they could see the boulders on the sea floor. Monte Solaro had taken on the bluish color of the moonlit sea. Below them, the black silhouettes of seagulls floated on the wind currents.

Dozens of mega yachts, sailboats, and smaller pleasure craft moored in the bay, now as still as a lake; the myriad lights of the vessels twinkled in the shimmering moonlit sea.

The beauty of the magical night made Katarina so melancholy that she almost cried. How she longed for a man to love, a man to share such a romantic moment with her. She looked at Camilla to see if she was feeling sad as well, but her sister seemed transfixed, she was smiling gently. Katarina wondered what secrets Camilla was hiding from her.

"Do you ever get sad, Camilla, when you witness such beauty?" Katarina asked, as they made their way back down from the belvedere; this time, getting a bird's-eye view of the moonlit Chartusian monastery, the monumental Certosa of San Giacomo.

"I do Kati, and I admit there were times when I was not strong enough to confront such exquisite beauty without suffering. But I would prefer to suffer deep emotions rather than not experience any emotions at all. When I first came to Capri, I recognized in an instant that the beauty of the island spoke to the beauty I felt in my heart. It was like the passionate rendezvous of two lovers, which is why I wished to have a home here, to be a part of this island forever. Through sorrows and joys, this sacred union has prevailed."

"Do you think marriage can be like that—a sacred union, as you say?" Katarina asked, though she doubted that she herself would ever find a lasting love. Apart from the gift of her lovely daughter, her marriage had been a failure.

"Absolutely, I do believe marriage is meant to be a sacred union." Camilla's face was radiant in the moonlight. "Marriage can be the most difficult of all relationships, but it becomes a sacred union when it's based on mutual love and respect and not on dependence and control. It will happen to you Kati, and when it does, you will know to value and protect it. When lovers share everything in life, the good and the bad, the ugly and the sad, then it becomes a sacred union."

"And what if I fail—again?" Katarina sounded skeptical.

"There is really no such thing as failure, Kati. There is only life. We must not be afraid of failing when we fall in love; life without love would be unthinkable. Every time we give or receive love, our heart expands. We must never give up on love or stop searching for the divine beauty in everything that exists."

After their walk, the two sisters sat on the roof terrace of the villa with glasses of cognac; they watched the stars and listened to Neapolitan songs on Camilla's iPod, attached to old fashioned speakers.

"Up here on the roof, I feel closer to the divine than I do anywhere else," Camilla said.

LAST DAY TOGETHER ~ SUNDAY, AUGUST 15

"Kati, what do you say we go to church this morning? Today is Ferragosto, you know." Camilla was busy stuffing shawls into their canvas beach bags. "We are going to need these to cover our shoulders, and we can't wear shorts in church."

Katarina was surprised by Camilla's suggestion. This would be the first time she had attended a church service on Capri. In Norway, she only went to church for weddings, funerals, and baptisms, and, of course, they all went to church on Christmas Eve.

"I'm a little surprised that you want us to go to church," Katarina said.

"Since this is the first time you're in Italy on the holy day of Ferragosto, I think you should observe the local customs, don't you think?" Camilla said.

"Yes, I suppose so. . ."

"The most important thing to remember on Ferragosto is to generously tip the people that work for you. I have tipped Zi' Bacco, you know, the caretaker, as well as Misha the gardener and Lina, my housekeeper. They have all taken the day off."

Katarina still wondered why Camilla wanted to take her to church. Did it have something to do with her dream? The death of her namesake, the Amazon warrior princess?

"It's the thing to do on Capri on the day of Ferragosto, you'll see," Camilla said as if reading Katarina's mind.

As they walked down Via Castello to town, the bells of the ancient campanile started to toll for mass. Katarina looked approvingly at her older sister. Camilla was wearing white linen pants and a white linen shirt, comfortable silver-colored sandals, and a fantastic straw hat by an American designer to protect her face from the sun. Black sunglasses completed the look. Katarina had chosen to wear a short white skirt, a blue cotton top, and no hat.

"Why is it called Ferragosto?" Katarina asked.

"The name comes from Latin, *Feriae Augusti*, the festivals of Emperor Augustus; they were introduced by him in 18 BC. It was a combination of several festivals that celebrated the harvest and the end of a lengthy period of intense agricultural labor. The calendar month of August is appropriately named after him. The Catholic Church conveniently believes that August 15th is the day God assumed the Blessed Virgin Mary into Heaven at the end of her life, and therefore it is a Holy Day of Obligation, making it a national holiday. Mostly it is an opportunity for Italians to celebrate together with their families while on vacation; you wouldn't believe the amount of food they prepare for the feast. Here on Capri, the restaurants will prepare elaborate dinners. For the finale, there will be spectacular fireworks at midnight."

Camilla finished her explanation just as they entered the little church square named after Ignazio Cerio. At least twice a day, Katarina would pass the white-painted facade of the ex-cathedral of Santo Stefano, admiring the baroque mixture of Moorish and Grecian elements that belonged so uniquely to Capri. But until this morning, she had never walked inside the building.

"Don't you think this church is a fantastical fairytale sculpture?" Camilla said.

Katarina nodded, smiling at her sister's fanciful description.

The ex-cathedral of Santo Stefano was packed full; they barely managed to squeeze into a pew. When Katarina looked around and saw that the church was filled with locals, she felt like an intruder, not just because she was not Catholic, but because this was the private sanctum of the Caprese. Glancing at her sister's profile, she could see that Camilla was totally at ease, and she relaxed. She closed her eyes, and soon the voice of the priest faded away.

"Did you have a nice nap?" Camilla was looking into her eyes, smiling gently. "It is time for cappuccinos."

As they were walking out of the church, a man came up from behind and tapped Camilla on the shoulder; it was Nicola Ferrante. Katarina knew him as a friend of Camilla, a *habitué* of Da Luigi.

"Kati, why don't you go ahead and get a table at Gran Caffè, I will be there shortly," Camilla said.

"Ciao Mario, how is it going?" Camilla flashed a brilliant smile at the waiter as she joined Katarina.

Mario smiled at the lovely blond-haired sisters. "Hey, did I see you two coming out of the church, and so early in the morning? I'm impressed. Now what are you ladies up to?"

"Today we are escaping from the masses, dear Mario. We are going to do what you locals do when you don't have to work; we are going to climb over the fence on Via Krupp and go swimming at Arsenale. What do you think, is it not an excellent idea?"

Mario nodded approvingly; he said he wished he could join them and avoid the sweltering day ahead on Ferragosto, always one of the busiest days of the year in the Piazzetta.

After a second round of cappuccinos, Camilla and Katarina left Gran Caffè and headed for Via Krupp. They found the gate to the pedestrian road open, by some miracle. Camilla didn't mention Nicola, nor did Katarina ask what he had wanted to talk to her about.

They climbed down the steep slippery trail from the lower part of Via Krupp to reach the area of Arsenale, a stretch of rocky shoreline mostly frequented by locals, as it was hard to access. Vito was there, a short, middle-aged man, sort of a recluse, with wild hair and bright blue eyes. For years, he had taken it upon himself to put out a sea ladder so that people could swim in the otherwise inaccessible sea. In this area by the grotto of Arsenale, bathing attire was optional. Camilla whispered to Katarina that she shouldn't go into the grotto itself, as it was often frequented by gay men who wouldn't appreciate her company.

They both chose to wear their bathing suits as well as snorkels and masks when they went for a long swim, staying close to the shore, as there were several hundred pleasure boats moored in the bay.

Still wet from the swim, they started the return trip up the steep trail. Upon reaching Via Krupp, they stopped to catch their breath. Camilla turned to Katarina, "I'm sorry Kati, I forgot to mention that I'm going out with some old friends for dinner tonight. Since they invited me, I find it awkward to bring a guest. You don't mind, do you?"

Katarina was taken aback by Camilla's words. She didn't know what to say or how to interpret the look on Camilla's face; her sister seemed strangely embarrassed.

"They are so much older than you; you would get bored, don't you think?" Camilla added while they walked side by side up the road.

Katarina couldn't understand why her sister had made plans for the evening without her.

"It's no problem," Katarina answered nonchalantly. "I was thinking of going to a party in Anacapri, at Gradola; they are supposed to be having a special Ferragosto celebration." She didn't see the point of mentioning that Giovanni, the man she had met at Da Luigi the day before, had said he was going to be there.

They made good progress walking up Via Krupp and took the fastest route home by way of Via Dalmazio Birago.

"If you want, let's have an aperitif together in the Piazzetta," Camilla said, as she put the key in the lock of the gate to the villa.

The long swim and the fast, vertical ascent of 200 meters had given them their workout for the day; they ate a light lunch and took a nap in the afternoon.

Admiring glances followed the beautiful blond sisters, dressed in long, flowing evening dresses, as they descended the broad flight of stairs, side by side, to the Piazzetta.

"Good Evening, Mario; two Bellinis please," Katarina said, smiling at the handsome waiter at Gran Caffè.

"I'm truly sorry Kati," Camilla said sadly, raising the fluted glass to her lips to take a sip of her drink. "Please forgive me for not spending this evening with you. I'll explain everything soon, I promise. Just give me a little more time."

Camilla lowered her voice, "You see, I thought I was in love, Kati, but it was an illusion. I was flattered, that is the truth of it. My vanity got the better of me and caused me to become a fool. I wanted to tell you about him . . . But it's all over now. I couldn't tell you about it any sooner—because—" Camilla's voice quivered.

Katarina feared her sister was going to cry.

Camilla took another sip of the Bellini, and when she looked at Katarina, there was a warm smile on her face and a sparkle in her eyes when she spoke:

"I'm in love—again. I want to dance! I want to sing! Love is life's glorious music."

At half past eight, they embraced and said goodnight in the Piazzetta before parting ways; Camilla walked up Via Longano toward the restaurant Le Grottelle, and Katarina headed for the taxi stand.

That was the last time Katarina saw her sister alive.

CHAPTER 12 - TESTIMONY

MONDAY, AUGUST 23

I'm in love—again. I want to dance! I want to sing! Love is life's glorious music . . . The memory of Camilla's last words to her on the fateful night of August 15th brought tears to Katarina's eyes. Enough crying, she told herself, and got up from her lounge chair to give the bougainvillea on the roof terrace a much-needed watering. The sun was high on the horizon and the temperature was rising, promising a scorching hot day. While watering the plants, Katarina's cell phone rang.

"Signora Kallberg, this is Chief Inspector Monti."

"Yes?"

Katarina had met the inspector when she went to the police station to report her sister missing.

"Would you mind coming down to the station, so we can get a deposition?"

"Of course, I'll come right away."

"And please bring your passport," the chief inspector added.

Katarina walked slowly down Via Castiglione, too lost in thought to enjoy the panorama. She was in no hurry to get to the police station, and struggled to push away the memory of her previous visit and the long agonizing hours of waiting alone at the villa until Captain Arcuzzi called to inform her that her sister had been found. Then having to accompany him to Naples to identify the body.

To distract herself from the memory of seeing Camilla in the chilly morgue, she directed her attention to the stone-paved road in front of her, recalling the history that Camilla had shared. The difficult construction of the private switchback road, Via Castiglione, was begun at the end of the 19th century and completed in 1938 by Count Galeazzo Ciano and his wife Edda, daughter of Benito Mussolini, to have access to their villa by car.

The castle for which the road was named was spectacularly situated on a limestone crag overlooking Capri and the surrounding sea. The story of the castle at the top of the hill fascinated Katarina. Twelve Roman villas were constructed on Capri during the reigns of Emperors August and Tiberius. Sometime around the year 1000, this castle was built on top of the ruins of one of the Roman villas; it was fortified between the 10th and the 11th century to protect the citizens from the barbarian invasions. Camilla had shown Katarina remnants of the protective walls and towers that once connected the castle with the town of Capri. Below the castle grounds, a path led down to the largest cave on the island, the Grotta del Castiglione, where the people of Capri would hide from the Saracen assaults during the middle ages.

The British occupied Capri in 1806 during the Napoleonic Wars when Joachim Murat, Napoleon's brother-in-law, was King of Naples. They used the castle in an unsuccessful attempt to defend the island against Murat and his French and Neapolitan troops. Afterwards the historic castle fell into neglect and came under private ownership.

Via Castiglione was opened to the public in the 1990s—a great advantage, Camilla had said; it meant she could take a taxi home, a rarity on Capri, or even own a car, since she had a parking space.

Katarina had learned as much about Capri and its history as she could fit in during the annual summer visits, and she knew her way around the island. Unfortunately, Camilla had never pointed out the location of the police station. Six days ago, when Katarina went to report her sister missing, she had mistakenly gone to the municipal police station near the town hall in the Piazzetta. By the time she had reached the state police station on Via Roma, she was frantic with worry when she spoke to the chief inspector.

When the police showed up at the villa the previous day to ask her if she had an alibi for the night of August 15th, she couldn't help laughing. She had laughed at Max when he asked her the same question. Now that she realized she could be a suspect, there was no reason to laugh.

"Good morning, Signora Kallberg, please take a seat," said Chief Inspector Monti

The Inspector sat officiously behind a wood desk with her dachshund perched on her lap.

"Please give your passport to my deputy, Captain Arcuzzi. He will write down your deposition. You're already acquainted, I understand."

Captain Arcuzzi nodded. He was the officer who had taken Katarina to Naples to identify her sister's body, and who had come to the villa the day before. The Captain was sitting at a desk in front of a computer screen.

"May we proceed in Italian, as on your earlier visit?" Chief Inspector Monti asked.

"Yes, if I don't understand something, I'll ask," Katarina answered.

"Kallberg, that is your maiden name?"

"Yes, I kept my maiden name when I married, so did my sister."

The questions came in rapid succession about her marital status, occupation, residence, and family. Then followed questions regarding her activities between arriving on Capri on Friday, August 13th and reporting her sister missing on Tuesday, August 17th. Captain Arcuzzi was typing as fast as he could on the computer keyboard.

"You reported your sister missing on the morning of August 17th. When and where was the last time you saw your sister alive?" inquired the chief inspector.

"In the Piazzetta at about 8:30 pm on August 15th."

"Where did you go after that?"

"I took a taxi to Gradola in Anacapri to go to a party."

"Why weren't you and your sister together that night?"

"She had an invitation to join old friends; I preferred going to a party."

"Can anyone verify your presence at the party?"

"I didn't know anybody there, and I only stayed for a brief time, not long enough to meet anyone. I felt tired that night, and I soon left."

"Really—Signora Kallberg, you didn't meet anybody?"

"I don't remember talking to anyone in particular. I took a bus back to town and walked straight to the villa and went to sleep."

"Did anybody see you on the bus or on the way to the villa?"

"I wouldn't know."

"Do you have any alibi for the time of your sister's death between 11 pm on August 15th and 3 am on August 16th?"

"I guess not, but I did not kill my sister."

"Did you look for a suicide note, Signora Kallberg?"

"I looked all over the house; I didn't find one."

"Why did you wait till August 17th to report your sister missing? What were you doing on August 16th?"

"I woke up early on August 16th and decided to go for a walk. The door to my sister's bedroom was closed when I passed her room on my way downstairs, so I thought she was still sleeping after a late night out. I hiked up the path to the top of Monte Solaro, and from there I followed the ridge to Migliera and down to Faro. I took a dip in the sea, had lunch, and headed back to Capri by bus, then I walked up to the villa." Katarina took a deep breath.

"That's a very long hike, Signora Kallberg, I'm impressed," said Chief Inspector Monti, managing a half smile. "And then?"

"Camilla was not at the villa when I returned; it was about 6 o'clock. When I went into her bedroom, the bed was made, and everything seemed normal. I couldn't phone her as I saw that she had left her cell phone on the make-up table. I assumed she had woken up late after her night out and that she had gone to the Lido of Da Luigi to swim. Often she stops in the Piazzetta afterward and doesn't return to the villa until 8 or 9."

Katarina took another deep breath before continuing.

"Anyway, I wasn't worried about her at that point. I had left a note in the living room to let her know that I was going for a hike. The note was still there on the table, and I assumed she had read it. But when she wasn't home by nine o'clock that night, I was frankly getting a bit upset. I thought she had gone straight out to dinner from the Piazzetta, as often happens, but I thought it strange that she would go without me, especially since it was the second evening we were not together. Anyway, I was tired after the long hike and went to bed early. When I woke up the next morning, on the 17th, and opened Camilla's bedroom door and my sister still wasn't there, I got really anxious. That's when I decided to report her missing."

"So, Signora Kallberg, when you were here on the 17th, you told us your sister had given you a detailed list of her funeral arrangements. Can you shed any further light on the possibility of your sister having committed suicide? What was her state of mind?"

"I've no idea why she would do such a thing. Her state of mind seemed reasonable. I don't believe she killed herself."

"Are you aware of your sister's testament?"

"No, I'm meeting with her lawyer in a few days, but Camilla did say—" Katarina hesitated.

"Yes, Signora, please continue."

"Well, she told me I was going to inherit her home on Capri."

"Were you also aware that you are the beneficiary of a life insurance policy worth two million dollars?"

Katarina gasped. "No, I had no idea."

"The insurance has a clause for nonpayment in the case of suicide. Is that why you are insisting it could not be suicide? So that you can claim the two million dollars in addition to the home on Capri?"

"No, I knew nothing about the insurance money, and I did not kill my sister!" Katarina said in an angry voice.

The chief inspector gently caressed the dog's soft ears. "How is your present economic situation, Signora Kallberg? You told us you were recently divorced. Is it possible that the suicide letter conveniently disappeared?"

Katarina hadn't noticed the steeliness of the inspector's gray eyes until now. "As I told you, I have a job in Norway; I am earning a decent living."

The chief inspector stood up from her desk and put the dog on the floor. She walked over to the window and back. Then she sat down once again and looked directly into Katarina's eyes.

"Do you know Max De Angelis?"

"I saw him for the first time at the funeral."

"Was he a friend of your sister?"

"I don't know, I think so."

"Did you know that he is a special investigator working for the insurance company investigating your sister's death regarding her life insurance policy?"

"No!"

Katarina was furious. She had been duped. Max had said nothing about his job or the reason for his visit. Why had he pretended to be a friend of Camilla? she wondered. Why had he come to the funeral and even kissed her sister? Was it possible that he was even Camilla's lover? Maybe his company hired him to prove that Camilla had killed herself, so they wouldn't have to pay the two million dollars.

The chief inspector appeared to be reading her thoughts: "Max De Angelis said he had never met your sister before. They were both in San Francisco when your sister took out a life insurance policy in the office where Max De Angelis works. His father worked at your sister's villa for many years. All just coincidences, do you think, Signora Kallberg?"

"I—I don't know." Katarina's voice was barely audible.

Katarina stepped back outside into the warm sunlight on the street. Seething with anger, she walked up busy Via Roma. Max De Angelis, damn him! He had so easily deceived her. How naïve she had been to trust some guy that suddenly showed up at her sister's funeral, somebody she had never even heard of before. How stupid could she be? He was a private detective on a mission to prove her sister had killed herself. How crazy was that? He wasn't a friend of

Camilla; he didn't even know her—well, at least, that's what he had told the police. And he didn't have an alibi; he had told her so himself. Could Max De Angelis be the murderer?

And now she was in trouble with the police as well, as if she didn't have enough trouble. She had lied to the police about her whereabouts on the night of Camilla's death. She hadn't wanted to lie, but she felt that she had no choice. She would just have to live with the lie, even if it made her a suspect.

The police had kept her passport and requested that she not leave the island, except to visit the lawyer's office in Naples if she gave them advance notice.

Katarina passed by the taxi station and the lines of people waiting for buses and entered the pedestrian area. Just as she was about to pass Bar Alberto, she stopped; the ice-cream counter looked very tempting. Yes, an ice cream was what she needed to cool down her fury. She squeezed into a chair at a table in the last row. The waiter brought her a large glass bowl with three scoops of ice cream. Heavenly. Licking the last of the ice cream off the spoon, she almost convinced herself that she had done the right thing by lying to the police.

Only one week ago, after she and Camilla said goodbye in the Piazzetta for the last time, Katarina had embarked on her own adventure.

Chapter 13 - A Taxi Ride

Sunday, August 15

As the stretch taxi sped towards Anacapri, Katarina let her body sink deeply into the luxurious lavender leather seats. The taxi's convertible top was down, and the warm evening breeze caressed her face. How lucky she felt to be back on Capri, to breathe freely again. The long, drawn-out divorce proceedings of the past year had been brutal. She was so very worn out.

Now on Capri with her sister, she could feel free and alive again—even laugh the way she used to. When was the last time she had truly laughed? Katarina closed her eyes and took a couple of deep breaths. There were times when it would have been easier to give up, to stop fighting for an end to her unhappy marriage. Only her little daughter's eyes had kept her going; for just one more day she would put on a mask and make small talk. When the evening came, she would collapse exhausted into bed and sleep through the night. And yet, she would wake up tired the next day. This went on day after day, week after week—how many months had it been?

Camilla had been there for her throughout that difficult year. Only with Camilla could she truly be herself and let her guard down. At times, she would break down and cry on the phone, but only when her daughter Anna was not around to hear it. With Camilla, there was no need for pretense; Camilla just listened. She would always say, "Katarina, darling, this will soon be over, and when that is, you will come to me in Capri for a holiday—"

Someone honked their horn; Katarina opened her eyes as they passed the statue of the Madonna bathed in the bluish light of evening. The larger than life statue of the Virgin Mary was set into a cleft of the rock wall on the side of the road. She noticed the taxi driver making a small, almost imperceptible sign of the cross over his chest. How reassuring his gesture was; it comforted her that a cab driver, who must have passed this statue thousands of times, still honored the Madonna, making a silent prayer for their safe passage on the nerve-racking hairpin turns of this spectacular road carved into the mountainside.

To the right side of the taxi was a protective railing, so close she could almost touch it; at the edge of the road, the cliff dropped straight down 305 meters.[8] Across the dark sea, she saw the lights of

---

[8] 1001 feet

Naples. The city's waterfront road, Via Caracciolo, gleamed like a string of pearls.

Katarina turned her head to look behind her. Lit up under a dark sky, the town of Capri fanned out between the hills of San Michele and Castiglione. The lights of boats and luxury yachts moored down at Marina Grande twinkled like diamonds. Beyond Capri, the lights of Massa Lubrense on the mainland made it seem as if the Sorrentine Peninsula was an extension of the island.

The taxi driver kept glancing in his rearview mirror; he couldn't help himself. The beauty of this woman struck him the moment he opened the door for her; but there was something more than beauty that attracted him. Her eyes were gently closed, and her face looked peaceful. Her tiny upturned nose was the cutest nose he had ever seen, and the sides of her mouth turned up ever so slightly, as if she was smiling to herself. He didn't talk, guessing that if she wasn't sleeping, she wished to be left alone.

Katarina didn't open her eyes again until the taxi stopped; they had reached her destination—the end of the road above the Blue Grotto. Another taxi pulled up just ahead of them. Katarina watched as a man and a woman stepped out; they were laughing, and then they embraced and walked down the narrow path towards Gradola.

It was Giovanni and—a woman.

Who is that woman? Katarina wondered, feeling embarrassed. What was I thinking? Just because Giovanni talked to me—and flirted a little—that didn't mean he was interested in me. All Italian men like to flirt.

Katarina hadn't thought to ask Giovanni if he was going by himself to the Ferragosto party when he mentioned it to her at Da Luigi yesterday. Suddenly, she realized that he had not personally invited her to meet him there. Katarina, you idiot, what in the world are you doing here? she chided herself. I can't go now. Why would I go to a party all by myself where I don't know anybody? I would look desperate. Of course, they would all be couples. Why didn't I think of that before?

Katarina's anger at her own stupidity upset her so much that, for a moment, she thought she was going to vomit. All it took was a few flattering words and a pair of passionate eyes for me to make a fool of myself; she cursed herself silently.

The taxi driver stood politely outside the taxi holding the door open for her, but she didn't move. He looked at her stony face, but she didn't notice him; she was looking past him. He turned his head and saw the backs of a couple walking, arm in arm, down the path. Is she staring at them? he wondered.

Something stopped him from saying anything to her. She just sat there, motionless. All was quiet; only the noise from a restaurant in the distance filled the silence.

"Take me back—please."

Her voice was so faint that he had to strain to hear it. The driver closed the door and returned to his seat to start up the engine.

After a few turns up the road, he couldn't restrain himself any longer. "Do you know that it is Ferragosto today?" he said.

"Yes."

He drove in silence for a while.

"So, what're you doing for Ferragosto?"

She took her time before answering. "Nothing."

The taxi driver continued driving slowly up the dark curvy road.

"Well, at least you must eat something somewhere."

"Eat—" she said. "I'm not hungry." Her voice sounded sad.

The driver turned on the radio. Some modern rock music was playing; he turned it off. He slowed down the taxi even more; he was not in any rush to get Katarina back to town.

Food—absolutely not—I'm not hungry, Katarina insisted to herself; but her stomach did not agree. After swimming at Arsenale, she and Camilla had eaten a light lunch to save their appetite for a Ferragosto feast. The more Katarina thought about food, the more she felt famished. How silly, she thought. First, I make a fool of myself, and now all I can think about is food. She laughed.

Laughter, how she had missed it. She kept laughing, listening to the strange sounds coming from deep within her belly. Before getting married, she had always laughed so easily; but it wasn't long before her husband started complaining that she laughed too much. Thank

God, I left him, she thought. Now I can laugh, even at the silliest things, whenever I want to.

Katarina felt so much lighter, but she was even hungrier now; unfortunately, there wasn't much in Camilla's fridge.

"Do you know any place where I can get a decent meal in Anacapri?" she asked the driver.

"I do, yes." He turned his head and smiled, wondering what had happened to change her mood. "By the way, I'm Amedeo."

"*Buonasera* (Good evening), Amedeo. I'm Katarina. Can you drive me to that place to eat or drop me off nearby? I don't mind walking a bit." Katarina knew that getting to many dining places in Anacapri required walking.

"I can drive you there; it's only a short walk from the road. The food is good, and the price is even better."

"That sounds perfect," Katarina said, letting out a sigh of relief as she leaned back.

Amedeo drove a while longer, and then he said, "My mother-in-law lives in Sorrento."

Katarina didn't say anything; she figured he wanted to make small talk.

"My wife is from Sorrento."

She let him chat on.

"My wife and my children are celebrating Ferragosto in Sorrento with my wife's family—" Amedeo paused. "Unfortunately, I had to work today."

"Too bad for you," Katarina said.

Amedeo cleared his throat, "Luckily she cooked a meal for me."

"Lucky for you."

Amedeo cleared his throat again, glancing at Katarina's face in the mirror.

"Too bad we each have to eat alone on a night like this."

She took it as innocent banter, the flirtation that was habitually going on in Capri and even more so in Naples.

"Yes," she laughed, "too bad."

Katarina had noticed how handsome Amedeo was when he opened the door for her, and she stepped into the taxi. He was tall and well-built with a broad chest, a flat stomach, and narrow hips. His dark curly hair was cropped short, and his warm smiling eyes were brown. The crisply ironed turquoise shirt set off his bronzed tan. She had noted these details, then filed them away. Do I have to notice every handsome man I come across now that I'm divorced? she asked herself, conceding that there weren't that many truly handsome men. This one, though, she had to admit, was one of them.

"I think you are one of the most beautiful women I've ever seen," he said.

Katarina laughed again; she knew it was just a game, but she enjoyed it anyway.

Encouraged by her laughter, Amedeo continued. "I don't want you to jump to the wrong conclusion, but it might be fun to have a glass of wine and some delicious food together. Nobody should eat alone on the night of Ferragosto. I started my shift early, and you are my last customer."

The invitation was tempting. Katarina thought about it for a moment, why not?

"You're right," she smiled. "Better not to be alone on Ferragosto night. Okay, so where are we going?"

Amedeo swallowed hard. "Well, everyone knows me—"

Katarina got it—the lead in. Naturally, he couldn't risk being seen out with her, since he was married. Amedeo did seem like a gentleman. She contemplated what would happen after dinner, with the wife and children away, but she wasn't able to imagine anything; her mind refused to go there.

"You mean dinner at your home, don't you?"

Amedeo sighed with relief; she understood.

The whitewashed house was tucked into the foothills of the mountain overlooking the plateau of the town of Anacapri. Everything was perfect—the table on the tiny patio, protected by walls covered with fuchsia bougainvillea; the million stars against the dark sky, a waning gibbous moon shining brightly above the dark mountain. The sparkling white wine was cold, the food delicious, the night air warm. They chatted. They laughed.

Amedeo admired Katarina's naked body resting peacefully on top of the bed sheets; her lovely skin was flushed pink in the morning light coming through the window, and her wild blond curls made a halo around her face—how perfect she was. She must have sensed his presence as her eyes opened; their indescribable shade of green was even more alluring by daylight.

Katarina stretched like a cat. They had not slept much, but she felt alive and energized. She couldn't remember when she had last felt this good.

She smiled when she saw Amedeo standing there in his shorts with a tray of espresso and a slice of cake. "Torta Caprese!" she exclaimed. It was the local flourless chocolate and almond cake.

Amedeo smiled back at her, relieved that she did not appear to regret anything. "I need to get to work soon. Shall I take you home first?"

After breakfast, she tucked her uncombed curls under an old tattered fisherman's cap Amedeo gave her and zipped his windbreaker over her long evening dress. It was a short walk before they reached his taxi cab; luckily, they didn't meet a soul on the way.

The ride from Anacapri to Capri and up the hairpin turns of Via Castiglione to Villa Ciano was exhilarating, with dazzling views. Katarina sat in the back seat of Amedeo's open-air stretch taxi, enjoying the magical spectacle as the rising sun illuminated the island. Putting her feet up on the row of folded seats in front of her, she stretched her arms up to the sky, and spontaneous fits of wild, free laughter were carried away by the wind.

She slipped quietly into the house and crept up the stairs. Camilla's bedroom door was closed. Glancing into the mirror in her room, she giggled at her silly image; she had forgotten to return Amedeo's fisherman's cap. She removed the cap and her dress and hung them over the coat stand, then climbed into bed and fell asleep the moment her head hit the pillow.

CHAPTER 14 - DOWNHILL AND UPHILL

C limbing down the steep lower part of Via Occhio Marino was just as demanding as climbing up the footpath, which is why a rope railing was installed for the less agile to grab onto; but neither Max nor Raffi needed to use it. That was the way of life on Capri: going up, *vaco 'ncoppa*, as they called it, or going down, *vaco 'o vascio*. Walking up and down endless stairs and paths was the only way to get around for the majority of the island's inhabitants. The temperature was pleasantly fresh, and the hot morning sun had not yet reached Via Occhio Marino.

Max glanced at his cell phone: it was 9:55; they had left Bar Funicolare at 9:40; they would be on time for their 10 o'clock appointment.

"So, who are these people we're visiting?" Raffi asked.

"Ciro and Emma Imperatore are from Naples, and as you know, they were present at the restaurant that night with Camilla. They are the owners of this villa; that's about all I know. They're expecting us."

Max and Raffi came to a wrought-iron gate set into a stone arch at the bottom of Via Occhio Marino. "This is it, I believe," Max said, as he pressed the bell at the side of the gate.

The gate swung open. They walked down a terracotta tiled stairway to a large cobblestone courtyard surrounded by ancient stone walls. Terracotta urns filled with colorful plants lined the walls, and a giant pink bougainvillea, the size of a small tree, stood in the center of the courtyard. All around were gnarled olive trees planted in stone tubs.

Signor Ciro Imperatore was waiting for them outside the wooden entrance door. What little he had left of hair was blond; his eyes were light blue, and his skin was pale. He wore casual slacks and a short-sleeved cotton shirt. Max guessed that he was in his late forties. After introductions, Ciro Imperatore led them through the living quarters to reach the loggia.

The vaulted ceilings and walls of the rooms were painted stark white; the floor was an intricate pattern of handmade milk-white Vietri tile. The comfortable chairs and sofas were covered in white fabric. Antique wall sconces, old paintings, and majolica plates hung on the walls; statues in niches and a few strategically placed antique furniture pieces completed the elegant décor.

Signor Imperatore's wife was standing on the old stone floor of the enormous crescent-shaped loggia when Max and Raffi entered. Emma Imperatore could have been her husband's sister, as they looked so much alike; she was short, with blue eyes and blond coiffed hair, and was wearing an apricot-colored summer dress. Further introductions and some small talk followed. Max apologized for intruding on their peace and quiet. He explained his professional background and the reason for his visit.

"Please sit down. Will you join us for an espresso?" Signora Imperatore gestured to a seating area on the loggia.

Max and Raffi sat down in the wrought-iron armchairs facing Emma and Ciro Imperatore, who seated themselves on a long, cushioned bench built into the stone loggia wall.

"Feel free to ask us anything you wish. We are glad to help in any way we can. We are not formal, please call me Ciro."

"Yes, please do call me Emma," chimed in his wife.

Max marveled at the hospitality and friendliness of the Imperatores. He would have thought this fair-haired couple was from northern Europe, were it not for their manners, language, and gestures—all characteristics of upper-class Neapolitan society.

A housekeeper brought out a silver tray with cups of espresso and a plate of cookies, placing it on the glass coffee table between them.

Max took a cube of raw brown sugar with the silver-claw tongs and dropped it into his porcelain cup. Raffi watched him and did the same.

Max felt it was the right moment to get down to business. "Since I understand you were friends of Camilla, could you tell me if you think it's possible that Camilla committed suicide?"

"Why don't you go first, Emma," offered Ciro.

"Yes, my darling," Emma said. "No, I don't think Camilla was the type to commit suicide, but I wasn't a close friend. We had, of course, met at mutual friends' dinner parties, and she often attended our annual summer parties; but we do not frequent the same beach club."

Ciro nodded. "I agree," he said.

Max stirred his espresso with a small gold-plated spoon, noting that his porcelain demitasse cup was gold-plated as well—on the rim, the handle, and on the inside. "Do either of you remember seeing her carry a purse at the party that night, a purple evening purse? And do you recall whether Camilla was wearing a diamond necklace?" he asked.

Emma and Ciro shook their heads; they didn't remember seeing either a purse or a necklace.

"Camilla looked lovely, as always," Emma said, as she passed the plate of cookies. "Please, would you care for a *quaresimale?*"

Max bit into the almond cookie; this was his favorite kind of cookie. He had a weakness for them since childhood, when he liked

107

to dunk them in milk; as a grown-up, he dunked the *quaresimale* in wine.

Emma continued. "Ciro and I sat at the opposite end of the table from Camilla that night, so we didn't get to converse much with her."

"Do you know if she was involved—romantically with anyone?" Max asked, as he spooned out the last drops of the excellent espresso.

Ciro glanced at Emma, who shook her head as if answering his silent question.

"Well, we had heard a rumor that there was someone new in her life, but you know rumors, they can't be trusted, can they? We don't listen much to gossip," Ciro said.

"Is there anything else you might want to add?" Max asked. But the Imperatores had nothing else to say.

Holding the empty demitasse cup in his lap, Max discreetly turned it over. He recognized the blue fleur-de-lys Capodimonte mark used by the Royal Factory in Naples from 1771 until the factory closed in the early 1800s. Max had once dated a Neapolitan girl while studying mathematics in Naples. The first time he was invited to meet her wealthy parents, the mother had lectured him on the different marks on porcelain from Capodimonte while showing off her valuable collection. Max remembered details significant and insignificant; it wasn't conscious, but he knew it sometimes annoyed people when he shared this kind of information, so he often kept it to himself.

Raffi took another *quaresimale* when Emma passed the plate around, then he stood up and excused himself, saying that, if they didn't mind, he would like to take some pictures of the view from the villa.

Max admired the remarkable panorama from where he was sitting, even more so, because he was able to get an unusual view of Capri only seen from the handful of villas in this area. Most impressive were the two mountains rising to their height from the sea: the smaller Monte Castiglione capped with the medieval stone castle stood in the foreground; behind it was the majestic Monte Solaro.

"The neighboring villa is said to be built on the grounds of one of the twelve Imperial Roman villas on the island, is that right?" Max asked.

"Yes, the very ground on which we are standing must have been part of the ancient Roman complex," Ciro said.

"We have wondered to which Roman God it was dedicated," said Emma, laughing.

They all stood up when Raff returned. It was time to move on.

Ciro Imperatore accompanied them to the gate. "Hamm," he made a small cough. "Our next-door neighbors, Giuliano and Elena Moretti, are good friends; the gate to their villa is over there." He pointed to a neighboring gate. "They were close friends of Camilla; maybe they know something that will be of help in your investigation." Ciro paused for a moment and then he said, "Yes, and the Ferrante's, Nicola and Maria Antonietta, who live further up on Via Occhio Marino, at Villa Chiara, they were also friends of Camilla. You might want to pay them a visit as well."

A CARD CAME

A Sri Lankan housekeeper dressed in a white tunic came to open the gate when Max and Raffi rang the doorbell; he escorted them down a long stairway to the garden where the Morettis were lounging beside the swimming pool with their two small grandchildren. Max recognized the middle-aged couple from the funeral.

"Yes, we knew Camilla very well," said Elena Moretti, after they had made the necessary introductions. "It is terribly sad, a tragedy."

"What can we offer you, an espresso maybe?" asked Giuliano Moretti.

Raffi and Max looked at each other and smiled. One could never visit anyone on Capri without being offered an espresso. Raffi accepted the offer, but Max had reached his quota for the morning.

"Please, just a glass of water," he said.

After the housekeeper had brought glasses of sparkling water and a cup of espresso for Raffi, Max started to ask questions about Camilla. It soon became clear that the Morettis didn't know much.

They had been at home on the night of Ferragosto entertaining guests for dinner, followed by a card tournament of Buracco; eight couples were present. After enjoying a midnight snack, their guests had left around one o'clock in the morning.

"I don't think it had anything to do with my cooking," said Elena.

"Of course not, my darling," said Giuliano. "Nobody else got sick."

It was clear from their faces that Raffi and Max had no idea what they were talking about.

"That night one of our guests—Nicola, Nicola Ferrante, got sick to his stomach, so he left early; luckily, he lives just up the road," Giuliano explained.

"Do you remember what time Signor Nicola Ferrante left?" asked Max.

"I think it was early in the tournament, around ten maybe," Elena said.

"And Nicola Ferrante's wife, when did she leave?" asked Raffi.

"Maria Antonietta? She had a partner in the tournament, so she left with all the others. Like I said, it was around one o'clock," Giuliano volunteered. "Why don't you pay Nicola and Maria Antonietta Ferrante a visit, they were also friends of Camilla, they live right up the street in Villa Chiara," he added.

Raffi rang the doorbell at the Ferrantes; a three-storied ocher-colored structure higher up on Via Occhio Marino. While they stood waiting at the door, Raffi explained to Max that he had often visited this villa as a child and that it was built by a wealthy sea captain in the mid-nineteenth century. Among the many properties on Capri formerly owned by his once wealthy family was a large villa only a stone's throw away.

Nobody came to the door. Max shrugged, and he and Raffi continued winding their way uphill on Via Occhio Marino until the road flattened into Via Campo di Teste.

"Will you join me for lunch at my sister's? She's making *pasta con piselli* (pasta with peas)," Max asked, as they made their way back into the center of town.

"Wouldn't miss it for the world," Raffi grinned. "You know how much I love Mona's cooking."

"We didn't get much out of the morning, did we?" Max said as they entered the stone archway of his sister's home on Via Posterula; he sounded discouraged.

"No, we didn't, but the espresso was tops, and so were the *quaresimale*," Raffi laughed. "And you, lucky devil, you have a hot date with Katarina tonight."

CHAPTER 15 - TIBERIUS BATHS

"Let's walk down to Marina Grande by way of *La Scala di San Francesco*,"** Max suggested, as he and Katarina left the Piazzetta. While walking side by side down the steps of St. Francis, they didn't meet a single person. The bay of Naples spread out in front of their eyes like a shining mirror, illuminated by the brilliant rays of the sun as it disappeared behind Monte Solaro.

"I have a dinner surprise for you," said Max with a smile.

"I like surprises—sometimes."

Katarina's smile quickly faded, and she fell silent. She was still seething with anger from her visit to the police station that morning. What was she doing here with Max? she asked herself. Was Max a friend of her sister, or wasn't he? Why hadn't he told her about his investigation and the insurance policy? Could Max be Camilla's ex-lover or the new lover? Maybe he was the reason for her suicide—

that is, if she was wrong and it was indeed a suicide. Or was Max her sister's murderer?

Max glanced at Katarina, admiring the beauty of her face aglow in the soft golden light. He wondered why her face looked so closed, even resentful. Yesterday morning she had seemed to enjoy his visit; now she was a different person. Max realized he knew nothing about her—and worse, he didn't know whether Katarina had anything to do with the death of her sister. After all, Katarina had no alibi, and she did have a motive. Could Katarina have murdered her sister?

They walked in awkward silence, keeping their eyes on the chipped cobblestones of the old steps. They were both embarrassed about the moment on the roof terrace when their eyes met and ignited a spark of desire. There was no denying their instant mutual attraction.

"Look at that giant tree; we call it the Belshazzar myrtle," Max said, breaking the silence. "Here on Capri we love the myrtle. Have you ever tasted liqueur made from myrtle berries, *liquore di mirto?*"

A small smile escaped from Katarina's tightly pressed lips. "No, I haven't, but Camilla once told me that myrtle was sacred to Venus, the Greek goddess of love, and that Greeks and Romans used myrtle for curing diseases."

"My sister Mimì makes liqueur from the myrtle berries that grow on Anacapri. I'll get you a bottle, what do you say?"

Katarina couldn't help herself; she smiled and nodded.

The footpath crossed Via Don Giobbe Ruocco, and the town of Marina Grande came into view. The harbor and its cluster of homes were awash in burnished copper light as the setting sun reappeared from behind the mountain ridge and painted the sky purple and orange.

They passed the auxiliary pier at Darsena, where vehicles and passengers were lined up for *la nave veloce* (the fast ferry), leaving at 8:15 pm for Naples. There were no more scheduled departures from the island and only one last arrival from the mainland—*il traghetto* (the slow ferry) would arrive at 9 pm and dock overnight on the main pier.

Most of the cafés and tourist shops catering to day-trippers were closed by now, only a couple of restaurants and bars had stayed open. Via Christofero Colombo, the main road along the waterfront, was peaceful at this hour; void of day-trippers, it was shared by locals and the privileged visitors who stayed on their yachts or in one of the few hotels in the harbor.

While Max stopped to talk with every other Caprese along the way—and he knew practically everyone—Katarina got a chance to look at him. He was handsome, no doubt about it. There was an untamed wildness about him, with his unruly black hair, sharp facial features, and intense brown eyes with golden flecks. The way he moved his body, he reminded Katarina of a sleek black panther.

"This is the surprise, Katarina," Max announced, stopping suddenly. "We are going to have dinner at Bagni di Tiberio, the Baths of Emperor Tiberius. We must wait here for their boat."

"I have been there," said Katarina. "But never for dinner. What a surprise!"

They stood waiting on a private wooden pier behind the ferry and funicular ticket booths. Katarina looked out across the long, curved bay of the pebbled beach and saw a motorboat approaching. "Ah, I see the boat is coming. Look over there," she said.

"We are lucky; the restaurant of Bagni di Tiberio is rarely open in the evening," explained Max, as they puttered along the seashore in the *gozzo* (motorboat), leaving the lights of Marina Grande behind them. Only a stripe of gold remained as the last trace of the sun that had set behind Ischia, Capri's neighboring island.

There, out on the dark sea, the night seemed so magical that Katarina's anger melted away. The closeness of Max's body seated beside her on the teak bench was intoxicating, and the half dozen other passengers on the boat became invisible to her.

High on the dark mountainside, Katarina saw the headlights of cars traveling on the implausible road cut into the rock wall, and she remembered her taxi ride from Capri to Anacapri on the night of Ferragosto, the night Camilla died. Only eight days ago, she had embarked on her impetuous adventure with Amedeo the taxi driver. Somehow, *I must contact Amedeo to warn him about the police, to* tell him about the death of my sister, Katarina thought. But how will I find him?

"Those are the Phoenician Steps," Max said, interrupting Katarina's thoughts, as he pointed to a string of lights zigzagging their way up the steep rock face of the mountain. "Did you know there are 921 steps? They were not actually built by the Phoenicians, as the name suggests, but were constructed by the ancient Greeks between the sixth and seventh century BC."

"I walked the Phoenician Steps twice, both up and down," Katarina said in a proud voice. "Going down is harder; the steps are so tall."

Max seemed to enjoy playing the part of a tour guide. "Apart from the steep old trail of Passetiello connecting the two towns, the Phoenician steps were the only link between Anacapri and the rest of the world until the paved road between Capri and Anacapri was completed in 1878."

Max went on to tell her that water was now brought to the island through pipes on the ocean floor. "The supply of fresh water is a problem on the island," Max explained, "since neither Capri nor Anacapri has any wells. The only source of fresh water, apart from rainwater, is a spring near the port, so the water was brought to the island by boat. Consequently, when the rainwater collected in cisterns was depleted, Anacapri's womenfolk were once obliged to walk down the 921 Phoenician Steps and climb back up with a heavy jug of water balanced on their heads."

"I've seen old paintings of the woman from Anacapri carrying water jugs on their heads. With their incredible posture, they were beautiful," exclaimed Katarina.

"Look, isn't this a magical place?" Max said, touching her shoulder lightly as the little beach came into view.

The only sign of habitation was a typical white Capri villa, belonging to the owners of the beach establishment, tucked into a dark bay under the looming mountain. Above the narrow strip of pebbled beach was a long wooden terrace lined with beach cabins painted white and green.

As the boat pulled alongside the pier of the restaurant, Katarina felt her pulse quicken in anticipation of their dinner together; the touch of Max's hand resting on her bare skin added to her excitement.

"Thank you," Katarina said, smiling brightly to the boatman, who offered his arm as she stepped onto the small wooden pier.

They walked up the steps from the pier to the entrance of the restaurant, illuminated with hanging lanterns, and were greeted at once by the owners and staff; they received all the guests, not only Max, whom they knew well, as warmly as if they were greeting their own family.

"This is where I learned to swim, you know," Max said to Katarina as they sat down at their table. He pointed to a narrow u-shaped cove. One side of it was protected by boulders; on the other side were traces of the ruins of the baths built by Roman Emperor Tiberius.

"They call it *la piscina,* the swimming pool, because the water of this protected little cove is so shallow. The locals like to come here with their children in the summer. But be careful if you come to swim in the *piscina*; I don't remember how many times I have cut my feet on the sharp rocks."

Katarina glanced over at the cove of *la piscina.* In the distance beyond the calm sea, she could make out a barely visible dark pyramid shape.

"Ah, there is Mount Vesuvius," she said, shuddering. She recalled the tragic fate of the people living below the volcano two thousand years ago, when a deadly cloud of volcanic gas, stones, and ash, spewing as high as 33 kilometers [9] destroyed the Roman cities of Pompeii, Herculaneum, and Stabia. "Is it true that the volcano is still active?" she asked.

Max was quick to explain that the volcano had erupted regularly since then, and was still active; the last major eruption, in March of 1944, lasted for days and destroyed many villages, depositing ash as far away as Capri.

---

[9] 21 miles

"Did you know there was once a funicular cable car on Mount Vesuvius?"

"Really?" said Katarina.

"Well, in fact, a cable car opened there in 1880, but was destroyed by the eruption of 1906. It was rebuilt, but then it was irreparably damaged in the eruption of 1944. Since that time, building on the slopes of Mount Vesuvius is forbidden, as it is one of the most dangerous active volcanos in the world and a population of three million people live nearby."

Their waiter came up to the table. "*Buonasera, e benvenuti* (Good evening and welcome)," he said with a smile, and proceeded to recite the menu and the specials for the evening. Katarina knew that if one was a local or a habitué on Capri, a written menu was customarily not presented unless asked for. Chilled white wine and mineral water were brought to the table, followed by bread and various plates of delectable *antipasti* (appetizers).

The boat dropped off another load of guests, then another, and soon the place was filled with excited vacationers and locals moving from table to table, shouting and greeting each other, as many were old friends. They were like one large boisterous family.

When Max and Katarina had started on their *linguine con vongole verace* (linguine with local baby clams), Max summoned the courage to ask her the question on his mind.

"So, are you afraid of me?"

"This is the best *linguine con vongole* I have ever had," said Katarina, as she expertly rolled the linguine and clams around her fork.

"So?" Max smiled, wondering why she hadn't answered his question.

"I was at the police station this morning, and—" Katarina sucked a tiny clam off its shell, avoiding looking at Max while she searched for the right words.

"The police told me that you are here working as an insurance investigator regarding my sister's life insurance. So why did you pretend to be a friend of Camilla? Why were you at the funeral? And one other thing: Why did you deceive me into thinking you were willing to help me?"

Max paused to refill their wine glasses before speaking. The coldness in Katarina's voice had an effect on him; he felt like a nasty son of a bitch for not telling her the truth.

"Believe me," he finally said, searching in vain for Katarina's eyes that stayed fixed on her plate. "I had no wish to deceive you or anyone. True, I should have told you about my work right away, and I admit I had no legitimate reason for being at Camilla's funeral. But I wanted to learn whatever I could about her death. And then, well—" Max lowered his voice, "when you urged me to kiss your sister, I felt I couldn't decline."

Katarina responded in a hard, resentful voice, enunciating each word: "But you and I have conflicting interests, isn't that true? You hope to prove that Camilla committed suicide, so your company won't have to pay me two million dollars. I, on the other hand, will swear that Camilla did not kill herself, not because I stand to get two million dollars if she didn't, but because I know my sister."

Katarina hoped the sting of her words had hit their mark. She took a forkful of linguine, struggling to control her fury at being betrayed by Max. She tried to convince herself that she had not been attracted to Max, or that, in any case, the attraction had now died. In her heart, she knew otherwise. She felt a pressure building up behind her eyes; it had started at the police station, and she fought back the tears. The linguine grew thick in her mouth, and she barely managed to swallow it. You are not going to cry stupid tears just because a pair of golden-brown eyes spoke lies, she told herself.

Katarina kept her head down while blinking hard, muffling her next words, "And you said we were going to find out the truth together? Please explain what you mean by that."

Max tried to compose himself, scooping up the last of his linguine with a piece of bread.

"This is what I can promise you. I am only interested in finding the truth. I promise you that I'll search for the truth no matter what that takes."

Max's eyes searched for Katarina's, and this time, when she raised her eyes from her dinner plate and looked at him, there was no anger.

After dinner, Max suggested they walk back up to the town of Capri from the beach by way of the lesser-known paths.

They walked side by side up the dark footpath of Via Fenicia under a starlit sky and turned left on Via Marucella. Most of the whitewashed villas along the path were owned by locals. Their abundant garden lots were filled with rows of grape vines, lemon, fig, and nut trees, as well as staples like eggplant, squash, tomatoes, and herbs. The scent of jasmine and lemon mixed with the musty smell of damp earth in the cool night air. Only the occasional barking of a dog interrupted the silence.

"Tell me about yourself, Catari," Max said. "You don't mind if I call you Catari, do you?"

Katarina was reluctant to break the magic spell of the night to talk about her painful past. Walking with Max along the quiet fragrant paths had lifted her spirits and the sting of his betrayal had gradually softened and given way. Now the stillness of the night sweetly embraced her, and she felt peaceful.

"Well, this past year has not been easy. I'm recently divorced. I have a twelve-year-old daughter named Anna. I'm a high school language teacher, and I also do translations from English to Norwegian as a freelancer. Usually, I come to Capri during my vacation in July, but this year I obtained a leave of absence for the month of August."

"Why did you get divorced, if you don't mind me asking?" Max probed.

Katarina sighed; it was hard to answer this question in a few words. She stopped walking and looked over at Max.

"My husband is OK—I mean, he's not a bad man; that was not it. I just never felt I could be myself with him. I suppose he didn't like my extroverted personality when we were with my friends. He often got angry with me for no reason—maybe it was jealousy, who knows? In the end, it was the insane anger that did it. Maybe he was angry because he believed I didn't love him—not enough, anyway."

Katarina sighed again. "He was right. I didn't love him enough to stay, and just as important, if I had stayed, it would have meant I didn't love myself enough."

Max gently touched her shoulder in sympathy. "I am also divorced," he said.

"Really?" Katarina was surprised.

She hadn't expected it; she had not even contemplated the possibility that he was ever married. When they had tea together on the roof the day before, she had noticed he wasn't wearing a wedding ring. The touch of his fingers on her bare shoulder felt even better than in the boat earlier that night. When he removed his hand, she hoped he would put his arm around her shoulders. He didn't.

They turned off Via Roma by Hotel Capri and started the walk up to Villa Ciano on the winding road of Via Castiglione. The road was dark at that hour. Max took Katarina's hand.

"So, what happened to your marriage, why did you get divorced?" Katarina asked.

Max sighed. He didn't know quite what to say. He had never discussed his divorce with anyone, not with friends—not even with his own sisters.

"I don't know . . . I guess things changed between us."

Katarina sensed it would be better if she didn't ask him any more questions.

They walked on in silence until they reached the villa. The iron gate was locked. Katarina reluctantly withdrew her hand from Max's to get the key in her purse.

"Shall we have a nightcap on the roof terrace?" she asked.

Max wanted to, why not? he thought. There was a magnetic attraction between them, and they both knew it.

"Maybe another night," he said.

Katarina lay wide-eyed and sleepless in bed, thinking about Max and what it meant that he had turned down her invitation for a nightcap. His rejection was painful—she felt like a fool; she had imagined the attraction was mutual. There was something mysteriously compelling about Max. He's dangerously handsome, she thought.

Suddenly she sat straight up in bed: What if Max was the man Camilla told her about, the man she said she was in love with?

Chapter 16 - Villa Moneta

R affi was, as was his daily routine on Capri, sitting on the panoramic little terrace of Bar Funicolare working on his iPad, as usual, when Max showed up. "Good morning," he said with a wide grin, "how was your hot date last night? Too hot to touch I bet—after all, she is a suspect in your investigation, isn't she?"

Max ignored his friend's bantering. "Do you feel like walking up to Villa Moneta to talk to the Aragones?" he asked, "I have to do some more investigative work."

"Sure," Raffi stuffed his iPad in his backpack and went to pay his bill.

"Come on, Max, don't leave me in the dark. How did the evening go last night with the hot sister?" Raffi probed again, as they crossed the Piazzetta and headed up Via Longano.

"With Katarina? Fairly good, I think, given the circumstances. It was a bit awkward though. When she went to give her testimony to the police yesterday, she learned about my role in the investigation of the insurance claim. Naturally, she got upset. She also learned from the police that I have no alibi for the night of her sister's death. I don't think she believed me when I told her I had never met her sister Camilla."

"That all does sound a bit awkward. Did you learn anything about the relationship between the sisters? Why wasn't Katarina with her sister at the restaurant?"

Max hesitated before answering. "Well, you know, the police had already given her the third degree, and I didn't want to sound like a bloody police officer, so I didn't ask her much."

From Via Longano, the two friends turned a corner, continuing on Via Sopramonte. Locals passed on their way to work, running errands or shopping for groceries. Mothers with children in tow were heading for the beaches, as the school term hadn't yet started.

Sopramonte was one of the most densely populated areas of Capri. Houses were stacked on the hillside, one on top of another like building blocks, rising ever higher as they climbed towards Monte San Michele. Max had a childhood friend whose family lived in a house that was one hundred steps straight up the hill. His friend's grandmother had a weak heart and could never leave the house, as she wouldn't have made it back up without being carried. Below Via Sopramonte, the steep alleys and stairways led down to the *quartiere* and the church of St. Anna and Via delle Botteghe, the busy and narrow shopping street.

Raffi was not going to let Max get off that easily. "What did you talk about then, you rascal? It was a romantic evening, right? Great food, I bet. Did you make sure to get her safely back to the villa?"

Max grinned. "Yeh, Katarina got home quite safely, I can assure you. Since I don't know if she played a role in the death of her sister, I thought it prudent not to get involved..."

"Bah—the way I see it," Raffi said, in a mischievous tone of voice, "there might be an advantage to getting as close to Katarina as you can manage—to learn as much as possible about the case."

"Maybe—" Max didn't feel comfortable with Raffi's suggestion, but he couldn't argue against the possible value of it. He changed the subject. "How's the lawsuit going?" Max asked Raffi, as they arrived at the intersection of La Croce and turned uphill on Via Tiberio.

Max knew that Raffi was involved in a legal case concerning a family property on Capri. Raffi's family had owned dozens of properties on the island before his father went bankrupt and left the island with his wife and children to start a new life in America.

"I'm seeing the lawyer tomorrow, but it's going as slow as molasses." Raffi squinted in the bright sunlight. "I don't have my hopes up, I can tell you that. As you know, these property cases here can drag on for generations."

Max glanced at Raffi's closed face. He was aware that his friend had suffered a forced exile from Capri; it couldn't have been easy losing everything. Maybe it was easier to be born poor like himself, to come from nothing and work your way up, rather than being born wealthy and privileged like Raffi and then losing it all.

They passed the restaurant Lo Sfizio, as well as the primary school, and the children's playground, and a few minutes later, they arrived at their destination. Villa Moneta's wrought-iron gate supported by massive columns was an impressive sight.

"I couldn't find a cell phone number for the Aragones, and no registered landline either. We'll just have to try our luck," Max said, pressing the doorbell.

Nobody answered. He rang again.

They were on the point of giving up when a couple appeared. "I'm Giuseppe Aragone, and this is my wife, Matilde. I don't think we have been introduced." Signor Aragone bowed towards Max. "We saw you at Camilla's funeral, and we wondered, didn't we Matilde, why we had not had the pleasure of meeting you before. Please, do come in."

Max introduced Raffi and himself, then they followed the couple down the long *viale* (pathway) flanked by colonnades; of the many colonnades on the island, these were certainly among the most impressive. Neither Max nor Raffi had ever been to Villa Moneta, which was constructed in the mid-seventeen hundreds. The land was once a part of the vast Roman imperial complex of Villa Jovis. It was speculated that Emperor Tiberius had built a secret tunnel between Villa Jovis and the site of Villa Moneta, in case he needed to make a rapid escape.

The overgrown foliage behind the colonnades created the shade of a dense forest, and the moss-covered cobblestones, littered with pine needles and dried leaves, gave the *viale* the appearance of neglect. Even the humblest of villas on Capri often had stone colonnades; only the grandest villas had colonnades made of marble, like the residences constructed on Capri by the ancient Romans.

Villa Moneta was no ordinary building; it was a large, strangely asymmetrical two-story structure. The stone staircase leading to the second floor was built on the exterior, a common feature of many of the ancient buildings on Capri. Surrounding the spacious cobblestone courtyard was a maze of bushes, palms, and tall oppressive pine trees.

"Please, do seat yourselves," said Signora Aragone, pointing to four old wicker chairs placed on the loggia in front of a tall arched lattice door painted green.

Everywhere Max and Raffi looked, there were high noble arches and gigantic urns filled with greenery. Apart from a royal purple bougainvillea climbing one wall, there were no blooming plants.

Signora Aragone brought out a bottle of mineral water and some mismatched glasses.

Max guessed the couple were in their early fifties. Signora Aragone was a petite and gracious woman. She wore an artsy patterned orange cotton dress and flip-flops. Her curly chestnut-red hair fell loosely down her back. Her pale complexion was flawless; she wore no make-up except for a dark burgundy nail polish on her delicate hands and feet.

Signor Aragone was exceptionally tall. He had a mass of wavy, salt-and-pepper hair, dark bushy eyebrows, and a prominent nose. He did not apologize for being in his striped pajamas and silk robe, or for wearing his torn slippers. Neither Max nor Raffi was surprised; it was common practice among certain gentlemen in Naples to spend an occasional day or two lounging around in a robe.

Max got to the point at once, explaining his assignment of the Camilla Kallberg case, and his visits to Signora Troisi, the Imperatores, and the Morettis, and then he asked if the Aragones were friends of Camilla.

"Why don't you start, Giuseppe," said Signora Aragone. She stood behind her husband's chair, affectionately wrapping her arms around his chest.

"Yes, I will Matilde, thank you, my sweetheart. Yes, we became acquainted with Camilla and her husband Daniel the first year they came to Capri, didn't we? What a pity he passed away so young. Daniel was a most intelligent and compassionate doctor. He was a man who loved his wife more than anything in the world. It was terribly hard on Camilla to lose him."

Giuseppe Aragone rambled on. "You may not know that I'm a surrealist painter; I keep a studio here in the villa and one in Naples. Capri continues to inspire many of my paintings. We bought this place because it once belonged to the great Neapolitan painter Carlo Siviero. Are you gentlemen familiar with his work?"

He paused to look at Max and Raffi, who shook their heads. "Like I said, we have been close friends with Camilla for many years, since the very first time she came to my vernissage in the oratory of the Monumental Church of St Michael the Archangel on Anacapri. My wife adored her, too; why don't you tell them, Matilde?"

"Yes, we were both very fond of Camilla and we had many wonderful dinner parties together. Do you remember, Giuseppe, that year when we had the big party here at the villa and the electricity went out for the whole night?"

"Oh, do I remember. A magical evening. We all dined outdoors on long tables under the stars with hundreds of candles everywhere. The cook had to prepare food by candlelight; luckily in our kitchen, we have a gas stove. We had invited over sixty of our closest friends, and we had hired the musician Aziz who brought his guitar. We danced and danced—right here on the cobblestones. Oh, how Camilla loved music and dancing! We don't believe she could ever have willfully ended her own life. She was typically the first one out on the dance floor and the last to leave the party."

"Wonderful that you have such good memories," Max said politely. "Signora Aragone, could you please tell me if you remember whether Camilla was wearing a diamond necklace on the night of Ferragosto when you were together at the restaurant? And do you happen to recall if she was carrying a purse?"

"Yes, I do think she was wearing her diamond necklace and she had a purple purse; I thought it was outrageous with the peacock colors of her dress. Am I right, Giuseppe?"

"Yes, yes, you're always right my dear. She might have worn a necklace, though I can't say I remember that she did—or if she had a purse."

"Do you remember anything unusual about that night?" asked Max. "Might she have gone to meet someone after you had dinner together, maybe a friend or a jealous lover?"

"I remember she was rather quiet, not at all herself, don't you think so, Giuseppe?"

"Of course, you are quite right, Matilde. I thought she was not feeling well, since she left before dessert. Jealous lover you say? Well, hard to know. What do you think, Matilde? Nicola Ferrante was pretty stuck on her, for years now, if you ask me."

"Giuseppe, do behave yourself; you know very well Nicola is married. I hardly think it's proper, and we don't really know anything about it, do we? So, he was sweet on her, but it doesn't mean anything, does it?"

"I thank you both for being so forthcoming. One more thing." Max was a bit embarrassed. "I apologize for asking you this question.

Camilla died sometime between 11 pm and 3 am; you were together that whole time, I assume?"

"Of course, we understand totally, don't we Matilde? Yes, we left the restaurant sometime before midnight and after we passed La Croce, we sat down on a bench on Via Sopramonte and watched the terrific Ferragosto fireworks over Hotel Quisisana. When it was over, we went to the Piazzetta for after dinner drinks with Pia and Claudio, the Giordanos. When did we finally get to bed, my dearest?"

"I think it was around half past two in the morning, and unless you snuck out, Giuseppe, and ran to Belvedere delle Noci and back before I woke up, yes, we were together the whole time. I slept so soundly I would hardly have noticed if you were missing."

The Aragones laughed heartily together.

Signor Aragone accompanied Max and Raffi down the *viale*. "By the way," he said, as he opened the gate, "Does Nicola Ferrante have an alibi?"

"I don't know, why do you ask?" Max answered.

"Well, the thing is, we saw him the night of Ferragosto. It was sometime after the fireworks had finished, so it must have been around twelve-forty-five. We were sitting in the Piazzetta when he passed us."

"Not that suspicious, is it?" Max asked.

"No, but what is strange is that he didn't stop to greet us. I'm sure he saw us, but he pretended not to. Perhaps it means nothing, but it seemed unusual. Good luck with your investigation, boys."

Signor Aragone closed the wrought-iron gate behind him, re-tied his robe, and shuffled back down the long *viale*.

"What do you think Max, did we learn anything from the Aragones?" Raffi asked as they made their way down Via Tiberio.

"Not much. We still don't know for certain that Camilla had a necklace or a purse; but since at least two of the women present that night say she wore a diamond necklace, it seems likely. Only one person, Matilde, recalls Camilla having a purse with her; and I believe her as she seemed to be certain. I called the Giordanos this morning, you know the couple who returned to Padova and who were also at

127

the dinner with Camilla, but neither of them remember anything particular. We don't know why Camilla left the party early or why she didn't bring her sister, or why she accepted an invitation to the restaurant in the first place. And we don't know the identity of the person that Camilla was talking to when she passed under the restaurant Da Tonino within earshot of Domenico. "

"Well, if she didn't kill herself," Raffi said, "the most likely reason to go to the belvedere would be for a rendezvous, don't you think? So far, Nicola Ferrante doesn't seem to have an alibi, and maybe he was in love with her. He was seen in the Piazzetta after midnight. Theoretically, he could have done away with Camilla either before or after he was seen in the Piazzetta, couldn't he? And why was Ferrante in the Piazzetta if he had left the card tournament at the Morettis at 10 o'clock due to a sudden illness. Then, what about the sister of Camilla Kallberg, how could she have done it?"

"The way I see it Raffi, the only way for Katarina to have killed her sister would be to have lured her to the belvedere by setting up a false rendezvous with somebody. That implies that Katarina knows who the mystery lover is, right? And wouldn't somebody have seen Katarina walk there and back? Of course, it is possible that she disguised herself; that's easy enough to do. I noticed an old Greek style fisherman's cap hanging in Katarina's bedroom on top of an evening gown; somehow that didn't make sense, and the cap looked much too big for her. I thought it was rather strange."

Max and Raffi were back at La Croce, the intersection of Via Tiberio, Via Croce, Via Sopramonte, and Via Matermania, when Raffi changed the subject of conversation. "Did you notice them, Max—Signor and Signora Aragone? I mean they seemed so affectionate towards each other, didn't they? And they appeared to have fun together."

Max nodded. "Yes, I suppose so. Yes, they did seem to care for each other."

"Have you thought about it, Max? I mean, what about us when we get to be that old, what will we be like? Will we be weird old lonely geezers, or will we be with a woman we love and who loves us back?"

Max didn't have an answer; it was a useless exercise to speculate about the future, he thought. The possibility that he would grow to be a lonely old man terrified him; it was better not to think about it.

"I think I will walk down to the beach, to Da Luigi by the Faraglioni," Max said. "Since Camilla spent most of her summer days at Da Luigi, the staff or the patrons may know something. Katarina told me yesterday that she was going to be there, and as you pointed out, I have a few questions for her I didn't ask last night. Why don't you tag along, Raffi? That way, you will get to form your own opinion of whether she is a murderer or not."

"Thanks, but my aunt is expecting me for a lunch get-together with some of my cousins. You go and enjoy yourself, will you? And like I said, you might as well get closer to your suspect. Do you have your swimming trunks?"

"When I'm on Capri, I always wear my swimming trunks under my pants."

"You rascal. Always prepared for all circumstances," Raffi laughed.

"Shall we hook up in the Piazzetta for a drink later?"

"Absolutely, see you around half past seven."

CHAPTER 17 - FARAGLIONI

TUESDAY, AUGUST 24

M ax was excited about the prospect of seeing Katarina again; he decided to take the shortest route to Faraglioni. After parting with Raffi at La Croce, he went up Via

Matermania, turned right and walked down Via Cercola, and made a left turn on Via Tuoro. From there, he went down the steps of Scala Tuoro and arrived on Via Tragara.

The scenic Via Tragara, home to several of the more exclusive hotels and villas on the island, ends at the Belvedere of Punta Tragara. Turning down the narrow path of Via Pizzolungo, just before the belvedere, Max managed to avoid looking at Hotel Punta Tragara, where ten years ago he had spent his honeymoon with Tara.

He skipped down the irregular steps of a steep path that split off from Via Pizzolungo and snaked its way down the cliff to the shore, where Capri's legendary Faraglioni rocks jutted straight up from the depths of the sea.

The moment he stepped onto the familiar path and heard the shrill, high-pitched mating calls of the cicadas, Max felt as if he had come home. The sharp, resinous fragrance of the coastal pines made him realize how much he had missed this part of the island, where the trees grow perpendicular to the steep slope, as if perpetually yearning for the sea. This is the place where Max had come as a child to escape his problems. When he was older, he would take girls there for romantic walks after dark.

Through the pine trees, he could see the monolithic Stella, queen of the Faraglioni rocks, connected to the shore by a narrow strip of land. Her smaller brothers, the sea-bound stacks, called "Di Mezzo" and "Lo Scopolo," followed in her train. The short, stubby Monacone islet stood by itself, as if guarding the entrance to the port of Tragara. Max smiled; the sight of the peaks was like seeing family after a long absence.

Two small rabbits nibbled on the undergrowth along the path, and dozens of lizards flittered in and out, competing for Max's attention; he greeted them all like old friends as he walked along.

He stopped at the curve overlooking the bay of Tragara; in ancient times it was used by the Romans as a port. It was a ritual for Max to stop at this spot and gaze down at the sea; his eyes feasted on the myriad shades of blue and turquoise. Nestled in the little bay, at Stella's feet, was Da Luigi, the beach establishment. Dozens of bright blue parasols were scattered on its rocky ledges and cement terraces.

Max recalled the first time he climbed to the top of the Stella Rock; he had just turned eighteen. The sea that day was choppy, and the windblown sea swirled into Stella's underwater hollow and erupted, showering spectacular fans of spray from the waves onto the rocks. Viewing it from above, while hanging for dear life onto a rope high above the crashing waves, had been scary, but it was spectacular theater. The howling wind and the roaring waves had made it impossible to communicate with his climbing partner, Francesco. That sly old mountain climbing legend, who led the climb ahead of him, was out of sight; he hadn't bothered to give him any instructions, and Max had been too proud to ask. In fact, he hadn't even revealed to Francesco that he had never climbed before in his life, with ropes or otherwise. Cursing himself, Max made it through his debut climb unscathed, despite his obstinate refusal to ask for advice. "Pride has a price," Tara used to tell him.

After passing the turnout for Fontellina, the other posh beach establishment beside the Faraglioni rocks, Max walked down the steps leading to the terrace of the Da Luigi restaurant and snack bar.

Chiara, the daughter of the family who owned the beach concession at Da Luigi, greeted him with a smile, "We haven't seen you for ages, Max, what's up?"

"I've missed coming here, believe me. I'm here today because I'm investigating the death of one of your patrons, Signora Camilla Kallberg."

Chiara looked surprised. "Such a sad ending of her life. But don't the police handle that?"

Max explained that he wasn't in competition with the police, just tying up the loose ends of the paperwork needed by his insurance company.

Chiara furrowed her brow. "I don't get it, why would she want to kill herself?"

"I don't know, but that does appear to be a possibility. But if she didn't kill herself, do you think it could have been a crime of passion?" Max asked.

"Crime of passion? Well, she certainly could have aroused passion, but she never confided in me. Why don't you ask the *bagnini* (the beach attendants) and the waiters—and of course, the *habitués*; they may know something. Good luck, Max."

A Young Witness

As Max walked down the stairs to the beach, a young girl licking an ice-cream cone blocked his way. The girl looked straight at him. "She was a close friend of mine," she said, in a stern tone of voice.

"Pardon me?"

"I overheard you and Chiara talking. Camilla and I were friends. We met here when I was six years old. I loved her very much."

"And you are?"

"My name is Sara, what's yours?"

"Sara, it's a pleasure to meet you. My name is Max De Angelis. Please call me Max."

The young girl was exceptionally beautiful, with long, straight blond hair, blue-green eyes, and golden-bronzed skin. Her intelligent eyes showed a hint of mischief. She looked to be about fourteen.

When Max suggested they sit down somewhere to talk, Sara led him to a stone bench near the pier for the shuttle boat between Da Luigi and Marina Piccola.

Sara explained that she was staying on Capri with her grandparents, who owned a summer residence on the island; they were from Naples and she always spent part of her summer with them. Like Camilla, they were habitués of Da Luigi. She went on to tell Max about her happy times with Camilla, swimming and having lunch together on the terrace.

Sara listened attentively while Max explained more about the investigation. She was very curious about the circumstances surrounding Camilla's death and was not timid or disturbed by this discussion.

"I don't see why she would have killed herself; she was always so happy. And I doubt that it was an accident because Camilla wasn't clumsy. Someone must have murdered her," Sara said.

"Who do you think that might be?" Max asked.

Sara shrugged her shoulders, "Maybe somebody who was mad at her."

"Why would anybody be mad at her?"

"Maybe she broke someone's heart."

"And who Sara, do you think that person would be?"

"Well, we wouldn't necessarily know, would we?" Sara lowered her voice to a whisper. "There is Camilla's friend Nicola, of course; he's from Naples. I think he was in love with her for many years. Nicola's beach chair is right over there; that's his regular spot. He always comes alone without his wife, but he's not here today." Sara pointed to an outcrop with a single empty beach chair. "Maybe he hoped that after she got over the death of her husband, he would have a chance. Maybe he got angry. Maybe he pushed her off the cliff. I remember the day before Ferragosto—"

Max's pulse quickened. Was he finally going to learn something? "Yes, what do you remember? Try to remember every little detail, even if it seems irrelevant."

"Like I said, it was Saturday, the day before Ferragosto. I had been here on Capri for a week, and I was looking forward to having lunch with Camilla that day, but her sister Katarina had arrived the day before; so, they had lunch together, of course." Sara communicated with her body as much as with her voice, emphasizing every other word with a hand gesture or a facial expression.

"Had you met Katarina before?" Max asked.

"No, Camilla introduced her to me that day. I understand she usually visits Capri in July, and I am on Capri mostly in August."

"And can you tell me what happened that Saturday?"

"Well, when I climbed up the ladder after a swim, I recognized the voices of Camilla and Nicola talking. They couldn't see me as I was out of view below them. They seemed to be having a fight. Nicola sounded furious."

"Do you remember what they said?" Max asked.

"I wasn't listening intentionally, you know, but it was hard to miss their loud angry voices. I remember something that Nicola said to Camilla. He said, 'I'm fed up with the way you're treating me. One day you'll get what you deserve!'"

134

Sara's reenactment of a man's speech was spot on, Max thought. "Hmm, anything else you can remember, Sara?"

"Yes, later when I saw Camilla's sister having an espresso with a man up at the bar, I decided to join Camilla on her *lettino* (sun lounger), and we sat next to each other and chatted for a while. The truth is, I had an important question to ask her." Sara paused; for the first time, she seemed unsure of herself.

"And what was that?" Max asked, gently coaxing her.

"Well," she continued, "I wanted to know—how does one know when it is real love? Camilla said that whether one is young or old, haste is not a good thing. She said that if a boy loves you, then he will wait for you. And she talked about hormones, that I should not confuse hormones for love. She said that both the male hormones and the female hormones are necessary and useful, but they are useless for knowing real love. 'Search in your gut for intuitive knowledge, do not search in the heart. If you feel at all uneasy in your stomach, it is better to take your time and wait.' That's what she said."

"Hmm," Max said. "Anything else?"

"Yes, first Camilla told me she hadn't always listened to her own advice, and then she said some very strange things." Sara stood up from the bench to face Max and folded her arms across her chest, as if she was an actress on a stage and Max was the audience. "I think these were Camilla's words, though I don't remember them exactly: 'Anybody can make a mistake. Believe me, Sara, one can be a fool at any age; nobody is immune to love. What happened to me is I fell in love with the idea of love. I fell in love with a man I admired for his intellect, a man who was crazy about me; he said he couldn't live without me. But that is not a good reason to be with a man, believe me. I knew in my heart I didn't love him. I was just living in the moment, and not thinking about the danger of my deception. Only now do I realize the damage that I did, and I'll have to face the consequences for my silly vanity.'"

Sara spoke slowly, carefully emphasizing each word. Max wondered if Sara was prone to exaggeration or whether she was aspiring to become an actress. The girl had a real flair for drama.

Sara's voice quivered, "That was the last time I saw Camilla alive. Those were Camilla's last words to me. Strange don't you think?

135

Don't you see? Someone must have killed her. You will find out who killed her, promise me you will!"

Sara's teary eyes were begging for his help. Max looked away, thinking he would have been better off not having met Sara; he feared he wouldn't be able to live up to her expectations. His boss Bob wouldn't be happy if Max found evidence proving that Camilla's death was not a suicide. Then he had a sudden change of heart; Sara's trust in him made him feel proud, how could he disappoint her? Turning towards her, he capitulated, "I'll do my absolute best to find out the truth, Sara. I can promise you that."

Max thought about the words Camilla had spoken to Sara: *I was not thinking about the danger of my deception and now I'll have to face the consequences.* Couldn't this be interpreted differently? he wondered. Wasn't it possible that Camilla had killed herself in order not to face the consequences of whatever she had done?

"By the way, do you know if Camilla's sister is here today?" he asked, as he got up from the bench.

"Yes, actually I spoke to Katarina before I went to get an ice cream. She had just gotten her red *palloncino* (inflatable ball) out of the locker; you know the one you need when you swim outside the roped boundaries, and she said she was going to swim to Villa Malaparte."

"That's a long way, was she going alone?" Max asked.

"Yes, I told her it was better not to swim alone, but she went anyway. Well, if you don't have any more questions, I think I will go for a dip. See you later."

Sara dove into the sea. When she surfaced, she expertly kicked off and dove deep to the bottom; she was like a fish in its element.

A TASTE OF SALT

After borrowing a pair of swimming goggles and fins from the *bagnino* (beach attendant), Max dove underneath the boundary rope protecting swimmers from the boat traffic and swam into the bay. A few minutes later, he passed the cave of the Coral Grotto, and with a steady crawl, he followed the coastline, staying as close to the shore as possible to avoid the danger of speeding boats. The water was calm and transparent, and the temperature was perfect.

The glorious underwater views never ceased to amaze Max with their variety. He swam through schools of shimmering fish, and saw giant starfish and limpets clinging to the steep rock wall along the shore. An octopus slid down a rock wall as he approached and camouflaged itself in a little cave; only the eyes were visible.

Crossing Cala del Fico towards Punto Masullo, he spotted Katarina lying on her stomach on the pier below Villa Malaparte. The boxy blood-red villa, bizarrely perched at the edge of a cliff rising straight up from the sea, appeared to be deserted; all the windows were shuttered. As Max started climbing onto the pier, Katarina awoke from her nap.

"What a surprise! Did you know I was here?" she said, giving him a hand up.

"Sara told me." Max grinned wide as he looked at Katarina. Her perfect slim body was tanned golden; her wild blond curls, bleached almost white by the sun. When their eyes met, they both smiled, knowing he had swum all the way there just to see her again. I was an idiot not to accept her invitation for a nightcap yesterday, he scolded himself.

The warm sun felt good on his skin after the long swim. They lay on their backs, side by side, while he told Katarina the history of Villa Malaparte. Max had once attended a play staged at the villa about the life of the eccentric Curzio Malaparte, who in 1938 had built a refuge for himself on Capri that he named *Casa Come Me* (A House Like Me) that was as peculiar as the writer himself.

"Nobody knew whether Malaparte was working for the fascists or whether he was plotting against them," Max said.

"Look at those steps cut into the rock; there are ninety-nine of them." Max pointed towards a staircase leading from the pier up to the villa structure. "An exterior staircase built in the shape of a reverse pyramid leads to the flat roof terrace, but the staircase has no handrail or support whatsoever—neither has the terrace. A freestanding curved fence that looks like a sculpture stretches across the roof; it has no function as far as I could tell—"

Max paused, glancing at Katarina; he was glad to see that she appeared interested. "The play about the life of Curzio Malaparte moved from room to room in the villa. I remember a quote by Malaparte: *Today I live in an island, in a sad, harsh, severe house, which I built myself, solitary above a rock overlooking the sea: a house that is the ghost, the secret image of my prison. The image of my nostalgia.* The last act of the play was recited, would you believe, by an actor while riding a bloody bicycle on the roof. It seems he was reenacting Malaparte's habit of bicycling on the roof for daily exercise. The actor on the bicycle suddenly lost his balance, and he would have gone straight down the stairs and over the cliff to the abyss below, had he not somehow magically regained his balance just in time. We all held our breath."

Max paused again and rolled over on his side to look up at the strange architecture built by the troubled but talented writer and journalist. Instead, he found himself looking straight into the bright green eyes of Katarina.

He kissed her.

On their return, swimming along the rocky seawall, they marveled at the color of the sea below the waterline; the water was every imaginable shade of brilliant blue, more varied and intense than either of them had ever seen.

Back in the cove of Tragara, they swam into the Coral Grotto and dove down to touch the fine sand on the sea floor. The light coming from the cave entrance had turned the water a dazzling translucent turquoise color, and as it lapped against the sides of the grotto, they could see the red coral covering the walls of the grotto just below the waterline.

Treading water, they kissed again.

DA LUIGI

"Good afternoon, Signora Katarina; good afternoon, Signor Max," said Sergio the waiter, greeting them as they sat down for lunch at Da Luigi's restaurant. "It's a pleasure to see you, and this time not under the sad circumstances of Signora Camilla's funeral."

"Good afternoon, Sergio," Katarina said. "Thank you, again, for helping to carry the casket."

"I was grateful for the honor; I shall miss her dearly," Sergio said.

Discussing the menu with Sergio, Katarina and Max decided on sharing a whole grilled fish, a plate of grilled vegetables, and a bottle of white wine; a Greco di Tufo from the hills of Avellino in central Campania.

Max and Katarina had chosen to sit next to each other during lunch so they could both enjoy the view of the sea and the Amalfi Coast in the distance. To their right, the Faraglioni rock Stella towered over them, and the steep cliffs of Capri rose to the left. The only residence within view, apart from the little villa next to the Lido, was the white two-story Villa Solitaria perched majestically on the cliff.

"Do you know the Roman legend of Monacone?" Max asked Katarina, pointing to the rocky islet straight ahead of them.

"Camilla and I went snorkeling around Monacone. I admired the abundant underwater life, but I don't know anything about a legend."

"It is said that Masgaba's tomb is on Monacone," Max began. "Masgaba was African, the Roman emperor Augustus' personal architect, and a favorite among his retinue. It is thought that the phrase *Apragopolis*, 'Land of Do-nothings,' was given to Capri by Emperor Augustus; originally, it was associated with the rocks of Monacone, where the favored elite enjoyed taking *apricari*, sun baths, beside the sea. It was discovered that in Roman times the rocky islets on this eastern part of the island might have stood twelve meters [10]higher above the surface."

"Imagine how impressive the Monacone and Faraglioni rocks must have been!" Katarina exclaimed.

"How is the grilled *orata* (sea bream)?" Sergio asked as he refreshed their wine glasses, only one-third full, before placing the bottle of Greco di Tufo back in the ice cooler.

"The *orata* is perfect, thank you," Max answered.

Katarina nodded in agreement and smiled.

---

[10] 40 feet

"Did you know that the Ancient Greeks devoted the *orata* to Aphrodite, the goddess of beauty, since it was considered to be the most attractive and tastiest of fish?" Sergio added before excusing himself.

"I didn't know fish had to be attractive to be tasty," said Katarina with a laugh. "In Norway, we say, the uglier the fish, the better."

"For me, any fish is beautiful as long it is in the water," Max said. "Maybe the sea bream was considered attractive in ancient times because of the golden colors between its eyes. Gold, beauty, power, and divinity seem to have gone together since gold was discovered thousands of years ago."

"Camilla's diamond necklace, the one that has mysteriously disappeared, had a heavy ornate gold chain," said Katarina.

"I see," Max nodded. "Then the necklace must be quite valuable. It may seem strange to you that it has disappeared, but actually, the necklace could easily have been stolen at the morgue in Naples."

"You're right, I thought about that, too."

While waiting for their coffee, a double espresso for himself and a café Americano for Katarina, Max decided he had better get down to the business of figuring out whether Camilla had killed herself or not. His office was pressing for an update. "Catarì," he said gently, "I would be grateful if you could tell me everything that happened from the time of your arrival on Capri to when you reported your sister missing. Try to remember every little detail."

Katarina looked out at the water and began telling Max the story of what had happened between Friday, August 13th, and Tuesday, August 17th (omitting the part about her little adventure with the taxi driver); she felt as if it had all happened to someone else. When she had finished speaking, she turned to face him. Her beautiful green eyes darkened.

"I wonder if there is anything I could have done to prevent Camilla's death? If only I hadn't let her go alone that night. I ask myself over and over again if there was anything I could have done, anything at all. I should never, never have left her side." Tears rolled down her cheeks. "I can't stop seeing the image of Camilla, the way she looked the last time I saw her alive. I'll never forget it." Katarina used the table napkin to wipe her tears. "At the same time, I feel strangely fortunate," she whispered.

"Fortunate?" Max asked in surprise. He wondered if Katarina meant that she was the beneficiary of Camilla's two-million-dollar life insurance policy as well as heir to her sister's house on Capri.

"Yes," Katarina managed a small smile, "fortunate in two ways. First, I feel lucky to be alive. It's as if everything in life has become more precious, more beautiful—especially my daughter. It feels as if I am truly seeing everything for the first time, and I feel so very blessed."

Max vacillated between believing her and giving in to his ingrained suspicion of human nature. She couldn't be such a great actress, could she? he thought. Compassion won him over, and he touched Katarina's hand. Tears glinted in the corners of her eyes.

"The other reason I feel fortunate is to have that special memory of my sister. How beautiful Camilla was on the last night of her life." Katarina squeezed Max's hand in appreciation of his support. "It's not only the memory of her beauty that I will always cherish, but her beautiful soul that showed itself that night. The sparkle in her eyes and the tenderness when she spoke to me were so full of love, a love that I know included me. *Love is life's glorious music!* That is what my sister said."

CHAPTER 18 - SUSPECTS

K atarina went to read a book on her *lettino* after she and Max had finished lunch, while Max spoke with the *bagnini* (beach attendants) and several of Camilla's acquaintances. Max then interviewed the barman and the woman who cleaned the establishment. Lastly, he spoke with Sergio and Peppino, the waiters at Da Luigi that had known Camilla for many years, and who had served as pall bearers at her funeral.

To ponder what he had learned, Max went to rest on a lounge chair beside Katarina, under the shade of a blue canvas umbrella.

Everyone he spoke to at Da Luigi had known Camilla well, but he was unable to uncover any new evidence to build a case for suicide. The majority didn't think suicide was in her character, but Max knew this was often the response of friends and family members. None of them believed that she had any enemies. Apart from the young girl, Sara, nobody else he talked to had come forward with the names of any lovers; there were some vague hints from Camilla's friends, but nothing concrete.

When Max asked each of them what they were doing on the night of Ferragosto, only one person, Sergio, lacked an alibi. Sergio told him that he had been scheduled to work as an extra at the Canzone Del Mare restaurant that night, but at the last minute, he had called and canceled, as he wasn't feeling well. He returned home from Da Luigi at 7 pm and laid down in the guest bedroom, because it was the coolest room in the house, and fell asleep. His wife, who had been at choir practice when he returned home that evening, was unaware that Sergio had not gone to work that night and was asleep in the guest bedroom. The next morning at 6 am, Sergio went in to wake her up before leaving for work.

And what about Nicola Ferrante? Max wondered. The Morettis had mentioned that Nicola became sick the evening of Ferragosto and excused himself from the card tournament at ten o'clock. Signor Aragone said he had seen Nicola at a quarter to one in the morning. Two hours and forty-five minutes would have been plenty of time for Nicola to walk to Belvedere delle Noci and back, but why would he have passed the Piazzetta? It was not on his way home. So, it appeared that he didn't have an alibi. From what Sara had said about Nicola threatening Camilla the day before Ferragosto, it sounds like he could be a suspect.

To Max's mind, Sara's testimony was not conclusive, especially in view of the conflicting interpretations for Camilla's comment about "facing consequences." Was Camilla killed as a consequence of something she did? Or did Camilla kill herself because she could not face the consequences of the damage she had inflicted on someone?

He considered the hypothesis that Camilla's new love interest had broken off the relationship, and unable to live with the disappointment, she had killed herself; her lover, afraid that he would be accused of murder, did not come forward to the police. Although there were many interpretations for Camilla's words, Max believed that somehow a man had to be involved. After all, Domenico had overheard Camilla talking to someone when she passed by his restaurant that night. And Camilla had told Katarina that she was in love with someone.

If Max wanted to prove that Camilla killed herself, he would have to find her past lover or her recent lover—or both.

Frustrated by his inconclusive speculations, Max asked Katarina if she wanted to go for a short swim; she readily agreed.

After drying off on the beach, they walked in silence from Da Luigi up the steep hill to Via Tragara. Their silence was not only from shortness of breath while climbing in the hot sun; they were both thinking about the significance of their kisses.

Katarina wondered whether kissing Max had been the smart thing to do. She still knew nothing about Max's life or his connection to Camilla. That first kiss had been nice—more than nice, she admitted to herself; the second kiss was even better. But how could she trust him when he was still trying to prove that Camilla killed herself? Why didn't he believe her when she told him her sister would never do such a thing?

Max wasn't sure why he had kissed Katarina. No doubt it had not been a wise move to get involved with a woman who may have murdered her sister to inherit her house and claim the life insurance. The kiss didn't really mean that much, he reasoned. The effect of sun and sea was intoxicating, and the body of Katarina even more so. How does the song go—*A kiss is but a kiss. . .* Or maybe what Raffi suggested was true. Maybe he was just trying to get close to her to learn more about the case. It couldn't be that he was actually falling in love... or could it?

After the steep climb from Faraglioni, the light breeze felt good on their sweaty skin as they sauntered back to town on Via Tragara.

"Ah, there is Nicola, he was a good friend of Camilla." Katarina pointed to a man in front of them pushing a baby stroller; a little girl held onto the handle of the stroller.

Katarina introduced Nicola Ferrante to Max.

"So, Max De Angelis, are you the brain to solve the mystery that is challenging the little gray cells of our local authorities?" Nicola asked sarcastically.

The snide remark wasn't lost on him, but Max knew that he had to tread lightly. He began to make small talk about the sultry summer weather and the Naples soccer team.

Nicola interrupted his chit-chat. "I heard you went to interrogate my friends, the Morettis?"

"We exchanged a few words, yes. Lovely people the Morettis, aren't they?" said Max.

"Oh, come on, don't play games with me. You're not kidding anybody."

"What do you mean, Signor Ferrante?"

Katarina bent over to talk with the little girl to distract her from hearing what her grandfather was about to say; his face was red with anger.

"What I mean is, you think I did it. You think I killed Camilla. I understand they told you I left the party early. Wasn't feeling well, stomach trouble. My wife stayed behind at the party until the end of the card tournament. We had a babysitter take care of our grandkids that night, so we could go to the Morettis'."

"Can the babysitter provide you with an alibi for the time between eleven o'clock and three in the morning?" Max asked.

"No, she can't—after I left the tournament, I decided some fresh air would be good for my indigestion, so I went for a stroll before I walked over to the Piazzetta to buy cigarettes and then went home. It was sometime after one o'clock; by then my wife had returned and the baby sitter had gone home."

Katarina touched Nicola's arm. "I'm sure you didn't kill Camilla; I know you cared for her. You couldn't have done such a thing."

"Yes, I cared for her, you're right," Nicola said, glaring indignantly at Max, and still simmering with anger.

"Thank you for the explanation, Nicola," Max said curtly.

They left Nicola and his two small grandchildren at the entrance to I Giardinetti (the playground) and walked over to the Piazzetta.

Max and Katarina found themselves a table at Grand Caffè and ordered two glasses of fresh squeezed grapefruit juice to replenish their energy after the hike uphill from Faraglioni.

"Let's make a list of possible suspects without alibis, shall we?" Katarina suggested.

"Okay, first on the list is me, second is you," Max said laughing. "Then there is Nicola and the waiter Sergio. That makes four of us."

"Did you notice that Nicola didn't deny killing Camilla?" Katarina said excitedly. "And on my last day with Camilla, she sent me away so that she could talk to him alone, strange don't you think?"

Max was surprised by Katarina's comment. She seemed eager to frame Nicola as a suspect without concrete evidence of foul play, but he decided to ignore it for the moment.

"And then there is Emilio," Katarina burst out, "Camilla's lawyer. This morning he called and asked me to come to Naples for a reading of her testament the day after tomorrow. He has no alibi. I asked him straight out. He said he was at home alone on Ferragosto. His office was closed that day, of course, and the following day. He could easily have arrived on Capri at nine o'clock by the last ferry and returned on the early morning ferry. Oh, and I just remembered, Emilio keeps his motorboat on Procida. What if he wasn't in Naples that night, but on his boat on Procida? The boat is fast; he could easily have made it back and forth to Capri in no time at all. I just had an idea, Max. Why don't you come with me to her lawyer's office on Thursday? That way you will meet Emilio."

"Okay, I'll go with you to Naples," Max nodded, even though he couldn't see why Emilio would be a suspect, "assuming the police give me permission to leave the island. Now we have five suspects. Who else?"

"I've been thinking about Lorenzo; he was one of the pallbearers at Camilla's funeral. He was a dear friend of Camilla, but I don't know much about him. Camilla would hire him whenever she wanted to take a trip around the island or go to Nerano or Positano on the mainland. When I was invited to his home for dinner after Camilla's funeral, I walked into the kitchen and overheard Lorenzo's daughter saying something strange to her mother. When the daughter returned from Naples on the night of Ferragosto, she saw her father's boat

146

pull into port. Lorenzo's wife told her daughter that she must have been mistaken; her father must have been leaving the port, not arriving, because he had been hired by an American couple for a boat ride to Nerano for dinner. You know Nerano, don't you?"

Max merely nodded; he didn't care to point out that he was from Capri and was familiar with Nerano, a quaint little fishing village by the sea on the Amalfi Coast.

◆ ◆ ◆

One of Tara's favorite things to do when they were on Capri was to spend the day on a boat and swim in the clear waters of the islets of Li Galli, followed by a seaside dinner at the restaurant Il Cantuccio in Nerano while watching the sunset.

Max felt a pang of sorrow when he remembered the very first time he took Tara to Nerano. It was during their honeymoon on Capri, and he had borrowed a *gozzo* (motorboat) from a friend. How well he remembered the boat ride back to Capri, sitting beside his wife at the stern and steering the boat under a starlit sky.

The memory of the adventure they had together after returning to Capri from Nerano was even more painful, tearing open the wound in his heart.

Later that night, they had decided to visit Capri's magical blue grotto, *La Grotta Azurra*. Max and Tara were in luck; the tide was low and the sea calm—ideal conditions for visiting the grotto. The sky was clear, and a full moon illuminated the sea. Max anchored the *gozzo* to a buoy, and they swam naked through the narrow opening into the grotto.

Once their eyes had adjusted to the darkness, the water and surrounding walls of the cave shimmered a fluorescent blue. Their naked skin glimmered in the water, and the ripples from the movement of their bodies made the water sparkle like champagne.

They climbed up on a ledge at the rear of the cave and stepped carefully on bare feet into the dark interior. In the faint light, Max took Tara's hand and led her to an inner chamber with three connecting passageways that opened to the dark blue lagoon. There in the dark, they made passionate love.

◆ ◆ ◆

Katarina looked at Max with concern. She didn't know how to interpret the dark stony look on his face. Was he regretting their new intimacy? she wondered. He seemed so far away, so lost in thought; and he seemed unaware that he was touching his good luck charm.

The red coral amulet in the shape of a hot pepper hung from a chain around his neck and rested in the little v-shaped dip in his collarbone, right above Max's sun-bronzed chest.

In an instant, Katarina was transported back to the delicious moment in the coral cave when his chest pressed against hers and their lips met in a salty kiss.

When she reached over and touched his shoulder, Max jumped.

"Sorry, I didn't mean to startle you," she said.

"No, no, not at all, sorry, I drifted off for a moment. I heard you saying something about Lorenzo and Nerano; please go on—"

Katarina resumed her story. "Yes, so that night after Camilla's funeral, when Lorenzo drove me back to the villa after dinner, I asked him if the fireworks had been any good in Nerano on Ferragosto. He said they were great, which does not correspond to being seen by the daughter coming into port in Capri early in the evening. I wondered what time he had gotten home to his wife that night, but I didn't ask."

"Hmmm, that means we have six possible suspects so far—all men except for you," Max said.

He wondered about Katarina's determination to help him find suspects; he thought she seemed a bit too eager. But then, again, he might have behaved the same way had he been suspected of murder. Then it hit him: he *was* suspected of murder.

CHAPTER 19 - A SEXAGRAM

M ax said goodbye to Katarina, who went home for a quiet evening, and he headed to Hotel Gatto Bianco to change his clothes; he was going to meet Raffi in the Piazzetta for an aperitif.

After a quick shower in the Kennedy suite's luxurious bathroom, Max pulled on a pair of black jeans and selected a pale blue cotton shirt. He rolled up the sleeves of his shirt to his upper arms, and slipped on his super light track shoes—black with a gray and red stripe, without socks. His cell phone and slim wallet went into the specially designed zippered pocket along the side seam of the jeans.

Raffi was waiting for him beside the clock tower in the Piazzetta, impeccably dressed in a pair of white jeans, a turquoise polo shirt, and dark blue suede loafers; his ever-present camera was slung across his shoulder.

They crossed the Funicular square to admire the dramatic purple sunset over the bay of Naples. After Raffi had taken a couple of photos, Max gave him an update on his investigation.

"You had a great swim and a delightful lunch with the fair lady—sounds like you're not overworking yourself. And you're keeping Katarina all to yourself, you rascal," Raffi joked. "You still haven't introduced me to her."

There was some truth to it, Max thought; he wasn't ready to share Katarina with Raffi, not yet anyway. Raffi had a way with women; he seduced them all with his charm—or, at least, most of them.

"So, as of now, there may be as many as six suspects from what you say, including you and Katarina?" Raffi asked.

"Yes, and Katarina has the most obvious motive: the insurance claim and Camilla's home on Capri."

"Well, my dear friend, you are mistaken if you haven't considered your own motive; you could be wooing the fair Princess Katarina to get the villa and two million dollars to boot," Raffi laughed.

Max tried to laugh, but the laugh got stuck in his throat; all he could manage was a cough, as he shook his index finger at Raffi.

"Just joking, of course. On the other hand, from what you've told me, there is quite a lot pointing to suicide, isn't that true?" Raffi said. "And if it was indeed suicide," he continued, "and Katarina knows the insurance won't pay, then she is eager to find other suspects, right?"

"Right Raffi; I've considered that myself."

"Maybe the beautiful Katarina destroyed a suicide note written by Camilla?"

Max sighed, "Yes, I've thought about that possibility, too."

"This Piazza is not just a square, you know," Max said, as they sauntered back to the bustling Piazzetta in search of a table.

"Of course, I know that," Raffi said in a mock indignant tone. "It is THE square."

They were in luck; a couple got up from a table at Piccolo Bar, freeing up a table in the next to the last row.

"No, no Raffi, what I meant is that the Piazzetta is shaped like a six-pointed star." Max said as they sat down.

"I have never thought about the Piazzetta as a star—just full of wannabe stars."

"Imagine, Raffi, that you're on a stage with six entrances and six exits," Max said. "How many different options would that give the actors for entering and exiting the stage."

"What do you mean?" Raffi placed his camera on the table. It had been a long and sweltering day; he wasn't in the mood for a math quiz.

"Just think about it, the Piazzetta has six entrances that also function as exits; I will count going clockwise, starting appropriately at the bell tower:

1. The grand entry between Palazzo Cerio and the campanile.
2. The arch to Via Acquaviva between Bar Caso and Piccolo Bar.
3. The arch to Via Longano between Piccolo Bar and the Municipal Hall.
4. The arch to Via Le Botteghe between Municipal Hall and Grand Caffè.
5. The entry to Via Vittorio Emanuele between Grand Caffè and Bar Tiberius.
6. 'The grand gallery,' as I call it. The broad stairway between Bar Tiberius and Palazzo Cerio leading to the church of Santo Stefano."

"You're right, Max. Six entrances and six exits in the Piazzetta. I've never thought about it that way. So what?"

"Yes, thirty-six options for entering and exiting the stage—that's what we have right here in our own famous little square, my friend. In the Piazzetta, we get to be actors and spectators at the same time. Marvelous, isn't it? That is certainly one of the fascinations of the Piazzetta."

Raffi tapped the top of his head, the gesture for *matto*, a total cuckoo. The sun must have gotten to Max, he thought—or was it possible that his friend had fallen in love?

Max ignored Raffi and continued his discourse. "It was Tara who pointed out that the Piazzetta has the shape of a six-pointed star or a hexagram. The Romans called it a sexagram. Tara said that it's also a mandala called a *shatkona yantra* in Sanskrit."

Upon hearing Tara's name, Raffi perked up and started to pay closer attention. He had been best man at the wedding of Max and Tara. Would this weird topic give him some insight as to why they had split up? Max had never told him, and Raffi had never asked.

"Sounds pretty sexy to me, Max," said Raffi.

Max tried in vain to flag down one of the waiters of the café while he continued his discourse, ignoring Raffi's remark.

"Well, if the Piazzetta is a six-pointed star, everyone who comes here should feel welcome. Think about it: the sexagram has had significance for virtually every culture and religion throughout civilization, from the ancient Egyptians up to the present." Max looked at Raffi to see if he still had his attention; surprised that he did, in fact, appear to be interested, he continued. "The sexagram symbolizes creation itself. So, you see, the energy of creation is here in the Piazzetta."

Max leaned back in his wicker chair and surveyed the scene in the square. A young waiter appeared; neither Max nor Raffi knew him. They ordered a couple of single malt Scotch whiskeys on the rocks with chasers of mineral water.

"Okay, so what did the Piazzetta represent to Tara?" Raffi asked.

"To Tara, the Piazzetta was the very heart and soul of Capri. She said that the interlacing triangles of a six-pointed star symbolize the union of two opposite forces: active and passive, darkness and light, and so on. Since one can't exist without the other, they are one. And—" Max paused as the bell in the campanile chimed once, indicating three minutes before the hour, "and—that is, if you're still interested—"

"Yes, yes, go on Max, please enlighten me," Raffi teased.

"Well, Tara explained that in the Eastern philosophy she was studying, the mystical union of the two triangles represents, like I said, creation, occurring through the divine union of male and female. The upward triangle of the sexagram symbolizes the Supreme Energy of Being, standing for the focused aspects of masculinity. And the downward triangle symbolizes Mother Nature, representing the sacred embodiment of femininity."

The young waiter walked up to them and placed their drinks and bar snacks on the table.

"Let's drink to the union of male and female!" Raffi raised his glass. He wondered what had happened to Tara since the divorce. Was she happy?

Chapter 20 - My Heart's Desire Beach

Wednesday, August 25

Not a soul was in the Piazzetta when Max passed the square just before six in the morning on his way to swim in the bay at Marina Piccola. Dawn was his favorite time of day on Capri, the hour when few people were awake, and the sun had not yet risen behind Monte Tuoro. The eastern sky was painted a hazy rose and lavender, and the gray rock of Monte Solaro was wrapped in a cloud of mist.

From Via Roma, he tucked into the underpass at Due Golfi to access the pedestrian path leading to the public beach. Max virtually flew down the familiar stairs of Via Mulo. The grand villas with their elaborate gardens and gates raced past him like a movie on fast-forward. Max was a kid again; this was his kingdom, his Capri, and he had it all to himself.

The sea was a shimmering mirror as Max skipped down the final steps to the shore of Marina Piccola; not a ripple disturbed its glassy surface.

The local fishermen were out on their boats and the quiet was only interrupted by the squawking calls of herring gulls. When Max stepped onto the smooth pebbles of the small beach, every worrisome thought dropped away.

Max immersed himself in the water, surrendering his body and mind to the sea. Coming up for air, he sighed with satisfaction, like someone who has returned to a lover's embrace after a long absence. With long even strokes, he crossed the cove and swam along the shore below the imposing rock wall, heeding every little underwater bend and every submerged rock; all of it was illuminated with a deep blue, almost supernatural, light.

There must be a God! he thought, much as he had often declared that he did not believe in God.

When he had swum as far as Punta di Mulo, a fishing vessel passed close to shore; seagulls encircled the boat with their shrill cries, eager for fish remnants. Max raised his hand, mid-stroke, in a greeting of solidarity to the fishermen, grateful to be sharing this magical early morning hour with them.

Swimming past the bend of the shoreline and beyond the sunlit bay, the water temperature suddenly cooled, and the ocean floor dropped away. Nothing to see now; the rock wall alongshore was devoid of light below the surface of the water. Max turned around and swam back towards Marina Piccola with a smooth and steady crawl stroke, his muscles performing on autopilot, and his breathing long and even.

The half-hidden minuscule beach he knew so well came into view. A warning sign that said, *Attenzione caduta massi (Beware of falling rocks)*, was posted on the beach to keep anyone from climbing up on the shore to rest or sunbathe. The temptation was too strong; an illicit paradise was beckoning.

Max slid into shore on his belly and carefully pulled himself onto the beach; he stood up, then wobbled across the slippery pebbles. He laid down on his stomach and closed his eyes. The heat from the sun and the stones beneath him warmed his cold body.

Then it all came rushing back—the memory of that morning ten years ago. There was nothing he could do to prevent himself from thinking about it now. This is where it had all begun; on a hot summer day just like this one, he had gone for a swim to Punta di Mulo and stopped to rest on this beach. Every little detail was etched vividly into his memory. He wondered, was it always like that when someone falls in love for the first time?

TARA

When Max met Tara, he had just turned twenty-eight. It was September, and he was back on Capri for a vacation. He had worked hard, going through the ranks to become an insurance investigator at UGI in London, a global firm with fifteen offices worldwide.

He was swimming back from Punta di Mulo when he saw her, a young woman lying on her back on the forbidden little beach. Max swam closer and closer to shore, straining his eyes to see her. Was this the same woman?

The evening before, Max had seen a woman run down the steps from the church to the Piazzetta. She was dressed in simple white attire, with her long blond hair in a ponytail, her sandaled feet barely touching the stairs as she flew down the staircase. What was it about her? Max wondered. He couldn't stop staring. Never had he seen a woman move so effortlessly; she seemed self-assured, yet so unaware of her striking beauty. And then—as if on wings—she raced across the funicular square to the railing overlooking the sea. There she stood, gazing at the sky, still as a statue, her face aglow from the light of the sun setting behind Monte Solaro.

Max was transfixed. He had the strange sensation of seeing the sunset through the unknown woman's eyes. The sky was every imaginable shade of purple, orange, red, and yellow, with colorful rays of sunlight splayed out and mirrored in the sea. If Max had been bolder, and a bit less concerned with making a fool of himself, he would have walked over to her to say something—anything. But he didn't. He hadn't wished to seem like just another jackass trying to make a pass at her.

Yes, it was her! No question about it. This was the same woman who had run down the steps to watch the sunset. She was lying on her back with her eyes closed, her long wet hair fanned out over the pebbles.

Max crawled as quietly as possible onto the shore at the far end of the little beach and sat down. The woman's fair skin showed the beginning of a suntan. Her slender body was perfectly formed, barely covered by her simple white bikini. Was she asleep? She didn't make any movement or open her eyes. He didn't mind waiting; he felt he would gladly have sat there on the beach forever, just watching her.

Suddenly, he got scared. The woman was completely motionless. Was she alive? He got up and walked towards her; when he cleared his throat to say something, he started coughing.

She sat up. "Are you OK?" she said, startled.

Looking into eyes as blue as sapphires, he was speechless.

Her lips parted into a broad smile. "I apologize, you probably don't speak English," she said.

"I d-do speak English," he stuttered.

"I'm Tara," she said.

Tara had been traveling through Italy and had planned to spend just one day on Capri, but she became so enchanted with the island that she decided to stay for a week. Since she worked as a freelance book designer and part-time yoga instructor, she had the freedom to set her own schedule.

When Max proposed to Tara four days later, Tara laughed and said, "If you move to San Francisco and you have a job, I will think about it."

Six months later, Max managed to get transferred from London to the company's office in San Francisco.

The following September, they were married in the municipal building in the Piazzetta and spent their honeymoon at Hotel Punta Tragara, one of the most romantic hotels on Capri. With the help of an inheritance from Tara's grandmother, who had raised Tara, they were able to buy a house in San Francisco and soon adopted a kitten. Tara learned Italian, and they spent their vacations on Capri.

Seven years after their wedding ceremony, they signed the divorce papers.

CHAPTER 21 - EYES OF SILVER

The pain from the pebbles digging into his cheek made Max realize he had fallen asleep lying on his stomach; he rolled over and sat up. A swimmer was headed straight towards him. How annoying, he thought. This was *their* sacred beach. Tara had named it "My Heart's Desire Beach," and Max was in no mood to share it with anyone; he stood up to leave.

The swimmer was a woman. She floated towards the beach until her belly touched the pebbly shore, and the waves gently rocked her body back and forth. She pulled herself up onto the shifting pebbles of the beach, the waves lapping over her legs. Rotating onto her buttocks, she pushed herself up to a wobbly standing position. Then she looked Max over, from head to toe.

Max was amused by her careful maneuvering and a bit intimidated by the way she scrutinized him. Her almond-shaped eyes were a smoldering silvery gray, *occhi d'argento,* the Capresi called it. The color reminded Max of the eyes of a rare Javan leopard he had once seen in the Tierpark Zoo in Berlin. She looked him over as if he were prey, or a horse for sale. He was about to ask if she wanted to see his teeth, but thought better of it; instead, he smiled uneasily and offered his arm for support.

Unsmiling, she wrapped her small hand halfway around his flexed upper arm; together they made their way over to a boulder. She sat down and gestured for him to sit next to her.

"*Sono Graziella,*" she said.

Ahh, she was Italian, as he had guessed, and from the way she pronounced the vowels in "Graziella," Max was fairly sure she was a *ciammurr,* a local girl from Anacapri.

"*Sono Max,*" he said.

She must be around thirty, he thought. Her features recalled the Moorish influence on the island. Her brow was low and broad, the chin was prominent, and her lips were slightly turned up at the corners. She was of medium height, with long, raven black hair, and her tawny brown body was sensuous and curvy.

They sat in silence for a while, letting the morning sunlight and the sun-heated boulder warm their bodies.

He wasn't aware of how much time had passed, as they sat there silently, hips touching, when she turned her head and looked up into his face. Again, he felt he was being measured, but he didn't mind.

"So, Max, are you alone?" she asked.

◆ ◆ ◆

Max watched his oldest sister Mona while she worked. Her head was bent over the ancient Singer sewing machine, with her feet tapping the treadle; she was making thin gold leather straps for glamorous hand-made Capri sandals.

Max was sitting on a narrow bench at the dining room table, eating a heaping plate of *spaghetti alla chiummenzana*, made just the way their mother had made it for them. He was hungry from his long swim. Mona prepared the local pasta dish with the classic ingredients: fresh tomatoes, local dried oregano, garlic, hot pepper, virgin olive oil, and fresh basil. A liter bottle of local red wine was on the table; Max poured a little into a kitchen glass.

"Mona, you are the best cook, almost as good as Mama," Max said, scooping up the rest of the sauce with a piece of *pagnotta* (rustic bread).

Mona looked at Max with contentment. After he and Tara got divorced, Mona had been worried about him, though she hadn't said anything. Max was so proud, and so hard on himself; she hadn't wanted to interfere in his life. She admired her handsome brother, with his sun bronzed and fit body, his bright, intelligent face and flashing dark eyes. His longish hair was shiny, and even more unruly than usual after his swim.

"How was the water?" she asked.

"The sea is blissfully clean—let's hope it stays that way." Max got up from the bench and bent down to kiss his sister on the cheek. "You know, I feel I may be finally getting over the divorce."

"That's great, Max. I am so happy to have you here again on Capri," she said, with tears of joy.

Slipping down the stairs and through the ancient stone courtyard off Via Posterula, Max was exuberant. He looked at his cell phone; it was just past two o'clock. In six hours, he was going to see Graziella again. Had her silvery eyes shown a hint of promise when she invited him for dinner?

There were certain things one didn't share with family. His date with the exotic and sensuous Graziella, who had risen like a siren from the sea, was one of those things better kept a secret.

161

Chapter 22 - Into the Woods

Graziella was sitting on her silver Vespa scooter in the parking lot at Due Golfi waiting for Max. She was dressed in a chic black skirt and jacket, wearing high-heeled sandals and a fire-red helmet over her long black hair. It was fifteen minutes past their appointed meeting time at eight o'clock when Max sauntered up to her. He didn't see the point of explaining that he'd been delayed at the police station waiting for a permit to go to Naples with Katarina the next day.

Without saying a word, Graziella handed him a helmet; no sooner had he mounted the bike and strapped on the helmet than they took off, forcing him to grab her waist and hold on tightly as they sped towards Anacapri, the other town and municipality on the island. Riding up the busy road, Max held his breath whenever she took advantage of a wide turn to pass a slower vehicle. An oncoming truck driver angrily sounded the horn while the Vespa hugged the centerline; sweat dripped from Max's forehead into his eyes.

Once they got past the treacherous hairpin turns and the road flattened out, Max relaxed from the harrowing ride. The warm rush of air on the summer night felt good on his clammy face. The further away from the town of Anacapri they got, the less traffic there was on the road. Holding onto Graziella's tiny waist while they sped down the long dark road of Strada Faro di Carena felt intimate and erotic.

Turning off the main road, Graziella pointed the scooter straight down a narrow, bumpy country lane. Barely lowering the speed, she made a 180-degree turn, put on the brake, and came to a full stop. She jumped off the scooter, removed her helmet, and shook out her long hair.

"We're here! Hurry up! My mother is surely waiting with the pasta water boiling," Graziella said.

She parked the scooter and led him through the property gate. The property was large by Capri standards, about two acres of fields planted with vegetables and fruit trees. They walked past Graziella's white-washed *casetta* (little house), built in the Capri vernacular style, and turned down a long lane leading to her mother's dwelling; a complex consisting of three small houses built in the same style, surrounding a small courtyard illuminated by candles in lanterns.

"We take care of most of the gardening ourselves," Graziella said with pride. "My mother makes jams, liqueurs, dried herbs and so on, all organic from our *orto* (lot)."

"My father passed away when I was little, so my mother raised me by herself. This is our little paradise away from everything," Graziella volunteered. She gestured for him to sit down at a table covered with hand-painted majolica tiles in the middle of the courtyard.

"Have you always lived here?"

"I left the island once as a girl. I went to Naples to become a nun, but I found out being a nun wasn't for me," she said, looking sideways at Max as if to judge whether he was surprised. "This place pulled me back; this is where I'll die. I couldn't imagine living anywhere else."

She poured water from a ceramic jug into a cobalt-blue glass goblet and drank thirstily before continuing. "I don't know how you felt leaving Capri, but it couldn't have been easy for you. You know what they say about us: *I Capresi sono attaccati all'Isola come le patelle agli scogli* (The Caprese are attached to the Island like limpets to the rocks)."

Max laughed; he knew exactly what she meant.

"It's hard to maintain this place, not only because of all the physical labor, but also it costs a lot to keep everything going. We hire laborers to help with the planting and the harvest. I work in the reception at Hotel Scalinatella now, and I love my job. Ah, here she is. Max, I'd like to introduce you to my mother, Angela."

Dinner was perfect; the pasta sauce was prepared with organic produce from their garden, including the herbs, garlic, and virgin olive oil. Graziella's mother, a charming and lively woman, was delighted by Max's visit. He told them about his job assignment on Capri while Graziella and her mother listened attentively. When he mentioned the name Camilla Kallberg, Angela became visibly excited and interrupted him.

"Oh dear, I knew Camilla Kallberg very well! She often came here to buy my dried herbs and jams!" Angela exclaimed. "You remember her, don't you Graziella?"

"Yes, of course," Graziella nodded. "She was a great lady; how sad to hear what happened to her."

Angela wiped a tear from her eye, "Yes, it is very, very, sad." She sighed, and slowly cleared the plates from the table.

Moments later Angela returned from the kitchen with a bottle of liqueur and three tiny glasses. "Camilla loved my myrtle liqueur; please do try it, Max." Angela passed him a shot glass of the dark crimson liquor.

"Don't tell my sister—she makes an excellent myrtle liqueur, but I think yours is the best I've ever tasted," Max said, smacking his lips.

Graziella's mother smiled, pleased at his praise, and then furrowed her brow.

"Something happened to Camilla recently; I can't put my finger on it, but I'm known to be intuitive. She wasn't herself the last time I saw her about a month ago, that's for sure."

"Really, in what way had she changed?" Max was curious to learn more.

"Let me think a moment," Angela said, closing her eyes. "Camilla was such a happy soul, but lately, there was a dark cloud over her—it was like she was under the spell of something or someone."

"Do you think she might have done away with herself?" Max asked.

"I don't know for sure—but as I said, I see it as a darkness that came over her."

She opened her eyes and looked quizzically at Max. He was about to say something in response to Angela when Graziella quickly changed the topic.

She got them laughing, telling funny stories about her time as a nun in the monastery. Then she joked to Max that she had never had a steady boyfriend, because she had never wanted to be with a "boy," she wanted somebody that was grown up—a *manfriend*. In her opinion, there were too many boys on Capri and hardly any men.

After dessert and another glass of liqueur, Max accepted Graziella's offer to drive him back to town. They shot straight up the country lane with a roar. Stopping at the main road, she turned her head to appraise Max with her silvery gray eyes. Without saying a word, she steered the handle of the scooter to the right, and they sped down the dark road going west towards Faro, the Lighthouse of Punta Carena, in the opposite direction from the towns of Anacapri and Capri.

Parking the scooter, they wandered up the hill towards the magnificent old lighthouse, the second brightest one in Italy; it had guided sailors in those parts for a hundred and fifty years.

The giant octagonal tower, painted with vertical red and white stripes, was built on top of a two-story building perched on a rocky precipice high above the rough waters of the bay. From out at sea, the precipice resembled a *"carena,"* or hull, of a ship. The lighthouse beacon rotated, blinding them with bright flashes of light every three seconds as it illuminated the rocks and the sea below.

Turning away from the light, they hiked down a path leading to a plateau overlooking the waves crashing on the shore.

They sat down on a smooth rock and gazed at the glimmering water and the blinking lights of fishing boats. Max breathed in the familiar salty aroma of the sea and drew Graziella closer to him.

Without saying anything, he got up and extended his hand to Graziella. Hand in hand, they headed towards a path that led into the dark woods.

CHAPTER 23 - A STAKEOUT

K atarina lingered in bed, reliving the moment with Max at the coral grotto the day before when their lips had met in a passionate kiss. She remembered the taste of salt on his lips and the thrill of his tongue seeking hers.

Reluctantly, she forced herself to get out of bed and take a shower. When the cool water hit her naked body, she knew what she had to do: find Amedeo, the taxi driver, and talk to him before the police did. She only knew his first name, where he lived, and that he was married with kids and that he drove a white taxi with a lavender interior. Going to his house was out of the question; she needed to talk to him without arousing any suspicion—especially from his wife.

An idea came to her; she would pass the day waiting for Amedeo at one of the taxi stands. She would hire him, and then they could talk in the taxi. As far as she knew, there were three taxi stands on Capri. The one on Via Roma next to the bus station was neither a comfortable nor an inconspicuous place to wait. The Marina Grande taxi stand had a café within eyesight where she could wait, but it was a busy place with a lot of commotion. Marina Piccola was quiet, with a restaurant right across from the taxi stand; that was her best choice.

Everything she needed to be comfortable for the day went into her handbag: a small cashmere sweater, a rolled-up silk shawl, sunscreen, a make-up bag, her iPhone, a portable charger, and her iPad to work on translating articles from English to Norwegian for a business magazine.

Looking over her wardrobe, she decided on a blue sleeveless dress and a pair of blue and white sandals. Seeing her image in the mirror, she laughed; who was she getting dolled up for, Amedeo? She borrowed a hat from Camilla's collection, one with a wide brim to protect her face from the sun. While putting on her sunglasses to step outside, she realized she had forgotten something; she ran up to her bedroom to get Amedeo's fisherman's cap and stuffed it into her handbag.

There were five tables on the sidewalk outside the restaurant in the little dead-end square of Marina Piccola, all facing the sea as well as the taxi and bus stands. Katarina sat down at the table closest to the restaurant entrance. Perfect, she thought, glancing at her watch— the Capri Time watch Camilla had given her, with the symbol of the campanile in the Piazzetta on the dial. It was ten minutes past ten.

Two taxis were waiting for a fare, but neither one had a lavender interior.

Gregorio, the owner of the restaurant, came out to her table, looking puzzled. He wondered who this elegant, beautiful woman was. Then he recognized her as the sister of Camilla.

"How nice to see you again." Gregorio's kind voice and smile made Katarina feel right at home.

"And you, as well."

"Please accept my condolences; I am so sorry for the loss of your sister. If there is anything I can do to be of help, please just ask."

"Thank you, Gregorio. Could you please bring me a café Americano and a cornetto?"

Gregorio went into the restaurant and came back carrying a tray for Katarina.

Once finished with breakfast, Katarina started working on the translation, interrupted by the frequent arrival of taxis. Now and then a few of the taxi drivers would walk into the café; she wanted to ask if any of them knew Amedeo, but thought better of it.

Every fifteen minutes or so, a little red bus brought a new load of beachgoers; the passengers spilled into the square and down the steps to the sea. Taxis dropped off more beachgoers. The interiors of the taxis were colorful, but none of them were lavender.

Then she saw Max. He was sitting at the window of a bus just leaving the square; she caught a glimpse of his profile. It seemed strange that Max had boarded the bus without coming over to talk to her—maybe he hadn't recognized her with the hat and sunglasses.

What do I really know about Max? she asked herself, recalling the morning after Camilla's funeral when Max had showed up at the villa. Now she feared, as she had a couple of days ago, that he was the man her sister had told her about, the man Camilla had said she was in love with. The unexpected sight of Max on the bus had shaken her. Could Max be the murderer? she wondered.

The hours passed; it grew hot in the square. Taxis came and went, but still no sign of Amedeo. She found it hard to believe that only ten days ago, they'd had that carefree adventure. So much had happened since that night. Suddenly she had a chilling thought: Was it possible that she and Amedeo were having sex at the time when Camilla died? She felt sick with a sudden remorse. What was I thinking? How stupid to have a casual affair, and even stupider, with a married man.

How did Camilla die? Could she have killed herself after all? No. Impossible! Camilla would never do such a thing. It must have been an accident or murder. But who would want to kill Camilla? Max?

Gregorio interrupted her tormenting thoughts. He set a cold bottle of mineral water on the table and raised the sun umbrella. She

removed her wide-brimmed hat and sunglasses and tried to return to
her work.

She had barely managed to translate one paragraph. when her cell
phone rang; it was her ex-husband. "Katta, Petter here."

"Yes?"

"Damn it, Katta. Last night you were on NRK, national television
news, did you know?" Petter was enraged. "Your daughter went to
school this morning thinking that her mother might be involved with
her aunt Camilla's murder. For God's sake Katta, seems you're a
suspect in the case."

Katarina was stunned; she had never expected to be on national
television. "They had no right to say I was a suspect. By law that's
not allowed, you know that."

"They didn't state it outright, they just said that you were
requested to remain in Italy for questioning regarding the death of
your sister. But you know how the damned media somehow makes
it seem as if a person is guilty."

"I didn't kill Camilla, Petter. You must know that. It's true that
the police will not let me leave the island of Capri for the moment,
but I'm sure everything will be resolved soon. Please explain to Anna
that it's all a misunderstanding, just standard police procedure. Tell
her that I'll be back home as soon as I can."

"I want you to get your ass on an airplane as soon as possible.
Anna needs you. I have called the embassy in Rome, and they will
send a representative if you need one."

"Thanks, Petter, I do appreciate that, but let's wait until I've been
charged with a crime, which I don't think will happen. Don't you
think it's better not to blow this out of proportion and give the media
a field day?"

"The damned media. But bear in mind that you may need the
embassy's help. And don't answer your cell phone if you don't know
who it is; no reason to talk to the media. Got to go, busy here at the
office; goodbye Katta."

"Good point, thanks Petter. Goodbye."

Only a short exchange of words with her ex-husband, and she
was exhausted. It was often like that with Petter. He tired her out; he

was consistently busy and often angry—mad at her, mad at the world. Granted, it wasn't his fault that she was on national television. And he had called the Norwegian embassy in Rome; that was sweet of him.

Katarina tried to enjoy the delicious lunch in front of her: fried baby calamari, a freshly caught grilled fish, and a salad of sliced artichokes—all perfect with the half bottle of chilled white wine. As she pecked at the food on her plate, she kept an eye on the taxi drivers. Only a couple of the other street-side tables were occupied; most of the patrons were dining on the scenic upper terrace.

An hour after lunch, she ordered a café Americano. Then she called Chief of Police Inspector Monti and received her verbal permission to leave the island for a reading of her sister's will at the lawyer's office in Naples the next day. Had Max gotten police permission to leave the island and go with her? she wondered. Two more hours passed; by now, the sun had disappeared behind Monte Solaro and the beachgoers were lined up for buses and taxis to return to town.

Twilight descended on the tiny square. Few people stood in line for the bus at this hour, mostly workers from the closed beach establishments. Only an occasional taxi dropped off a fare. A couple of giant seagulls paraded up and down the quiet road. The sea and the sky had merged on the horizon into an intense opaque blue and the Faraglioni rocks cast dark shadows on the sea. Monte Solaro's towering presence loomed overhead.

Katarina had all but given up on finding Amedeo's taxi that day, and she went inside the restaurant to pay her bill.

"By the way, I find the taxis amazing here—so stylish, with such luxurious interiors," she mused to Gregorio, who was about to close the cash register and go home. "How many taxis are there on Capri? You seem to know all of the drivers."

"You are right, they all pass by here eventually. I don't know how many taxis there are on Capri, but I could find out. Do you want to know the number of taxis on Capri or the number on Anacapri or both?"

Katarina was taken aback when she realized her mistake. "I had no idea there were two groups of taxis. Does that mean there is a different taxi stand for the Anacapri taxis?"

"That's right. Generally, the Anacapri taxis wait at Piazza Vittoria for a fare, and the Capri taxis wait at the stand on Piazzetta Martiri d'Ungheria at the end of Via Roma. They all have routes to Marina Piccola, of course, but the taxis from Anacapri come here less often."

"I see, thank you." She silently scolded herself: What an idiot I am!

Katarina splurged on a cab; she had no time to waste. It was possible that she would still find Amedeo in Piazza Vittoria. Sitting in the back of the stretched open-top taxi, while speeding up the hairpin turns all the way from Marina Piccola to Anacapri was exhilarating; it reminded her of the night with Amedeo.

The ice cream wasn't bad, but she hardly touched it while waiting at the table at Bar Due Pini in Piazza Vittoria, only a few meters from the Anacapri taxi stand. Several white taxis were waiting; none had lavender seats.

Katarina called her mother-in-law in Norway and gave her an overly positive review of her situation, trying to discredit the report by the national media. Then she spoke with Anna; her daughter's worried voice was unbearable to hear, and she had to force herself to sound cheerful.

An hour passed before Katarina gave up all hope of finding Amedeo; she paid her tab and got in line for the bus. The road between Capri and Anacapri was busy; apart from the constant stream of cars, the preferred method of transportation seemed to be scooters and mopeds.

Suddenly she saw Max; she was sure it was him, even though he was wearing a helmet. It was the second time she had spotted Max that day. He was on the back of a silver scooter with his arms around a girl. The girl wore a red helmet; her long black hair was flying in the wind as they drove past. Where are they going? she wondered. Who is that girl?

A sharp pang of jealousy stabbed her heart.

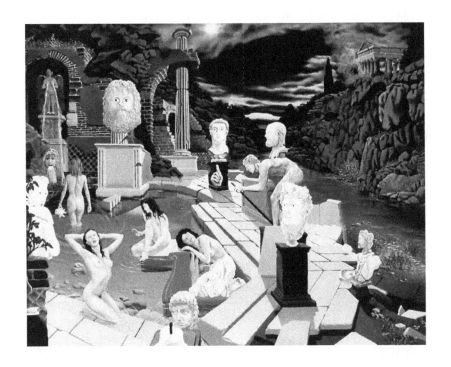

CHAPTER 24 - A TEMPTRESS AND A VIXEN

FRIDAY, AUGUST 27

Max had no desire to open his eyes and get out of bed. He was savoring the memory of Graziella's body rocked by the waves as she slid onto the beach; and even more enticing, the silver-eyed beauty's sun-bronzed body dripping with water. The erotic evening at Faro with the irresistible siren had made him feel alive again. That was two days ago.

Then he remembered what happened the day before. Horrified, he sat straight up in bed with wide-open eyes, recalling his experience at the Baths of Nero while in Naples with Katarina. He could have died in that steaming inferno! Katarina, who had seemed so sweet and harmless, now seemed dangerous. Had she bewitched him with her beauty? Was she the murderer of her sister?

Max crossed the Funicular Square to find Raffi sitting at his usual table in the shade on the terrace above the funicular rail. The morning was hot and humid, promising a muggy day. Naples and the mainland had disappeared into a white-hot haze.

"Ah, the prodigal son of Capri. You must have solved the mystery by now. Why else would you have gone AWOL for two whole days? Unless, of course, you were romantically detained; in that case, don't expect instant forgiveness." Raffi's rebuke couldn't mask his delight at seeing Max.

"Hey, Raffi," Max said, without acknowledging his sarcastic remark. "Actually, I met a girl on the beach Wednesday morning—" he was interrupted by a waiter, who took his order.

"*Veramente* (Really)!"

Max took his time before continuing the story. He looked out over the bay of Naples; the sea was calm, crisscrossed by white streaks from the wakes of boats and ferries arriving and departing. The waiter brought Max his order, and he emptied four packets of cane sugar into his double espresso, stirred it, dunked the *cornetto* in the coffee, took a sip, then nibbled on the cornetto—a drawn-out ritual that Max seemed to relish. Raffi's impatience mounted, but Max pretended not to notice. The taste of the bittersweet espresso and the flaky buttery pastry melting on his tongue calmed his anxious mind.

"Well, are you going to tell me about this girl or not?" Raffi's patience had run out.

Max didn't know what to say. How could he explain the complex emotions he had experienced since he last saw Raffi, just two days ago? The euphoric evening with Graziella had made him feel like a roaring lion in tune with nature, with the entire world. His depression had loosened its grip; it was the best he had felt since the divorce.

Max had not been celibate after the divorce. But every time he had a casual sexual encounter, usually while traveling for work, he felt even worse about himself, and lonelier than before. The women he slept with always seemed to want something from him that he couldn't give them. Sex wasn't enough. Neither had it been for him. Without passion, lovemaking was reduced to a physical act. His casual encounters had become rarer and rarer until, a year or so ago, he decided to stop looking for them altogether. So, what was different with Graziella? Max didn't know how to put it into words. Was it different because she didn't need anything from him, or because she was a local girl? Or was it that he was finally getting over Tara?

Raffi waited for Max to say something. What the hell had happened to Max? he wondered.

"We had a magical night together," Max said at last. "She's a beautiful girl, rather unusual, Anacaprese. It felt—like when I was young and carefree."

"So, will you meet this unusual girl again?" Raffi was curious as to who the girl was, but he knew better than to ask her name. Gentlemen didn't share the names of casual girlfriends.

"No, I don't think so, nothing planned for now." Max seemed lost in thought.

Raffi wondered if Max had fallen for the Anacaprese girl. "And what about the lovely Katarina? You still haven't introduced her to me, you know. Weren't you supposed to go with her to Naples yesterday for a reading of her sister's will? How did that go?"

When Max paused again before answering, Raffi was beginning to wonder if Max was getting himself involved—with two women.

"Yes, you're right, I did go to Naples with Katarina yesterday. When we got to the lawyer's office in the morning, we found out her lawyer was detained and couldn't see us until the afternoon. Since we had some time to waste, Katarina suggested we visit the Baths of Nero." Max spoke slowly, and he seemed distant. "Do you know about this natural sauna from Roman times? It's inside a cave with ancient stone walls—"

"Yes, I've been there. What the hell were you doing in the Baths of Nero taking a sauna in August!" Raffi cried out.

Max didn't heed Raffi's comment, but continued telling the story in a faraway voice.

"I was in the sauna . . . it was very humid . . . like being in a steam room. I could hardly see Katarina because of the vaporized mineral salts in the air. The temperature in the baths is usually around 53 degrees Celsius.[11] But the temperature of the thermal waters heating the natural stoves fluctuates—sometimes it gets extremely hot. I can tell you it was hot in there—no doubt the hottest sauna I've ever been to—"

Raffi worried about Max's state of mind; it was as if he was still inside the steamy hot sauna in the depths of the cave.

"—and, as you probably know," Max continued, "the emissions of steam come from live volcanic activity in the region. Well, it was so filled with steam in there I couldn't see anything, and the stone floor was slippery. And then—I don't know how it happened, but I must have slipped and fallen. The guy that found me said I passed out, I don't know for how long."

"You passed out!" Raffi cried.

People stared at them from the nearby café tables.

Max lowered his voice. "A man dragged me out of the sauna, a stranger who said he stumbled over me while I was lying unconscious on the floor. He may have saved my life. This stranger told me that for a few scary minutes he was not sure I was breathing; he was prepared to give me CPR, but then my chest started to rise. When I regained consciousness, I had no idea where I was; it scared me." Max shuddered, touching his *curniciello*. "I must have hit my head on the stone floor and blacked out. I still have a large bump on the back of my head. Somebody at the baths brought me a pack of ice to put on it."

Raffi was visibly shaken. "And where was Katarina?"

"Well, she said the sauna had been too hot for her—so she went back outside—earlier—without telling me—she said she was shocked when she saw the man dragging me out."

Raffi was flabbergasted; he didn't know what to say. The whole situation seemed strange. He couldn't understand how a woman could even think of relaxing in a sauna when she'd just lost her sister—and in the hot month of August, of all times. And it seemed peculiar that she would leave Max in the sauna without saying anything.

---

[11] 127.4 Fahrenheit

Raffi was worried about his best friend's state of mind; he thought that the incident had traumatized Max, and he felt it wise not to leave him alone. Perhaps Max felt that way himself, because he was easily persuaded to go with Raffi to visit his cousin Assunta, who lived up on the Torina hill.

How involved was Max with Katarina? Raffi wondered, as they left Bar Funicolare. Why hasn't he introduced me to this mysterious Norwegian woman by now? What kind of person is she? Is she a vixen? And who is this temptress Max just met? Looks like my old friend Max is getting himself into some deep water.

CHAPTER 25 - THE BREAK-IN

T he residential maze of Torina situated above the saddle of
Due Golfi was only accessible by footpaths. From Via
Torina, it was all uphill. Max and Raffi walked past the old

whitewashed houses spread across the green slopes below Monte Solaro. It was unbearably hot, and the mountain peak high above them was shrouded in a white cloud of humidity.

"How's the case coming along?" Raffi asked, feeling the need to think about something other than Max lying unconscious on the stone floor of a hot sauna.

"It's up to the police, you know, but I haven't seen any evidence indicating that it's not suicide. On the contrary, everything points to that conclusion—which, of course, is good for me."

"Do you ever feel conflicted, Max? I mean, what if you found some evidence the police don't have, and it's to your advantage not to give it to them, would you keep silent?"

"It is up to the police to do their job; I have no obligation to tell them anything, unless—" Max sighed, "unless it's in my interest to do so."

"Hmm, then I imagine it could be a tricky situation, morally speaking, at times," Raffi said.

At the top of a narrow footpath, an old two-story house came into view. Assunta's house had an exterior staircase; it was originally an old farm house where the domestic animals were sheltered on the first floor. It was the highest house on the slopes of Torina; the rock wall of Monte Solaro shot straight up behind it.

When they got to the house, Raffi and Max were drenched in sweat after the long uphill climb. Raffi's cousin Assunta gave them a hearty welcome; she and Max hadn't seen each other in years. She was a short, black-haired woman with an ample waistline. Despite years out in the sun, her dark skin was surprisingly supple, as soft and unwrinkled as a child's, Max noted.

While she prepared their lunch, Max and Raffi went up to the roof terrace to use the outdoor shower. They stripped off their clothes and stepped under the ice-cold spray of water. While showering, they enjoyed the spectacular eagle's-eye view of the rocky southern coastline of Capri and the iconic Faraglioni rock formations.

The three of them sat down at a table on the patio; Max and Raffi were bare-chested, as Assunta had insisted she hang up their sweaty shirts to dry on the clothes line. Far below, the town of Capri stretched out, misty and dreamlike in the afternoon heat. The plate of pasta she had prepared for their lunch, with local beans, *"chichierchia,"* as they called it, was superb; so was the local wine and the homemade fig tart she had prepared for dessert.

Max reclined in a lounge chair after lunch, while Raffi chatted with Assunta in the kitchen. Looking over at the Castiglione hill rising above Due Golfi, he could make out the blue and white sun umbrella on the roof of Villa Ciano. He wondered if Katarina was there. After his frightening experience at the baths in Naples, he was worried that he had been wrong about her—perhaps she was capable of murder after all.

His cell phone rang; it was Katarina.

"I'm at the Villa, Max. Camilla's home has been ransacked! Everything is a mess; you wouldn't believe how bad it is. The police are on the way now. Please, could you come over?" Katarina's voice sounded weak and desperate.

Max and Raffi took Via Castiglione from Via Roma up to Villa Ciano. Halfway up the road, they met a blue Alpha Romeo 159 police car heading downhill; it stopped in the middle of the narrow road. Two police officers in uniform stepped out; one of them was Captain Michele Arcuzzi, Deputy Chief of Police.

"Good afternoon, De Angelis. Kallberg called you?"

Max nodded. "Good afternoon, Captain. Muggy day, isn't it? Yes, Kallberg called me, anything you can tell me?"

"*Bah*. Very strange case. It appears someone was searching for something. No forced entry. Signora Kallberg thinks the hidden spare key was likely used. Nothing seems to be missing, as far as Kallberg can tell."

"Fingerprints?"

"We took some; likely a waste of time. Whoever used the spare key would have taken the trouble to wipe it clean before replacing it."

"When did it happen?"

"*Bah*. Kallberg says she left the villa around ten. The housekeeper discovered the mess when she came to work at one-fifteen; she called

Kallberg, who was at the beach; she called us as soon as she got home."

"The custodian Zi' Bacco?"

"We spoke to him. He came to work at noon; said he didn't see anybody."

"How is the Camilla Kallberg case going otherwise, Captain Arcuzzi, any clues?"

"*Bah.* So far, Katarina Kallberg seems to be the only suspect with motive and opportunity. Can't rule out the possibility that she faked the break-in to divert suspicion away from her. She certainly could have done it before leaving the house. Her story about returning from the party at Gradola by bus on the night her sister died doesn't pan out. The bus from Grotta Azzurra to Anacapri runs hourly from a quarter to five in the morning to a quarter to eleven at night. Only one driver worked the route on the night of Ferragosto. When I showed him a picture of Katarina Kallberg, he insisted she was not on his bus that night. We asked the staff at Gradola. Nobody remembers seeing her there either. Bah. The question is, why is she lying? We're looking for the taxi driver who took her to the party. Maybe we'll find out something from him. Good afternoon." Captain Arcuzzi saluted them and returned to his car.

"The officer seems like a decent chap," Raffi said, as the police car drove out of sight.

"Hard to tell, but yes, he does seem less nervous when he is not in the presence of his boss, Chief Inspector Monti." Max frowned, remembering the unpleasant time in her office.

"It's strange that Katarina would lie about going to Gradola," Raffi said, as Max pushed open the unlocked gate to Villa Ciano. "But in any case, she doesn't have an alibi for the rest of the night. And the other thing, if she had wanted to kill her sister, why didn't she just push her over a cliff during the daytime and make it look like an accident? I mean, wouldn't that have been easier than staging a suicide?"

"Yes, I asked myself the same question. Maybe she thought suicide would cast less suspicion on her. And then when she found out about the suicide clause in Camilla's life insurance, she deliberately tried to confuse the police and me as well. She may be hoping to get a 'cause of death unknown' verdict. That way she would still collect the insurance money. Ah, here is the custodian."

Zi' Bacco appeared at the door of the utility room, an unlit cigarette dangling from the side of his mouth.

"The police were just here—again." Zi' Bacco lit his cigarette. "They asked me all sorts of stupid questions. Nasty, this break-in, isn't it? And here on Capri. What's the world coming to, you tell me? And it had to happen—of course—on the one day when I was late to work. I had to take my mother to the hospital this morning because she wasn't feeling well."

"So, obviously, you couldn't have seen anything. Did you work on the night of Ferragosto by the way?" Max asked.

"That's what those stupid police officers asked me. Yes, I worked that night; I work every night till two in the morning at Il Riccio— you know, the restaurant at Grotta Azzurra."

"And your mother, she is all right?"

"Thanks for asking about her. I'm leaving now for Capilupi Hospital to see how she is doing."

"Signora Katarina Kallberg called me an hour ago. Is she still here?"

"Yes, she is here. That poor girl, she is having a tough time since her sister passed away. You boys go and cheer her up, will you? If I were a couple of years younger myself. . ."

The moment Raffi met Katarina, he understood Max's dilemma. He was struck by her considerable charm and beauty. But that wasn't what most impressed him; there was something else about her, a certain lightness mixed with strength of character. Despite the difficult circumstances, she had a sparkle in her eyes. Now the reason Max hadn't introduced Katarina to him earlier was clear; the rascal wanted her all to himself.

If she was the one who killed her sister, she was an excellent actress. Nothing about Katarina seemed fake, Raffi thought, as they exchanged pleasantries. Could there be a reasonable explanation for what had happened to Max in Naples?

As they went from room to room surveying the scene, Max's brain registered every detail. The break-in wasn't as bad as he had feared; whoever had done this had been surprisingly considerate. Granted the house was a mess, with bedding, clothes, shoes, and all manner of things thrown about, but nothing was damaged. Dozens of books were scattered everywhere; Max examined the title page and the first page of every book.

"Who knew where the spare key was hidden?" Max said to Katarina as the three of them sat down on the blue sofas in the living room.

"I guess pretty much everybody—everybody who needed to know; certainly, the housekeeper Lina and the custodian Zi' Bacco, her gardener Misha, and I think the plumber and a handyman as well."

"When I was here the first time, I remember seeing a paperback on the nightstand in Camilla's room," Max said. "It was Virgil's *Aeneid*, the Italian edition. The book isn't there now, and I didn't see it anywhere else in the house. Have you seen it?"

Katarina shook her head. "No, I haven't, and it's odd that it's missing—because, as you may recall, this book had great meaning to Camilla."

"Yes, you mentioned at the funeral service that your sister had a dream about her namesake; the Amazon warrior princess from the *Aeneid*. It's too bad that I didn't look inside the book when I saw it," Max said. "Maybe it had an inscription, the name of someone."

"Of course, you're right! This book might give us a clue if we can find it!"

"Nothing else is missing—you're sure about that?" Max sounded skeptical.

Katarina shook her head. Excusing herself, she went into the kitchen, and returned carrying a tray with a bottle of mineral water and three glasses.

"There is something else that just occurred to me," she said, pouring water into their glasses. "I remember Camilla telling me that she had gone to the island of Procida for a couple of lovely visits this past year. I wonder if she might have met Emilio on Procida. I was reminded of this yesterday when we went for the reading of Camilla's will at his office in Naples. Is it possible that Camilla was involved romantically with her lawyer? Do you remember Emilio saying that he keeps his motor boat moored on Procida?"

"I remember something like that, but for now, it's only speculation," Max said. "Let's examine what we do know, shall we?"

Katarina and Raffi nodded.

Max consulted the notes on his cell phone and read them aloud:

"We have six suspects to date with opportunity: Max, Katarina, Nicola, Sergio, Emilio, and Lorenzo. Of those six suspects, there is only one suspect so far with a clear motive; that is you Katarina."

Max looked up from his cell phone; Katarina's angry eyes met his. Embarrassed, he looked down at the screen.

"Three items are missing: a diamond necklace, a purple purse, and a book—Virgil's *Aeneid*. Are we in agreement?"

Katarina and Raffi nodded.

Max continued, "I've made a list of questions; here they are:

o   If Camilla wrote a suicide note, where is it?
o   Why did Camilla write her will and plan her funeral a few weeks before she died?
o   Who were Camilla's most recent lovers?
o   Who was Camilla talking to on Via Dentecala outside the restaurant?"

"I'll add these new questions to my list," Max said, typing on his cell phone keypad as he spoke aloud.

o   Camilla's trips to Procida: With whom? When? Why?
o   Break-in at villa: Who did it? What was the intruder searching for? Was it found? Check alibis for time of break-in."

Max looked up at Raffi and Katarina.

"I, Max, hereby state that I have an alibi for the time of the break-in at Camilla's home. I was with Raffi," Max added, making them both laugh.

"Well, I have an alibi for the break-in as well," Katarina said. "I was at Da Luigi, though as the police pointed out, I could have faked the break-in myself before I left the house. Sergio the waiter was at the beach, so I assume he has an alibi. However, I didn't see Nicola at Da Luigi today."

Max put his cell phone away and emptied his water glass before looking at Katarina. "I've two more questions. The first question is, where is the iPod?"

Katarina's face went blank. "What are you talking about?"

"I'm referring to the portable speaker in Camilla's bedroom; it has an iPod slot, but I haven't seen an iPod. I noticed there was no iPod when I was here the first time. Do you know where it is?"

Katarina shook her head. "No, I don't know where it is, but I do remember seeing it. Camilla brought the iPod and the portable speaker to the roof to listen to music the night before she disappeared. Do you think it has any importance?"

"I've no idea, but now that you tell me you saw the iPod before Camilla's disappearance, I wonder if that was the item the intruder was searching for. I'll add the iPod to the list of missing items."

Max continued, "The intruder could have been looking for any of the missing items, and we don't know if they were found. Are we in agreement?"

Raffi and Katarina nodded.

"What was the second question?" Katarina asked.

The look of embarrassment on Max's face surprised both Raffi and Katarina. They waited for his answer.

"Mm, I don't remember," he mumbled as he swore silently at himself. Do you want to sound like an imbecile, Max? He realized it would be too personal and even embarrassing to ask Katarina why the old battered Greek style fisherman's cap he had seen during his first visit to the villa was no longer hanging over a silk gown in her bedroom. Max had in vain looked everywhere in the house for it during his search for missing items after the break-in.

Raffi glanced sideways at Max's closed face as they headed down the footpath of Via Castello towards the Piazzetta. He was curious as to why Max had backed off from asking his last question. Was Max trying to protect Katarina? He could understand how Max might have fallen for the Nordic beauty, and he'd obviously regained his passion for women since the divorce. Raffi had once envied Max for his loving relationship with his wife Tara. That all changed after the incident three years ago when he, Max, and Tara were on Capri. Max had never spoken to Raffi about the consequences of what had happened that night or the reason for the divorce that followed not long after.

The Piazzetta was a happening place on Friday evening; the atmosphere was charged with excitement on the last weekend in August, the end of the summer holiday for Italians. Max and Raffi grabbed the first table that became free at Gran Caffè. As soon as they sat down, Max's cell phone buzzed.

"What's up, Maxi boy?" Max cringed at the roaring voice of his boss.

"It is precisely a week today since I last called you. We are concerned about your daily e-mail reports; it seems you are at a standstill."

"Well Bob, no verdict has come from the police yet."

"But it does look like suicide, right?"

Max turned down the volume on his phone. "I'm working as hard as I can to get all the relevant facts. So far there is no indication that Kallberg was murdered or that it was an accident. Everything is under control, Bob."

"That's good to hear, good to hear. Hopefully, the case will get wrapped up in a few days and we will see you back in the office by next week. What's that noise, Max, are you in a club again?" Bob hung up before Max could answer.

Max avoided looking at Raffi's questioning face as he put his cell phone back into the zippered pocket of his jeans.

"Good evening, guys," Mario the waiter said as he approached their table. "How's the case going? Did you find out anything about the mysterious death of Camilla? It wasn't suicide, was it?"

"All I can tell you, Mario, is I just don't know." Max shook his head; he suddenly felt drained. At one moment, he thought the evidence weighed on the side of suicide; the next moment, he had his doubts.

After Mario had brought them glasses of single malt Scotch, water, and a plate of green olives, Raffi couldn't restrain his anger any longer. "Everything is under control, Max?" he said sarcastically.

Max didn't answer; he took a sip of Scotch and nibbled on an olive while surveying the frenetic activity in the Piazzetta.

"Apart from almost dying in a sauna, everything is OK, is it? And what about the missing items, and the list of suspects—is that all just for show so you can get close to Katarina? Is that it?" Raffi was fuming with anger and disgusted with Max.

Max looked at Raffi with pained eyes. "What do you want me to do? It's my job. Do you seriously expect me to tell my boss that I don't think it is suicide based on some missing items—a bloody purse and a book by Virgil? Oh yeah, and a dream about an Amazon warrior princess? Are you kidding me? Besides, I'm not paid to have doubts if matters are going our way; that's the job of the police. If they produce a verdict other than suicide, I'll express my doubts, not beforehand."

Raffi was furious; he opened his mouth to say something. Instead, he took a sip of his barely touched Scotch, left some money on the table, and got up. "Goodnight, Max. I'm tired, see you around," he said.

CHAPTER 26 - PEGASUS

Katarina was unable to fall asleep; she tossed and turned in bed while the thoughts in her brain went around and around in circles. It was inconceivable to her that Camilla would kill herself, and if it was not an accident, then who was the murderer? She could not rule out Max, in view of his peculiar behavior—first blowing hot, then cold.

Katarina reached for her cell phone and opened the notepad screen; she had decided to make her own detective list.

Times with Max over the past six days:

> *Saturday: Day of Camilla's funeral: saw Max for the first time.*
> *Sunday morning: Tea on the roof.*
> *Monday evening: Romantic dinner.*
> *Tuesday: We kissed.*
> *Wednesday: I didn't meet Max; saw him twice, riding on bus and with a girl on scooter.*
> *Thursday: Max went with me to Naples—*

Katarina stopped typing—a light went off. That's when things had really changed. Since their visit to the Baths of Nero, Max had treated her as if she were a leper—or worse, as if he believed she was the murderer of her sister. Today, he had shown her no warmth or kindness, despite the ransacking of Camilla's home, officially "her home" now, according to Camilla's testament. In fact, he had pointed out she was the only suspect with both opportunity and motive.

The attraction between them was mutual, she was sure of it; but for some reason Max had withdrawn his affection. She felt hurt and rejected.

Then there was the problem of Amedeo, the taxi driver—the only one who could give her an alibi for the night of her sister's death. Her attempt at finding him had been a failure, an entire day wasted. Whatever had possessed her to spend the night with Amedeo, a total stranger, a married man, no less? It was useless trying to sleep; she slipped on a gown and went up to the roof terrace.

The fresh night air felt soothing on her hot skin. The starry midnight sky was clear and bright, but the moon was not visible. This must be the first night of the new lunar cycle, she said to herself, remembering that she had arrived on Capri two weeks ago, on the night of the full moon, Friday the 13th.

She reclined the chaise and leaned back to look up at the trillions of stars. Ah—how glorious! Close to the planet Jupiter, directly overhead, she recognized Pegasus, the constellation of stars named after the winged white stallion who flew to heaven to become Jupiter's thunderbolt-bearer.

To be as free and wild as Pegasus, that was what Katarina wished for now. Yet the thought that her night of freedom with Amedeo might cost him the breakup of his marriage, a marriage with two small children, horrified her. She knew better than anyone the viciousness of divorce. How could she have been so thoughtless? By thinking only of her selfish needs, she risked the ruin of a family. What if anyone found out— Max, for instance, or her daughter? She would be mortified.

Katarina felt that even if she managed to find Amedeo and explain that her sister had died the night she was with him, she couldn't use him as an alibi. If he told the police the truth that they had been together, he would risk ruining his marriage. If he denied being with her, she would lose her alibi.

Katarina tried to persuade herself that she didn't care whether Amedeo provided her with an alibi. But what if she was charged with murdering her sister? In that case, she might need one. She reasoned that if Amedeo first lied to the police to protect his marriage and then had to testify in court, his testimony wouldn't be believed. That could be a problem for her. She was ashamed of herself for considering her needs above Amedeo's.

Tracing the constellation of the winged Pegasus with her eyes, she suddenly knew what she had to do. If she wanted to be free, she had to be brave—like Pegasus.

There was no other solution; she would go to Chief Inspector Monti and tell her the truth. She would beg Monti to use her discretion when talking to Amedeo. Katarina hoped that since the inspector was a woman, she would understand her predicament.

Gazing at immortal Pegasus, she whispered a prayer: "Dear, dear Pegasus, please help me. I forgot what it means to live a life in freedom. I will no longer do things that cause me or anyone else to lie. I promise. But please, please protect Amedeo—and his family—and me."

CHAPTER 27 - JUPITER

SATURDAY, AUGUST 28

Max woke up with a start; he was lying on top of the bed linens drenched in sweat. Now wide awake, he looked at the clock; it was just past five in the morning. He shut his eyes, hoping to get a couple more hours of sleep, but he began thinking about the bad dream that had awoken him.

Tara is in the dream; she is naked, lying in bed on her tummy. Next to Tara there is a man—the world-renowned Ashtanga yoga instructor who stole Tara away from him . . .

Why did he keep torturing himself with the image of Tara and her lover? If he wasn't dreaming about it, he obsessed over it. Max knew it was useless to think about sleeping; he got up and pulled on his cargo shorts, a t-shirt, and sneakers. Five minutes later, he was striding uphill on Via Croce.

It was quiet in the fresh predawn hour; the stars were fading, and a trace of pink light showed in the eastern sky. Max passed by the minuscule San Michele, the oldest church on Capri. Then he crossed Via Cesina and continued up Via Tiberio, walking past gated villas and dark gardens. Since he had already come this far, he decided to go all the way up to Villa Jovis, the palace where Roman Emperor Tiberius had spent the last decade of his life.

Max didn't see much as he walked along; he was unable to shake off the dream about Tara and her lover. Why would Tara leave him for another man? He had asked himself that question a million times. He had loved his wife more than he had ever imagined it possible for a man to love a woman. She had been so much more than his wife and his lover; she was his soul mate, and his best friend.

Turning right on Via Moneta, he rejoined Via Tiberio higher up. Soon he came upon Villa Falconetta and the adjoining public park, Parco-Astarita, that Mario Astarita, a banker from Sorrento, had donated to the island. He didn't enter the park, but from the path he could see at least a dozen roaming goats. The wild goats seemed surprised to see anyone at such an early hour; they looked him over while chewing their cud. Each goat had different coloring, a mixture of brown, beige, and black.

How he missed his wonderful friend Signora Astarita, a niece of Mario Astarita, who had chosen to stay in her remote Villa Falconetta until the end of her days. Her life force had been incredibly strong. He wondered if the Peregrine falcons still built their nest on the steep cliff below the villa.

Max continued uphill until he walked up the last stretch of the road to the ruins of the magnificent Villa Jovis, the palace dedicated to Jupiter. The gate to the palace ruins was locked. Max looked around; there wasn't a single soul in sight, and in less than a minute, he had climbed over the two-meter [12]high gate. From there, he climbed several dozen stone stairs to reach the highest point.

There, above the ruins of the palace named for the supreme God of the Roman pantheon, stood the little chapel of Santa Maria del Soccorso, once a hermitage. Max wondered if this was the place where Roman Emperor Tiberius had stood when he received confirmation of the Roman crucifixion of Jesus Christ, the Jew from Nazareth. In front of the chapel was a bronze statue of the Madonna and Child; it was a copy of the original, destroyed by lightning. In Roman times, all places struck by lightning were the property of Jupiter. Maybe Jupiter was sending a message with his thunderbolt that this place didn't belong to any other god, Max mused.

When he walked around the chapel, he was met by a dazzling spectacle. A gigantic fire ball appeared over the shore of Salerno; the sun rose in all its splendor, casting a glorious light over the immense natural theater unfolding before Max's eyes. The distant mountain ranges, the islands, and the curving shore of the Amalfi Coast were bathed in the rose-colored light of dawn. Max looked in awe at the magnificent panoramic views. How strange, he thought, to be standing on the same spot where the reclusive emperor Tiberius once stood over two thousand years ago, seeing the same miracle of nature, the sacred ritual of the sun rising in its glory.

The present holds the past, Max thought, recalling that Jupiter was still honored once a week: *Giovedì* or Thursday is named after the mighty God—also known as Jove, Iovis, Zeus, Thor, Thunor, Thunrax, Guru, and Brihaspathi.

Max walked over to the edge of the precipice called *Salto Di Tiberio* (Tiberius Leap) and looked 330 meters [13] straight down to the incredibly clear sea. Instantly he felt dizzy; the transparent emerald and blue water beckoned him, and he took a step back. He thought

---

[12] 6.56 feet
[13] 1083 feet

about the fate of Camilla. Did she throw herself from the cliff at Belvedere delle Noci? What was it the Romans said, *Quid est Veritas?* (What was the truth?)

Max skipped back down the two-thousand-year-old cobblestone stairs and climbed over the gate. As he wandered down the solitary footpath towards town, Tara returned to his thoughts. Strangely, he no longer felt angry with Tara for leaving him. But could he ever forgive her? He asked himself what it was that Tara had done that needed forgiveness, but for the first time in three years, doubt entered his mind. What if it's not Tara that needs to be forgiven, what if it's me? he speculated. Was I the one who screwed things up? The idea alarmed him; it was too dreadful to consider, and he pushed the thought from his mind.

CHAPTER 28 - THE PROFESSOR

SATURDAY, AUGUST 28

M ax walked at a quick pace down the hill from Villa Jovis back towards the town of Capri. It was time to stop brooding about the past, he decided. The present is what matters. His empty stomach rumbled; he needed to get some breakfast before heading to the Police Station to talk to Chief Inspector Monti.

Last night, after Raffi had stormed out of the Piazzetta in a rage, Max had shared a bottle of wine with his friend Antonio, a hotelier at Hotel Gatto Bianco. He learned that the mayor was putting pressure on the chief inspector of police to wrap up the investigation.

"The mayor has lost his patience with the police," Antonio said. "It isn't good for the image of Capri as a tourist haven that the death of a foreigner remains a mystery; that leaves open the possibility that a murderer is loose on the island."

Antonio said that the mayor had suggested he ask Max, who had the advantage of not working and living on the island, to meet with Chief Inspector Monti; he wanted Max to hint at the incompetence of the local police to help bring the investigation to an end, and officially declare Camilla's death a suicide.

Max doubted he had any credibility with the police, but he agreed to see what he could do. Antonio was persuasive. By the time he and Antonio had finished the bottle of wine, Max felt fortunate that he was in a unique position to help his island keep a positive image for tourism.

Walking down Via Tiberio, Max had an uneasy feeling in his stomach, and he knew it was more than hunger. If the police declared Camilla's death a suicide, everybody would be happy. Well, everybody except Katarina; she wouldn't get the two million dollars, but she would no longer be suspected of murder and inherit the villa. Max could return to San Francisco with the expectation that a promotion and a hefty hike in his salary might finally materialize.

Strangely, these thoughts didn't make him feel happy or relieved. The idea of leaving the island made him feel sad.

Max stopped in the middle of the road, suddenly realizing that he didn't know what to say to the police. He knew what the mayor and his boss wanted, but how could he argue a case for suicide? What about Katarina's insistence that Camilla didn't kill herself? And the arguments pointing to suicide just weren't convincing. He didn't know what to do. He sighed deeply.

A familiar voice interrupted his troubling speculations. "I can't believe my eyes, Massimiliano De Angelis!" A tall, gray-haired man with a dog on a leash stood in front of Max with a big grin on his face.

Max's eyes lit up when he saw his retired mathematics professor. They were soon engrossed in memories of the days at the Liceo scientifico.[14] Max had been the best student in class and was a favorite of the professor. Il Professore, as everybody called him, invited Max up to his villa for a cup of coffee.

"This is Jacques, my closest and dearest companion these days," Il Professore said, looking admiringly at his dog as they walked east on Via Lo Capo.

"Ah, he's a beauty. Beauty and brains; you two are a perfect match," Max joked. The black and white cocker spaniel let Max caress his long ears.

Max talked about his job in the States and the specifics of the case he was working on while the professor prepared *la caffiera*, the old-fashioned stove-top espresso maker.

"You see," Max explained, "in the interests of my company UGI and its shareholders, I'm collecting as much background information as I can about the deceased policyholder. If the insurance claim is denied, and then disputed by the beneficiaries, it may be necessary to do a psychological autopsy, also called an EDA, an equivocal death analysis. It is far more common to do a psychological autopsy when the manner of death is undetermined, which could happen in this case. Of course, my company is hoping the police will declare it to be suicide."

Il Professore handed Max a cup of sweetened espresso. They carried their cups into the living room. The elegant room was a showcase for the professor's small, but eclectic collection of paintings by artists who had resided on Capri.

---

[14] Students typically study for five years, and attend the school from the age of 14 to 19. At the end of the fifth year all students sit for the *esame di Stato*, a final examination which leads to the *maturità scientifica*.

Max lingered in front of a large painting of the island of Capri; the subtle colors of the landscape were wonderfully portrayed by the artist, as if the island was suspended in the sea. Max guessed that it had been painted in the early morning light from Punta Campanella on the Sorrentine Peninsula, 4.2 kilometers[15] from Capri. In the bottom right corner of the pale shimmering sea, he read: "J. Talmage White, Capri 1881."

The professor chuckled when he saw the surprised look on Max's face. "Yes, it is indeed a painting by James Talmage White," he said. "Did you know that White was the first artist to open a studio on Capri—1861, I believe. White came into possession of Villa Mura, Cà del Sole, and Villa Alba. Those grand villas became a reference point for Italian and foreign artists and intellectuals for many years. He also co-founded the non-Catholic cemetery with other foreigners living on the island."

The professor cleared some newspapers off the floral chintz sofa, and they sat down. Jacques jumped into an armchair covered in faded burgundy velvet. "You were talking about the kind of information needed for a psychological autopsy," Il Professore reminded Max. "What kind of background information are you looking for?"

"Well, as I said, when the manner of death is undetermined, a psychological autopsy is sometimes requested; typically, it includes an extensive impartial investigation. The decedent's life, right up until the time of their death, is put under a microscope."

Max took a sip of his espresso. "It's rather complicated, and I'm not qualified to give a final opinion. I am only authorized to find as much preliminary information as possible as early as possible after the death."

"This seems like a suitable job for you, Max, with your keen insight and statistical research skills. Tell me, what do you think so far, was it a suicide?" Il Professore asked.

Max hesitated before answering. "Between you and me, the case of Camilla Kallberg is not an easy one."

"I knew Camilla. I am a habitué of Da Luigi as was she. I saw her on the night of Ferragosto when I took Jacques for a walk after

---

[15] 3 miles

having dinner at my sister's house; it was around eleven o'clock, I think."

"You did? Where?" Max was astounded.

"We—that is, Jacques and I, were returning from Piazzetta delle Noci when Camilla Kallberg came towards us. It was on Via Dentecala, near the entrance to Da Tonino; I assumed she was meeting friends in the restaurant. I bowed to her, and she smiled and nodded."

"Who was with her?" Max was thrilled. Would he learn the identity of the mystery person that Camilla, according to Domenico, was talking to on the street that night?

"What do you mean? Nobody was with her; she was alone."

Max raised his eyebrows in disbelief. "Are you sure?"

"Absolutely."

CHAPTER 29 - A FISHERMAN'S CAP

SATURDAY, AUGUST 28

s soon as Katarina had finished watering the plants on the terrace, she ate a small breakfast in the kitchen, then hurried out the door and walked down Via Castiglione to the main police station.

Chief Inspector Monti was alone in her office when Katarina was shown in; not quite alone, as the little brown dachshund was lying patiently by her feet under the desk.

"One moment, Signora Kallberg, I will be with you shortly," Inspector Monti said, her eyes glued to the computer screen.

What kind of a woman was the chief inspector? Katarina wondered. The inspector was undoubtedly particular about her appearance; her straight, shiny black hair was cut just below the ears; her bangs, cut with razor-sharp precision, barely touched her finely arched black eyebrows. Pearl earrings and a thin silver bracelet suited her severe yet feminine personality. She was wearing the same dark red shade of lipstick as the last time Katarina had seen her. At eight o'clock in the morning, she was perfectly put together.

The inspector turned to Katarina, "Good to see you, Signora Kallberg. We were about to call and ask you to stop by. Please sit down; I have a couple of questions for you."

The inspector's steely gaze flustered Katarina, and she averted her eyes.

"Do you have any further information regarding Max De Angelis? Was he acquainted with your sister before her death or not?"

Katarina hesitated, "I don't know for sure, but I have no evidence that they knew each other."

"We have been informed that he was observed kissing your sister in the casket after the funeral service in the church. Can you confirm that?"

"Yes."

"Strange to kiss a dead stranger, don't you think?"

Katarina didn't answer.

"And then, about your alibi. Do you recall any further details from the night of August 15th?"

"Mm—that's why I'm here." Katarina's heart was pounding.

"Go ahead."

The inspector listened without interruption while Katarina told her the story about the night of the taxi ride to Anacapri. She recounted the bare facts in an emotionless voice without dwelling on the details. To her own ears, it sounded like someone else was telling the story; it all seemed so distant, as if it had happened a long time ago to somebody else. Her pride prevented her from making any excuses for her behavior.

"I was hoping—" Katarina said in a soft voice, "I hope that you will use discretion when confirming my alibi, so as not to cause any marital conflict."

Chief Inspector Monti stood up and pushed back her chair. The little dachshund came to all fours.

Katarina waited, feeling downcast and ashamed; like when she was a kid in school and the teacher found out she hadn't done her homework.

"We are not in the business of causing unnecessary harm," the inspector said, putting the dog in her lap as she sat down in the chair beside Katarina. "If this person, I will call him Signor A, confirms your alibi, it's unlikely we will need his testimony in court."

Gently stroking the dog's back, she turned to Katarina. "What about De Angelis, anything else you can tell me about him, anything at all that comes to mind?"

Katarina felt herself blush upon hearing Max's name. "I—really can't think of anything," she said, hoping the chief inspector hadn't noticed.

"I would caution against getting too involved with De Angelis; he may not have your best interests at heart," the chief inspector said.

Katarina blushed again. Damn, she thought, and took a breath to compose herself.

The chief inspector changed the subject, "Well, is there anybody else you can think of who might have had a reason to do away with your sister?"

Katarina vacillated as to whether she should mention the names of any of the four men she thought could be involved, but decided against it; she had no concrete evidence. She surprised herself by mentally excluding Max as a suspect.

"No, I can't think of anybody who would have wanted to harm Camilla. But I recollect Camilla saying that she had visited the island of Procida a couple of times in the spring. If she didn't go alone, who was with her? Maybe it would be possible for the police to find out?"

"We will look into it." Inspector Monti placed the dog gently on the floor and stood up. The audience was over.

"That's a fantastic haircut, by the way, is your hairdresser on Capri?" Katarina dared to ask.

"Yes, Gino at Pronto Charme," the chief inspector said while suppressing a smile.

"That was my sister's hairdresser as well," said Katarina. "Maybe Gino knows something about Camilla that we don't; I will talk to him."

Reaching deep into her handbag, Katarina pulled out Amedeo's old fisherman's cap and placed it on the desk. "I borrowed this. Uhmm—would you kindly return this to—uh —Signor A, and please—if possible, please be discreet."

Chief Inspector Monti couldn't help but smile at the sight of the raggedy old cap.

As soon as Katarina Kallberg had closed the door behind her, the inspector picked up the phone. "Arcuzzi, get a hold of Max De Angelis; have him come to my office right away."

Chapter 30 - A Kiss of Death

After the happy reunion with Il Professore, Max headed back to town in a better mood. He squeezed into a chair next to Raffi on the terrace above the funicular track. Raffi nodded but kept working on his iPad. Max ordered a sandwich and a bottle of mineral water.

Raffi was still angry with him, Max noted. It wasn't as if Max didn't understand Raffi's anger; he himself seriously doubted that Katarina had murdered her sister. But Max was just doing his job. He was hired to work for a private company, he was not in public service as a police officer. Raffi should understand that.

Raffi had appeared to be quite charmed by Katarina when they met. Was it possible that Raffi was playing their old boyhood game of competing for the same girl? he wondered. They had fought by every possible means to win the game. Or could it be that Raffi was genuinely interested in Katarina?

Max's cell phone rang. *"Buongiorno,* Arcuzzi here. Chief Inspector Monti would like to see you in her office."

"All right, Captain, I'll be there as soon as I can."

Max was in no hurry to see the chief inspector; she could wait. While eating the sandwich he had ordered, he waited in vain for Raffi to say something.

"The chief inspector wants to talk to me, I'd better go," Max finally said.

"Well, you'd better go then," Raffi said.

"How about hooking up tonight? I was thinking of having dinner at Da Tonino. My old mathematics professor is coming, and I'll invite Katarina as well."

"OK," Raffi nodded.

Max chuckled to himself as he got up; he had put out Katarina as bait, and Raffi was on the hook.

An old fisherman's cap was lying on the desk in front of Chief Inspector Monti; it was the first thing Max noticed when he entered her office. It was the same cap he had seen in Katarina's bedroom the day he was invited for tea at the villa, he was sure of it. And he didn't see it hanging on the clothes rack or anywhere else after the break-in, so Max knew there was something "fishy" about this cap, something personal that Katarina was hiding. What was it doing on Monti's desk?

"Good morning, Chief Inspector Monti," Max said cheerfully. "Good morning, Captain Arcuzzi," he added. The Captain was standing by the window. Without waiting for an invitation, Max sat down. Forcing himself to avert his eyes from the fisherman's cap, he looked straight into the chief inspector's eyes with a feigned indifference. "What a coincidence, I was about to come here just when you summoned me."

"Good morning, De Angelis—what a coincidence, yes," said the inspector dryly.

"How is your investigation going, Chief Inspector? It seems to be dragging on, but then I don't suppose you get many cases quite this complicated on this little island." Max spoke with deliberate slowness and more than a hint of sarcasm. "May I inquire on behalf of UGI when we may expect a final report? I assume that by now you have concluded it was suicide?"

"Rest assured, you will be notified as soon as we have a report, which we hope to have very soon." The chief inspector's voice matched the iciness of her eyes. "Perhaps you have forgotten the customs of this country, but here, we do not make hasty conclusions that will turn out to be wrong. If you discover any new evidence, feel free to share it with us."

"Of course, Chief Inspector. May I have copies of the coroner's report and any photos taken at the scene where Kallberg's body was found? It's essential for my final report. I understand the police have confiscated Kallberg's laptop and cell phone, could I have access to them?"

"We will arrange for copies of the photos and the coroner's report. Captain Arcuzzi will call you when they come in. However, her laptop and cell phone will not be available to you—that is confidential information."

Max nodded.

"If you don't mind, De Angelis, I have a question for you." Chief Inspector Monti paused for a moment. "You were observed kissing the deceased—Camilla Kallberg—when she was lying in her coffin. Do you have an explanation?"

"Guilty as charged. Since when is kissing a crime?" Max said in a nonchalant tone of voice, pretending he was not caught off guard by the direct question fired at him by the chief inspector.

"And you maintain that Camilla Kallberg was a total stranger to you?"

"Yes."

"Do you make it a habit, De Angelis, to kiss total strangers—in this case, a dead stranger?"

Max felt the urge to laugh; the question was ludicrous. He managed to restrain himself from laughing, but was betrayed by a small twitch at the side of his mouth.

Captain Arcuzzi was standing at attention; he was in full uniform. His back was as straight as a board and not a muscle moved on his face under the stiff blue police cap.

"Do you think this is funny, De Angelis?" said the inspector. "I personally find nothing funny about it, but as you clearly do, please enlighten us so we may share in the joke."

Max thought he saw a glint of humor in her gray eyes; he suspected she might be on the verge of laughter herself.

"You're right Chief Inspector, it's not a laughing matter, but I can assure you that it was only my ridiculous desire to behave correctly and beyond reproach that got me in trouble. You may not know about it, since you did not grow up here in Capri, but on this small island, correctness is an acquired tool for getting along with everyone. What happened is that everybody got in line to put a flower in the coffin; I didn't want to draw attention to myself, since I had no business being there, so I stood in line like everyone else. Katarina Kallberg had invited us to kiss her sister; I thought it would be rude to refuse her request, so that's why I kissed her."

The chief inspector raised her eyebrows until they disappeared underneath her bangs.

"So, De Angelis, let me get this straight. You kissed a woman—a dead woman—who was a total stranger—on the mouth—out of correctness?"

CHAPTER 31 - CAPRI DIEM

T he sight of Max and Raffi standing beside the campanile raised Katarina's spirits. It wasn't every day that two handsome men were waiting to escort her to dinner. Their admiring glances and compliments didn't hurt either, and she was glad she had gone to some length to look her absolute best. Katarina thought Max looked particularly attractive; she admired the fit of his slim black jeans over his narrow hips. The sleeves of his blue cotton shirt were rolled up, showing off his sun-bronzed muscular upper arms. She felt the urge to run her hand through his long, unruly black hair, then she noticed that he had an angry look on his face. What was he upset about now? she wondered.

"So, Max, tell us what happened when you were summoned to the police station this morning?" Raffi said, as they stopped to admire the view of the town from Via Sopramonte.

Katarina looked at Max in surprise. "I was at the police station this morning as well. Are there are any new developments regarding my sister?" she asked anxiously.

Max's face darkened. "No, there is nothing new," he said in a gruff voice. "Let's get moving, the Professor is waiting for us at La Croce."

Katarina noticed the surprised look on Raffi's face, and she wondered what Max was hiding.

Raffi took Katarina's arm as they walked through the restaurant to the round table set for five in the corner of the patio. He pulled out a chair for Katarina and sat down to her left. The Professor sat to her right and Max sat across from her. A seat was left empty between Raffi and Max for Domenico, the manager of the restaurant, in case he could join them later. Katarina noticed Max looking at her in a peculiar way. Apart from complimenting her in the Piazzetta, Katarina realized he hadn't spoken a word to her the whole way up to the restaurant.

All the tables on the terrace of Da Tonino were filled on this final Saturday in August. Most of the patrons were Neapolitans on vacation; they were talking, laughing, and gesticulating while enjoying the food and wine in the company of friends. Many would soon leave Capri. Some of the luckier ones would return for the occasional weekend; others would not return until the following summer. The knowledge that summer was ending made them especially exuberant.

It was as if they wished to devote every minute of their precious time in paradise to life's pleasures. The memories of their time on Capri would sustain them through life's relentless pressures and inevitable demands until they could return to the island of dreams once again.

To Katarina, it seemed as if the older patrons were even more lively and free-spirited than the younger ones. Did older people know better than the young how things could go wrong in the blink of an eye?

On Capri, Katarina had learned that friendship was precious to Italians, and especially so to the Neapolitans. One time at a party, Camilla had whispered to her, as if it were a secret, that friendship with Neapolitans was often for life and could demand sacrifices. Friendship might even be sacred, Camilla had said.

Katarina scrutinized the faces of the men sitting around the table. Max's friend Raffi had the noble face of someone trustworthy, and she had liked him from the moment Max introduced him to her. It seemed as if she had known him her whole life, even though they had only met the day before. Max's retired mathematics teacher, whom they called Il Professore, had a learned and distinguished face that commanded respect; but his eyes betrayed his soft heart.

Then she looked at Max, with his sharp angular features, high forehead, and straight nose; his handsome face had become quite familiar to her. And yet she could only guess at what went on behind his cool facade. Could she trust him or not? Had he been her sister's lover?

She remembered their first kiss in the Cala del Fico. Closing her eyes, she could almost taste the salt when their lips met. When she opened her eyes again, they were magnetically drawn to Max's. His dark, penetrating eyes reminded her of a falcon; they looked straight at her. She felt her cheeks flush with heat.

Domenico came over to join them, with a cheery smile; his sister-in-law had arrived to relieve him of duty for the night. The waiter brought over a chilled bottle of white wine from the 10,000-bottle wine cellar; a Gennaro Picariello Fiano di Avellino. Numerous plates of delicate and unusual antipasti were passed around the table, and comments on the food were solicited and exchanged with ruthless honesty; not the tiniest ingredient or sensory experience went unnoticed.

"Melancholy thoughts are inseparable from joy and beauty, don't you think?" Domenico said, after the waiter had cleared the appetizer plates; he was looking directly at Katarina.

Katarina felt embarrassed; she didn't know how to respond to the question.

"Could it be that the spectacular eternal beauty of Capri forces us to face the fact that we will all die?" Domenico added, glancing at everyone around the table.

"You are thinking about Camilla, aren't you?" Katarina's voice quivered. "Are you saying that because of her joy for life and her appreciation for beauty, she threw herself from the cliffs!"

"No, no, Katarina," Domenico said. "That is not what I meant at all. On the contrary. Mindfulness of our mortality is essential to make us realize the importance of the moment. In other words, when we experience the beauty and joy of living, we realize that our life on this earth will one day end. Therefore, one must live life fully every single moment as if every day was the last. It is above all true when one sees the glory of nature, and the nature of Capri is spectacularly glorious, isn't it?"

Katarina's face lit up. "Oh Domenico, I see what you mean! It's a famous saying, 'seize the day,' in Latin it's *carpe diem*, right?"

Domenico smiled at Katarina, "Brava. *Carpe diem* is an aphorism; I'm glad that you are familiar with the expression. But did you know that here on Capri we have our own interpretation of it? We call it 'Capri Diem.' It means to live each day on Capri as if it were the last day of your life, with joy, and in search of beauty."

"Let's toast to that, shall we?" Raffi raised his wine glass.

After the toast, Raffi said in a mock serious voice, "I live in grave danger in my quest for beauty."

"What danger is that, Raffi?" Max asked.

"I've heard it said that when one finds beauty, one desires to be a part of it forever." Raffi looked directly at Katarina.

211

Katarina was bewildered; was Raffi talking to her or speaking in general terms? To hide her pleasure over the apparent compliment, she turned to the professor. "What does beauty mean to you, Professore?"

The professor smiled, "Ah, *la bellezza*, beauty, what is it? I believe that everyone and everything one observes with close attention becomes more beautiful as time passes; how else to explain some people's love for the ugliest creatures in the world?" Then he smiled tenderly and said: "As they say, beauty is in the eye of the beholder. For instance, Jacques, my cocker spaniel—he is the most beautiful creature in all the world to me."

"All this talk about beauty doesn't help to explain why Camilla fell to her death," Max said in an impatient tone of voice. "Now that we are all here together, let's examine what we know about the night she disappeared. Il Professore last saw Camilla alone on the road just below this wall. Domenico overheard her while she was talking to someone. Those two statements are not compatible. Since Domenico didn't hear a second voice, I think it's likely she was alone, and either talking to herself or on a cell phone and therefore—"

Katarina interrupted Max. "Camilla's cell phone was on the nightstand, remember?"

Katarina suddenly remembered that *other* kiss; Max kissing her sister lying in the coffin. It was odd, she thought. Why did Max kiss Camilla if he didn't know her? Again, she wondered if Max and Camilla had been lovers—maybe in San Francisco?

"Of course, Katarina, I know that Camilla's cell phone was on her nightstand," Max continued. "But we haven't considered the possibility that Camilla had a second cell phone, have we?"

"You may be onto something, Max; I mean, it wasn't likely your sister would be talking to herself, would she Katarina?" Raffi said, gently touching her arm as if to show his solidarity.

"So, the way I see it," the Professor said, "since no other phone was found, and her purse is missing, it's possible that the phone is inside her purse lying somewhere on the side of the cliff or at the bottom."

"Exactly!" Max exclaimed.

The second course arrived, and they all grew quiet while enjoying the sumptuous pasta dish with mussels, *tortelli cacio e pepe con cozze e lime.*

"Let's be logical and examine the simple facts," Max said, after the waiter had cleared away the plates. "Camilla was in love. Camilla was planning to reveal secret information to her sister. Camilla was afraid for her life for unconscious or conscious reasons."

Katarina, Raffi, Domenico, and Il Professore looked at Max as he continued.

"I'm not a psychologist, but I took a course on psychological autopsy. All the people who knew Camilla concur that she was a sane, happy person. I've found no evidence that she had a reason to commit suicide, nor was a suicide note found." Max took a breath; they all waited eagerly to hear his next words.

"What we know is that Camilla had a dream about dying that caused her to make special arrangements for her funeral. The dream may have expressed an intuition. Intuition often comes from unconscious facts. My conclusion so far is that Camilla was very afraid of something."

"So, then, you agree that she was killed!" Katarina burst out.

"I can't say that for certain. So far there's no evidence that someone killed Camilla. All I'm saying is that we know she was frightened enough to make funeral arrangements and that soon after she had that dream, she did in fact die," Max said.

"That doesn't help much, does it?" Raffi said, sounding disappointed. "In fact, it doesn't help at all. If you can't prove anything to the police, they will declare the cause of death to be suicide, or at best, undetermined—neither of which is the verdict Katarina wants."

Max didn't respond to Raffi's remark.

"You will find the truth, Max," the Professor said. "You will use your head, and you will track down the murderer if there is one. I'm quite sure you will."

Max didn't say anything.

"What else do we know?" asked Raffi. "Is there anything new?"

"Well, I went to talk to Gino today, Camilla's hairdresser," Katarina said. "Camilla told Gino that she was madly in love. Gino said he could testify that it was true by looking at Camilla's glowing face."

"Good Catarì, but did you find out who she was in love with?" Max asked.

"No, Gino didn't know, and he hadn't seen her with anyone special, but I did find out something else—" Katarina paused. "Camilla told Gino she'd decided to give away her diamond necklace because she was no longer interested in wearing expensive jewelry."

Max looked at her in surprise. "Did Gino tell you the name of the person she planned to give it to?"

"No, Camilla didn't say."

"If Camilla wished to give away her necklace," Raffi said, "why not give it to Katarina or someone else in her family? Is it a coincidence that she gave it away just before she died?"

"I don't believe in coincidences," Max said drily.

Katarina looked at Max's grave face. Suddenly, she felt a chill go down her spine. What about the coincidence that he and Camilla had lived in San Francisco at the same time, and that they were both free after Camilla lost her husband and Max divorced his wife. What about the coincidence that Max's father worked as Camilla's gardener for many years? Was it just a coincidence that Camilla took out a life insurance policy at Max's company, and that he was on Capri when she plunged to her death? Or was everything planned?

Katarina's eyes narrowed, and when she spoke to him her voice was unusually sharp: "How strange, Max, your life seems so full of coincidences—or are they *not* coincidences?"

Chapter 32 - Lido del Faro

Sunday, August 29

L azing around in bed in his luxurious hotel suite, Max thought about the conversation at the restaurant with Katarina, Raffi, Il Professore, and Domenico. It had been interesting to hear their different opinions, but they still didn't know what had happened to Camilla. Max refused to give up his conviction that by discovering the facts he would solve this mystery, but he'd begun to realize that there was more to it than facts; something beyond the logic of a usual investigation.

Tara had always said that things happen for a reason. Did fate bring him to Capri? If it was all meant to be, what was the meaning of it? Was he somehow destined to meet Katarina?

The cell phone alarm interrupted his useless speculations. It was time he got up, he had an appointment to meet Katarina and Raffi by the clock tower at ten o'clock. Reluctantly, he rolled out of bed.

While walking back to town with Raffi and Katarina after their dinner at Da Tonino the night before, Raffi had come up with the idea that the three of them spend a day at the beach. Katarina was thrilled by Raffi's suggestion they go to Lido del Faro. Max didn't like the idea at all, but he couldn't think of any reason for not joining them. Why was Raffi suddenly so eager to go to a lido, and on a busy Sunday of all days? Max asked himself as he stepped into the shower.

Max was on his second espresso in the hotel's breakfast room when Antonio came over and joined him at his table. He wanted to know if Max had been able to put any pressure on the chief inspector to hurry up their investigation.

"The mayor is mad as hell, as you can imagine, Max," Antonio said. "The media is having a field day over this mysterious death here on the island. The police have to wrap up this case, the sooner, the better, and we hotel owners feel the same urgency, as you can imagine."

"Well, I spoke to the chief inspector about it; she made it clear to me that she is the one in charge, but I doubt she is immune to the political pressure."

"Let's all hope so; I don't believe the woman was murdered, not here on Capri," Antonio said. "Ah, I see Ugo Vitale is here; he is a loyal patron and friend of mine. You two have something in common. Like you, Ugo is an avid mountain climber; he has even climbed Mount Everest. Ugo is also renowned as a writer. His young daughter Beatrice is with him at the hotel, but I don't see her; she is probably still sleeping. Come with me; I'll introduce you."

Introductions were made, with Antonio relating that Max was a mountain climber, and that he was on Capri representing an insurance company in the United States, whose client was a Norwegian woman who had died on Capri.

Antonio returned to the reception and Max exchanged some pleasantries with the famous mountain climber before excusing himself; he didn't want to be late for his appointment with Katarina and Raffi.

Raffi splurged on a taxi to take them to Lido del Faro on Anacapri, on the westernmost point of the island. The beach establishment was packed, as could be expected on a Sunday in August. To Max's surprise, Raffi had reserved sun loungers on a waterfront terrace tucked into the cliff-side, and to avoid the crowds in the restaurant, he had organized a wine and tasting menu to be served on their terrace that afternoon. What the hell, Max thought, Raffi must be really taken with Katarina. Apparently, he had decided to make every effort to impress her, so he could outmaneuver Max.

Below their terrace, the views of the sea and sun-bleached cliffs lining the tiny cove were dazzling. Max's irritable mood passed as soon as he dove into the crystalline deep blue water. They all went snorkeling along the rocky shore. Later, they soaked up the sun and then lounged in the shade under an umbrella.

Lunch was perfect. They started with a *degustazione di mare*, a tasting appetizer with four different seafood samples; next was ravioli filled with burrata, mussels, shrimp, and zucchini flowers. Each dish was paired with a different wine. Dessert was a Torta Anacaprese lemon cake.

On Max's request, the waiter brought glasses of mirto (myrtle liqueur). Max was about to raise his glass for a toast, in the hope of reminding Katarina of the time he showed her the Balthazar myrtle tree, when he was interrupted.

"Let's go for a stroll to see the lighthouse," Raffi said, and pulled Katarina to her feet.

They went up past the impressive Punta Carena Lighthouse to the lookout point where they could see the Faraglioni stacks in the distance. Then they walked down to the public swimming area, packed with locals, to watch the bravest youngsters dive from the high craggy rocks into the sea.

Suddenly a woman's voice cried out, "Max, Max, *sono qui, sono qui,* I'm here!" The woman used the ladder to climb out of the water, and threw her arms around Max.

"This is Graziella," Max said with a sheepish smile, as she clung to him with her wet body.

Katarina recognized the woman at once; she was the one on the silver Vespa scooter with Max as passenger on the night she was trying to find Amedeo in Anacapri. With her voluptuous body, long raven-black hair, and dark sun-bronzed skin dripping with water, Katarina had to admit Graziella was stunning. She felt a pang of jealousy in her heart—was this young woman Max's lover?

The four of them went to Da Antonio for margaritas, a local hangout above Faro's public beach. Sitting on tall bar stools, they watched the sun as it turned into a glowing ball of red light and slipped below the horizon into the sea.

"What a coincidence that we should meet by the sea, once again," Graziella said, raising her margarita glass to toast Max, while shooting him a teasingly provocative glance. "And what a coincidence that we should be together again by the lighthouse of Faro." She stroked Max's coral amulet with a finger before lingering in the groove of his suntanned chest.

"Yes, how strange, Max—your life seems so full of coincidences," said Katarina, unable to control the sarcasm in her voice. "Didn't you tell us yesterday that you don't believe in coincidences?"

Max had nothing to say; he licked the rest of the salt off the rim of his cocktail glass.

Katarina couldn't stand to watch Graziella, and the way she acted as if she owned Max; she turned her attention to Raffi. "I understand you live in the states. How long are you planning to stay on Capri?"

"Sadly, I have to leave tomorrow to visit my wine suppliers in Tuscany and Veneto. I'll return on the eighth of September for a few

218

days before leaving for California. I've got a fantastic idea, Katarina, why don't you accompany me to Tuscany and Veneto?"

Katarina laughed at the impromptu invitation. "If only I could Raffi, but I'm afraid the police on Capri wouldn't like the idea very much. I'm still a suspect, you know."

"Then, will you visit me in California one day soon?"

"Maybe, who knows?" Katarina smiled at Raffi.

Max's irritation with Raffi escalated by the minute: What the hell does Raffi think he's doing, hitting on Katarina? We're not boys playing games anymore.

Again, it was Raffi who was the big shot and insisted they take a taxi back to town. They said goodbye to Graziella, who roared off on her shiny silver scooter, and then the three of them slid into a white seven-seat stretch taxi.

Katarina gasped; the interior of the taxi was lavender. The driver turned his head, and she recognized him in an instant—it was Amedeo.

Max felt uncomfortable sitting by himself in the middle row while Raffi and Katarina occupied the last row of the cabriolet taxi. None of them said a word during the long ride back to town. The silence was unbearable. Raffi's courting of Katarina was awkward, and Katarina's coolness towards him was distressing.

Max sighed as the taxi sped in darkness down the hairpin curves from Anacapri towards the bright lights of the town of Capri. Then suddenly, he saw it: The cap.

On the dashboard of the taxi was an old tattered fisherman's cap. It looked identical to the one that he had seen lying on the desk of Chief Inspector Monti—and identical to the cap in Katarina's bedroom at the villa. Could this be the same bloody cap? he wondered.

The driver opened the door for them. Max was about to ask him where he had gotten the fisherman's cap, but he thought better of it; he would just make a fool of himself. The exchange of words that followed left him dumbfounded:

"Ciao, Amedeo, *grazie*," said Katarina.

"Ciao, Katarina, *grazie a te*," said the taxi driver.

It had been a perplexing day, Max thought, as he left Raffi and Katarina in the Piazzetta. Although the weather, the swim in the sea, the food, the wine—and, not least, the sunset, had all been perfect, he was left with a bad feeling that he had screwed things up. Not only had he gotten no closer to discovering the manner of Camilla's death, but now both Raffi and Katarina seemed upset with him. Had they made plans to meet for dinner? He felt guilty that he was not sad that Raffi was leaving Capri the next morning.

Introducing the exotic Graziella to his friends had been embarrassing. Graziella was an alluring woman, and the possibility of meeting her again was tempting, but only if he were to meet her secretly. Theirs was not a dating relationship; their relationship was happily free of any expectation that it would turn into something more than a casual affair. At least that was what Max thought, and he had assumed that Graziella felt the same. Now he questioned his relationship with Katarina. Did he have feelings for her? By the time he walked into his hotel, he still hadn't found the answer.

Matisse, the longhaired white Persian cat—and mascot of Hotel Gatto Bianco, was sitting on the reception counter, and was hard at work licking his bushy tail. Matisse was the last in a long line of white cats bringing good fortune to the hotel named for a white cat found on the grounds of the family-owned hotel in 1950. Renato was sitting at the reception desk; he was one of the owners of Hotel Gatto Bianco, and the brother of Max's good friend Antonio.

"Good evening, Max, how are things going with your case?" Renato said, as he looked up from reading a book.

"Good evening, Renatino. The case is going slow. Everything is at a standstill. That's a well-used book you're holding; what's the title?" Max knew Renato was an avid reader.

"Ah, this book was written by me, my dear friend: *Minima Capraria – 51 racconti brevi alla ricerca del Capri Diem (Minima Capraria — 51 short stories in search of Capri Diem)*. I wrote these stories a long time ago. The book is out of print now, and this is the last copy I own. It is an imaginary journey into the myth of Capri."

"Just yesterday I heard someone use the phrase, 'Capri Diem.' I

220

had never heard it before."

"I believe I am the person who coined the term Capri Diem; it's a play on words from the Latin aphorism, *carpe diem*, 'seize the day.' As you know, I enjoy playing with words."

"Remind me, what's the origin of *carpe diem*?" Max asked.

"No doubt you've heard of Horace—the leading lyric poet during the time of Roman Emperor Augustus. Horace used the words *carpe diem* in an ode; it says that the future is unforeseen, and that one should not leave future happenings to chance, but should do all one can today to make one's future better."

"That's something to sleep on, isn't it Renatino? Good night. Tomorrow is another day; maybe it's time for *carpe diem* on Capri."

"*Sogni d'oro*, golden dreams," Renato said.

CHAPTER 33 - IF NOT NOW, THEN WHEN

MONDAY, AUGUST 30

M ax woke up and got straight out of bed to open the shades. It was daybreak. Now was the time to act, he could feel it in his gut. What was that phrase Renatino used last night? *Carpe diem*, yes, seize the day. Even if it wasn't in his company's best interests, he had to try to find out the truth. Camilla had feared something was about to happen to her, and he needed to find out if her fear was justified. It was time he listened to Katarina, who insisted that her sister was murdered.

"Screw my boss!" Max exclaimed out loud.

The police hadn't done a damn thing to solve the case, except to harass him and throw suspicion on Katarina. There is no way around it, he'd have to climb the cliff at Belvedere delle Noci to look for that missing purse or whatever else he could find relevant to the case.

He would have to climb down from the top of the cliff, Max reasoned, to reach the area where Camilla's body had been found. Going solo top-roping was ordinarily tricky, but it would be especially dangerous at Belvedere delle Noci, because of the porous limestone rock on the island. To his knowledge, nobody had ever climbed the area before, and for good reason, and therefore no recreational climbing road had been established. If he started the climb from the bottom, he would have to cut through thick brush to reach the rock face; it would be harder to spot the purse and the dangers would still be the same.

Max decided to walk over to the police station to get the photographs he had requested of the location of the body at the site, and then visit Il Professore to ask his advice; he also had to see about borrowing some rock-climbing gear from his friend Luigi.

While waiting for the police station to open, he went into Bar Due Golfi. As he was standing at the counter finishing his double espresso, he heard a familiar voice.

"Good morning, Riccardo, fresh orange juice please, no ice, no sugar."

Riccardo, the owner of the café, looked up from the espresso machine: "Good morning, Inspector."

Max turned around. Chief Inspector Monti was standing behind him in full uniform, holding her brown dachshund.

"Signor De Angelis, good morning," she said.

Max bowed, "Good morning Chief Inspector Monti, may I hold your dog while you drink your juice? What's his name?"

"Montalbano," she answered, passing him the little dachshund. "Ah, named after the famed Sicilian Commissioner," Max said, cradling the dog in his arms. "Montalbano[16] is your boss, I assume, since your title is Vice Commissioner?"

She didn't smile at Max's lame attempt at humor.

Thirty minutes later, after first calling to make sure the professor was at home, Max arrived at his house on Via Lo Capo with police files tucked under his arm. He didn't know how he had managed to persuade Chief Inspector Monti to release all the information she had on the investigation, but he suspected it might have had something to do with his enthusiasm for Montalbano, her friendly dachshund.

While waiting for the *caffiera* to brew, the professor got a magnifying glass, and they examined the blown-up aerial photographs of the location where the body was found. Neither the purse nor any of the other missing items were visible.

"I remember your lesson on gravity," Max said. "According to Galileo, two bodies of different masses, dropped from the same height, will touch the ground at the same time in the absence of air resistance. Hence any two objects that are subject only to the force of gravity will fall with the same acceleration, and they will hit the ground at the same time. Do you think it's possible that the purse could be near the place where the body landed?"

"A possibility, but not a guarantee; the area is large, and there are obstructions such as jagged rocks and tree branches," Il Professore answered.

Max looked discouraged.

"I think I can help," Il Professore said as he passed Max a cup of sweetened espresso. "I have friends at *il commune* (city hall). I will ask them for a topographic map with elevation data for that area of Capri in a digital format. I can then use the science of photogrammetry to make measurements to find the exact position of the surface point

---

[16] Inspector Montalbano (Italian: Commissario Montalbano) is a fictional detective created by Italian writer Andrea Camilleri in a series of novels and short stories.

of the body, although that won't necessarily be close to where a thrown purse would have landed."

"Excellent idea to do a land-surface analysis," Max said, while caressing Jacques's head; the cocker spaniel had put his chin on his thigh. "How much time do you think it will take to complete these calculations?"

"After I get the maps from city hall, which as you know depends on the 'mood' of my friends there, it will take me a day or so to do the calculations," Il Professore said.

"Great to see you again, Max," said Luigi, the owner of Le Grottelle Restaurant.

Max got to the point right away, explaining that he would like to borrow rock climbing equipment to search for evidence at Belvedere delle Noci. He also asked Luigi for a pair of rock-climbing shoes and a handheld drill.

"No problem, I have everything at home. Luckily, we have the same shoe size. I have a Bosch Bulldogs drill," Luigi said. "Make a list of everything else you need. If you come back tonight, the equipment will be here waiting for you. But you shouldn't go climbing in that area alone, you know; it's dangerous. Why don't I come with you?"

"Thanks, Luigi, but you have a wife and family to consider; I don't want you to take the risk. I, on the other hand, don't have anyone to worry about. I'm single now, as you may have heard, and my parents passed away. I'll climb alone; I don't want to take responsibility for anyone else."

Max sat down at a table beside the wall close to the grotto and let his waiter Giovanni choose lunch for him. As soon as he had finished the delicious plate of *scialatielli ai frutti di mare* (fresh pasta with seafood), he gave Luigi the list of equipment. Before leaving, he reserved a table for two for dinner; then he waved goodbye to Mama and Costanza in the kitchen before hurrying up to Belvedere delle Noci.

Surveying the area below the top of the cliff, Max found it was not ideal for solo top-roping. There was no suitable tree to use as a bomber anchor; so, as he had thought, he would need a charged hand drill for placing the anchors into the rock wall.

Walking back to town on Via Matermania, he called Katarina; she was at the villa working on a translation project.

"Do you want to join me for dinner tonight at Le Grottelle?" he asked. "I want to discuss some ideas with you about looking for evidence that your sister was murdered."

Katarina's excitement strengthened his resolve to take matters into his own hands. They agreed to meet for an aperitif in the Piazzetta at seven.

Max was early; he hated being late for anything. All the tables in the Piazzetta were occupied. When Max took a position outside the shop of La Parisienne to wait for a free table, a man waved to him from a table at Piccolo Bar, gesturing to join him. Max didn't recognize him at first; then he realized it was the mountain climber Antonio had introduced him to in the hotel breakfast room: Ugo Vitale. Max looked at the clock in the campanile; he still had fifteen minutes to wait for Katarina, plenty of time to say hello to Antonio's friend.

"This is my daughter Beatrice," Ugo said. "Please, we would be honored if you joined us for an aperitif."

"Thank you, but I'm waiting for a friend," Max said.

"Then why don't you sit with us while you wait," Ugo offered.

There was no way he could excuse himself without appearing rude; Max sat down. Ugo did most of the talking. He was charming and seemed eager to hear about Max's mountain climbing. He had heard from Antonio that Max had gone to Thailand to climb the limestone crags at Railay. Max's trip to Thailand hadn't gone well; his depression after the divorce had caused insomnia and he had cancelled the rest of his climbing adventure to return to the states.

"Did you just arrive on vacation?" Max asked, turning to the daughter to change the subject.

"We got here on Thursday," Beatrice replied.

"So how do you spend your days on Capri?" Max asked. He guessed Beatrice was around fifteen or sixteen. "Do you have friends on the island?"

"No, I don't know anybody here," Beatrice said in a sad little voice. "We go swimming on the public beach at Marina Piccola during the day, then I read after dinner and go to sleep early, while Papa goes for an evening stroll on Via Tragara." The girl looked down, "You see, I lost my mother last year," she added in a teary voice.

Max didn't know what to say; why did this young Neapolitan girl confide her loss to him?

His cell phone rang; it was his boss. He excused himself and went to take the call standing at the side of the café.

"It has been ten days, Max," Bob said, "when are you going to wrap up this case?"

"Well, there are still some matters to pursue in the investigation."

"Just three days ago, you said the police were expecting to close the case and declare it a suicide, what has changed?"

"I don't know Bob; several indications make me question the idea of suicide—"

"What the hell are you talking about, Max? You doubt it is suicide, you say? Is it necessary to remind you that it is not your job to question anything? That's the job of the police."

"I know, but—"

"Damn it, Max, it sounds like there is nothing we can do now but wait for the police to close the case. Drop the investigation and get on a flight back to San Francisco—tomorrow."

The line went dead.

Katarina was radiant when Max met her in the Piazzetta that evening; she was overjoyed that Max had finally taken her side. They decided against having an aperitif in the busy square. Instead, they took a leisurely walk up to the restaurant in the twilight hour, stopping to watch the spectacular views as the sea and sky changed from iridescent azure to cobalt blue.

"Look at the moon!" Katarina exclaimed. They had stopped to rest and were looking at the town of Capri in the distance behind them. In the western sky was a waxing crescent moon. "A couple of nights ago I saw a glowing translucent ring around the dark moon.

Did you know that it is called earthshine, and that the dim glow on the darkened portion of the moon is light reflected from Earth?" she added.

Max nodded absentmindedly, only half listening to what Katarina was saying. He was worried about the consequences of his decision to go against his boss's order to leave Capri and return to San Francisco. And he was concerned about the weather forecast for Capri—a rainstorm was forecast for the following evening. These sudden storms hitting Capri in the middle of summer were often ferocious and could cause severe damage. That was a problem for Max, as the rain increased the danger of climbing on porous rock. If there was no change in the forecast, Max decided he would have to go early the next morning. It was too bad, but he couldn't wait for the professor's calculations. If necessary, he thought, he could do another climb after the storm had passed; the second time would be easier. But would he have lost his job by then?

Dinner at Le Grottelle was perfect. Katarina was in a great mood, laughing and enjoying the food and the wine, and chatting with their waiter Giovanni and Gregorio, the pizzaiolo. She seemed to have recovered from the awkwardness of meeting the audacious Graziella.

It wasn't until Max went to pay Luigi and returned with a large red backpack that Katarina's bright face dimmed.

"What's that?" she inquired, with a look of bewilderment.

"It's a haul bag," Max said. "Let's get back to town. It's late," he added, as he hoisted the backpack over his shoulders, snapped shut the buckle of the back strap, and buckled the hip belt.

"What are you hauling? Looks like it's full of stuff," Katarina said, walking beside him out of the restaurant.

"Mountain climbing gear."

Katarina looked puzzled, "What for?"

"Mountain climbing."

"Where are you going mountain climbing?" Katarina said in an exasperated tone of voice.

"Here on Capri, of course," Max said. "I am going to search for that goddamn purse of Camilla that you said is missing."

"You mean on those steep rocky cliffs? Isn't that dangerous?"

Max shrugged his shoulders and discovered the haul bag was very heavy.

"You are not going alone, are you?"

Max nodded. "Better alone."

"Can I come with you?"

Max laughed, "Sure, how much mountain climbing experience do you have?"

"None."

"Some other time then," Max said.

"When are you going?"

"Tomorrow morning, early," Max answered.

They were walking down the steep part of Via Croce when Katarina suddenly stopped.

"No, I just won't let you go!" she said insistently. "It's too dangerous, especially going alone. I can live without knowing what happened to that purse, I can live with being suspected of killing my sister, and I can live without finding her murderer, but I cannot live with you risking your life. I can't permit it."

Max felt a rising anger; he had made up his mind, and after all the effort he had gone to, he was not about to be stopped. "There's a storm coming tomorrow night. It's better to climb before it rains; otherwise, the evidence might be harder to locate."

"Going alone is insane." Katarina raised her voice in anger: "I forbid you to go!"

What was Katarina's reason for wishing to stop him? he wondered. Was she afraid he would find evidence incriminating her, or was she genuinely concerned for his life? In any case, he might as well lie and tell her he wasn't going; at least then she would stop bothering him.

"Maybe you're right," he said, "it would be better to wait for the professor's calculations, although I don't know if they will make much of a difference."

"What calculations?"

After Max had told her about the professor's offer to help, Katarina calmed down.

They arrived back into town and stepped into the arcade of Max's hotel off Via Vittorio Emanuele to say good night. Katarina made one last plea, "So, you won't—"

Katarina was suddenly interrupted as a man came down the steps of Hotel Gatto Blanco and turned to Max. "Good evening, Signor De Angelis. Ah, I see you have an Osprey Variant, great bag—you went night climbing?"

Max smiled out of politeness; he didn't see the need to explain why he was carrying a mountaineering backpack at that hour. "I wish you a pleasant evening, Signor Vitale," he said.

"Who was that?" Katarina asked when the man was out of earshot.

"Ugo Vitale—he's a famous mountain climber and writer from Naples. He and his daughter are staying at my hotel."

"Maybe he'd want to join you on your climb at Belvedere delle Noci?"

"I'll see, though I don't really know him well enough to ask—"

"So, you won't go tomorrow then?" Katarina asked

"No," he lied.

She kissed him on the lips. "Thank you for wanting to help," she said.

CHAPTER 34 - SABOTAGE

TUESDAY, AUGUST 31

The view from Belvedere delle Noci was dramatic. The craggy peaks of the island's eastern cliffs glowed pink in the early morning light. Leafy branches clinging to the rock walls rustled in the wind; a herring gull rode the current a few meters below.

Max dumped his heavy backpack on the pavement and surveyed the scene in front of him. The ripples on the sea made him apprehensive; the wind was picking up—a sign that the weather was changing. Checking the weather app on his phone, his fears were confirmed: the day would be increasingly cloudy with rain showers and the possibility of thunder storms forecast for the evening. He stuck his cell phone back into the right pocket of his cargo shorts and zipped it shut; in the left pocket he had his cell phone charger and his wallet. He exchanged his black Nikes for Luigi's climbing shoes. Then he started his methodical preparation for the solo top-roping climb, pleased with his decision to climb that morning, rather than risk hazardous conditions after the storm.

◆ ◆ ◆

The tops of the pine trees were swaying in the wind when Katarina stepped onto the roof terrace with her late morning breakfast tray. It wasn't a good day for swimming, she realized, but it was just as well; she had received a new translation project by email. She got to work on her laptop.

Two hours later, she heard someone calling her name from the courtyard; it was Misha, Camilla's gardener. He came up to the terrace; after untying the ropes securing the giant umbrella, he closed it and took the precaution of laying it flat on the terrace floor.

"There's a storm heading this way," he said, as he helped her carry the cushions inside. "Often the storms pass by the island, but it's better to take precautions."

Katarina walked down to town. The Piazzetta was packed with tourists and vacationers; the wind and fast-moving rainclouds had kept people off the beaches and leisure boats. She did her grocery shopping, then headed straight home when the wind started to pick up.

Back at the villa, Katarina decided to call Max to invite him for dinner. When he didn't answer, she left him a voice message. An hour later she called again; still no answer. What had happened to Max? she wondered. Was he ignoring her on purpose, or was something wrong? She shivered at the thought. Unable to relax, she grabbed Camilla's windbreaker and was out the door.

Gusts of wind hit her face while running down the footpaths to Hotel Gatto Bianco. The receptionist informed her that Max was not at the hotel, and that she had not seen Max all day.

Am I being silly to worry about Max? Katarina asked herself. He promised he wouldn't go climbing today, didn't he? Her anxiety got the better of her. She went back out into the wind and hurried up to Le Grottelle restaurant to ask if they had seen him.

Luigi shook his head; he hadn't seen Max. "It is possible he went climbing at Belvedere delle Noci," he said. "Did you know I loaned him some equipment?"

Katarina nodded; she was unable to hide the anguish in her voice when she asked Luigi to go with her to the belvedere.

It was twelve minutes past four when they arrived at Belvedere delle Noci. Katarina remembered it afterwards, because she had checked the time on her white Capri Time watch, the present from Camilla. Later, Katarina would remember every detail of what happened; it was as if she had been forced to live through the death of her sister—a second time.

"Max is here," Luigi said; he was standing next to Katarina leaning over the protective railing. "Look, he must have used my drill to create three anchor points just below the top of the cliff. They're connected via rope into one clip-in point, the master point."

"I see," Katarina said.

Luigi stood on tiptoes. "I can see the shiny top of the carabiner that's clipped into the master point. It seems fine."

"I'm surprised he's still down there," Luigi added. "If he got an early start this morning, I would've thought he'd be finished by now. Can you call him again on your cell phone?"

When there was no answer, Luigi pulled out a whistle. "Max should respond to this; there's a whistle attached to the backpack."

The worried look on Luigi's face, after repeated sharp blows on his whistle got no response, and brought Katarina to the brink of panic. "If anything has happened to Max, it's all my fault!" she burst out. "I was the one who talked him into looking for that stupid purse!"

"No, no, you mustn't blame yourself," Luigi protested. "I know Max, he is a *testa dura* (hardhead), he will do whatever he thinks best."

Luigi blew his whistle again. They stood by the railing, watching the whitecaps on the rough sea while listening for a response. None came.

Luigi got down on his belly and stuck his head through the railing, straining to see if he could spot Max, while Katarina looked on nervously. "I can see the metal anchor leg carabiner clipped into the master point; it's pear shaped." Then he got a shock—the rope that was supposed to run through the anchor leg carabiner was not there! He blinked hard. Could it be possible that Max was not attached by the rope? It was possible. There was no rope!

Katarina was alarmed by the look of horror on Luigi's face when he got up from his belly. "What's wrong?" she asked.

Luigi hesitated, then he said, "There is no rope running through the anchor leg carabiner."

Katarina was speechless. "Wh-what does that mean?" she stammered.

"I don't know, it's inexplicable—it could be an accident—" Luigi's voice expressed his fear; he paused, then he said, "—I hesitate to say it, but I wonder—if it's sabotage—"

"Sabotage!" Katarina cried in a shrill voice.

"I'm calling the police," Luigi said.

It was two hours before they heard the chopping sound of helicopter blades over the howling wind.

"Come, we'll go to my restaurant and wait for news," Luigi insisted. Katarina was shivering uncontrollably despite her wind jacket. She was in shock. "There is nothing else we can do here; it's all in the hands of the expert rescue team—and in the hands of God," he added softly.

Please God, please keep him safe, Katarina begged silently, repeating the prayer with every step she took on their way back to Le Grottelle.

To Katarina it seemed an eternity had passed before the police called Luigi with the information that Max was found and hoisted up into the helicopter and that he was still alive, but in critical condition and being transported to emergency care at the Cardarelli Hospital. By then it was too late for Katarina to catch the last boat from Capri to Naples.

While running home from Le Grottelle, the skies opened, and torrential rain poured down on Katrina; the roads under her feet turned into small rivers. She arrived at the villa soaked to the bone, just as the first lightning split the sky over Monte Solaro. An eruption of rolling thunder echoed from the mountain. She fumbled for the keys and entered the house. A second flash of lightning was followed by an earsplitting bang and all the lights went out.

She crept upstairs in the dark, stripped off her wet clothes, climbed into bed and pulled the bedcovers over her head; she felt utterly alone—and scared, scared for herself and scared for Max.

CHAPTER 35 - CARDARELLI HOSPITAL

K atarina didn't sleep a wink all night, praying that Max would be safe. Rain kept battering down on the roof long after the thunderstorm had moved on. Camilla had spoken about the violent thunderstorms and torrential rains that would sometimes hit Capri, but this was the first time Katarina had personally experienced it.

When the lights came back on, just past five o'clock, she got out of bed, packed an overnight bag, and walked down to the port of Marina Grande by way of the steps of San Francesco. The rain had stopped by then, but the sea was wild and the hydrofoils to the mainland were all cancelled for the day. Having just missed the ferry leaving at six-forty, she had to wait for the next ferry at ten-twenty.

It took her a while to get through the bureaucracy of the front desk at Cardarelli Hospital. She had to lie and say that she was Max's fiancé to be allowed to visit him. Then they insisted on giving her his personal belongings—his cell phone, charger, and wallet. When she finally entered the emergency ward and found Max, he was hooked up to intravenous lines and monitors; his face was black and blue and so swollen that she hardly recognized him. She suddenly felt faint and had to go out in the corridor and sit down for a few minutes before she felt strong enough to go back in and look at him. His face was expressionless, and his body was so still she couldn't even tell if he was breathing.

A nurse appeared and explained that Max was unresponsive; he was in a coma.

"Is he going to be all right?" Katarina whispered.

The nurse smiled and said in a soothing voice, "We were told he landed in some trees or bushes when he fell; that might have saved his life, but it cut up his face a bit, nothing serious. Imaging tests show he broke his left collar bone. However, we don't know the extent of the injury to his brain."

Katarina waited until she was out in the corridor before she burst into tears. Dear God, Max must make it, he just must, she prayed.

When she had calmed down, she called Chief Inspector Monti and told her that she was visiting Max in the hospital, and she didn't know when she would be returning to Capri. She also told the inspector that she didn't care whether she had permission or not. Monti wasn't pleased and made Katarina promise to inform the police of her whereabouts. Monti also reminded her that according to Italian law, she could not check into a hotel without legal identification, and the police had her passport. She hung up on Monti.

Katarina fumed, the damn police, they hadn't done anything to find her sister's murderer. And Max might end up dead because he tried to help her!

She found Camilla's lawyer Emilio in his office at Piazza Trieste e Trento. He understood at once that Katarina was in a state of shock and took her to his apartment on Via Santa Lucia. After swallowing two shots of cognac, she got undressed and fell asleep in his bed.

CHAPTER 36 - INTERMEZZO

SEDUCTION - WEDNESDAY, SEPTEMBER 1

Thehe touch of a hand caressing her naked back woke Katarina; she stirred and raised her head from the pillow.

"Just relax, your back is full of knots. You deserve a massage, my dear," Emilio said. "I'm told I'm quite good at it," he added.

His strong hands went to work, expertly kneading oil into the tense muscles along her spine. She had difficulty relaxing, still shaken by the discovery that someone might have tried to kill Max; not to mention the anxiety of watching him as he lay helpless and unresponsive in a coma. She reproached herself silently. It will be my fault if Max doesn't recover. He risked his life for my sake.

"Don't move, I'm going to put on some music," Emilio said. He got up and left the room.

Katarina sat up in bed, draping the sheet around her naked body, and looked around. She must have been sleeping for several hours. The bedroom was dark, except for a faint orange light filtering through the tall shuttered windows from the streetlights two stories below. The street was surprisingly quiet in the early evening, despite being in the center of Naples. Emilio had explained to her, as they walked over from his office in Palazzo Zapata, that Via Santa Lucia now had limited access for automobile traffic.

Magnificent piano music filled the room as Emilio returned carrying a small portable Bluetooth speaker. He placed the speaker on the nightstand and picked up the jar of coconut oil. Katarina lay back down on her stomach on top of the sheet.

"Do you like Brahms?" he asked. Without waiting for her answer, he said, "I like his Opus 118 played by Radu Lupu. This piece is called Intermezzo in A-minor, *Andante teneramente.*"

So, Emilio is a classical music lover, Katarina thought, realizing how little she knew about him. She didn't know much about Brahms either. She remembered seeing a grand piano in the living room and felt stupid that she hadn't asked Emilio whether he played.

Slowly and methodically, he massaged her back, then he ironed out the tension in her shoulders and neck. The piano music and the aroma of coconut oil being rubbed into her skin calmed her anxious mind, and the stress and worry over Max faded away. With each exhalation, she felt herself sinking deeper and deeper into the mattress.

"I'm going to massage your feet; you'll love it," Emilio said, as a new piece started playing

The acupressure massage of her feet felt heavenly; Katarina's fear melted away.

"The piece playing now is Intermezzo in F-minor. *Allegretto un poco agitato*," Emilio said. "Some aficionados call this sensuous musical signature the key of love."

The key of love, what an unusual expression, Katarina thought. What was it that Camilla had said on their last evening together? *I'm in love—again. I want to dance! I want to sing! Love is life's glorious music.* Was Emilio one of Camilla's former lovers? she wondered. Was Emilio the man Camilla had been in love with before she died. A sudden chill shot through her: Was Emilio the one who murdered her sister? He was on the list of suspects, wasn't he?

The mattress moved, and Katarina jumped when Emilio climbed onto the bed; she tried to sit up but was restrained by Emilio's hands on her shoulders.

"Take it easy, my dear, I was getting a kink in my back from standing over the bed. I'm almost finished, just relax." Emilio's voice was commanding. Katarina had always admired his clear and formal sounding Italian, spoken with a distinctive Neapolitan accent.

Emilio spread the oil up and down her legs, massaging the muscles of her inner thighs. When he pinned her spread legs apart with his knees on the inside of her calves, and his hands started stroking ever higher on her thighs, Katarina realized how naïve she had been. This was no ordinary massage.

Her body ached for intimacy; it would have been easy to let go, to give in to the sensuous pleasure of the moment. Apart from her impromptu adventure with Amedeo, the taxi driver, she had not had any sexual attention for an awfully long time. She felt herself yielding to Emilio's touch.

The image of Max's handsome face appeared, and she wished he was giving her the massage instead of Emilio. The memory of his kisses filled her with longing. But then she remembered how Graziella had touched Max's bare chest, making her mad with jealousy. If Max preferred Graziella to her, then she may as well give in to Emilio, who clearly wanted her.

"What's the name of this piece?" Katarina asked when the music changed again, looking for a way to stall his intentions.

"This is the Intermezzo in E-minor. It's called *Andante, largo e mesto* — it has a motif from *Dies Irae.*"

Katarina had no idea what *Dies Irae* was.

Emilio must have felt her resistance to yield to him; he took his time, waiting for her to make a sign that she would accept him, while kneading the oil onto her buttocks.

"You are lovely," Emilio whispered into her ear. "You deserve this."

Deserve sex? Katarina asked herself. What a strange choice of words. Does Emilio think he's doing me a favor by having sex with him? Am I a charity case? His comment emptied her of desire, and she suddenly felt sad. The Brahms music started to annoy her.

"Please, Emilio, I must get up. I need to go to the bathroom."

When she came back from the bathroom wearing Emilio's bathrobe, he was lying naked in the middle of the bed waiting for her.

DOWN TIME - THURSDAY, SEPT. 2 - SATURDAY, SEPT. 4

"Caffè Gambrinus is my favorite morning hangout," Emilio told Katarina, as he led her inside, finding them a quiet table in the rear of the café. "This is Naples' most famous café and a meeting place for intellectuals and artists since 1860. Not only that, it has a grand piano," he added with a smile.

"Remember this," Emilio said, after the waiter had brought their order, "My home is your home for however long you wish. I promise you that I will not bother you with my advances unless you ask for them, and I will always be there for you when you need me."

Katarina could only nod; she was too embarrassed to look Emilio in the eyes.

Emilio paid for her café Americano and cornetto and left her to go to his law practice in the seventeenth-century Palazzo Zapata, right across the street.

Katarina looked around at the elegant art nouveau interior of the historic café, while she pondered what had happened the night before—or rather, what had *not* happened. A single sentence whispered by Emilio, *You deserve this,* had saved her from yielding to his seduction in a moment of weakness.

She had to admit that Emilio had behaved like a perfect gentleman when she returned from the bathroom and explained that she was not ready for a sexual encounter in her present state of mind. They got dressed and Emilio took her for dinner at a restaurant just a block away. Once back in Emilio's apartment, she slept soundly through the night in the narrow bed of the empty maid's room.

Katarina stepped out the door of Caffè Gambrinus and walked quickly down Via Toledo towards the metro station to take the subway to Cardarelli Hospital.

Seeing Max in the hospital bed, hooked up to all kinds of monitoring equipment and feeding tubes, just like the day before, brought her to tears. She held his hand for hours and told him irrelevant details about her life, but received no sign that he had heard a word of it. That evening, when she caught the last hydrofoil back to Capri, she barely noticed the half-moon that shone high above the island.

Katarina spent the next two days traveling back and forth from Capri to Cardarelli Hospital with Max's two sisters, Mona and Mimì. They waited in vain at Max's bedside for him to regain consciousness. When Katarina called Chief Inspector Monti to ask for the return of her passport, it was denied; they had not yet closed their investigation. Every night she spoke to her daughter Anna, assuring her she would soon be home and that everything was all right. She listened to Anna chatter about school, and friends, and her handball practice, and forced herself to sound cheerful and enthusiastic. Her nights were long and lonely.

TEMPTATION - SUNDAY, SEPTEMBER 5

On Sunday morning, Katarina walked down from the town of Capri to Marina Grande, taking the steps of San Francesco, preferring to get some fresh air and exercise instead of taking the funicular. While she stood in line to buy her ticket for the hydrofoil to Naples, she noticed a large crowd of people on the terrace of the beach club, Le Ondine. Among the crowd were men and women in swimwear with black numbers written on their greased shoulders or backs. A banner was swinging from the club's railing: MARATONA DEL GOLFO CAPRI-NAPOLI - FINA WORLD GRAND PRIX. (Marathon Swimming: Capri—Naples).

Suddenly she heard a man's voice behind her. "Katarina, *ma sei ancora a Capri?* (you're still on Capri?)" She turned around to see Lorenzo, Camilla's handsome muscular boatman, looking at her with a big smile on his sun-bronzed face.

"*Carissimo* (dearest) Lorenzo," Katarina smiled back, surprised at how happy she was to see Camilla's friend again.

"How're you doing? I haven't seen you since the day of Camilla's funeral," he said.

"Oh Lorenzo, you won't believe everything that's happened." Katarina felt as if she was about to cry. Lorenzo must have sensed it; he took her arm and led her to a bench overlooking the beach. They sat down, and she told him most of what had happened, omitting the personal details.

When Lorenzo put his big arm around her shoulders and hugged her tight in response to her sad story, Katarina burst into tears.

"Thank you, Lorenzo, for listening," she sniffed.

"You've had a miserable time. I think it's time you let someone take care of you for a change," Lorenzo said. "I've a job to do today. I have volunteered to follow the race participants in my boat to make sure they make it safely from here to Naples; it's a 36-kilometer (22 mile) race. Why don't you keep me company? We'll stop at Aldo's shop and get him to prepare us some sandwiches for lunch. There's plenty of water and wine onboard."

Katarina nodded, "OK, why not? Can you let me off in Naples? I'm going to Cardarelli Hospital to visit Max."

"Sure."

They walked along the waterfront of Marina Grande to reach il Porto Turistico, the port for pleasure craft, where they boarded a beautiful blue gozzo with a magnificent mahogany finish all-wood deck.

"She is a seven-and-a-half-meter Open Cruiser from the Aprea Brothers in Sorrento," Lorenzo said proudly. "Her name is Rachele, after my mother," he added, with a touch of reverence.

"How many swimmers are participating?" Katarina asked, as Lorenzo skillfully maneuvered Rachele out of the narrow and busy port entrance to reach the sea facing the public beach on the other side of the commercial pier.

"There are, I think, 21 men and 18 women racing to win this final event of the World Grand Prix marathon. It's one of the most celebrated events in its field, you know," Lorenzo explained. "They say open-water sea marathons are much more tiring than marathons on land."

She looked at Lorenzo sitting in the high captain's chair, waiting for the race to start. Lorenzo exuded strength and masculinity. He was tall, with a broad chest and big muscular thighs and upper arms. Had there been something more than friendship between Camilla and Lorenzo? she wondered. Was that why Camilla had refused to hire any other boatman? Katarina recalled how she had wished Lorenzo would spend the night with her after Camilla's funeral, so she wouldn't be alone with her unbearable grief. Now she wondered if Camilla had ever spent a night with Lorenzo. What about the fact that he was married? That would explain why her sister had kept their relationship a secret.

"Your wife doesn't come with you on the boat?" Katarina asked brusquely.

"Most of the time she is busy with housework and our two teenage children."

"I see."

A whistle blew, and the race started; all the swimmers dived into the water at the same time. Katarina found it exciting to watch the ultra-distance swimming event while aboard Lorenzo's boat. There were dozens of other support boats following the swimmers, many with loudspeakers, some with TV and film crews.

As they followed the race, Lorenzo asked Katarina about her divorce and about Anna, and about how shared custody worked in Norway. Before she knew it, Katarina had practically told Lorenzo her whole life story, especially the details about the marriage falling apart. Strangely, she had risked baring her heart to a man she hardly even knew. Before this conversation with Lorenzo, only Camilla had

244

been privy to her innermost thoughts. She felt unburdened from talking with him, but wasn't sure what had made her open up to him.

What about Camilla and Lorenzo? she asked herself again. Did he have an alibi for the night of Camilla's murder? Katarina remembered that Lorenzo's daughter had said she saw her father's boat pull into port in the early evening. Lorenzo's wife had said the daughter must have been mistaken; Lorenzo would have been leaving the port, not arriving, because an American couple had hired him to take them to Nerano for dinner.

"Do you remember the night of Ferragosto, the night Camilla died?" Katarina blurted out. "You were out on your boat?"

"Of course, I remember. It was a confusing night. I was halfway to Nerano with clients, an American couple, when they received a phone call that another couple wanted to join them, so I had to return to port to pick them up."

Katarina was embarrassed by her suspicions; she should have known that Lorenzo would never hurt a fly.

Katarina was suddenly hungry; she got out the delicious sandwiches and Lorenzo got a bottle of sparkling white wine from the cooler.

When he turned his face towards her to make a toast for her future, she noticed the color of his eyes; they were green like the sea. Too bad he's married, she thought. Otherwise—

The race took longer than she had predicted, and Katarina didn't get to Max's hospital room until six-thirty. It was pointless to think about returning to Capri that night; the last boat, the slow ferry, was leaving Naples at 7:40 pm.

Max appeared lifeless; only the monitor confirmed that he still had a heartbeat. She rested her head on Max's bed, closed her eyes, and prayed silently for his recovery. Then she prayed for strength to be a good mother to Anna, and she prayed for forgiveness for suspecting innocent people; lastly, she prayed that she would one day find a man like Max or Lorenzo, who would be there for her. When she opened her eyes, it was dark outside. The idea of spending the night in the hospital chair was not inviting, and she was hungry. She called Emilio; he was home.

"Of course, you must come here. I'll take you out for dinner. My home is your home; feel free to sleep wherever you like."

A PROPOSAL - MONDAY, SEPTEMBER 6

Katarina spent the night in the maid's room. The next morning, she and Emilio had breakfast together at Caffè Gambrinus before she took the metro to the Cardarelli Hospital. There was no change in Max; he was still unresponsive. Overcome with desperation, Katarina asked the nurse if she could speak to Max's doctor. Doctor Palumbo showed up an hour later. He seemed a serious and dedicated physician, but he had no information regarding Max's prognosis. *"Pazienza, ci vuole la pazienza* (Patience, one needs patience),'' was all he said, before he left in a hurry to continue his rounds.

Katarina had just received a new translation project; she sat down in a chair next to Max's bed and got to work on her iPad.

At twelve o'clock her cell phone rang; it was Emilio. "It's a gorgeous sunny day. Let's have lunch by the sea at the Borgo di Marechiaro. I'll pick you up in fifteen minutes outside the main hospital entrance." He didn't wait for her answer before he hung up.

Emilio pulled up in a dark grey Maserati, jumped out, and opened the door for her. They drove past the port of Mergelina and up the winding panoramic Via Posillipo along the coast of Naples, continuing down narrow picturesque streets to Marechiaro. Emilio left the car with a parking attendant.

When they walked into Cicciotto, it was obvious that Emilio was a longstanding valued customer of the restaurant; they were seated on the terrace under an umbrella at a table with an enchanting view.

They were sipping their espressos after lunch, when Katarina got the courage to ask the question that had been on her mind. "Were you and Camilla lovers?" she asked, as she looked across the shiny blue Mediterranean Sea; the saddle shaped island of Capri lay on the horizon.

"No, Camilla and I were close friends, but I confess to something else." Emilio tried in vain to make eye contact with Katarina. "I've been in love with you ever since we first met on Capri three years ago."

Katarina ignored his declaration. "What about the night Camilla died, you said you were alone, is that right?"

"I lied. I was with a girlfriend. I didn't want to tell you about her, since she doesn't mean anything to me."

"Really." She avoided looking at Emilio, fixing her gaze on the humpbacked peak of Vesuvius in the distance.

Emilio must have sensed Katarina's skepticism; he reached out and touched her hand. Katarina wanted to pull her hand away, but didn't.

"Hear me out—please. I've fallen in love with you. Maybe you don't love me now, but when we get to know each other better, you may grow to love me. I want to marry you, Katarina."

A million thoughts raced through Katarina's head as Emilio drove her from Marechiaro back to Cardarelli. Marriage? with Emilio?

"I'm flattered, and honored—" she started, looking over at Emilio after he stopped the car in front of the hospital entrance, "but—"

Emilio got out of the car and walked around to open the door for her. "I understand— It's all right, my dear—I just wanted you to know how I feel about you."

As the Maserati disappeared down the street, she followed it with her eyes, not knowing whether she felt relief or regret.

HOPE - MONDAY, SEPTEMBER 6

Max was not sure where he was, but he could see everything clearly. It's as if I'm watching myself from above—from the ceiling, he thought. He was lying on a narrow bed. Wires were strung between his body and monitoring equipment. Why am I in a hospital? Am I sick? he wondered. He didn't feel sick; in fact, he felt fantastic. Suddenly he was no longer seeing himself from above, but was lying motionless on the bed, unable to move. "Hey, get me out of here!" he cried out. But nobody came. A voice called his name, "Max! Max!" It was Tara's voice. "I'm here!" he cried, but she didn't hear him. "Over here!" he repeated, but it seemed she was too far away to hear him. A woman dressed in white appeared and kissed him. He recognized her—it was Camilla. "Come with me," she said.

Max opened his eyes and looked around the room; at first, he didn't know if he was alive or dead. Then he saw the monitoring equipment next to his bed and felt a sharp pain in his shoulder and knew he must be alive; but he found no pleasure in this realization. He closed his eyes and drifted back into unconsciousness.

The cables connecting him to the monitors broke, and he was lifted off the bed and pulled up through the roof out of the hospital. The freedom he felt was indescribable. Everything was stunningly bright; he was spun around and around in a spectacular light show . . . just above he saw the figure of Camilla standing with other bright luminous figures. He reached out to them, but they faded and slipped away, enveloped in a bright white mist, and he began spiraling down. "Wait, I don't want to go back!" he cried. "This is too beautiful. Wait for me, Camilla!"

Katarina walked into Max's hospital room. She went over to his bed and stroked his forehead. "How beautiful you are, you must live," she said in a whisper, with tears rolling down her cheeks. She bent down to kiss his closed eyes and his lips.

A familiar voice was calling him. "Come back, Max! I'm here, waiting for you! Come back!" It was Tara's voice.

"Tara, where are you?" Max shouted. Then he opened his eyes and blinked in surprise to see Katarina's worried face hovering over him.

"You are back!" Katarina cried.

Max closed his eyes and drifted into a deep sleep.

Katarina called the nurse to say that Max had been conscious. Half an hour later, Doctor Palumbo walked into the room. When he learned that Max had regained consciousness for about ten seconds, he patted Katarina on the shoulder and said, *"C'è la speranza, abbia pazienza* (There is hope, have patience)."

"C'è la speranza— C'è la speranza— C'è la speranza," Katarina sang to herself as she rushed to catch the last hydrofoil to Capri.

CHAPTER 37 - THE GETAWAY

"Good morning, how is our patient doing?" Doctor Palumbo asked, addressing the nurse attending to Max. "Good morning, Doctor. The patient is still unresponsive. His vital signs are stable."

Max wished the annoying voices would shut up and leave him alone, so he could get back to his beautiful visions. Suddenly a hand moved across his chest and shoulders, and he winced in pain.

"Ah, so you are awake then, Signor De Angelis?"

Max opened his eyes.

"Can you hear me?"

"Yes," Max said.

"Do not move your arm, it is in a sling to protect your shoulder."

"Where am I?"

"You are in Cardarelli Hospital in Naples. I'm Doctor Palumbo, your physician."

"Why am I here?"

"You've been unconscious for seven days. Do you recollect mountain climbing on the island of Capri?"

Max was confused. What was the doctor talking about? What was he doing here in a hospital?

Doctor Palumbo held Max's x-rays up to the light. "Your left collarbone is broken, right in the middle; most likely it happened when you fell."

The fog started to clear from Max's brain. "I sort of remember... eh... preparing... for a climb," he mumbled.

"Do you remember what day of the week you went climbing?"

"I am not sure... maybe... it was on Tuesday? What day is it today?"

"Today is also Tuesday, but Tuesday the 7th of September. Very good, very good, looks like your memory has not suffered."

Doctor Palumbo looked at the x-rays again. "Hopefully, no surgery will be necessary. Keep wearing the sling for ten days, and I recommend you rest for a few weeks, both physically and mentally, since you have just come out of a coma due to a traumatic brain injury. You don't want to take this situation lightly. Get plenty of bed rest and limit your exercise to short walks." Doctor Palumbo's stern voice made his recommendation nothing short of a command. "You must remain in the hospital for a minimum of three more days to make sure that you are stable and safe to leave after such a serious injury. You are very lucky to be alive. I wish you a good day." Doctor Palumbo scribbled some notes on Max's chart and left the room.

The nurse helped Max sit up in bed and gave him a glass of water. On the nightstand was his cell phone and charger; he picked up the phone and found it was fully charged. Checking his messages, there was one from his boss Bob; it was dated Monday, September 6th. He played the message on the phone speaker: "Max, I've not heard a word from you for seven days. Didn't I tell you to drop the case and get on a plane back to San Francisco? You don't even bother to pick up the damn phone when I call you. So where in the hell are you? You are fired, Max!"

So, he was fired. Max didn't give a damn. He might be dead for all Bob knew, and his boss had the audacity to fire him. Screw him!

Max felt a shooting pain in his shoulder. How the hell did I fall? he asked himself. He had taken every precaution.

Next, he called Katarina. She was thrilled to hear his voice and said she would come to the hospital right away. The nurse brought Max cookies and tea, and made him swallow some pills to alleviate his pain. Feeling drowsy, he soon fell asleep.

When he woke up, Katarina was sitting beside his bed.

"Welcome back to the world of the living!" she said as she helped him sit up, adjusting pillows behind his back.

He nodded weakly and took a sip of water.

"Just so you know, I pretended to be your fiancé, so I could visit you in the hospital. I was here every day you know—I was sick with worry. The hospital gave me your wallet, cell phone, and charger; your wallet is in my handbag."

Max managed a weak smile, "Fiancé, eh? Thanks for looking after me. I'm sorry to have caused you so much trouble."

"No trouble at all," Katarina said in a soft voice, knowing she would never forget the awful days and nights fearing for Max's life. "You're alive—and conscious, that's all that matters. You should call your sisters, they are very worried about you, they came to visit while you were in a coma."

"How did I end up in the hospital?"

Katarina told him the whole story of how she and Luigi had gone to the belvedere to look for him, and when Luigi suspected sabotage, he had called the police and Max had been rescued by helicopter.

"Thanks, Katarina."

"By the way, I told your friend Antonio at Hotel Gatto Bianco what happened to you and about Luigi worrying that it was due to sabotage. When I asked Chief Inspector Monti to investigate the possibility of sabotage, she said that Captain Arcuzzi had already checked it out, but had not found any evidence of it. I didn't call Raffi, thinking it would have caused him to cancel his business trip to come to your side. I was praying every day that you would regain your consciousness."

"Where is your amulet?" she added, placing her hand on his bare chest showing through the opening of the hospital gown.

Max's face darkened when he reached for the *curniciello* he always wore around his neck and it wasn't there. Katarina searched the room but found nothing. Max rang the nurse, who said she would ask around, but in the end, nobody had seen a necklace or an amulet.

"You told me you were not going to climb alone, Max. You could have died; you should have listened to me," Katarina said in an accusatory voice when they were alone.

"Maybe I should have. I don't know how it happened—I took every precaution. It's strange, but I seem to remember looking up and seeing a face just before I fell; it was vaguely familiar, but I don't remember who it was."

"Concentrate, maybe you will remember. Was it a man or a woman? Was the face young or old? Close your eyes, maybe it will come to you," Katarina suggested.

Doing as told, Max tried to remember the exact moment before he fell. The blurry image of a man's face appeared; it was not a young man's face, and if he had to guess, the man was Italian. Suddenly a vision came to him of a man sitting in the Piazzetta at Piccolo Bar and waving at him. "I got it, I got it!" he cried. "It's that mountain climbing guy, Ugo Vitale. Do you remember the man that talked to us outside Hotel Gatto Bianco on the night we were returning from Le Grottelle? He commented on the backpack I was carrying; it was the night before I went climbing."

"Do you think this guy Ugo Vitale could have sabotaged your climb in any way?"

"Well," Max replied, "I guess it's possible, but even if he did, he would have removed any traces of foul play by now. The question is, why would he want to sabotage me?"

His fingers were already busy tapping the browser on his cell phone, looking up Ugo Vitale. "Here's a picture of him climbing . . . and it appears his latest book was published three years ago. Now I remember why the name Vitale was familiar to me; if I'm not mistaken, I saw a couple of his books in Camilla's living room on my first visit. I wonder if they're still there—or if somebody took them during the break-in?"

"I can find out when I get back to the villa," Katarina said.

"It says here Vitale climbed Mount Everest, which I knew already—wait, here it says his wife died while climbing with her husband during a tragic accident in the Alps—just last summer!"

"Do you think Vitale was on Capri when Camilla died?" Katarina asked.

"Well, maybe not, because I remember his daughter Beatrice saying they had arrived on Capri on Thursday. That would have been August 26th, the night before the break-in at the villa. So, theoretically, Vitale could have been the one to search Camilla's house. Let me call Hotel Gatto Bianco."

After assuring Antonio that he was okay, Max expressed his suspicion of possible sabotage by Ugo Vitale. He also told him that the police seemed disinterested in investigating the possibility of sabotage. Max begged Antonio to give him the dates of when Vitale was staying in the hotel; Antonio initially was reluctant but relented. Ugo Vitale and his daughter had checked into the hotel on Saturday, August 14th, and checked out on Monday, August 16th. Then they had checked back in on Thursday, August 26th, and were still registered as guests at the hotel. Antonio also shared the good news that he had reserved Max's suite for him while he was in the hospital.

"Great, Antò, thanks. Please, I need your help, can you let me in by the back entrance of the hotel tonight? I'll call you with the exact time once I get back to Capri. And Antò, it's crucial that not a soul knows that I am on Capri when I return."

Katarina stared at Max in surprise as he put his phone down. "Tonight?"

"Yeh, we've got no time to waste. If Ugo Vitale is the one who sabotaged my climb, I've got to get back to Capri to look for that evidence before he realizes I'm alive and goes looking for it himself—that is, if he hasn't already done so, and I'm too late."

"You are in no state to go mountain climbing!" Katarina burst out.

Max thought about it and realized she was right; defeated, he sank back into the pillows. In a flash, it came to him: he would call his friends Paolo and Franco for help. They were two of the expert *Scoiattoli* climbers, the famous mountain climbers from Cortina.

Luckily, Paolo answered right away. Max explained the situation, and Paolo called him back half an hour later to confirm that he and his brother Franco would take a flight to Naples the following morning with all the necessary climbing equipment.

"I've to get out of here," Max said to Katarina, who had eagerly followed the conversation. "I can't wait three more days to get discharged from the hospital."

Katarina shook her head and said skeptically, "I don't know if that's a good idea in your condition; besides, I don't see your clothes here, or your shoes either. Are you going to leave the hospital in a hospital robe and slippers?"

"Mmm, you're right, but I don't have a choice. For now, I'll have to leave behind my clothes and Luigi's climbing shoes and his backpack with the gear, assuming the hospital has it. I don't want to raise suspicion by asking for it. Why don't you see if you can find a wheelchair somewhere in the hallway? I think it will look less suspicious if you wheel me out of the hospital; you can help me wrap this blanket around the gown."

Nobody paid any attention to Katarina as she wheeled Max down the long corridors and out the main entrance of Ospedale Antonio Cardarelli. Luckily, they found a taxi waiting at the curb and wasted no time getting in, leaving the wheelchair behind.

Max told the driver to step on it, as they were in a rush to catch the last ferry to Capri, from Porta di Massa; but on the way, they needed to make a short stop at the Forcella open-air market close to Piazza Garibaldi.

CHAPTER 38 - REJECTION

With the help of Katarina, Max removed the sling around his arm, changed out of the hospital gown, and pulled on a black pair of jeans, a black t-shirt and the sneakers he had bought at the Forcella market, then replaced the sling, while the taxi sped towards the port of Massa. Then he put on the cap and sunglasses he had bought.

"Wait here," he told Katarina, as they stepped out of the taxi at the port.

She watched him walk over and talk to the driver of a small truck in line at the ferry terminal. Returning, he took Katarina's arm and led her to the back of the truck. Katarina climbed in first, and since Max's shoulder was out of commission, she gave him a hand to pull him up.

"It's an advantage not having to pay, but I also don't want anyone to recognize me," Max said, as they sat down on a dirty blanket between the crates on the floor of the truck. "You never know who might know me around here; secrets are hard to keep on Capri. These guys are old friends. They won't tell anyone."

The disadvantage of concealing themselves was that they had to stay in the cramped, airless van during the eighty-minute ferry ride from Naples to Capri. Max fell asleep with his head on Katarina's shoulder; her neck began to ache, but she didn't mind.

The van dropped them off at Piazzetta Strina, the taxi drop-off point at the entrance to the town of Capri. Max checked the time on his cell phone—it was 21:40 (9:40 pm). Katarina and Max hurried up the steep stairs of the Rampe di Santa Teresa to reach the square in front of the Church of Santissimo Salvatore. They were relieved to find themselves alone in the small square, but took the precaution to climb to the top of the church steps to sit down out of view. Max swallowed one of the pain pills he had managed to buy at the Forcella pharmacy; he tried to soothe his aching shoulder by holding his elbow with the opposite hand.

"Do you think anybody saw us?" Katarina asked.

"No." Max shook his head.

He removed his sunglasses and black baseball cap; his hair fell loose in a wild disarray. Katarina thought Max looked surprisingly good for someone who had been in a coma for a week.

"Santa Teresa is the *quartiere* where I grew up, you know. Would you believe I was once an altar boy in this church?" Max's voice had a touch of nostalgia. "This baroque church was founded by a woman from Capri at a time when nuns were not even allowed to sit in the church. Amazing, isn't it? The nuns used a secret entrance from the adjoining nunnery to enter the church and hid themselves in the gallery during services."

"Yes, truly amazing what those women managed to do," Katarina said. "They sure knew where to build their convent. This view is unforgettable."

They sat in silence admiring the view of the bay of Naples spread out before them. The night sky was clear, and the air felt pleasantly cool after being cooped up in the hot airless truck. Katarina draped her cashmere sweater over her shoulders.

She secretly wished that Max would kiss her; the warmth of his body pressed close to hers was intoxicating. The idea came to her to invite Max up to the villa for a plate of cheese and a glass of wine on the roof terrace.

"What do you say we go to my—"

Max interrupted her: "I'd better get back to the hotel for some rest."

She was unprepared for his next words: "Don't wait for me to call tomorrow; the Cortina boys and I will handle the situation from here. And don't call me, I'll be too busy. I'll call you when I can. Good night."

"Alright, Max, good night," Katarina said, bewildered by his brusqueness.

After calling Antonio to tell him he would be at the back entrance of Hotel Gatto Bianco in two minutes, Max hurried up the side alley of the church and disappeared through the Traversa Santa Teresa archway.

Katarina walked alone through the medieval arch on Via Castello, and stopped halfway up the road to rest and take in the view. The town of Capri lay under the bright canopy of millions of stars; a waxing gibbous moon adorned the crest of Monte Tuoro.

By the time she reached the villa, she was feeling sad and confused. Max had given her the brush off—what was that all about? His behavior seemed ungrateful—almost cruel, after all the long days in Naples waiting at the hospital and worrying that he might not come out of the coma, and then helping him to escape. She was overcome by loneliness. Her body ached to be hugged and it took her a long time to fall asleep.

CHAPTER 39 - A PLAN

WEDNESDAY, SEPTEMBER 8

The buzz of the alarm clock at six in the morning cut through Max's sleep like a chainsaw. For a moment, he wasn't sure if he was still asleep, in the middle of a torturous nightmare. The persistent throbbing pain in his collarbone felt like someone was hitting him over and over again with a sledgehammer. He groped blindly for his cell phone and silenced the alarm. If he went back to sleep, the pain would disappear.

Just as he was drifting back to sleep, the telephone rang on his nightstand. He fumbled to pick it up with his eyes still closed.

"Listen, you said you wanted to know as soon as Mr. Vitale appeared; well he is having his coffee now in the breakfast room." Renato's muffled voice was barely audible.

Max held the receiver in one hand as he stumbled out of bed, and bent over, as the phone cord was barely twenty centimeters long. "OK, if he leaves the hotel, call me, will you?"

His left shoulder and arm were useless from the broken collarbone, and his legs could barely hold him up; they shook like leaves. What the hell's happened to the muscles in my legs? Max winced in pain as he fumbled to put on his jeans and a t-shirt. Swearing under his breath, he pulled on the cheap sneakers he had bought at the Forcella market; luckily, they didn't need lacing. Stuffing his wallet and cell phone into the pocket of his jeans, he headed for the door, then returned to the bedroom to grab the baseball hat and sunglasses he had bought to disguise himself. As the door closed behind him, he heard the phone ring; ignoring it, he dashed down the stairs and through the lobby to the front desk.

Upon seeing Max, Renato raised an index finger and pointed toward the double doors of the front entrance; Ugo had left the hotel.

Max scrambled clumsily down the front steps and got to the hotel's arcade in time to catch a glimpse of the back of the man he assumed to be Ugo disappearing around the corner. Hurrying to the end of the arcade, he peeped out and saw the man walking down Via Vittorio Emanuele; he followed him.

The street was deserted at that hour; the boutique windows lining the street mirrored the rosy glow of sunrise. Max kept a bit of distance from Ugo, now and then taking advantage of the shop entrances to hide, in case Ugo looked back.

Ugo seemed unaware that he was being followed as he continued along Via Camerelle. The brim of his crumpled beige beach hat was pulled low over the forehead; his eyes were fixed on the deserted pedestrian road in front of him. A bulging black backpack was hanging from his shoulders. His steps were short and measured, but quick and efficient. Max summoned all his strength as he dashed between hiding places to keep up with Ugo.

Max kept a safe distance until the end of Via Camerelle, where Ugo turned left. Ignoring the pain in his shoulder, Max sprinted to the corner and up the incline towards the Evangelical Church. Hiding in the doorway of the church cellar, he saw Ugo continue on Via Tragara. He waited for a minute before following him; it was going to be trickier on Via Tragara, as there were few hiding places between the hotels and villas.

What if Ugo is heading to Belvedere delle Noci to look for Camilla's goddam purse? Max asked himself. What can I do about it? Max knew that he had no right to try to stop him; he had no evidence of any foul play.

Max's mind raced to come up with a plan.

Suddenly Ugo stopped, turned around, and headed straight towards him. Max's heart skipped a beat; there was no time to escape. In a split second, he ducked into a space beside a gate pillar. Damn it! he thought. I'm such a fucking idiot. Ugo is bound to see me.

Max leaned against the gate and pulled the baseball cap over his sunglasses, hoping that Ugo wouldn't notice him; he would become invisible by blending into the black iron gate. Miracle of miracles, when he leaned against the gate, it gave way and swung open. In the blink of an eye, he was inside, quickly closing the gate behind him. Thank God! Now what? he wondered.

This would be an excellent time to find out whether he had any little gray brain cells left after being in a vegetative state for a week. If Ugo hadn't seen him, then he must have changed his mind about something, Max reasoned. Was he was going back to the hotel, or if he had decided to take a different route to Belvedere delle Noci, which way was he going? There were two other ways to get there. Ugo could turn right at the Evangelical Church and go up Via Cercola, then continue on Via Matermania and Via Dentecala. Or instead of taking Via Cercola, he could take Via Tuoro to the end, and from there, climb the steep path towards Monte Tuoro (the "Semaforo" they called it), and descend to Belvedere delle Noci.

Max knew where he was; on the grounds of the enormous and impressive Villa Capricorno, constructed around 1890. As a child, Max had often sneaked into the garden when the gate was left open and the gardener was too busy to notice him. He liked to play among the exotic oriental plants. Now the columned walkways, patios, and pergolas, and the villa itself were in a state of disrepair, giving it an air of past grandeur, and making it even more beautiful in Max's eyes.

Max went through a long walkway flanked by columns to reach the villa's massive main gate. The gate faced the road that ran past Ruggiero's nursery and led up to Via Tuoro bordering the upper garden of Villa Capricorno. Max quickly found the hidden button, and the gate swung open from the inside; when he peeped out, he saw Ugo hurrying up the road and turning right on Via Tuoro. So, just as he had imagined, Ugo was likely headed towards Belvedere delle Noci.

Outside the gate of Villa Capricorno, he stopped as the songs of hundreds of birds in the villa's giant old trees filled the clear morning air. He didn't move, just listened, recognizing the various songs of the migrating birds that summered on Capri; he knew the distinctive song of each species from childhood. The birds' cheerful chirping calmed him, and he realized he had been an idiot to chase after Ugo. He had been running around like a chicken without a head. If his mother had been around, she would have said: *"A capa, 'a capa Massimì, addó' sta'* (Massimì, have you lost your head)?"

Max had no plan as to what he would do if he followed Ugo to Belvedere delle Noci. How could he stop Ugo from climbing once he got there? Max struggled to get his damaged little brain cells functioning. His head throbbed. The pain of his broken collarbone felt—if that was possible— even worse. As much as he hated taking any medicine, he must get back to the hotel and take a couple of those pills, soon—very soon.

Out of the blue, it came to him; he finally had an idea. The pain pills would have to wait.

Chapter 40 - Deception

"Renato, this is Max. Please transfer me to Signorina Beatrice Vitale," Max said, speaking into his cell phone as he hurried back towards Hotel Gatto Bianco; this time, by way of the Reginaldo Giuliani Road above Ruggiero's nursery.

"You must be kidding, it isn't even seven o'clock. Even the roosters are asleep on Capri," Renato whispered. "Signorina Beatrice usually comes down to breakfast with her father around ten."

"This is no joke." Max searched for the right words; he might just have to lie a little, since it was possible that Renato was going to listen in on his telephone conversation with the girl. "Her father may be in danger of having a climbing accident. It is imperative that I talk to her right away." It wasn't a total lie, Max reasoned to himself; he wouldn't deceive Renato if it were avoidable.

Renato didn't seem convinced, but transferred the call to Beatrice Vitale's room.

"Helloo Beeatriisce, I'm a veery clouse friend of your faather—"
Max had added an American accent to top off his female
impersonation.

"Who?" Beatrice sounded as if she were still asleep.

"W-well, we have not met —yet, but you must listen to me veery
cayerfully," Max continued in a sugary-sweet, high-pitched voice.
"Sweeetheart, your faather's life is in graave danger, I think he's
risking his life. . . he has suffered soo soo much, now he deeesperately
needs YOU to stop him."

"What are you saying, I don't understand—"

Beatrice sounded drugged more than half asleep, Max thought.
"You must get dressed immediately and go to Belvedere dellei
Noocai, your father is in danger; only YOU can convince him to stop
the climb. Go nauooow, it's a matter of life and DEATH."

"Go where?? My father's life is in danger? What do you mean?"

Max continued, "Go to Belvedere dellei Noocai. Go down to the
hotel desk; they will tell you hauow to get there."

He ended the call, then at once redialed Hotel Gatto Bianco.
"Renato, believe me, this is a matter of life and death. Yes, I know
the voice sounded crazy—but trust me, I beg of you, there was a
good reason for it. I'll explain later. Please, do whatever you can to
get her out of the hotel as soon as possible. I will handle it from
there."

Twenty-two precious minutes passed while Max waited
impatiently in the arcade of Hotel Gatto Bianco with the hope of
casually intercepting Beatrice. Enough time to regret he hadn't taken
a chance and gone back up to his room for the pain pills. He was
well aware that his plan hinged on the cooperation of Beatrice as his
unwitting accomplice. Max knew that he had no proof of anything.
Ugo may indeed have killed Camilla and attempted to kill Max as
well, but he had no evidence to prove it. But if Ugo was at that
moment preparing to climb the cliff at Belvedere delle Noci, then
some evidence MUST be there. If Max's hunch was correct, he had
to stop the Neapolitan mountain climber before he found the
evidence and destroyed it.

Beatrice finally made an appearance, slowly descending the stairs to the arcade as if she were sleepwalking. She was wearing a crumpled pink summer dress; her large Bambi eyes were tear-filled, and her long black corkscrew curls were in disarray.

Max managed to put himself squarely in her path. "Lovely day for an early morning stroll, isn't it Signorina Beatrice?"

"Sorry, I've no time to talk— How do you know my name?" Beatrice tried to pass him. Max spun around to walk through the arcade alongside her.

"I'm a friend of your father. Don't you remember me? We were introduced in the Piazzetta. Where are you headed in such a hurry? I'm going for a walk myself. Maybe we're going the same way?"

The girl burst into tears. "I've no idea where I'm going, someplace called Belvedere delle No. . . noc—"

"Ah, Belvedere delle Noci, I know exactly where it is. The belvedere has an impressive view from the top of its incredibly steep and dangerous cliffs."

Max gently took hold of the girl's upper arm; he was worried that she might slip, as she was obviously upset and disoriented. "Please permit me to escort you; that way you will not get lost."

"*Grazie*," the girl said in a tearful voice.

They passed the tennis courts on Vicolo Sella Orta, turned right on Via Fuorlovado, and went up the steep Via Croce. Max continued to steady the girl with a firm but gentle grip on her slender arm. Even so, Beatrice struggled to climb up the steep incline; she grabbed onto the handrail at the side of the footpath, as if to pull herself uphill. No doubt her choice of footwear made it even more challenging; she wore little golden sandals with a heel, hardly designed for hiking the hills of Capri.

"Tell me a bit about yourself," Max started, "What is it that you like to do more than anything else?"

Beatrice dried her eyes with the back of her hand before answering, "I like to read—and—sometimes—to write."

"Really," Max tried to hide his surprise, "so you want to be a writer, like your father?"

"No, I don't want to be a writer," she snapped. "Papa was never happy writing his books. Mama loved to write; she wrote all the time, but what good did it do her? She never published anything. She told me Papa said it wasn't any good and threw everything out. I don't get it, why even bother to write at all?"

"How did she know it wasn't any good, did she try to publish it?" Max asked. He wasn't interested, but he didn't wish to upset her by mentioning her mother's tragic death—at least not for the moment; that would come later.

"No, Mama said a woman's role was to support her husband. She said one artist in a family was one too many, meaning my father. He's not so easy to get along with. Mama wanted many children, but they only had me." Beatrice sighed. "Frankly, I never understood why Mama was writing so frequently—I mean, when she wasn't cooking or cleaning or taking care of me."

By now Max's shoulder joint was throbbing with excruciating pain; he wished he had an icepack and a couple of the pain pills back in his room. He was getting impatient with their slow pace up the hill. Max knew his plan to stop Ugo had to work; it was the only plan he had. It was time to start preparing Beatrice for her upcoming performance; he changed the topic of the conversation to rock climbing. "Well your father enjoys writing those books that make him famous, and he loves climbing mountains, right?"

She was suddenly more animated. "Yes, Papa preferred climbing peaks; he was only happy when he was climbing. He never liked being in Naples. Our happiest times were in the mountains." Then she added, in a sad little voice that would have broken anybody's heart, "That was a long time ago."

Passing the Croce intersection, the road flattened out, but the long climb up Via Matermania loomed ahead. The familiar rumbling sound of an electrical delivery cart caused Max to turn his head. Was this the answer to his prayer? Wonder of wonders, it was Gregorio, the pizza maker from Le Grottelle. He was sitting tall and proud on the seat of an electric cart delivering fresh supplies to the restaurant.

Max raised his hand to stop him. "Please, Gregorio, could you give us a lift?"

"Hop on."

They squeezed in, shoulder to shoulder, next to Gregorio on the hard and narrow bench, the only seat of the delivery cart. Beatrice was in the middle; she glanced up at Gregorio towering over her, and he smiled kindly and winked. She blushed.

The sun rose, warming their faces and promising a hot day, despite it being September.

They jumped off the cart at the place where the miniscule chapel with the *Madonnina del Divino Amore* split the road. Gregorio continued on Via Arco Naturale, and Beatrice and Max headed down Via Dentecala, the road high above the Matermania cave and Cala del Fico.

Max decided it was time to direct the conversation to his purpose. "So, why are you going to Belvedere delle Noci?"

Beatrice's tears started to flow again. Good, Max thought, tears were not bad for his purpose.

"Papa packed his climbing gear last night—he said he might do a small climb. When I asked if I could come along and watch, he said no—that I needed to rest. He believes that I have a mineral deficiency and that is why I'm so often tired," she said.

"Do you sleep a lot?"

"Yeah, I do. Papa doesn't let me go out by myself at night. He says, 'the climate,' as he calls it, at night on Capri isn't suitable for young girls. When he's on Capri, Papa likes to go out for a stroll in the evening, so after dinner, he gives me the vitamin pills, and I go to sleep. I usually wake up around ten in the morning, and then we have breakfast together."

"I see." Max was skeptical about those vitamin pills. She had seemed almost drugged to him earlier that morning, and her father had managed to slip out without waking Beatrice. Then he wondered about the night of Camilla's death: Had Ugo drugged his daughter?

"Maybe Papa has a girlfriend. I received a strange scary telephone call from a woman this morning—" Beatrice continued.

She sighed heavily. "He has been depressed and angry for so long, even before my mother's—passing away. It isn't any fun to be around him; I can tell you that. It isn't good for a man his age to be alone." Her voice had the weary tone of a grownup, not a teenage girl.

Max cleared his throat; he had to risk it: "Maybe he has lost his girlfriend—as well."

"We must hurry!" she cried. "I'm so worried about Papa climbing—after that strange telephone call. What if that woman was telling the truth? —What if my father is in danger?"

"Yes, Belvedere delle Noci is a dangerous place to climb; I almost got killed climbing there myself and ended up in a coma. It's a bloody miracle I'm alive." Max was surprised at the emotion in his voice; he had no need to fake it.

"Hurry, get me to the belvedere—we must run!" Beatrice pleaded.

She took off ahead of Max. Max thought her attempt at running in her fancy sandals was short of pathetic, but he admired her guts. With her long skinny legs, she reminded him of a bolting gazelle. Max felt conflicted; guilty that he had scared the poor motherless girl, but glad that she was now rushing to find her father. The persistent throbbing pain in his collar bone and shoulder worsened as he labored to catch up with her.

Via Dentecala ended in Piazzetta delle Noci, the first and largest of the three terraced lookouts. An older woman was kneeling in front of a *Madonnina,* set into a niche of the rock, to place a bouquet of flowers at the feet of the small statue of the Virgin Mary. She was short and a bit stocky with thick arms. Her flower-patterned dress reached to her calves and two long grey braids fell down her back.

"Signora Immaculata Ferrara!" Max was jubilant. "How wonderful to see you again. Heaven must have sent you; this little Signorina desperately needs your help."

He continued, after taking a breath. "This is Beatrice. Her father is climbing alone at the Belvedere delle Noci. We must stop him. You know how dangerous it is there. This dear girl has already lost her mother to a climbing accident. Please come with us, we must save him!"

"Of course, Max – I will help you if I can," Immaculata nodded as he helped her to her feet.

"Where to now?" Beatrice asked impatiently.

Max pointed to the broad incline of steps just ahead of them; they would have to climb the steps to reach the path towards the third belvedere. Beatrice removed her sandals and started running barefoot, a shoe dangling from each hand.

How did this little gazelle know the way? Max wondered, wincing in pain as he trotted behind, trying to steady the left arm with his right hand.

Immaculata, in thick-soled sensible shoes, followed as fast as she could for her 79 years, now and then stopping to catch her breath.

Beatrice stopped at the plateau of Piano delle Noci, looking lost and bewildered. Max was close behind her. He sent her down the path so that she would arrive before him at Belvedere delle Noci— in case Ugo had not yet started climbing; Max didn't want to confront him. He followed Beatrice at a distance.

"Daddy, Daddy! Come up, come back up!" Beatrice screamed, while leaning far over the railing, her tears streaming uncontrollably down her cheeks.

Max grabbed her arm while trying to stay back to avoid being seen by Ugo from below.

"How far down is he?"

She ignored Max. "Daddy, Daddy! I need you. I need you!" she sobbed hysterically.

Max did not hear a response, only the distant shrill cries of seagulls.

"Daddy, Daddy . . ." was all she managed between sobs.

"Can you see him?"

She shook her head.

Max didn't know what else he could do; he hoped Immaculata would arrive soon. He waited impatiently, holding onto Beatrice's arm for what seemed like an eternity. Then he got an idea.

"I can see your father is using the same bolt that I drilled into the rock wall. And I can see the anchor leg carabiner attached to it, but the rope running through it has frayed. It might break, and your father could fall and DIE."

She bought Max's lie and screamed at the top of her lungs, "DADDY!!!"

Immaculata entered the terrace while Beatrice was screaming and took charge at once; she leaned her head over the railing, wisely managing not to touch the fence with her body.

"YOU. Get up here. NOW!" her voice was loud and commanding.

There was only silence below.

"NOW!" the old woman commanded. "This little girl has lost her mother, she needs her father. NOW."

"DADDY—DADDY!!" Beatrice's shrill voice could have awakened the dead.

Max could not imagine any father being immune to such suffering.

Finally, Ugo's voice shot up from below, "OK—OK, coming up."

The words were loud and clear; they were sweet music to Max's ears. Perhaps Ugo hadn't gotten far enough down the cliff to find the purse. Max could only hope so.

CHAPTER 41 - PUNTA TRAGARA

Max didn't stay around to witness the wrath of Ugo, who was bound to find out that Max had lured Beatrice to the belvedere by a hoax telephone call. There was also no time to lose. Max had to be at Hotel Gatto Bianco to meet the Scoiattoli climbers from Cortina; he decided to return by taking the old hunting trail from Belvedere delle Noci to Via Pizzolungo.

The last words Max heard in the distance, as he was hurrying away, were from Signora Immaculata Ferrara scolding Ugo. "We have already had one tragic death at this place, as well as a serious accident. Take your daughter with you; go and enjoy the beautiful life the good Lord has given you."

The pain in Max's collarbone was excruciating. He barely managed to stop himself from screaming and his legs were shaking from exhaustion, as his muscles had atrophied to an alarming degree during his week's confinement to a hospital bed. Just concentrate, he told himself—take one step at a time. The irregular stone steps were steep; some were missing, some damaged. Why did the Romans make their steps so bloody high? he mused. Their legs couldn't have been longer than mine.

When Max was a boy, he had gone quail hunting on this trail. To make a blowgun, he had "borrowed" a few of his mother's sewing needles and stopped by the electrician's shop to get a piece of plastic electrical tubing. Max would stick a needle into a spitball of wadded paper and load it into the tube. He became adept at using his blowgun to kill quails for his mother to cook. One day, however, when he picked up a felled bird, it was still alive. The tiny bird's heart was beating fast as he held it in his palm to examine the wound; only the skin was nicked. He closed his fist gently around the bird and held it toward the sky, then he spread open his hand and released it: the bird lifted its wings and flew away. From that day on, he never hunted again.

Max stopped and sat down on a stone step to rest. His keen eyes caught a pair of Peregrine falcons gliding from the precipice towards the sea. Ah, at least there was one couple left of the nearly extinct birds of prey on the island. They built their nests just below Villa La Falconetta, named after them. When a third falcon came swooping down to join the two, it filled him with hope for their future; how beautiful it was to watch the three of them.

Max got up and continued down the old trail; the Scoiattoli brothers would be arriving at the hotel soon. He decided that he would personally pay for their expenses. Max suddenly realized that he had lost his job and wouldn't get paid for the investigation he was doing now. No matter, the important thing was to find out the truth. At least I'm free, he thought, not as free as those falcons, but all the same free—at least for now.

The trail ended at Via Pizzolungo; he turned right. Shortly after, he passed the desolate "haunted" Villa Solitario and came up on Villa Monacone, named for its view of the Monacone islet, part of the Faraglioni rock formation. When he came to this villa, Max always thought of Thomas Mann's' daughter Monika, who had lived thirty-two years of her life in Villa Monacone with Antonio Spadaro, a Capri fisherman who made miniature wooden ships in bottles for tourists.

Max had met Monika Mann years ago on one of her solitary walks along Via Pizzolungo. She was sitting on a bench at a viewing point at dusk. The sun had set early; the January temperature was barely above freezing. He sat down beside her on the bench, and they struck up a conversation.

Monika Mann first talked about her love of Capri and its natural beauty, and spoke about her life as a writer. Then she confided in Max that she was Jewish and had fled Europe in 1940. She had survived a shipwreck in the Atlantic Ocean caused by a German submarine attack by clinging to a piece of wood for twenty hours. She paused for a moment before finishing her story. Then she explained that she had lost her husband in that wreck; three times she had heard her Hungarian husband, Jenö Lányi, call out her name before he went under.

They sat together in silence looking out at the sea. The last thing she said to Max was: "My lover Antonio Spadaro died last month; my time on Capri has ended, and I'm leaving in a couple of months."

Max wondered if Capri and Antonio the fisherman had become Monika Mann's lifesaver. Would he, like Monika, find his lifesaver somewhere, with someone? He knew that a job alone would never be a lifesaver for him. Could he live on Capri—or anywhere without love?

As Max started the final ascent up Via Pizzolungo towards Via Tragara, Hotel Punta Tragara appeared in all its glory. The terracotta colored hotel, hovering high above his head, seemed as if it was sculpted out of the rock face.

The sight of the hotel pierced Max's heart like a thorn. This was where he and Tara had spent eight glorious days and nights together on their honeymoon. Room number 38. They had chosen the room because it was the least expensive; it was tiny with no balcony, but there was a spectacular view from the wide window. Max recalled every detail of the little room, the red color of the walls, the red tiles in the bathroom; how exotic their little love nest had seemed to them – how perfect.

The sound of crickets grew louder as he walked up the last part of Via Pizzolungo. On his honeymoon, the rhythmic high-pitched clicking of the crickets had seemed sensual, even erotic to him. It was as if the cricket's chirping accelerated as their bodies inflamed with passion, creating background music for their ecstatic lovemaking. That was ten years ago, in September, but he remembered it as if it were only yesterday.

As soon as he had ascended the path and entered the square in front of Hotel Punta Tragara, his vision blurred and the tops of the Faraglioni rocks started to spin. The pain in his collarbone added to a throbbing headache and now—this heartache. His legs started to tremble, threatening to collapse; he had to sit down and rest for a moment.

There were four benches in Tragara Square facing the sea, but all of them were occupied. The bench underneath a gnarled oak tree had a single occupant; a woman with a long blond ponytail. I must be hallucinating, Max thought, as the ponytail and the nape of the woman's neck looked just like Tara's. Then he remembered that he hadn't had anything to eat or to drink since he left the hospital last night; he felt dizzy and utterly exhausted. He staggered over to the bench, collapsed into the seat, and passed out.

CHAPTER 42 - LA CONCHIGLIA

WEDNESDAY, SEPTEMBER 8

When Max opened his eyes, he was lying on his back on a bench looking straight into the deep blue eyes of—TARA.

Tara seemed as surprised to see Max as he was to see her. She was leaning over him; and despite the tears in her eyes, her face was beaming with the most radiant smile he had ever seen. Am I still in a coma—or dreaming? Max wondered. He reached out and touched the back of her pale slender hand. A small electrical current ran up his arm. He was awake!

What's Tara doing on Capri? And what is she smiling about?

He shut his eyes again; he could not bear looking at Tara, knowing they were no longer together. It was too much for him; his chest tightened, and he felt as if he was being strangled. When he found the courage to open his eyes, he looked straight into her eyes, and this time he let himself drown in their bottomless depths.

Tara burst into laughter. How he loved her laugh; it was big, real, and deep.

Was she laughing at him? How ridiculous he must appear laying helplessly on a public park bench. He struggled to sit up and winced from the pain; he had forgotten about his left shoulder. Tara gently restrained him by placing her hands on his wrists.

"Take it easy," she said. "I know about the accident."

"How . . ." His voice trailed away.

"Why . . ." he continued, but was not able to form a sentence.

Tara said, humorously mocking him: "Just the Max I remember, you still want to know everything, like right away, don't you?"

◆ ◆ ◆

Back in his suite at Hotel Gatto Bianco, Max swallowed two painkillers with half a bottle of mineral water and collapsed onto the bed, waiting impatiently for a bit of relief from the relentless throbbing pain in his left shoulder.

The words of Doctor Palumbo at Cardarelli Hospital came to him: *You must remain in the hospital for a minimum of three more days to make sure that you are stable and safe to leave after such a serious injury.* Well, Max reflected, guess I didn't take Doctor Palumbo's advice.

The hotel phone rang; it was Antonio at the reception desk.

"Hi Max, Renato told me what happened this morning, how you lured Signorina Beatrice out of bed, you rascal," he said, laughing.

275

"Your friends from Cortina have a message for you; they have arrived in Naples and are departing for Capri on the 11:35 hydrofoil. They tried to call you, but your cell phone may be turned off."

Max reached into his jeans pocket for his cell phone; the screen was blank; the battery was drained. "Thanks, Antò, I'll tell you about everything later, what time is it?"

It was already a little past noon. Max knew he could not afford to waste any time. The boys should arrive at the hotel around one o'clock. He reminded Antonio to make sure that no one knew he was in the hotel or even on Capri, except his friends from Cortina. Luckily, Antonio trusted him; he and Antonio went a long way back as friends.

"And Antò, can you send me up a triple espresso, some sugar, and a bottle of mineral water? We will talk later. And please, let me know if you see Signor Ugo Vitale or his daughter."

Max stepped carefully into the shower. He managed to shampoo his hair and bathe with one hand; then he shaved and put on a clean t-shirt—navy blue with light blue borders, like all his t-shirts. He preferred to keep things simple. Using one hand, he threw the clothes and fake Nikes he had bought at the Forcella market into a drawer and managed to pull on his skinny, low-waist Italian summer jeans and his own track shoes, while he made a mental note that he would have to replace the climbing equipment and climbing shoes he had borrowed from Luigi. He still had the use of his hands, which was good news; though, better to avoid using his left shoulder. To protect it, he slipped his arm into the sling from the hospital.

Max felt something was not right; he touched the notch between his collarbones, recalling that his *curniciello* was missing. Had it been stolen by one of the staff at the hospital? That wouldn't be too unusual in a case where the patient's death had been noted. He had looked at the medical chart himself indicating that he had been pronounced dead. Naturally, if he were dead, he wouldn't have any use for the necklace.

He poured four packets of sugar into the triple espresso that the kind porter had brought up to his room and sipped it slowly. The porter Abeysinghe Ampitiya Rajapakse Gedera was known by all on

Capri as Alberto, but back in his homeland Sri Lanka, he was known as "The Ambassador to Capri" for all the assistance he offered his compatriots on the island.

Ah, the taste of good espresso! He was feeling a lot better. The pain pills were starting to take effect. Max became aware of the demands of his stomach; he was starving. The idea of getting some decent food was tempting. Max's knew in his head that he should stay put and not risk an encounter with Ugo, but his tummy used a different logic. There wasn't much time before the Cortina boys would arrive, and they might want some lunch as well.

Max pulled on the baseball cap he had bought at the Forcella market in Naples and tucked his unruly black curls behind the ears. Luckily, he still had his black Maui Jim sunglasses. Three minutes later he was inside his favorite take-out, Capri Pasta.

Further up the alley of Via Canale, he made a quick stop at the supermarket cooperative to pick up a bottle of red Aglianico wine from the hills of Vesuvius, and a bottle of Ferrarelle sparkling water. Back down Via Canale, he made a final stop at the bakery for the last crucial items: a crusty loaf of *sciuscella* and some *taralucci* (the small round delicious local crackers that are boiled before baking).

Turning the corner into the crowded Via Le Botteghe, he spotted Ugo and Beatrice coming straight towards him. Max slipped into the side gallery and ducked into La Conchiglia bookstore; he didn't think they had seen him.

"Can I help you?" asked the owner, Ausilia, by way of greeting.

"I'm just browsing," Max said curtly. He picked up a book at random and pretended to look at it; through the store window he watched Ugo and Beatrice walk into the pharmacy across from the bookstore.

"Do you read a lot?" Ausilia's pleasant voice expressed a note of irony. Max caught it, as few things ever escaped him, but he didn't answer.

Some minutes passed before Ugo and Beatrice came out of the pharmacy and continued on Via delle Botteghe towards the Piazzetta. Good, Max thought. That way I'll be able to beat them back to the hotel by taking Vico S. Tommaso. He quickly paid for the book he had pretended to read; it seemed like the right thing to do. As he opened the door to leave, he turned towards Ausilia to say goodbye.

She smiled broadly and said, "Good day and good reading. Maybe you would enjoy the book even more if you tried to read it right-side up."

CHAPTER 43 - THE SCOIATTOLI ARRIVE

Max reclined his weary body on the big bed in the Kennedy suite. When the hell would the Cortina brothers get to the hotel? Did the bloody hydrofoil break down? It was after two o-clock and Max's impatient nature had gotten the better of him.

The book Max had bought at La Conchiglia was lying on the nightstand; it was titled *L'isola del Dio Nascosto* (*The Island of the Hidden God*), written by Riccardo, Ausilia's husband. He read a few pages to distract himself from his speculations about the likelihood of the Cortina brothers finding evidence related to Camilla Kallberg's death. He could just imagine what the boys would think when they found out they were going to "rescue" a purple evening purse.

Why did the author Riccardo say that on Capri, God was hidden? Max wondered. Was there even a God? If there was a God, then Max felt he must have been hiding from him since his divorce. He slammed the book down on the bedside table; it was impossible to concentrate.

His thoughts turned to the dream in the hospital in which Tara had appeared to him. What did it mean that right now, she was there on Capri?

Tara had been raised by her Buddhist grandmother, who named her after the mythical Goddess Tara. Tara told Max that there is only one Goddess Tara, but that she has different attributes. White Tara protects and brings long life, inner peace, and spiritual acceptance. Green Tara is a fierce goddess who overcomes obstacles and saves one from danger. Tara is also an archetype of inner wisdom; one that guides and protects us as we navigate the depths of the unconscious mind, and helps to transform consciousness into a personal journey of freedom.

Max hadn't paid much attention to what Tara had tried to teach him during their marriage; he was usually preoccupied with work, even when he was at home. Now, after his accident and nearly dying, Tara's spiritual philosophy began to feel more relevant to him.

He thought about the last time he had seen her in San Francisco and what had happened between them that night, but quickly turned his attention to the moment a few hours ago when he was lying on a bench under an oak tree gazing into Tara's eyes.

◆ ◆ ◆

"Just the Max I remember. You still want to know everything, like right away, don't you?" Tara had said, while her hands were ever so lightly massaging his shoulder. At that moment, he had no pain in his collarbone, no anxiety in his stomach, no thorn in his heart.

Max felt he could have stayed on that bench at Punta Tragara forever, enjoying the magic touch of Tara's hands, but then her eyes darkened, and she removed her hands and said, "When I called my neighbor Betty-Anne from India last week to ask about Principessa, I found out that our precious cat had gone missing. Fortunately, Betty-Anne's phone number was on Principessa's collar tag; someone found her and brought her home. Betty-Anne is busy fattening her up."

She sighed and continued: "It feels like ages since I last held Principessa; I miss her adorable little face so terribly much." Tara's eyes misted over. "Betty-Anne also told me that you had called her to say that you'd received an assignment while on vacation here that had delayed your return; she said she'd take care of Principessa until one of us gets back. Then I decided—" Tara paused.

Max waited, filled with wonder as she spoke. Tara's eyes were mesmerizing.

Tara looked up at the twisted oak branches above their head. "I decided to come and look for you here on Capri. I flew from Kerala in India via Dubai and Milan, and got here two days ago. I called your cell phone yesterday from my lodging at Villa Helios, but there was no answer, and I didn't leave a message. Then I called your sister Mona, who told me you were in a coma at the Cardarelli Hospital in Naples. I went there at once."

Max couldn't believe what Tara was telling him. Why did she come from India to look for me? he asked himself. He had so many "whys" to ask her, he hardly knew where to start.

"When I got to Cardarelli Hospital and finally found the pavilion and the room you were supposed to be in—that hospital is a labyrinth; you had disappeared. The nurse called a doctor, I think his name was Palumbo, and he was furious. He said you'd left against medical advice."

Max felt guilty; the good Doctor Palumbo, he had meant well.

"I came back to Capri and called Mona again, and she was shocked that you'd left the hospital. She was also glad, since that meant you were no longer in a coma. She said you'd been staying at Hotel Gatto Bianco before the accident. When I went there to look for you last night, the receptionist told me you weren't registered at the hotel."

Ah, my faithful friends, Max thought, acting exactly as he had instructed them.

"So here I am on Capri!" Tara threw her hands up in the air. "Interesting, isn't it? how I happened to find you here at Punta Tragara—or did you find me? Which is it? You tell me."

Max was tongue-tied. What did it all mean? he wondered. Tara had told him an amazing story, but she hadn't revealed anything at all about her feelings. Her reason for coming to see him on Capri was just as hidden now as when she had first started explaining everything.

Max's eyes sought Tara's, and for a split second, he thought he saw everything he would ever need to know about what is important in life.

◆ ◆ ◆

While resting on the bed in his hotel room, Max almost forgot about his friends from Cortina, soon to arrive; he was excited at the prospect of seeing Tara later that day. They had agreed to meet in front of the church of Santa Stefano. Maybe then he would learn why she was on Capri.

The hotel phone rang on the nightstand; it was Antonio: "Your friends are on the way up."

The brothers—Paolo, nicknamed *Smalzo,* and Franco, nicknamed *Fantorin*—were members of the famous mountaineering club called *Gli Scoiattoli di Cortina d'Ampezzo* (The squirrels from Cortina d'Ampezzo).

Max had met Paolo and Franco the year before on a rock-climbing vacation on the limestone crags at Railay, Thailand. On his first night there, they struck up a friendship while sitting next to each other drinking beer at the counter of the Bang Bang Bar. The following day, they climbed the Thaiwand Wall together, the incisor of stunning rock that dominates Rai Leh West beach.

Railay, or Rai Leh, is known as the ultimate out of the way and laid-back jungle gym for rock climbing fanatics. For Max, it had been yet another attempt at escaping his dark moods after the divorce. But the quiet slice of paradise filled his heart with too much loneliness. Despite four days of breathtaking climbing and swimming in clear green waters, his nights were black holes of sleeplessness. He escaped on a long sleepless flight back to San Francisco to drown himself in work.

The brothers from Cortina had since kept in touch with Max to inform him of their high-risk endeavors at Rai Leh to replace the fast corroding and decaying stainless steel bolts with costly titanium bolts.

Paulo and Franco dropped their heavy backpacks filled with climbing gear on the majolica-tile floor of the suite.

"Hi Max, this place isn't bad. You don't look like someone who just came out of a coma; you sure know how to exaggerate, man," Paulo teased, as he removed his Oakley sunglasses and grinned wide, showing off a row of perfect white teeth. His muscular upper arms stretched the fabric of the red polo shirt, embroidered on the left sleeve with the logo of a white squirrel. Max knew the logo was a reminder of the conquest of K2 in 1954 by the founder of the *Scoiattoli*.

They went out on the private terrace of the suite and spread the containers of food from Capri Pasta on the wrought iron table. The fragrance of orange and lemon trees drifted up from the garden and mingled with the aroma of the local dishes: roasted peppers, cold calamari salad, a savory tart, and *funghetto di melanzane* (eggplant with tomatoes).

After Franco dipped his *sciuscella* crust in olive oil and swallowed it with the last sip of wine, he turned his angular weather-beaten face towards Max. "Now, tell us everything."

"Let's get going boys, grab your gear. I'll tell you everything you need to know while we walk up to the belvedere. We will stop to meet with my old professor along the way. He'll provide us with a map and some calculations of the terrain."

CHAPTER 44 - CATS AND LIZARDS

T he morning passed like so many of Katarina's mornings on Capri, except for one crucial difference: Camilla was not there, and she never would be there, ever again. While

Katarina went about her morning routine, doing everything the two of them had always done together, she talked to herself—or rather, to her sister.

"This isn't fair, Camilla. How could you leave me?" She startled herself when she realized she had spoken the words aloud.

To distract herself from her thoughts, she went into the courtyard with Camilla's garden scissors and began cutting off the dead heads of the hydrangeas. The night had not been a good one; she had tossed and turned for hours, recycling the same troubling questions. Why would anyone want to kill my sister? She now wondered whether Ugo Vitale might in fact be the murderer, as Max had suspected. After Max claimed that he had seen books written by Ugo Vitale the first time he came to the villa, Katarina looked all over for them, but couldn't find any. Was Ugo Vitale the person who broke into the house to cover up that he had any connection to Camilla?

And then there was Max. She didn't know what to think about Max. For days, she had been worried that he would die, just like Camilla. She cared about him—a lot. But after he had come out of his coma and they were safely back on Capri, he had given her the brush-off. What Max had said still infuriated her; she remembered his brusque manner and tone of voice: *Don't wait for me to call tomorrow; the brothers from Cortina and I will handle it from here. And don't call me, I'll be too busy. I'll call you when I can. Good night.*

What did he mean by excluding her from the investigation? Did he still suspect her as the murderer? If the feeling she felt for Max was mutual, as she hoped it was, then why had he treated her like that? She tried to convince herself that his sharp words were meant to protect her, but her heart wouldn't listen. And she couldn't forget that Max had cried out the name of his ex-wife Tara, when he was in a coma. What did it mean?

When she stood up from cutting the flowers, a bright green lizard slid down to the courtyard from the rock wall behind the jasmine vines, followed by a lighter green lizard. They lifted their little heads to look up at Katarina.

"Camilla isn't here—anymore." Katarina was surprised to hear the words spontaneously coming out of her mouth.

Camilla had unashamedly talked to the lizards in the courtyard every day. She told Katarina that she always recognized them when they came to greet her; Katarina had never doubted it. What could she say to Camilla's lizard friends?

She sat down on the doorsill of the apartment. "I miss her, too—terribly," she said, and covered her face with her hands. A river of tears started to flow.

A long time passed as she sat there in the garden crying her heart out. When she looked up with bleary, tear-filled eyes, she was amazed to see that the pair of lizards were still there, looking at her with their tilted little heads and funny protruding eyes as if waiting for an explanation, or so it seemed.

"So sorry—" she said.

Katarina got up and went for a stroll around the garden. Nothing cheered her up, and her one-sided conversation with Camilla continued.

"OK, I know you didn't kill yourself, for heaven's sake, and I know it is selfish of me, but I need you. You were my pillar, you were my only sister and my best friend."

Turning off the garden path and maneuvering around a large thorny agave plant, she found the little oval patch marked with small round stones surrounded by weeds. It was the final resting place of Camilla's cat Arjunì, who had died after fighting a heroic battle with a big black nasty dog.

"Dying a warrior is the noblest death," Camilla had said.

Camilla had grieved deeply over the loss of her beloved Arjunì, *Il Re di Castiglione* (The King of the Castle Hill), as she called him. Last summer, on the night he died, they had both been at the villa. Katarina would never forget it.

◆ ◆ ◆

Arjunì never made any noise other than purring, except on two dramatic occasions, with Camilla and Katarina together on Capri as testimony.

286

The first time was in the middle of the night when they were awakened by loud heartrending screams. Alarmed, they went out on the balcony of Camilla's bedroom. Arjunì and another cat were below in the courtyard; they were in a desperate fight over a female cat waiting above on one of the flowered terraces. Neither Katarina nor Camilla had ever seen a cat fight like this; the screaming could have awakened the dead, and the fighting was fierce and bloody.

"We must save Arjunì!" Camilla insisted. "He's such a smart one; I bet he picked the fight right here, so we would help him out. That's his son he is fighting; he's much stronger and younger. He's also wild, not half domesticated like Arjunì. It's about who's going to be the reigning king of Castiglione. Come!"

At that, Camilla threw a nightgown over her naked body and ran down the stairs, grabbed an umbrella, and opened the front door. Wielding the umbrella like a spear, she chased the son of Arjunì out of the courtyard, down the *viale*, and out the gate. The wild cat ran down Via Castiglione with Camilla chasing after him, umbrella raised high. Arjunì jumped up on the stone fence to get a better view of Camilla chasing his son down the road; he seemed astonished.

Once back in the house, Camilla put on Arjunì's favorite music. It was a live recording of Vladimir Horowitz playing a piano concerto in Moscow, that after her husband's death, Camilla would listen to with Arjunì every evening before she went to sleep. Arjunì's front paw and ear were bleeding, but he was purring as loud as ever as he lay in his usual spot on the blue entry rug, while they cleaned his warrior's wounds with vodka.

They didn't know what had happened to the female; she was nowhere in sight. This wasn't his "regular" fiancé, the little black Nedina. Arjunì didn't seem concerned; he had always had more than his fair share of females. Nobody ever saw the son around the villa again.

The second time Arjunì made a terrible noise was on a dark moonless summer night after a fatal fight with a black dog. He lay bleeding on his blue-and-white striped pillow on a lounge chair outside the villa's front entrance. For days, they had been nursing a neck wound from Arjunì's fight; a German-born woman veterinarian had come over from Naples to give him antibiotics, but the wound was deep, and the infection had spread.

The scream started from Arjunì's belly; it sounded like rumbling thunder and crescendoed to a high pitch. It was the most bloodcurdling scream either of them had ever heard. It was the cry of Death.

The next morning, they found the lifeless body of Arjunì in the garden.

◆ ◆ ◆

"The cat loved her, too."

Katarina spun around, startled to hear a voice; she hadn't heard anyone approaching. Zi' Bacco, Camilla's caretaker, was standing behind her looking at Arjunì's resting place. He had always scared Katarina a bit, although she knew Camilla had been very fond of him. He was short and stocky. His trousers were too long and bunched up over his muddy shoes. For a belt, he used a piece of old rope; but the knot often came loose, and the pants would fall to his hips; he continually untied the rope, pulled up his pants, and re-tied the rope. His face was unshaven, his dark hair uncombed. An unlit cigarette hung from the side of his mouth; Katarina had never seen him without a cigarette.

"I was the one who dug that resting place for the cat, you know," Zi' Bacco said proudly. "I found the rocks and planted the flowers around; I even put in the wooden cross. Your sister would often visit, you know."

They walked back together towards the villa. Zi' Bacco sat down on a bench and glanced up at Katarina as he lit the cigarette. "Do you miss her?" he asked.

Katarina looked into the eyes underneath the caretaker's bushy eyebrows for the first time. How compassionate his mild brown eyes were, how concerned and warm his voice was; she was surprised. She had never looked closely at Zi' Bacco, as Camilla called him; preferring his *sopranome* to his given name, Pasquale. Katarina sat down on the bench next to the caretaker; pressure built up behind her eyes, and she started to cry, yet again.

"I know, I know, I miss her, too." Zi' Bacco fished out a dark blue handkerchief from deep within his trouser pocket and offered it to her.

She took it, if a bit reluctantly, as she didn't wish to offend him. She knew it was one of the cardinal rules of Capri never to offend anyone who extends a kindness. She wiped her eyes on Zi' Bacco's soiled handkerchief.

CHAPTER 45 - GOOD NEWS AND BAD NEWS

K atarina still hadn't heard from Max. Her Capri Time watch showed a quarter past one. She got angrier and angrier as she thought about Max's words: *Don't wait for me to call. The boys and I will handle it* . . . Her cell phone interrupted her ruminations; she picked it up on the first ring, thinking it was Max finally calling her. "Hello."

"Signora Kallberg, this is Chief Inspector Monti. Could you please come down to the station right away?"

"Yes, of course—what does it concern?"

"You will soon be informed of that. Good day."

"Good day, Inspector."

Katarina walked down Via Castiglione, still puzzled about what had happened with Max in the square at Santa Teresa. The memory of his physical closeness made her tremble, and her pulse quickened. When was he going to call her?

"My apologies, Signora Kallberg, for asking you to come on such short notice." Chief Inspector Maria Maddalena Monti was sitting behind her desk; underneath it, the little dachshund was laying at her feet. "Please sit down." The inspector gestured to the chair facing her.

Katarina noticed with a woman's discerning eye that the Chief Inspector's police uniform fit as perfectly as if it had been tailored for her. She was wearing the same red shade of lipstick as last time, complimenting her black eyebrows and gray eyes.

"I will get to the point, and then I have some information to share with you. One of my officers saw you, yesterday, getting on the hydrofoil for Naples, is that correct?"

"Yes, that was me. I went to visit Max De Angelis in the hospital. I thought I had your permission—"

Chief Inspector Monti interrupted her, looking straight into her eyes: "Yes, we know you went to the hospital, that is not the problem; however, we tried calling Signor De Angelis in the hospital today, as we have some information for him, but were informed that he had left without the doctor's permission yesterday. Do you have any idea where he is now?"

"Eh, no, I don't know where he is now." It wasn't a lie, Katarina said to herself.

"I have bad news and good news. I'll give you the good news first." Chief Inspector Monti smiled, showing her pearly white teeth.

"You're free to leave the island. Your 'friend' the taxi driver has confirmed your alibi for the night of your sister's death, and there is no reason to involve him any further."

"Thank you, Inspector." Katarina's voice was hardly audible. How embarrassing it was to have her escapade revealed. Then she felt a profound sense of relief—her conduct that night wouldn't cause any problems between Amedeo and his family, and she was now cleared of the suspicion of murder. She took a deep breath; the day suddenly started to look brighter.

"Here's the bad news . . ." Inspector Monti pushed back her chair and faced Katarina; her eyes looked surprisingly sad.

"I am sorry to inform you, Signora, that our head office in Naples, La Questura, has concluded their investigation and have declared that the cause of your sister's death was suicide. If any added information becomes known, we will, of course, reopen our investigation."

Katarina was deep in thought as she walked from Due Golfi up Via Roma. She was convinced that the police were wrong. Camilla would never have killed herself, she was sure of it. Her only hope now was that the Cortina brothers and Max would find evidence to prove that her sister did not commit suicide.

The calls to Norway to tell her family she was now free to come home could wait. She was not ready to leave Capri—not until she knew the truth, even though she longed to hug Anna, the beautiful miracle that was her daughter. Katarina promised herself that she would bring Anna to Capri and teach her about the real Capri, the hidden Capri, the people of Capri—and most important, she would explore nature on the island with her. That was what Capri and Norway had in common, spectacular nature. Love of nature ran deep in her family's Norwegian blood.

Why didn't Max call? Her frustration was increasing by the minute. This decree not to call him seemed ridiculous. She felt she had a right to know what was going on.

"Signora Katarina, Signora Katarina!" The bright voice from across the street interrupted her thoughts. It was Lina, Camilla's faithful housekeeper.

Lina's long, thick chestnut-brown hair flowed loosely down her back, swinging from side to side with the movement of her well-formed hips, as she crossed the street to talk to Katarina. Lina had a cheerful disposition, with the gift of making everyone she met feel cherished.

"Dearest Lina, how are you?" Katarina said; at that moment, she realized how much she had wanted to see Lina.

"Thank you, Signora. I'm all right, but it's not the same without Signora Camilla. I've been with her for fifteen years, you know. But how are you doing? I cannot even imagine how hard it must be for you to lose your sister."

"I understand how you feel," Katarina sighed. "I miss Camilla terribly every minute of the day."

Suddenly it dawned on Katarina that she was now the owner of Camilla's home on Capri, and with that, came responsibilities. She had inherited the villa, but without the life insurance money, it would be difficult to maintain the property, as the yearly expenses were high. Lina had been coming to clean the villa every day since Camilla passed away; until now, it hadn't occurred to Katarina that she must pay Lina for her work. Katarina silently scolded herself for being so wrapped up in her problems: How thoughtless I have been!

"Please forgive me, Lina—I feel so lost without Camilla. But I suppose the good news is that none of us is a suspect any longer; the police have determined it was suicide."

"We know that's not even a possibility. Never will I believe it." Lina was emphatic. "Signora Camilla will rest in peace; she was ready for death, but she didn't take her own life. She would have wanted us to be happy. We must do the best we can."

"You're right, Lina, of course you are. And thank you for keeping the house in top shape. I want you to stay on as the housekeeper just as before. I'll find a way to maintain the house as Camilla did."

Just saying those words cheered Katarina's spirits. Yes! she thought to herself. I will find a way—with Lina's help. Hearing Lina using the word "we" had made all the difference; she knew they were going to make it—together.

After hugging Lina, Katarina walked to the Piazzetta and sat down under the shade of a sun umbrella at Gran Caffè.

Mario greeted Katarina warmly when he brought over her café Americano. "How's the investigation going with Max in the hospital? How's he doing—is he out of danger?"

Upon hearing the words "out of danger," it came to Katarina in a flash what she was going to do. "I think Max is going to be fine. At the moment, the investigation is—how shall I say it, up in the air." Or down a cliff, she thought to herself. "It's a shame, Mario," she continued, "but it appears the police have buried the investigation."

She made a quick stop around the corner from the square at the pastry counter of Bar Alberto, before passing through the arch between Piccolo Bar and city hall. The sound of the bell ringing in the campanile in the Piazzetta followed her as she walked quickly up the shady Via Longano. She counted three loud bells and three weak bells; it was three forty-five in the afternoon. She would have to hurry. Had the Cortina guys arrived? she wondered. And what about that writer, Ugo Vitale, was Max in danger?

CHAPTER 46 - A VOICE FROM THE GRAVE

WEDNESDAY, SEPTEMBER 8

P aolo and Franco, the Scoiattoli from Cortina, were expert mountain rescuers, not just professional climbers. They wasted no time getting ready for the descent. Pure poetry in motion, Max thought, as he watched the two brothers, *Smalzo* and *Fantorin,* organize their state-of-the-art climbing equipment. There were belays, pulleys, ropes, nuts, bolts, carabineers, chalk bags, and so on.

Max noted with envy that they had Metolius master cams for active protection as well as Petzl stop descenders with a self-braking function that allowed them to stop and maintain their position on the rope easily. The Petzl device could be rapidly installed or removed from the rope without disconnecting it from the harness. That would have been useful for my solo climb, he thought. Max was still unsure whether his fall had been due to an accident or foul play.

Franco opened a black bag sticking out of his backpack and pulled out a bunch of loose pieces. "We brought a couple of Minelab CTX metal detectors, just in case," he said. "We use them for rescues. They cost a fortune, but they're the best."

Within minutes, Paolo and Franco had assembled the pieces, explaining to Max some of the sophisticated features of the detectors. He was impressed. The detectors had a color LCD screen, advanced target discrimination, integrated GPS, search modes, a map screen, and navigation tools.

"We'll put on the headphones later," Franco said. The black Cordura bags attached to their belts with CTX clips contained pairs of waterproof wireless headphones with built-in speakers.

"OK, we're ready—give us the calculations," Paolo said, flashing one of his dazzling grins as he slipped his sunglasses into a Velcro secured pocket.

"Here they are." Max handed a laminated sheet to each of the boys. The sheets got rolled up and tucked into their belt bags.

He and the boys had met *Il Professore* on the way up, and they had gone over the sheets that mapped the terrain of the cliffs and forest below. The professor's computer-generated logistical calculations showed the estimated fall line of Camilla's body. The theory was that any object that fell from the cliff would take a similar fall line, but due to different weight calculations could land higher up, and then bounce down.

Smalzo was as smooth as butter, living up to his nickname; he was the first to go over the belvedere railing, knocking the first bolt into the porous cliff just below the edge, then rappelling about ten meters down and getting the second bolt secured. His older brother *Fantorin*, followed, his lean bronzed face lined with wrinkles from years of exposure to extreme elements.

Max was now alone at the Belvedere. He didn't like not being able to do the climb with the boys. Worn out from the pain and stress of a long day, he slumped down in exhaustion on the stone bench, closed his eyes and fell asleep.

Awakened by the sound of footsteps crunching on pine needles, he jumped up from the bench. Crossing the belvedere to look up the path, he held his breath.

Katarina appeared, walking carefully down the forest path to avoid slipping on the pine needles. Dangling from her hand was a package wrapped in blue paper and tied with ribbon; in the other hand, she held a plastic shopping bag.

"Catari!"

Katarina felt relieved when she heard Max's joyful welcome. Great, she thought, he isn't angry with me for ignoring his command to stay out of the action. She laughed with pleasure when she saw him safely in front of her.

"*Cosa sta succedendo* (What's happening)?" she asked, as she placed her bags on the bench. "Where are the boys?" She looked over the railing. "Let's hope they are safe; I don't care any longer if we find evidence or not. Camilla was killed, and nothing will bring her back. I don't want anybody else to get hurt."

"The Cortina Scoiattoli are expert rock climbers; they know what they are doing, don't worry," Max said, gently touching her shoulder, and leading her away from the railing.

Katarina seemed reassured. She sat down on the stone bench and opened the package; it was a beautiful *Torta di Mandorle*, a flourless chocolate and almond cake that she had bought at Bar Alberto.

"Torta Caprese, fantastic!" Max made a sign with his index finger as if he was drilling into his cheek, a gesture that means "delicious."

Katarina removed her Borsalino hat and shook out her shiny blonde curls, handing the hat to Max. He hung it carefully on a tree branch.

"We are celebrating that we are alive and that neither you nor I are murder suspects anymore—at least not to the police."

She added in a resigned voice, "The police have declared Camilla's death to be suicide."

"Oh, I'm so sorry."

"I've come to terms with their decision. You will get your job back, and I can return to Norway. I can't wait to see my daughter again."

Katarina reached into the plastic bag and triumphantly held up a bottle of honey-colored liquid.

"What? Ben Ryé Passito di Pantelleria—di Donnafugata!"

"Yeh, I got it from the bar at the Croce intersection on the way up. It's still cold from their fridge, and look, I borrowed a corkscrew from them."

The sight of Katarina sitting on the bench where he and Tara had once spent a passionate evening together made Max pensive. He observed her as she got to work opening the bottle; then she cut two slices of cake with a plastic knife, placed them on paper plates, and poured the dessert wine into paper cups.

Her beauty was so natural, Max thought, as he sat down next to her. There was nothing artificial, nothing fake about Katarina. She didn't play games with people. Katarina was self-assured, but not self-absorbed. Max had recognized their attraction the moment their eyes locked on the roof of the villa the day they met. He had desired her. So why hadn't they made love? Obviously, the circumstances of the investigation and their mutual suspicion had gotten in the way. But it was more than that – what was it? The answer came to him instantly: Katarina wasn't the kind of woman one fooled around with, she was the kind of woman one married, and he knew now that he wasn't ready for that. Katarina deserved someone who loved her and felt committed to sharing a life with her.

After they had finished eating their cake, toasting each other a few times with the divine wine from Sicily, Max spoke up. "Catari" he started, "I think it's time we talked. You deserve honesty, and—"

"Yes," she interrupted, "I already know." Staring at the bottom of her cup, she said, "You still love your ex-wife, right? It's OK."

298

She looked up into his eyes, and then reached for the bottle and poured more of the sweet golden nectar into their cups. With a touch of sadness in her smile and a tremble in her voice, she raised her glass and said: "Here's to us—and to each of us finding a person we love. May it be soon."

As they were about to take a sip of the Muscat wine, they were interrupted.

"What is love?" Ugo said. He stood towering above them. They hadn't heard him coming.

Katarina was the first to recover. She poured wine into a paper cup and offered it to Ugo.

"Please join us in a toast to love—whatever love is."

They all sipped silently. Max noticed Ugo glancing sideways at the ropes on the ground.

Ugo passed his empty cup to Katarina and broke the silence: "Who is climbing?"

"Friends," Max replied.

Silence again.

Katarina packed up the cake and the utensils and put the cork back in the bottle. Katarina and Max sat on the bench, waiting nervously, while Ugo stood by the railing with his back to them, looking down the cliff. He startled them when he started talking, as if to himself.

"Maybe I've never been loved. Maybe I've never loved. Maybe I don't know what love is. Do I even love myself? I don't know. Maybe I love my daughter."

Katarina and Max exchanged worried glances. They waited in silence, wondering what else Ugo might say. Just then, a sharp whistle came from below the cliff; it was the signal that the Cortina boys were starting their ascent.

Max, Katarina, and Ugo stood beside the pile of ropes, waiting expectantly. Franco was the first to arrive; he climbed over the railing and sat down on the ground to rest. Katarina pulled out a bottle of water and poured some into a cup for him.

"Thanks," he said. "You know, this climb is not that difficult, but it has its challenges."

Paolo soon followed over the railing. He looked at Max and grinned from ear to ear; then he slumped to the ground and drank the cup of water Katarina gave him in one gulp.

Max's heart was racing: Did Paolo's cocky grin mean they'd found something? After the brief introductions to Ugo, he couldn't help himself: "So?" he asked.

They were all mesmerized as Paolo got up from the ground, removed his helmet and harness, and sat down on the stone bench. He slowly unzipped his belt bag, and with dramatic flair, carefully pulled out something wrapped in a kerchief and placed it gently on his knees. When he unwrapped the kerchief, a small padded purse made of shimmering purple cloth came into view.

Max gasped—the purse! He was right; it had been there all along. Now to find out the secrets it might hold.

Paolo saw with satisfaction the stunned reaction of his audience as all eyes fixed on the purse. Ever so slowly, as if to heighten the suspense, he spread the kerchief on the bench and unzipped the purse. Paolo pulled out a small silver cosmetic bag and emptied its contents: a credit card, 300 Euros in notes, a tube of lip-gloss, and a silver powder compact. Next, he pulled out a key chain with a flashlight attached. The last item was a neatly folded cream-colored cashmere scarf, which he placed on his knees. Paolo turned the purse inside out and waved it back and forth to verify that it was empty. He grinned wide, immensely proud of his performance.

Max was inwardly cursing him with impatience.

Paolo slowly slipped his right hand into a fold of the featherlight cashmere scarf on his knees, and like a magician pulling a white rabbit out of a hat, he withdrew his fist with something inside it. He opened his hand with an air of triumph. Laying in his palm was the prize—a silver-colored iPod.

Attached to the iPod lightning connector was a small black device, about 5 centimeters wide and 1.2 centimeters thick. They all strained to see the letters on it: "B-l-u-e."

Max knew at once what "Blue" stood for; this was a Blue Mikey Digital plug and play recording device. It could turn an iPod into a sophisticated mobile recording device.

"May I?" Max held out his hand, and Paolo passed it to him.

Now came the test, was the iPod still working? Max disconnected the Mikey first. Then he pushed the sleep/wake button. The logo appeared. The iPod was alive and there was still a battery charge.

Max scrolled through the apps and found what he was looking for: "Voice Memos." He held his breath as he opened the application. The red dot recording button was dimmed; the last recording was either finished or paused. Max tapped "Done" next to the red dot.

An extensive list of named recordings came up; the last one was unnamed and dated August 15th, 11:56 pm. He believed the external microphone had to be attached to enable listening to the recording using the iPod touch built-in speaker, so he reconnected the Mikey.

Max tapped the arrow button to listen to the last recording.

"Today is the fifteenth of August—the holy day of Ferragosto—It is one year since I first started to record my thoughts and reflections. This morning the title for my book came to me—I will call it 'Capri Diem: A Memoir.' I've just had dinner with friends at one of my favorite restaurants. . ."

The sound of Camilla's voice made everyone jump. Katarina burst into tears.

The quality of the recording was excellent.

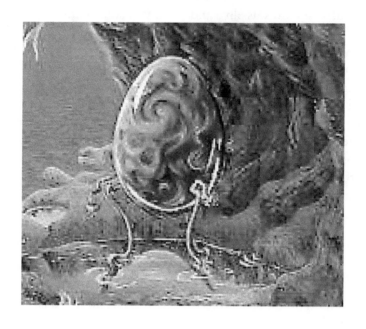

CHAPTER 47 - A RENDEZVOUS WITH FATE

WEDNESDAY, SEPTEMBER 8

C amilla's recorded voice from the past hypnotized them all. Katarina was speechless; she collapsed onto the bench next to Paolo and appeared to be in a trance. Franco dropped to the ground beside them. Ugo stood apart, leaning against a cement post of the railing. Max was standing a few meters away from Ugo, holding the iPod with the Mikey in his right hand. Everyone was feverish with anticipation to hear what Camilla was about to say next.

They listened to her musings about Ferragosto and how it all started in Roman times. Then Camilla changed the subject:

"I've decided to end the relationship with Ugo tonight. It pains me terribly to do so, but I must be honest. I now understand that I fell in love with an illusion. I fell in love with an image—an idea—a mirage of my dear friend, not who he

is. He is an exceptional writer—a great thinker, a poet. I admire and respect him. It's not his fault. I've finally realized my mistake—and I will ask him for his forgiveness. I was of course—I admit it—flattered by all the attention he showed me. That was my weakness."

Max noticed a bitter smile on Ugo's lips.

"The years after Daniel passed away were hard—I missed Daniel so very, very much—I was lonely. When I met Ugo, we had the best time because we were just friends—we knew it couldn't be anything else—he was married—in a way that protected me. After his wife's death everything changed. Oh yes—the passion he showed me was much desired. But strangely our relationship didn't seem real— it felt more like a performance. We agreed to wait before making it public—until a year had passed after his wife's fatal accident—especially because of their daughter. I need to find the courage tonight to tell him it is over—I should have done it a long time ago. My vanity stopped me. . ."

The recording paused, and they waited for about fifteen seconds before it resumed. *"My suspicions ruined the relationship for me—I started to see Ugo as an impostor or an actor. As I began to know him better—it seemed like he was two people—the one who wrote the books and the other—"*

There was silence on the recording for a few seconds, then Camilla spoke again; her voice sounded surprised. *"Ugo! You're early. I thought we were supposed to meet at the belvedere, not here on the path?"*

They all stared at Ugo. He appeared to have been struck by a thunderbolt, his face was ashen, his lips twisted. Max felt a cold shiver go down his back.

Ugo's loud voice came on the recording: *"Yes, I couldn't wait to see you, my darling little queen. I tried to call you a few minutes ago, but—"*

"Oh, I forgot to turn on that phone you lent me." Camilla's voice was hushed, they had to strain to hear the words. It sounded as if they were walking.

Ugo's voice came on again. *"I arrived early at Belvedere delle Noci. I came by way of walking up the old hunting trail from Via Pizzolungo. It was spectacular when the moon rose about an hour ago. I didn't meet a soul. But I grew impatient when you didn't return my call, so that's why I decided to walk down the path to meet you, my darling."*

The recording went quiet again. There was a faint sound of footsteps. Nobody moved or said anything; all were waiting for the revelation on the iPod.

Ugo's voice came on: *"Isn't this belvedere the most beautiful place in the world Camilla? And we have it all to ourselves. Look at the moon shining on the sea—"*
Camilla responded: *"Yes, it's spectacular. The moon was full just two nights ago, it's still so incredibly bright. Have you ever seen so many stars?"*

Max heard a note of sadness in Camilla's voice.

Ugo's voice: *"The night is magical, and you are the star that shines brightest among the countless stars. I couldn't live without you, my darling."*

Max shivered; it felt weird to be listening to the recorded voices of Camilla and Ugo while standing on the spot where they had been that fatal night.

There were some rustling sounds on the recording, and then Camilla's voice came on: "

Stop—please, Ugo! I have something difficult to tell you. Perhaps it would have been better to say this on a different night—but we have few chances to speak privately. It has not been easy keeping our relationship a secret and—"
"Can't it wait, my darling? A night like this is meant for love, not talking."
"No. I must tell you now. I must be honest with you, out of respect for you—and for myself."

There was a moment of silence on the recording before Camilla's voice continued.

"Ugo, please forgive me. It is entirely my fault—I can't go on. We must end this!"
"If you've found another man—I'll kill him!"
"You know I care for you very much—but we don't really know each other—do we? —Our love isn't real—you know it, too—don't you?"
"Nonsense. That isn't true! After everything I've sacrificed to be with you—I won't tolerate this. You will not leave me!"
"Please, Ugo—I beg of you—be reasonable—"
"Never. You will NEVER leave me!"

Silence on the recording.

"No. No! Ugo—NO!"

"I will kill myself if I can't even kiss you!"

"My dearest Ugo, you don't know what you're saying. Please listen to me. When you were married, we were just friends, remember? You knew that I never wanted to have a relationship with a married man. I admit that I enjoyed flirting with you—it was wrong of me to play that game. It wasn't supposed to get serious—but passion got the best of us—we were both lonely. And then when you lost your wife that changed things—but—I must be honest with you—I have found a new friend—"

"Never will another man have you. NEVER!"

"Please, Ugo—let me help you. I know how hard it's been for you since your wife's tragic death. You haven't been able to work at all. I want you to take this diamond necklace. I've no need for it. Here, look—this is how to open the safety lock—take it—give it to Beatrice—or you could sell it."

Ugo could no longer restrain himself. He leapt like a tiger towards Max and tried to grab the iPod. Instinctively, Max took a step backward and swung his right hand with the iPod behind him—and just in time. Ugo groped for the iPod, but Max gripped it tightly out of reach. Ugo changed tactics and went for Max's throat, pushing him back against the railing.

Paolo, Franco, and Katarina jumped to their feet, ready to spring on Ugo.

"If any of you take one more step, I will choke this son of a bitch to death and fucking push him off the cliff!"

Max's back ribs dug into the railing; he arched his back away from Ugo to relieve the choking, and shoved his hand between the rails behind him to keep the iPod away from Ugo; they cut like blades into his wrist.

Paolo, Franco, and Katarina stayed where they were—if they moved, the iPod would fall and break into pieces. Much worse, Max's life was at stake.

The recording was still running. Camilla's voice came on: *"What? NO—Ugo, you didn't! How could you throw the necklace down the cliff?"*

Ugo pushed Max further over the railing. "Drop it. Drop the fucking iPod!" he yelled.

Max felt Ugo's fingers squeezing his vocal cords; it wouldn't be long before he passed out. He wanted desperately to let the iPod slide from his hand, so he could take a breath.

"AHHHHHHHH!!" Ugo's daughter Beatrice came running down the path, screaming at the top of her lungs.

Ugo turned his head towards the scream and loosened his grip for a moment, giving Max enough time for a quick breath of air.

"STOP IT, DADDY! WHAT ARE YOU DOING?" Sobbing, Beatrice threw herself on the ground and wrapped her arms around her father's legs, trying to pull him away from Max.

Max got in another breath of air.

They all heard the next words coming from the iPod; it was Ugo's voice:

"You whore! You think you can find yourself another man—that you can just get rid of me? That you can buy me off with a stupid necklace? NEVER!"
Then came Camilla's sobbing voice: *"Stop it. Please—oh please—STOP IT! My God—please—"*

Muffled sounds came from the recording.

Ugo's voice: *"I destroyed my life for you! I ruined my career! I killed my wife to be with you! How dare you!"*
Camilla's voice: *"AAAAAAAaaaaaaa!"*

When Beatrice heard Camilla's high-pitched cry on the recording, she screamed again, a piercing wail that echoed into the hills. It shook them all to the core.

Then it was quiet.

"What in the name of GOD is going on!" Immaculata cried, as she walked onto the belvedere, her chest heaving from hurrying up the trail when she heard the scream.

Ugo let go of Max's neck. He reached down and gently removed Beatrice's hands from behind his knees. Beatrice was sobbing uncontrollably, tears streamed down her cheeks.

Max staggered to safety, his legs barely supporting him. His broken collarbone felt like a dagger being thrust into an open wound. Everything started spinning, faster and faster. Paolo and Franco dashed to his side. Paolo grabbed the iPod out of his hand, and Franco supported Max's head as he collapsed to the ground. Max was unconscious.

Ugo knelt beside Beatrice and dried her wet cheeks with his palms. He held her small face tenderly in his hands and looked into her tear-filled eyes. "Beatrice, my daughter, I love you. Always. Forgive me."

Ugo stood up. He looked at the scene around him.

Katarina and Franco were kneeling on the ground beside Max while Franco was feeling for Max's carotid pulse.

Paolo had wrapped up the iPod in his kerchief and was putting it inside his shirt.

Immaculata had closed her eyes and her hands were folded in prayer: "Santa Maria . . ."

Beatrice was kneeling on the ground beside her father, still sobbing.

In one quick leap, Ugo jumped up on a post between the railings and swan dived into the abyss.

The bloodcurdling scream from Beatrice as she watched her father dive to his death was a sound so horrifying that everyone who heard it would remember it for the rest of their lives.

Immaculata pulled the girl up from the ground and dragged her to the stone bench. Poor Beatrice was shaking uncontrollably. Immaculata held her close to her bosom, slowly rocking her back and forth like a baby, while she hummed a lullaby.

CHAPTER 48 - A TREASURE HUNT

WEDNESDAY, SEPTEMBER 8

"He has a pulse!" Franco cried in relief. "Is he breathing?"

Katarina was watching Max's chest, with her ear beside his mouth listening for the sound of his breath. "YES—Yes, he is! Thank goodness!" she cried.

"Great, I was beginning to worry. This day has been dramatic, to say the least. Let's give him some time to recover. Make sure he keeps breathing," Franco said as he got up from the ground.

Then he pulled out his cell phone and checked an app before turning to Paolo: "The time now is 18:02. The sun is setting at 19:23 and the moon will be rising at 19:19. There's no time to waste; we have 85 minutes max of daylight left. Luckily, the rising moon is a waxing gibbous at 92%, giving us good light."

Franco started to lay out his climbing harness. "Katarina, why don't you tell us about the necklace Camilla talks about on the recording?"

Katarina described the diamond and gold necklace that had once belonged to Camilla's mother-in-law, omitting the emotional details of the story.

"Ah, I see," Paolo said. "It sounds valuable. I'll try to find it for you when we go back down. The last time I saw Max in Thailand he was wearing some kind of necklace, with one of those Neapolitan things to ward off evil, but I see he's not wearing it now."

"Yes, I've seen it, too," Katarina nodded, "it was a platinum chain with a twisted coral horn, the *curniciello* they call it here. After Max's climbing accident, it disappeared, and he thought it was stolen in the hospital."

Max moaned and started to stir. To their delight, he sat up.

"What happened?" He reached for his painful throat, recalling how Ugo had tried to strangle him.

Paolo told him about Ugo's suicide leap.

Max was stunned to find out that Ugo had killed himself. "Where is Beatrice?" he asked as he looked around with a worried look on his face.

"Immaculata has taken Beatrice back to Hotel Gatto Bianco, she has promised to stay with her as long as necessary," Katarina reassured him.

Max fished out his cell phone and got Chief Inspector Monti on the line.

"Max De Angelis here, up at Belvedere Delle Noci. I want to report a suicide," he said in a hoarse voice.

They waited to hear the inspector's response; Max had put his cell phone on speaker mode. "If this is a joke, De Angelis, it is not appreciated."

While Max gave the Chief Inspector an account of Ugo's fatal jump off the cliff, the Cortina brothers quickly prepared for another descent. Back on came the harnesses, the metal detectors, and the Cordura bags; lastly, the helmets with ultra-wide headlamps.

"We'll look for Ugo's body first, just in case he should be alive. Then we will see. . ." Franco said. This time he was the first to descend.

Paolo reached into his shirt and pulled out the scarf with the iPod wrapped in it. "Here Max, you'd better take charge of this. We don't want anything to happen to it, do we?" He shot one of his dazzling smiles at Katarina. "You kids behave while we're gone."

The belvedere was again quiet. Max and Katarina stood by the railing and watched the seagulls glide along the steep walls of the coastal rock below, feeling relieved and grateful. The magnitude of what had just happened had the effect of rendering everything in life unimportant except one thing: being alive.

The sun had disappeared behind Monte Solaro and the cool humid night air of the island started to creep in. Katarina put on her cashmere sweater. They sat down on the bench to wait for the Cortina brothers to return from the climb. A big orange moon rose above the Amalfi Coast in the cobalt blue sky.

Watching the sea as it rippled with shimmering gold moonlight, Max had a strange feeling that he had forgotten something important. Then he remembered: What an idiot! How could I forget the meeting with Tara at seven o'clock? He called her cell phone number; a recorded message said that she was out of the country. It dawned on him that she didn't have a cell phone in Italy. He called her lodging, Villa Helios, but she wasn't there.

Katarina looked puzzled. He decided it was time to explain that Tara had arrived on Capri, and that he was supposed to meet her.

It was now seven-twenty. Max was feeling more desperate by the minute. He called her hotel again; this time he left a message for Tara that he had been detained for his investigation and left his number. The battery level on his phone was at 1%, about to die. They checked Katarina's phone—it was dead. He considered calling the Chief Inspector for help before his battery died as well, but his pride stopped him. He called his sister, but just as she picked up, his battery went dead.

"Listen, Tara will understand," Katarina said, "she knows you are involved in a case, right? She will go to her hotel, she will get your message and call you, she will realize your battery is dead." Katarina's logic calmed Max down a bit.

"Tell me how you and Tara met?" Katarina asked.

A loud whirring noise interrupted Max's story. A large white helicopter with a blue stripe flew over Monte Tuoro and came straight down towards the belvedere. It passed over their heads and went out towards the sea, then circled back and hovered directly in front of them, so close they could see two heads inside the glass cockpit.

"It's one of the newer AgustaWestland AW139 twin-engine helicopters acquired by the Italian State Police," Max yelled above the ear-piercing noise.

Next, the helicopter rose some distance above their heads. Katarina and Max plugged their ears with their fingers, but the noise was still deafening, and having the helicopter hovering so close was unnerving.

A large door on the side of the chopper slid back, and through the opening they watched a man wearing overalls, a helmet with a visor, gloves, and a harness sit down at the doorway and hang his feet over the edge.

A deployment bag secured by a rope inside the helicopter was thrown out. Katarina and Max couldn't see where the bag landed. The man in overalls jumped out and smoothly rappelled down the rope right in front of them and out of sight.

Shortly after, something that looked like a sled appeared at the side opening of the helicopter. Max realized it was a folded stretcher; it was roped down to the man below.

Some minutes passed, and the stretcher was hoisted up with a body tied to it by security belts. The body was covered by plastic sheeting from head to toe. As soon as the stretcher was pulled into the helicopter, the man below got hoisted up, and the door slid shut. The helicopter rose above their heads, slowly tipped into a turn, and was gone.

"That was fantastic!" Max exclaimed exuberantly as soon as they could hear each other again. Then he grew quiet. That could have been me, he reflected, lying dead on a stretcher.

A sharp whistle shot up from below—the expert climbers from Cortina had started their ascent.

For the second time that day, Paolo and Franco were back safely on the Belvedere.

"We have a couple of surprises for you guys," Paolo said, after they had packed up their gear.

Paolo's famous grin was wider than Max had ever seen.

CHAPTER 49 - FROM INDIA TO CAPRI

WEDNESDAY, SEPTEMBER 8

T ara sat on the bench at Punta Tragara with a soft smile on her lips: the pleasure of seeing Max again was immeasurable. Max had not explained why he had to rush off, only saying he was in the middle of an investigation, after he proposed they meet in front of the church in the Piazzetta at seven o'clock.

While tenderly stroking her belly with its growing miracle of life, Tara's thoughts went to Doctor Amrit back in Kerala, India. She sent him her silent prayers of gratitude, as he may have saved her life and that of the baby.

INDIA

Tara would never forget the many days of awful sickness in the ashram before she was admitted to the hospital; how worried she had been, not knowing what was wrong with her.

The fear of infecting anyone else in the ashram had stopped her from going to the common hall to eat or get filtered water to drink, making her weak and dehydrated. The fever, nausea, headache, and pain in her bones increased, and after a few days, she went by taxi all the way to the hospital in town. The doctor ran blood tests, but couldn't find anything, so she returned to the ashram and spent more long, lonely days in bed, getting weaker and weaker.

Another week passed, and when she started to sweat profusely, and developed a blotchy blood-red rash all over her body, she decided to return to the hospital.

On this second visit, she was examined by Doctor Amrit, who ran more tests. He discovered that she had dengue hemorrhagic fever and wanted to admit her to the hospital. She told him she was afraid to be a patient in a hospital in India and wanted to get on a plane back to America.

Doctor Amrit patiently explained that she could suffer life-threatening consequences if she were not treated at once. She was malnourished, fatigued, and in a dangerous state of dehydration—in no condition to go anywhere. He made her an offer she couldn't refuse, one that she would be forever grateful for: "Why don't you tell me tomorrow morning how you find the hospital, and if there is anything you are not 100% satisfied with, I will let you leave."

The administration of intravenous fluids and electrolytes to correct her imbalances had already had a beneficial effect by the time

Doctor Amrit visited the next morning. Tara was barely able to sit up, but she smiled with pleasure at seeing him.

"You will see, another twenty-four hours with this treatment and you will feel better," Doctor Amrit said.

He was right; by the third day she was weak, but beginning to feel like herself. The hospital care was better than she could ever have imagined. Doctor Amrit came to check on her every morning, and Tara looked forward to his visits. On the fourth morning, he pulled up a chair next to her bed and studied her chart for a moment; then he removed his black-rimmed reading glasses and looked at her.

"I think you have regained most of your strength, and as far as I am concerned, you are out of danger, and you can be discharged today."

Tara's heart sank; she wasn't at all ready to face the world. She was not going to risk returning to the ashram, where she could get infected by a different strain of mosquito, a danger she now knew was possible. She felt supported in her hospital suite, with all her needs taken care of. Where would she go? She felt too weak to get on an airplane.

"There is something I want to talk to you about—" Doctor Amrit hesitated. He appeared almost embarrassed when he looked at her chart again. "Did you know—" he paused to correct his grammar, "Do you know that you are pregnant?"

Tara was speechless.

Pregnant! That was a word she had longed to hear for a long time. How was it possible that she was pregnant now? It would have to be a miracle, she thought. She recalled missing her period after the long flight to India. But during the time when she was sick at the ashram, it hadn't occurred to her that she'd missed a second period. Seven months had passed since she ended her relationship with the Ashtanga yoga teacher. Then Tara remembered what had happened the night before she left for India. When she went over to Max's to drop off Principessa, their cat, he prepared a fabulous meal of linguine with fresh lobster, and they shared a bottle of wine. They had made a new vow together—to try to be friends. Afterwards they drank cognac in front of the fireplace and—well . . .

Her mind raced to calculate the weeks since that night: the baby would be about eleven weeks old—and the father was definitely Max.

Now aware of the new life inside her, Tara felt a wave of panic. Will the baby be healthy? she wondered. "Tell me doctor, do you think my illness has damaged my baby in any way?"

Doctor Amrit had read the concern on her face. "I think the baby will likely be fine, but I recommend we do an early prenatal ultrasound." He hemmed, after looking at her medical records again. "I assume you will keep the baby? I see you are not married."

Tara's face broke into a radiant smile. "Of course, I will, it's a miracle baby! Don't worry, I will be able to take care of my child."

Doctor Amrit let out a sigh of relief.

Tara was pensive, she felt scared. "Doctor, I don't feel ready to leave the hospital yet. Is there any way you could make a recommendation for me to stay for a few more days—until I get my strength back?"

"Didn't I tell you, you would love this hospital? I didn't expect you to love it so much that you wouldn't want to leave us," the reserved doctor said with a chuckle. "I will recommend that you stay for three more days due to your pregnancy and for you to have some tests. And then, if you like, you can stay with my family for as long as you like to recuperate."

Tara was so moved by his unexpected generosity that she didn't know quite what to say. She only smiled and nodded, as tears of joy trickled down her face. It seemed impossible to believe that she was about to become—that she was now a mother.

Gratefully, the ultrasound showed no abnormalities in the baby. Tara left the hospital with Dr. Amrit and stayed with his family for three wonderful weeks before making a tearful farewell. By then, Dr. Amrit, his mother, and his wife and their two children had all become like family.

CAPRI

The bells rang in the campanile, seven long and two short bells: it was seven-thirty. Why, of all times, is Max late now? Tara asked herself. She had waited over half an hour past the time of their appointment outside the church of Santo Stefano. She couldn't call Max, as she had left her cell phone behind in San Francisco. God knows where one would find a pay phone these days, she remarked to herself.

Tara went inside the church to sit down. The quiet, solemn interior of the church was comforting. She looked up at the high vaulted ceiling, unconsciously resting one hand on her belly.

Closing her eyes, she tried to meditate; her breath became smooth and even, but her mind was far from tranquil. What had happened to Max? What should she do?

Silently, she chanted the Gayatri mantra twenty-one times. Then she sat quietly, feeling the reverberations inside her body from the sacred mantra. A spiraling current started rotating counterclockwise in slow motion up her central spine; it paused in the chest and swung like a pendulum before rotating counterclockwise down her spine. The vibrating current travelled up and down her spine spontaneously a few more times. The experience filled her with blissful energy and gratitude. She rested both palms on her belly. "Thank you, God, for the wonderful life you have given me."

Tara got up from the bench and walked to the sacristy, unaware that the two-thousand-year-old tile beneath her feet came from the site of Emperor Tiberius's villa. She knelt in front of a silver statue of San Costanzo, the patron saint of Capri. "Dear San Costanzo, I offer you my respect. I beg of you to protect Max and keep him safe." It never occurred to Tara that it might matter that she wasn't Catholic. For her, spiritual worship had no religious boundaries.

Outside in the fresh air, Tara felt calm; she now felt positive that Max was okay. After the chilliness inside the church, she wanted to get a hot drink to warm her up. Glancing over to the Piazzetta, she didn't see Max or anyone else she knew. She crossed the Funicular Square. The sun had just set, and the sky was painted every imaginable shade of yellow and red.

Just around the corner from the crowded tables outside Bar Funicolare was a well-kept secret among the locals. There were three or four tables in a single row that had the advantage of being hidden

317

from the crowds. It was one of Tara's favorite spots. She ordered a cup of hot chamomile tea.

From where she sat, there was a stunning view of the bay of Naples bathed in a beautiful purple glow.

A surprised voice broke the quiet in Tara's little corner of paradise. "I don't believe my eyes. Tara!"

Suddenly, Raffi appeared in front of her.

"Raffi! You have no idea how glad I am to see you!"

Raffi was flattered. Tara's pleasure at seeing him was unexpected, though he had been her admirer from the very first time he laid eyes on her. Max had been the luckiest guy alive to marry her, in Raffi's view, and he blamed Max for the breakup. Raffi felt that he himself would never have messed up, not with a treasure like Tara.

"We have a lot in common, don't we?" Raffi said, as he sat down beside Tara and ordered chamomile tea. "This is my favorite table. I bring my tablet and manage my business from here, not bad, eh? What are you doing on Capri? Max told me you were in India. You must tell me all about it. I've always wanted to go there, you know."

In a pause between stories about India, Raffi got his chance. "Do you have plans for dinner?"

"Nooo—but, do you mind, could we try to call Max? I don't have a cell phone."

"Sure thing." Raffi wondered what had happened since he'd left Capri. He tried Max's number. "No answer."

"Could you try Hotel Gatto Bianco?" Tara asked.

The receptionist informed Raffi that Signor De Angelis was not a guest in the hotel.

Raffi was surprised. "Seems Max checked out. He was staying in Hotel Gatto Bianco when I left for a business trip a week ago—I just returned to Capri today. Max was in the middle of an investigation and I was helping him out. Haven't you seen him?"

Tara sighed, "Yes, I saw him earlier today, but only for a few minutes before he had to run off. He had just come out of the hospital yesterday…"

"What are you saying! Max was in the hospital?"

Tara told him the little she knew. Raffi was shocked to learn that Max had been in a coma in Cardarelli Hospital, but calmed down when she said he appeared to be doing relatively well. Now he understood why Max hadn't returned his telephone calls during the past week. Why had Max ended up in a hospital? he wondered. "Did Max tell you about his investigation?"

Tara turned to Raffi with tearful eyes. "No, he said he would explain later. I don't know what to do."

"Let's try to call Max again in a little while," Raffi said. "Shall we get a bite to eat in the meantime? Let's go to Cucciolo, my favorite restaurant? It is in Anacapri."

She nodded.

Passing the white columns alongside the square in front of Bar Funicolare, Tara pointed to Monte Solaro. "Look, Raffi. What are those strings of bright light towards the summit?"

"Oh, that's the Hermitage of Santa Maria at Cetrella. It's illuminated today in honor of the Virgin Mary's birthday. The church in the hermitage is open all day for liturgy. Spectacular, isn't it?"

Tara nodded. "If I had wings, I would fly up to the hermitage this minute," she said wistfully.

Where was Max? Tara wondered, as she walked arm in arm with Raffi towards the taxi stand—had he forgotten about her?

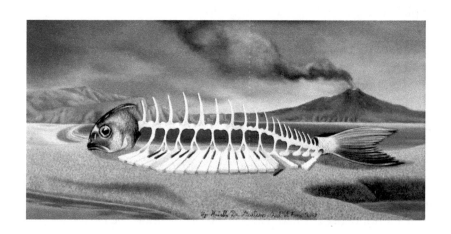

CHAPTER 50 - ABANDONMENT

The taxi speeded up the narrow hairpin turns towards Anacapri. The fresh night air brushed against their faces as they sat beside each other in the backseat of the open-air cab. Raffi put his arm around her bare shoulders; Tara didn't protest.

The taxi driver passed the town of Anacapri and drove down Via Grotta Azzurra, letting them off at the road to the ruins of Damecuta, another of the Roman villas built by Emperor Tiberius. From there, they took a ten-minute walk along an idyllic country lane to reach the restaurant Il Cucciolo.

Tara devoured her plate of risotto with seafood; she hadn't realized how hungry she was. Raffi had spaghetti with local lobster, finishing a bottle of Fiano di Avellino by himself, as Tara now abstained from drinking alcohol.

Between bites, Raffi tried to distract Tara from her worries about Max; he talked about his recent travels visiting his wine purveyors. "When did you arrive on Capri?" he asked, when he realized she was only half listening to his stories. "The night before yesterday, after a long and tiring trip from Kerala."

"You look as marvelous as ever!"

Tara didn't acknowledge his compliment. "Where do you think Max is?" she asked anxiously.

"Well, before I left, Max was investigating the suspicious death of a woman on Capri and he was spending a lot of time with the number one suspect, the sister of the deceased. Maybe he is with her," Raffi said nonchalantly.

Raffi looked up from reading the dessert menu. "Remember the last time we saw each other three years ago—at *La Festa Degli Emigranti*, the party for the Capri expatriates up at my friend's villa on Via Castello?"

"Mm—yes, I remember." Tara's face changed color; she didn't look well

"The desserts are scrumptious here; will you have one?" Raffi said.

"No thanks."

Raffi went on, "What an unforgettable evening that was—the dancing, the music, the entertainment—great food. I wish they'd have another party like it."

"Yes, it was—unforgettable . . ." Tara stared out over the Gulf of Naples. The islands of Ischia and Procida lay before them, their lights twinkling like stars in the black sea.

How could she ever forget that night, or the hellish nights leading up to it? There was not the tiniest little detail that she didn't remember about those nights. Life could be cruel; so many things one could forgot, but the pain and suffering from a betrayal were wounds that did not easily heal.

Those fateful nights had been the beginning of the end of her marriage.

Three Years Earlier

Tara was looking forward to the annual vacation on Capri with Max that summer. His work load and travel schedule had become impossible, but at least they'd have this time together. It seemed that all Max could talk about on the rare evenings when he was at home were his cases under investigation; to top it off, he was taking courses to advance his career. He had only a casual interest in Tara's work as a yoga teacher, and he didn't share her passion for Eastern philosophy or care for her circle of friends. When it came down to it, he didn't particularly like living in America; he said he didn't feel like he belonged there. In sum, things weren't working for them and the marriage suffered.

They'd had their first major disagreement earlier that year. Tara wanted a child, but Max wasn't ready to be a father. He said that he first needed to get a promotion so that he'd be able to spend more time at home. Tara went off birth control pills against Max's will, but months later, she still wasn't pregnant. She asked Max to go with her to consult a specialist; she was prepared to do whatever it took to get pregnant, including in-vitro fertilization. When Max refused to go to a doctor with her, they had their first real quarrel.

Tara hoped that the vacation on Capri would work its special magic on them and heal their relationship, but everything went wrong from the start.

The plane was late leaving San Francisco, so they missed their connection in New York. Put on the last flight out of New York to Rome, they were given separate middle seats. Her seat was next to two screaming toddlers, and she didn't sleep a wink. In Rome, her suitcase hadn't arrived. They filed a baggage claim, got on the train to Rome, changed for Naples, taxied to port, then took a hydrofoil to Capri. By the time they got to their hotel at five that evening, they were both exhausted. Max fell asleep fully dressed on top of their bed. To survive the exhaustion of the trip, Tara had indulged in two double lattes; one in Rome and one in the port of Molo Beverello in Naples while waiting for the hydrofoil.

322

After laying sleepless next to Max for an hour, she went down to the beach for a dip in the sea. She came back refreshed and snuggled up to him, but he grunted and pulled away.

It was ten o'clock by the time she managed to rouse him, and they went out for a pizza near the Piazzetta.

Max proposed they go out to the nightclub Anema e Core where his friend Guido, a popular singer and guitarist, was entertaining. Tara felt uncomfortable going out in her rumpled travel clothes.

"Why don't you go without me?" she said. "I'll return to the hotel and get some sleep."

She couldn't believe it when Max actually did go out to the nightclub without her. When she woke up the next morning, she was alone in bed.

◆ ◆ ◆

The waiter at Il Cucciolo brought Raffi a dessert; it was a *semifreddo pistacchio e nocciola* (pistachio and hazelnut semi-frozen dessert).

Raffi pushed the plate towards Tara after sampling the dessert himself. "Here, try a taste of this — it's delicious."

"Thanks, it does look good, but—" She pushed the plate away; a feeling of nausea had welled up, but luckily it passed, and she managed a smile.

"Raffi, there's something I've been wanting to ask you—about that night three years ago, when you and Max went to Anema e Core and I stayed behind at the hotel. After Anema e Core, you went to the other nightclub called Number Two, is that right?"

"Yes." Raffi shifted in his seat.

"Then Max went with some friends on a boat ride to a nightclub in Positano, right? Did you go with him?"

"Noo, I didn't." Raffi poured himself the last few drops of the bottle of wine.

"Did you know these friends? Max told me they were all too tired to take the boat back to Capri, so they slept overnight on the boat. Whose boat was it?" Tara knew that everyone from Capri pretty much knew everyone else.

"I don't know who owned the boat. I don't know those guys."

"How many were on the boat? Were they Italians?"

Small beads of sweat were forming on Raffi's forehead. "I don't remember anything. I probably had too much to drink that night—just like tonight."

Tara had never seen Raffi drunk or even tipsy before. She was starting to feel sorry for him.

"It's OK Raffi, I know you're covering something up. But you're not expected to lie for a friend. Don't lie to me Raffi, please—I'm your friend too. Max never went on that boat trip, did he? It was all a lie, wasn't it? Now that we are divorced, it's all water under the bridge—or in this case, no water under the boat, shall we say."

Aren't I clever, Tara thought, laughing at her little joke. Then for some reason, a nursery rhyme started repeating in her head:

Row, row, row your boat
Gently down the stream.
Merrily, merrily, merrily, merrily,
Life is but a dream . . .

Raffi wiped his forehead with the dinner napkin; his mouth moved, and he wanted to defend Max, but not a word would come out.

◆ ◆ ◆

Tara remembered the hellish details of what had happened three long years ago as if it had all happened yesterday.

Seven days after Max disappeared that night, she was sitting alone at Gran Caffè in the late morning, sipping her cappuccino and pretending to read a book, when Raffi, who had been Max's best man at their wedding, appeared in front of her.

"Tara, how great to see you, you look ravishing. Do you mind if I join you?" Raffi smiled as he sat down, placing his camera on the table. "I've been looking for you, and now suddenly the day seems brighter."

Tara understood from his overly cheerful voice that he knew what had happened to her and Max during their vacation; that Max had spent a week sleeping at his sister's, while she stayed alone in the hotel. "You're the one like the sun, Raffi—always shining." She managed a fake smile, keeping her dark sunglasses on so he wouldn't see the despair in her eyes.

They chatted about everything except what had happened between her and Max, while Raffi showed her some of the latest photos on his camera. When they ran out of anything to say, they sat in awkward silence.

"There's going to be a fabulous party at my friend's villa tonight, and you must come!" Raffi burst out.

Tara realized this must be the reason Raffi had been looking for her; he was feeling sorry for her. "Thanks, but I don't think so. No, I don't care to go, Raffi," she said.

"Nonsense, you have to come to *la festa degli emigranti* (the party of the emigrants) —it's for my friends who left Capri like myself and who are here on vacation. You just can't miss it. We're meeting in the Piazzetta at eight o'clock to walk up together. You must come!"

Tara took great pains in choosing her outfit that evening, selecting a long, flowing silk chiffon dress that draped her body in hues of blue that matched the ever-changing color of her eyes. She pinned her long blond hair on top of her head, showing her neck and shoulders to their best advantage.

Admiring looks greeted her when she made her appearance in the Piazzetta. Raffi told her she looked stunning. He proudly introduced her to his old friends, and she chatted with everyone as they walked up the hill on Via Castello to reach the elegant three-storied villa. The lively party of around sixty guests was in a beautiful garden setting overlooking the town of Capri.

Naturally, Max was at the party; she should have known.

The night air was soft as velvet. The stars twinkled, and the joy of the emigrated Caprese, back home on their magical island, spread contagiously to their companions, spouses, and friends.

Max watched as the friends he had grown up with on Capri circled Tara like vultures. The news about their separation had spread like wildfire.

Tara put on a brilliant act that she was in rapture over the beauty of the evening, and delighted by the company, the food, the entertainment. Her charm was irresistible to everyone and her bright blue eyes sparkled like sapphires. She ate and drank and laughed at the jokes of the hired Neapolitan comedian. She danced non-stop to the live music, her long blond hair, unpinned, swinging to the beat. When she broke out in a wild rock-and-roll dance, a ring of people formed around her watching and clapping; she drew them into the center, one by one, to take their turn dancing while the rest clapped. Tara was damned if she was going to let anyone see how much she was suffering on the inside that night, especially Max.

Max didn't choose to join Tara's admiring circle of dancers, but he pretended to have an enjoyable time. Now and then he stole a nervous glance at Tara. He started to relax when he saw her smiling at him; or maybe she was just smiling radiantly at everybody.

The party began to break up. Tara was about to leave with Raffi when she suddenly stopped at the top of the stairs exiting the villa, turned around, and walked back to where Max was standing. "Will you walk me to my hotel?" she asked him.

Raffi, left alone at the top of the stairs, watched Max and Tara as they descended the stone staircase of the grand old villa; two black silhouettes against the twinkling lights of the town of Capri below.

The live music ended, and the host put on a recording of the melancholy voice of Roberto Murolo singing "Malafemmena" (The Wayward Woman).

> *Si avisse fatto a n'ato*
> *Chello ch'e fatto a mme*
> *St'ommo t'avesse acciso,*
> *Tu vuò sapé pecché?*
> *Pecché 'ncopp'a sta terra*
> *Femmene comme a te*
> *Non ce hanna sta pé n'ommo*
> *Onesto comme a me. . .*

Paradoxically, the song was one of Raffi's favorites. The bittersweet song lyrics were written by Prince Antonio De Curtis, nicknamed Totò, and regarded as "il Principe Della Risata," the Prince of Laughter.

Three months after the night of that party, Max called Raffi. "Tara has left me. She wants a divorce," he told his friend.

CHAPTER 51 - A NIGHTMARE

THURSDAY, SEPTEMBER 9

Max was falling and falling . . . then he was a falcon flying, swerving up and down with the wind currents; it felt joyous, magnificently free and powerful. The scene changed . . . there was a body strapped onto a stretcher floating in the air; it swung around, and he looked to see who it was, but he couldn't see the face; it was covered with a cloth.

Max woke up in the big hotel bed in a cold sweat. The image of Ugo's dead body on the stretcher being hoisted into the helicopter earlier that night came to him. That could have been me, he reflected. Just days ago, I was bound to a stretcher and airlifted by helicopter—I was that close to death.

Ugo was dead, and he was alive. He had cheated death for now, Max thought, but eventually, death would come for him. What was the point of it all, if he was just going to die anyway?

He looked at the clock; it was two in the morning. As he got out of bed to get some water, the room started to spin; he sat back down on the bed. The throbbing pain in his shoulder and collarbone hadn't diminished, even though he had taken two pain pills before going to sleep at around midnight. Was it possible that the medication was making him dizzy? He resolved not to take any more of it.

I got lucky, he told himself. I survived the accident and I'm alive. Planning and hoping is important, but luck may be more important, he reflected.

He wondered about Tara, was she sleeping? He had felt terrible about standing her up for their appointment at 7 o'clock last. Thank God, he had finally gotten hold of her last night—on the third try; it was close to midnight. He remembered their conversation.

"*Pronto*, hello?"

Max sighed with relief upon hearing Tara's voice. "I've been so worried, I can't tell you how bad I feel about not being able to be there for our appointment. I was caught up in the discovery of—"

She interrupted him, "It's OK."

"Listen, I know it's late. I'll explain everything tomorrow. I wanted to make sure you were fine, are you?" There was silence on the other end; Max panicked, thinking they were disconnected.

"Tara, Tara, are you there?"

"I'm here."

"I'm so sorry about not showing up. I really couldn't help it."

"It's OK." Tara's second okay was as cold as the first one.

"What do you say, shall we meet now, and I'll tell you everything that happened?"

"No, it's late."

"So tomorrow?"

"Yes," Tara's voice was distant, "tomorrow night, eight o'clock in front of the clock tower, does that work for you?"

"Absolutely," Max said, cheerfully.

They said goodnight and Max sighed in relief; he would get a chance to see Tara and tell her everything that had happened.

Max had fallen asleep right after talking to Tara on the phone, utterly exhausted after the strenuous and dramatic day. Now he lay wide awake in the hotel bed staring at the ceiling, filled with a sense of despair. Why do I feel so hopeless? he asked himself. Shouldn't I feel grateful to be alive?

He was unable to go back to sleep—the dream of the man on the stretcher haunted him.

Then an image of his mother's face came to him.

His *mammina* was a perceptive woman; she always got straight to the heart of things. What was it she had said to him in that dream some nights ago?

A capa, 'a capa Massimì, addó' sta, che hai scurdato? (Little Massimiliano, where is your head, what did you forget?)

There was something he had forgotten, he felt the truth of it—but what was it? The murderer had been found, wasn't that enough?

His hand reached for his necklace. He had his *curniciello* back, thanks to the Cortina brothers. Finding the necklace had been a bonus. The boys had searched the site where he landed in the fall at the belvedere and found it under a bush. Tara had told him the coral amulet would protect him when she gave it to him; apparently, she was right. Max wrestled briefly with two unanswered questions before he finally drifted back to sleep.

Why was Tara on Capri?

What had he forgotten?

CHAPTER 52 - A LONG BREAKFAST

Te telephone woke Max. "Good morning," whispered Renato from the reception desk. "I do apologize for waking you, but you have an important visitor."
Max looked at the clock on his nightstand; it was 9:00. Guess I fell asleep, he thought. "Who is it?" he asked. If it was Tara, fine; if not, he wanted to go back to sleep.

"Dottoressa Maria Maddalena Monti, Vice Questore Aggiunto della Polizia di Stato," Renato said, as if announcing royalty. "I have accommodated Dottoressa Monti in the courtyard outside the breakfast room. Eh—" Renato cleared his voice, still whispering, "there is more privacy in the courtyard. Eh—luckily, she is in *borghese* (civilian clothes), and she brought—well, you'll see."

Max showered, taking more time than usual, as his left shoulder was still out of commission and his body ached as if it had been run over by a truck.

Although he was impressed that Chief Inspector Monti herself had come to see him, he didn't see any need to rush. Recalling the strange dizzy spell he had experienced during the night, he flushed the painkillers down the toilet. He pulled on a pair of navy-blue shorts, a light blue t-shirt, and sporty sandals. The door to the second bedroom in the Kennedy suite was closed; Paolo and Franco, his friends from Cortina, were still sleeping.

Chief Inspector Monti was sitting at a round majolica table sipping an espresso, while reading a newspaper. She sat erect on the elegant wrought-iron chair, surrounded by old statues and the exuberant display of flowers in the courtyard. Max appreciated that she was not in uniform, which could have needlessly alarmed the hotel guests; she was wearing a pair of perfectly tailored sky-blue slacks, a simple white blouse, and high-heeled navy sandals. Montalbano, her loyal dachshund, lay on the tile floor at her feet as usual.

"Good morning, Dottoressa Monti. What a pleasure to see you." Doctor of what? Max wondered, though he wasn't about to ask her. He bent down to caress Montalbano's head.

"Good morning, Inspector De Angelis. The pleasure is mine." Her voice was all sugar.

"If you don't mind, Dottoressa, I'll get some espresso." Max suspected that whatever was expected of him, it would be better if he were more alert.

He had a hard time suppressing his smugness. He had trumped Chief Inspector Monti! Not only had he found the evidence that Camilla was murdered, but he also tracked down the murderer. Once out of sight, he allowed himself a cocky grin.

"Breakfast, Dottoressa?" Max asked, with a trace of the self-congratulatory smile lingering on his face when he returned. "Personally, I'm starving."

A dignified waiter dressed in a white jacket, followed Max from the buffet table; he was carrying a large tray with a variety of pastries, cheese, marmalade, butter, two glasses of orange juice, two small cups of espresso, and two glasses of water.

While Max was eating with noticeable appetite and Chief Inspector Monti nibbled on the end of a *cornetto*, she politely thanked him for calling her from Belvedere delle Noci. She told him Ugo's body had been found and brought by helicopter to Naples;

apparently, she didn't know that Max had witnessed it all. The body had been identified by the next of kin, a-sister-in-law.

The inspector went on to explain that when she arrived at her office at eight o'clock that morning, she received a message to call Katarina Kallberg.

"Signora Kallberg has requested to meet us both here this morning. She informed me that you have evidence of who killed Camilla Kallberg. Please tell me what happened—"

The Chief Inspector was interrupted by Katarina, who came into the courtyard and greeted them with a cheery smile. "Good morning, Chief Inspector. Good morning, Max."

Max ordered café Americano for Katarina, and just as he began telling the Chief Inspector the story of what had happened the night before, he was interrupted—Paulo and Franco walked in. They were all smiles as well. Introductions were made, and the waiter pulled up two chairs while the Cortina brothers went to the buffet. They came back with café lattes and heaping plates of fresh fruit, muesli and yogurt.

Max started anew, "The boys came up from their climb, and Paolo showed us what he found. It was—"

"Good morning to you all!" Signora Immaculata Ferrara greeted them brightly. Her ample arm was wrapped around Beatrice, who stood beside her with downcast eyes; her shoulders were slouched and lifeless, her thin arms hung limply at her side.

Max couldn't begin to imagine her suffering. For a young girl to lose both parents was tragic enough. But to have to live with the knowledge that her father had killed two people, including her own mother, and then see him commit suicide right before her eyes— how would she recover from such trauma? It would require immense courage and strength.

The waiter reappeared with another table and two chairs. Immaculata brought over a selection of pastries and two glasses of juice from the breakfast buffet.

Montalbano got up on all fours and did an extended dog stretch. Wagging his tail, he looked expectantly up at his mistress, who lifted him up and put him on her lap, feeding him the end piece of her *cornetto*.

"OK, De Angelis, may we get on with —" the chief inspector began.

"Just a moment Chief Inspector," Max interrupted. "Beatrice, could you please go to your room and get those vitamin pills you've been taking?"

Max miraculously managed to tell the entire story without interruption before Beatrice came back with the pills.

"Where is the evidence? where is the iPod?" Chief Inspector Monti asked.

"It's in the safe in my room. I'll get it," Max said.

He made a quick stop in the reception to thank Renato for his help in solving the murder. Max paused to give Matisse a couple of strokes under his chin. Matisse well knew that the caresses were meant as much for another cat; he received affection from cat lovers every day. The sweet little face of Principessa came to Max. I will see you soon, he promised.

At the "ceremony" in which Max handed over the iPod and the Mikey to Chief Inspector Monti, Katarina clapped jubilantly, and the Cortina brothers joined in. Max beamed with pride as he showed the inspector how to get the recording to play.

Beatrice returned and gave the box of pills to Max and sat down. Her face was wet with fresh tears.

Katarina knelt beside Beatrice's chair and held her limp hands.

"*Colombina*, little dove," she said softly, "you don't know me yet, but I hope you will soon come to visit me in Norway. I have a daughter there your age, and I think you two will like each other. You are welcome to stay as long as you like. What do you say, will you think about it?"

Beatrice raised her head and gazed into Katarina's kind eyes. She nodded twice.

"I'll be waiting for you. Here, I've something incredibly special for you. Camilla, my sister, wanted you to have this as a gift; it once belonged to her mother-in-law. Please put out your hands."

Katarina pulled out a heavy gold necklace from the box in her handbag and let it gently spiral into Beatrice's open palms. The large diamond, encircled by a crown of gold, lay glittering in her small hands. Beatrice's eyes were wide with astonishment. "I'll keep the necklace safe for you until you are eighteen years of age, is that okay?"

Beatrice nodded twice. Katarina threw her arms around the orphaned girl and Beatrice clasped Katarina around the neck.

"Dear *Colombina*, you should know that it was only with the help of Paulo and Franco that I am able give you this necklace, they risked their lives to find it on those treacherous cliffs."

The two brothers beamed with pride as Beatrice rushed over to embrace them.

Max took the occasion to whisper into the chief inspector's ear:

"Could you please have those pills analyzed? When Beatrice told me about her father giving her these pills at night, it got me thinking—Are they actually vitamin pills?"

"I'll take care of it right away, De Angelis. I'd better get back to my office now."

Before the chief inspector could make her escape, Renato and a middle-aged woman approached. "This is Signorina Beatrice Vitale's aunt, she has come to pick up her niece," Renato said.

After introductions and a long teary hug of Beatrice, the aunt told them about the horrible experience of having to identify Ugo the previous evening at the morgue. She obviously hadn't yet been informed that he had murdered her sister, but had been told at the morgue that Ugo had committed suicide.

The chief inspector didn't get a chance to escape before Ugo's sister-in-law recounted a long, sad story after Beatrice left to pack her suitcase with the help of Immaculata.

"The poor man, Ugo, my brother-in-law, how he must have suffered; he couldn't bear living without Diana." She babbled on in a fast mix of Italian and Neapolitan. "I knew there were problems, my sister confided in me, God rest her soul. I promised her that I wouldn't tell a single living person, not even my husband." The aunt took a breath before continuing.

"When Ugo found a publisher for his first book, he decided not to mention that Diana had written large parts of it. Diana was a shy person, she didn't want to have anything to do with signing books and travel and all that stuff. Ugo was the one who was good at that."

Monti had sat down again, with Montalbano in her lap. Nobody could escape a Neapolitan woman with a story to tell.

"Diana, my poor little sister, now in heaven, she said Ugo didn't love her anymore, and that they didn't have any intimacy, so she started suspecting. She was very jealous my sister, and she threatened that if he had a mistress, well she was going to tell everyone that she had written those books. Ugo got angry at her for suspecting and on and on it went, they were always fighting, oh poor Beatrice —"

Sighing heavily, the aunt continued, "What happened next was a disaster; Diana stopped writing. If Ugo didn't love her, she said, there was no reason to write books with him. So, no new books came out; some money came in from the old books, but Ugo invested money in stocks and lost it all. They had to borrow money from us to pay the mortgage."

After polishing her thick glasses with a handkerchief fished out from the bottom of her roomy handbag, she picked up her story.

"Last year Diana came to me, saying everything was going to be fine. Ugo loved her after all. Now suddenly everything was all right, and they wanted to take a trip to the mountains, another honeymoon, just the two of them, and could I take Beatrice for a few days. I was happy to—you see, I have no children of my own, God didn't—"

The aunt blew her nose into the handkerchief. "Then my sister died in that terrible accident on the mountain," she sniffed. "Beatrice will be with us now, we'll take loving care of her, she needs a good education. That girl reads whatever she picks up; she has a good head on her, takes after poor Diana."

"Signora, duty calls, I must excuse myself." Chief Inspector Monti stood up and put on her sunglasses. "My sincerest condolences. I'm sure Signorina Beatrice will be well cared for. I wish everybody a good day."

The inspector's high-heeled sandals made rapid clicking sounds on the pavement as she hurried out of the courtyard and down the steps. Montalbano kept up the pace, the little dog's tiny feet skipping as fast as they would go, as he bounced down the steps behind her on his leash.

CHAPTER 53 - VILLA HELIOS

Max decided to go for a walk after his substantial breakfast. He strode up Via Croce past the Tiberio Palace Hotel and stopped to admire the gigantic old magnolia tree outside the entrance to Villa Helios. As a child, he used to put his palms on the gnarly trunk to feel the tree's vibrations.

The rare Australian fichus magnolia was planted on the grounds of the villa when it was built by the Swiss baroness Meta Von Salis in 1904. The trunk had grown so wide that it would take about a dozen people holding hands to encircle it, and Max couldn't even see the top of the tree when he leaned back his head.

Tara was staying at Villa Helios; whose striking octagonal towers and Moorish arches were visible from almost anywhere in the town of Capri.

Max stood outside the villa debating whether to go inside and ask for Tara or wait for their appointed meeting time at eight o'clock. Why so late? he wondered. Why not earlier in the day? His feet soon carried him through the impressive blue-tiled pillars flanking the entrance gate of the magnificent ochre-colored villa.

"Is Signora Tara De Angelis in?" He asked, slightly embarrassed. "Uh—my name is Max De Angelis." The fact that Tara had not changed her surname could give people the impression that they were still married.

The young man in the reception smiled courteously.

"No, Signora De Angelis is not here."

"Do you know where she went?"

"No, I don't know, unless—"

"Yes?"

"Well, I've seen her visit the garden, you might look there," he suggested.

Max made his way into the terraced garden. On the lower level was an orchard with fig trees, where an old man in a straw hat stood on a ladder picking figs and tossing them into a woven basket. Max picked a fig, eating it with gusto, skin and all. He had never adopted the custom of removing the skin from figs.

"I remember you, you *mascalzone* (rascal)," said the old man, peering down at him from the ladder, "you used to come in here and steal my figs."

There was no point in denying it. He and a group of three or four boys liked to raid the garden. While two of them stood guard, one of them—usually Max, would climb a tree and pass figs to the boys below.

"I'm sorry about that, but the figs tasted just as good back then as they do now," Max said with a grin.

"So, you were a rascal then, and you are a rascal now. Some things never change. At least you learned what a good fig from Capri should taste like."

"Sure did," Max said as he bit into a second fig, picked from a lower branch.

"So, you're looking for that lovely American woman, are you?"

Max nodded. He had no idea how the old gardener could know he was looking for Tara, but old people on Capri seemed to know everything.

"Maybe she's in the chapel," he said, tossing Max a fig. "Remember this: Forbidden fruit may be good, but the price you pay for it may cost you all you've got. Fruit grown in your own garden that you watch and care for is best—the reward you get is priceless."

Max was still chuckling over the old man's double entendre when he opened the door to the little chapel below the hotel. For a moment, he thought he had been transported to somewhere in Africa. Five dark-skinned nuns dressed in black habits and white veils were dancing and whirling to African drum music blasting from a CD player. Light streamed through the stained-glass windows, casting colorful patterns on the walls and dark swirling robes. Tara was not among the dancers in this unreal scene. He closed the door carefully; they hadn't even noticed him.

Back on the street outside Villa Helios, he looked at his cell phone. It was eleven-thirty. The meeting with Tara at eight o'clock seemed an eternity away. He decided to walk up the hill and visit Il Professore on Via lo Capo.

"Max De Angelis!" the Professor exclaimed with delight when he opened his door. "How lovely to see you. Do tell me everything."

"You shall hear every little detail, my dear Professor. It will give me great satisfaction," Max said, caressing Jacques, the black and white cocker spaniel. "But what do you say we take Jacques for a walk down to Annalisa's restaurant, Lo Sfizio, and have a plate of something to eat?"

They selected a table outside on the terrace, alongside Via Tiberio. Max went to the kitchen to chat with Bruno, Annalisa's husband and chef, to inquire about the specials of the day.

In between mouthfuls of heaping plates of spaghetti with seafood, Max managed to sum up the dramatic events of the previous day.

"Here's to you, Max!" said Il Professore, beaming with pride as he held up his glass of wine.

Every couple of minutes, they were interrupted by one of the Caprese passing on Via Tiberio who wanted to congratulate Max. News traveled fast on Capri, and it seemed he had become a minor celebrity.

Annalisa came out to greet them and they chatted for a while. When she offered them a grappa on the house, they couldn't refuse.

"Thanks for all your help, Professore." Max raised his dainty grappa glass. "And here's to justice!"

"So, you're out of a job now, is that right?" the Professor asked.

"Yes, let's drink to that," smiled Max, and they toasted again, emptying their grappa glasses.

"Will you walk with me down to town, Max? I have a meeting at the Liceo in the Certosa." The Professor picked up Jacques' leash.

"Of course."

"I've a very interesting proposition for you," Il Professore said with a smug look as they walked down Via Tiberio towards town.

"What are you proposing?"

"Let's have a gelato first, then we will talk about it," Il Professore said evasively.

CHAPTER 54 - THE CERTOSA

THURSDAY, SEPTEMBER 9

They stopped for gelatos at the counter of the Embassy Bar on Via Camerelle. Jacques waited obediently outside. The Professor had a sweet tooth and took his time deciding which flavor of gelato to order. After careful consideration, he settled on one scoop each of pistachio, hazelnut, and chocolate served in a wide glass cup.

"Max, there is something I would like you to consider," the professor said in a low voice.

Max was surprised at the professor's sudden seriousness; it didn't match his childlike pleasure licking gelato off his spoon.

"Maybe it's time for you to think about changing careers and do something different with your professional skills."

Max chuckled; he should have known the shrewd professor hadn't brought him along to visit the Liceo without a purpose. His curiosity was piqued.

"And what do you have in mind, Professore?"

Il Professore licked his lips, a little bit of gelato stayed on his chin.

"I will get right to the point. Our mathematics teacher at the Axel Munthe graduate school's scientific program in Anacapri, poor guy, was diagnosed with a brain tumor this past spring. We had hoped he would recover, but sadly we have just learned he will not be returning to teach this semester. We urgently need to find someone to take his place within a week. The meeting today in the Certosa is for the committee to review our candidates. Unfortunately, few teachers are available for the post at this time of year, and I am sorry to say, they are not very qualified."

The Professor paused, wiping his lips and chin with a paper napkin, before continuing.

"With your permission, of course, I would like to propose you for the teaching job. Wait— I can read your face, I know just what you are thinking. At least give me a chance to tell you about this position. Then all I ask is that you will think it over seriously. Take a little time to make your decision—but not too long, mind you, we must fill the job soon."

Max laughed. "How many seconds do I have to make up my mind?" he asked.

They walked down Via Cerio. In Max's youth, the road was nicknamed *Via dei Gelsi*, as it once was lined with mulberry trees.

The Professor continued making his argument. Max listened silently.

"Max, you have, without a doubt, the requisite education and qualification in mathematics. You were my best student. Besides, you have skills in computer science, logic, and statistics, and you did some tutoring, if I remember right. What you lack is teaching experience, but I will personally coach you on the art of teaching to get you started."

At the bottom of the street, they continued down the ramp to the Certosa while the Professor talked. "What you bring to the table is something unique, and I will emphasize that to the school board. You are a local boy who graduated from university despite hardship; then you succeeded in getting good jobs in London and San Francisco. What you offer is inspiration to the young boys and girls that they can become somebody like you by studying. It doesn't hurt that you also know the local culture and the dialect, of course. We need you here in Capri, Max."

The professor brought his passionate appeal to a close as they walked down the cobblestone path leading to the entrance of Certosa di San Giacomo, the Carthusian Charterhouse monastery founded in 1363. The medieval monastery was now used as a school, library, museum and for cultural events.

They walked through a long, dark stone corridor into the deserted and strangely colorless cloister. Massive pillars, severe in geometry compared with the rest of the architecture, supported four long wings with countless arches. The cloister was so large it would strike awe in anyone, Max reflected. He guessed it was almost as big as a soccer field. The unbroken series of cells ran along the cloister's northern, eastern, and southern sides.

Max had once visited the monks' cells after their restoration. He had never understood why these men would choose to live like hermits, praying and studying in silence in isolation from each other.

They entered the small and intimate side cloister, *il chiostrino*.

"You wait here while I talk to the board. Think about my offer and let me know what you decide. The board needs to make a prudent decision today. It is possible that our present teacher will

343

recover sufficiently to return to teaching, but the school board would guarantee your job for six months."

Il Professore pointed in the direction of a large door at one end of the little cloister.

"Perhaps you would like to go into the church to make your decision; it's a good place to think. Jacques, *rimani qui* (stay here)."

Jacques followed Max into the church next to the small cloister. Max didn't know if dogs were allowed inside, but as there was no one around to ask, he didn't see any harm in it.

The solemn austerity of the deserted church interior gave Max a feeling of peace—it was as if time had ceased to exist. He imagined how wonderful it would be to be left alone, to have a chance to think, not having any chores, not having a job, no stress, all one's needs taken care of, no lost love to worry about, no children and no problems. Suddenly, he had a better understanding of the Carthusian monks, even a touch of envy.

What about love? he wondered. Was the love of God enough for the monks? Did the monks love themselves, their fellow monks, as well as they loved God? Could love be rated? No, Max decided. Love could not be superior or inferior, it just was. If, however, one didn't have the security of food and shelter, love was hard to keep alive. He realized that he had overrated the importance of security; there hadn't been a balance in his life. After nearly dying, he understood that love needs tending, each and every day, or it will die.

Max knew his answer to the job offer before he even walked into the church. There was only one thing that worried him. What about Tara? What if, by some miracle, they got back together. Would she want to live on Capri? Looking up at the vaulted ceiling, faintly glowing with light from the stained-glass windows, he searched for a sign from the heavens . . . Nothing came.

Il Professore hadn't been gone more than fifteen minutes when he walked into the church to find Max with Jacques. "I gambled," he said with a grin. "Yes, I gambled, and I hope I won."

"You mean you decided for me?"

"Well, you got the job—at least for six months. I guessed what your answer would be. Was I right?"

Max chuckled. "*Certamente* (sure)."

Max and Il Professore were walking up Via Birago on their way back to town when Max's cell phone rang. The chief inspector's voice was unmistakable: "Signor De Angelis, would you mind coming to the police station to sign a statement, shall we say at six o'clock?"

Five minutes later, his cell phone rang again; it was Katarina.

"Chief Inspector Monti called me, seems we will both meet in her office at six. Shall we have a farewell drink together afterward? I just bought airline tickets for a flight from Rome to Oslo tomorrow. Oh, and I ran into Raffi. He's back on Capri and wants to join us, what do you say?"

"Fine with me. Tell Raffi to meet us around seven o'clock in the Piazzetta; I have an engagement at eight," Max said.

After wishing the Professor and Jacques a good evening, Max skipped up the stairs to Hotel Gatto Bianco, two steps at a time. Matisse was sitting on top of the reception counter. He must have smelled Jacques on Max's caressing hands because he yawned so wide that Max could see all his teeth, then he jumped off the table and strode off with his tail in the air like royalty.

CHAPTER 55 - MEETING A STAR

THURSDAY, SEPTEMBER 9

Tara threw open the windows of her hotel room in Villa Helios. She barely had a chance to enjoy the view of the town and hilltops of Capri, wrapped in peach-colored early morning mist, before nausea hit her. She dashed to the bathroom just in time.

As soon as she had recovered, she dressed in simple cotton pants and a loose top, and walked out through the lovely garden and down the steps to the little chapel below the hotel. Using her folded travel blanket as a cushion, she settled into a comfortable cross-legged sitting position on the floor of the chapel for her morning meditation and yoga practice.

During her light breakfast after the practice, Tara reflected on her purpose on Capri. She had a clear intention: to find out if Max still loved her, and if so, even more important, whether it was possible that they could live in harmony together with their child. Her hope of a reunion with Max had deflated like a balloon when he stood her up the previous night, and that disappointment stirred up memories she had wanted to forget.

But that was yesterday, she consoled herself. Tara felt this was a new day, a day to start fresh.

When Max told her the convoluted story of why he had disappeared that night on vacation on Capri three years ago, Tara had suspected it was a lie. Yesterday, Raffi had confirmed her suspicion, and now she felt much better knowing the truth. When she was sick in India, she had finally let go of her hurt over Max's suspected unfaithfulness; the difficult part was forgiving him for his insistence that he wasn't lying about it. And she recognized how she had been holding onto resentment toward Max for not communicating with her during their marriage. Now the important thing was not to repeat this mistake and move forward.

There were reasons she had set the meeting time with Max for eight—her recent habit of taking a short nap in the afternoon, and she didn't want Max to notice her belly, yet—and it would be easier to hide her pregnancy at night. And she wanted to look her absolute best.

Tara decided to go shopping. She wanted to make a change from her casual Indian-styled wardrobe to the local style. Avoiding the famous luxury brands, she found a sweet summer dress that concealed her slightly protruding belly. Then she headed for a shop that sold a wide selection of hats. Tara chose a straw-colored, wide-brimmed hat, the kind that she could roll up and put in her handbag. Next, she traded her well-worn Indian sandals for plain flat leather sandals handmade at Canfora's in Capri. Her final purchase, a pair of large black sunglasses, completed Tara's "Capri look."

Next on the agenda was a haircut at Pronto Charme.

"*Buongiorno!*" Gino greeted Tara as she entered the beauty salon. Tara had gone to Gino before and considered him a true artist. He remembered her, but it seemed that he didn't make the connection that she was once married to a Caprese. Since there was a half-hour wait for Gino, she went into the Galleria Gaudeamus, the courtyard behind the salon, to read her book.

The courtyard was empty except for a beautiful young girl who Tara guessed to be around thirteen or fourteen. She was sitting on a bench reading a small thin book. Tara sat down beside her and opened her own book. After a couple of minutes, she glanced over to see what the girl was reading, and discovered that the girl was doing the same. Their eyes met and they both laughed.

The girl was exceptionally lovely; she had a sweet smile and blue-green eyes with a touch of mischief. Without speaking, she held up her book, so Tara could read the title, *Montedidio* (*God's Mountain*) by Erri De Luca. The book cover was light papyrus gray with a small charcoal drawing of a bird's wing. Its simplicity appealed to Tara's professional instinct as a book cover artist, and she felt an immediate desire to read the book.

Tara nodded and showed the girl her book cover: *Kundalini Tantra* by Swami Satyananda Saraswati. On the book's cover was a blue human figure, encircled by a green serpent, seated in a lotus position on a bed of white and orange flames within a yellow square. On the vertical axis along the spinal column of the human figure were symbols of the seven chakras. It occurred to Tara that the two covers represented the respective stages of the young girl's life and hers. Her book's design was complex; the young girl's was simple.

"My parents are yogis, but I don't know much about Kundalini, and I know nothing about Tantra," the girl volunteered. "I go every year on a yoga retreat with my father. Are you American?"

"Yes, I am, and where are you from?"

"My father is from Rome, and my mother is from Naples, but I live in Genova with my mother and her boyfriend. My father lives in Rome with his girlfriend and our dog Athena; she's a mongrel and looks like a scary wolf, but she wouldn't hurt a soul. My grandparents have a summer house here on Capri. I'm waiting for my grandmother, who is having her hair done by Gino."

Tara was amused and smitten by the charmingly free-spirited and unpretentious girl. Her expressive hands were in constant motion as she spoke. Her skin had a light caramel suntan glow, and her long blond hair was tied in a thick side braid. Tara thought she had never seen a more beautiful girl.

"I'm Tara," she said. "I'm waiting for my hair appointment with Gino."

"I'm Sara," the girl giggled.

"Sara means 'star' in Sanskrit, did you know that?" Tara offered.

"Yes, I know—" Sara giggled again, "and Tara is known as the sav-i-our-ess—" she said, drawing out the word to twice its length. "Tara is a heavenly deity who hears the cries of beings—in misery—and she has compassion—is that right?"

The girl held a cupped hand over her mouth to suppress her giggling, and then continued:

"If I shine while you save, won't we make a perfect pair?"

They both giggled at Sara's silly declaration. Tara was impressed; was this girl for real?

Sara suddenly burst out: "Do you know that a murderer was found here on Capri yesterday? I overheard Gino telling my grandmother about it."

"What are you talking about?" Tara was doubtful; she wondered if the precocious girl was prone to making things up.

"Look!" Sara held up her book, opened to the title page.

The first inscription said: "To Camilla"; it was signed by the author, Erri De Luca. The second inscription, "To Sara," was signed Camilla Kallberg.

Seeing the blank expression on Tara's face, Sara realized that she must be a tourist who was not informed of the happenings on the island.

"Camilla, you see, is the one who was KILLED!" Sara said, jumping up from the bench and throwing her hands dramatically up in the air. "Camilla is a Norwegian woman who lived on Capri for many years. Until yesterday, the police thought she had killed herself. Camilla and I were close friends." Sara put a closed fist over her heart, "She gave me this book last month when she invited me on a boat trip. I knew all along that the police were wrong."

Tara listened with fascination as Sara unraveled her tale. It was beginning to sound convincing. Why would the girl fabricate all this?

"I met Katarina—the sister of my friend Camilla. She was suspected of killing her sister for her insurance money." Sara's eyebrows rose. "I told Katarina I didn't believe it at all, and I told my grandparents that, too, but they disagreed with me. I am so happy that I was the one who was right all along." Sara smiled with smug satisfaction.

"So, who found the murderer?" Tara asked, curious if she had guessed right that it was Max.

"His name is Max De Angelis. He came down to the beach to ask people questions about Camilla. I spoke to him, and then Katarina confided something to me a few days ago."

Sara lowered her voice to a whisper: "Katarina said she had fallen in love."

"You mean with—Max?" Tara asked. How strange to talk about Max with this girl who didn't know that she had been married to him.

"Well, she didn't actually say his name—but she didn't need to—" Sara paused for effect. "They swam into the coral grotto together— I know, because I was in the water close to the grotto, but they didn't see me. They stayed in there a long time—do you know what that means?"

"No, I don't."

"Well, usually, eh couples, you know, they go there for, you know—romance." Sara's eyes had a mischievous spark.

"Did you see anything?" Tara couldn't stop herself from asking.

"Nooo—I didn't stay. I'm not a spy."

Sara's imagination was certainly vivid, but she was quite perceptive for her age, not to mention observant as well. Tara wondered if Max was in love with Katrina? Was that why he hadn't shown up for their meeting?

"Now Max is a HERO," Sara continued, interrupting Tara's speculations. "And Katarina is RICH." Sara rubbed her thumb against the four fingertips of her hand. "She will inherit lots of money and Camilla's home on Capri. She will need the money. My grandfather is always complaining about the cost of keeping a home here; he worries whether I will be able to pay expenses when they are gone, as I am the one who will inherit the house." Sara sighed. "I'm the only grandchild you see, but I know I will find a way—I'll have to. Our villa is beautiful—and the garden is my favorite place in the entire world. I LOVE Capri!" She spread out her arms with her palms to the sky. Her face was shining like the star she was destined to be.

A woman dressed in a beige linen dress appeared in the courtyard and walked towards them; she was of medium height, sun-tanned and in good shape. Her dark hair was perfectly coiffed.

"Sara, here you are. You are not boring the lady with your tales, are you?"

"Of course not, Signora. It has been delightful to meet your charming grandchild. Now I guess it's my turn with Gino; it won't do to keep *il maestro* waiting. Good-bye *Stellina*, little star, we shall surely meet again—soon, I hope."

Sara pressed her slender body for a moment against Tara's pregnant belly as she hugged her. Although having met only a few minutes earlier, they felt a bond of budding friendship.

Is Max in love with this Scandinavian woman named Katarina? Tara wondered as she walked into the beauty salon.

Chapter 56 - Girlfriends

Thursday, September 9

Gino had almost finished cutting Tara's long hair, quickly and precisely snipping the ends, while complimenting her on her new dress and sandals, when Tara worked up enough courage to ask, "Who is this murderer on Capri, do you know?"

"Ah, the murderer—Ugo Vitale. He was from Naples, like myself, but I didn't know him; I only heard about him. He was a writer. The first book he wrote became a tremendous success. The title of it is *La Madonna e viva e sta bene a Spaccanapoli* (*The Madonna is alive and well in Spaccanapoli*). Are you familiar with Naples?"

Tara shook her head.

"Well, Spaccanapoli is the narrow street that traverses the old historic center of Naples. I grew up in the historic center, close to Il Duomo, the Naples Cathedral, which is known as the Cathedral of San Gennaro. San Gennaro, of course, is the city's patron saint, but you may not know that the Cathedral is dedicated to the Assumption of the Blessed Virgin Mary."

Gino laid down his scissors on the table and made the sign of the cross. "Yesterday, on the Virgin Mary's feast day, the murderer Ugo Vitale jumped off a cliff to his death."

"Why would he do such a thing?" Tara asked.

"Well, this guy, Max De Angelis, who is originally from Capri, proved that Ugo Vitale murdered a client of mine, a woman named Camilla. When De Angelis confronted Vitale with the truth at Belvedere delle Noci, he committed suicide."

Tara waited for Gino to continue, but he picked up his scissors and finished cutting her hair in silence. Assessing his workmanship, Gino concluded that it was perfect, and passed Tara a mirror so she could see the back of her head.

"That is a perfect haircut, thank you," Tara said. Getting up from the chair, she added, "How did this local guy find the murderer?"

"I don't know, maybe Carmen knows—she is the manicurist." Gino pointed to a small side room behind him where two manicurists in white coats were sitting side by side bent over on small stools. "Carmen told me this morning she was once engaged to Max De Angelis. I had no idea."

Luckily, Carmen had a cancellation and could fit Tara in for a manicure and pedicure. Tara studied the woman's face, looking for clues about her character; she wore no make-up and looked unaffected and kind. She was attractive and slim built, with curly light brown hair.

So, this woman was once engaged to her ex-husband? Max had never spoken to her about his past. She was burning to ask Carmen when and why it had ended. But she hesitated, not sure whether it would be better to come clean and tell her she had been married to Max before asking her questions about the murder investigation.

Next to Tara, a young woman was getting a pedicure by the other esthetician, named Adele. Soon the three women were engaged in a lively conversation in the local dialect. Tara tried to follow what they were saying. The two manicurists appeared to be teasing the young woman, whom they called Graziella, about her lack of interest in getting married, and all her rejected suitors.

"Men are a strange species," Graziella said. "When they want a relationship, or sex for that matter, they think all is required is that they find the 'perfect' woman. The man thinks the woman, the prey, will eventually relent, but that's not love, that's just a catch."

"Yes, I agree," Carmen, said. "If a man finds the perfect woman for him, he doesn't care if he is the perfect man for her."

Graziella continued, "I've made the mistake of having sex with men who think like that. But they weren't men, they were boys. Despite their age, so many stay boys forever. I have given up on sex, well almost—"

Adele looked up from painting the toenails of Graziella's perfectly formed feet. "We don't really want to take the hunter out of the man, do we? But after the hunt, we want a man who understands the risks of losing the catch. If the catch is going to stick around, the man needs to understand the value of it. It's a problem, because too many married men are out there doing their hunting outside the home. It destroys a lot of marriages."

"Not only men do this, Adele, but I wish women would stay away from married men," Carmen said. "So Graziella, what do you mean, *almost* given up? Let's hear what is going on."

Tara noticed the color of Graziella's face change. Was it possible that she was blushing? Tara was surprised, after hearing the young woman's bold words.

Graziella was a stunning, exotic beauty. Her Greek profile reminded Tara of the origin of many of the people of Capri and Naples. Her shining blue-black hair was long and wavy, and her complexion was nut brown. She seemed like a wild free spirit. Apart from the silver-gray eyes, she reminded Tara of the Anacapri girl in the painting "A Capriote" by John Singer Sargent. In the dreamlike Capri forest landscape, the girl Rosina was leaning sensuously into the twisted tree branches, her waist and arms supported by the serpentine branches in a way that made her seem as untamed and natural as nature itself.

Tara closed her eyes, pretending to be resting while the women continued their chatter.

"Yes, Graziella, come on, give us a hint—who is your latest prey?" Adele laughed.

"Okay, okay, but I'm not so sure you want to know, especially you, Carmen. If I am not mistaken, he is one of your ex-boyfriends —"

"Are you kidding? Who are you talking about? Any of my ex-boyfriends would be too old for you, you are putting us on —"

"His name is Max De Angelis."

Tara's eyes snapped wide open when she heard the word, "Max" —just in time to see the faces of Carmen and Adele staring in disbelief at Graziella.

"Why are you shocked? so what? He's your ex-boyfriend from a hundred years ago. And he's divorced. So, what's the big deal? He is a bit older than me, but he's a man—not a boy—he's experienced. And, as of today, he's a hero—a sexy hero, I would add."

Tara left the beauty salon and navigated her way along the narrow Via delle Botteghe, ducking left and right; the pedestrian road was crowded at the midday hour. She had no destination—her mind was a blank. After the dramatic revelation of a liaison between Max and Graziella added to the story about a relationship between Max and Katarina, and his earlier engagement to Carmen, Tara felt like she was in a horrid dream. What was she doing on Capri?

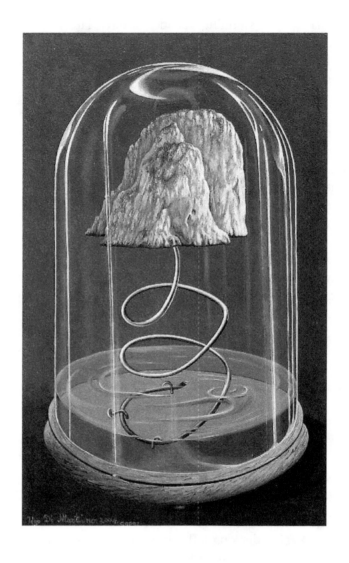

CHAPTER 57 - OPPORTUNITY KNOCKS

THURSDAY, SEPTEMBER 9

Tara jumped through the door of a shop to avoid colliding with a baby stroller pushed by a young couple, but she misjudged the distance and fell onto the marble floor.

Luckily, she landed on her butt. A salesclerk came running over and helped her up to her feet, then led her to a chair in the dressing room.

It was a bathing suit shop, with a large display of discounted bikinis. Tara believed that nothing happened by coincidence, so she decided to buy a new bathing suit, one that would fit her now pregnant figure. She asked the salesclerk, a tall dark-haired girl, if she could show her some one-piece bathing suits, but the store only carried two-piece suits.

"But you see, I'm pregnant," Tara whispered.

"I understand—you must be American," the girl said, smiling. "Here in Italy, few women wear a one-piece suit, whether they are pregnant or not. What is there to hide? Being pregnant is a celebration, isn't it? The women here like to show it off."

The girl brought her a few dozen bikini pieces. Tara quickly found a top and bottom piece that fit her, and she was not dissatisfied when she looked at herself in the mirror.

"With a figure like yours, Signora, you could be a movie star," the girl said with admiration as Tara left the shop.

The fall had made Tara acutely aware that she had to be more careful now that she was expecting a baby. She felt lightheaded, and recalled that she hadn't been able to eat much for breakfast and hadn't had any water for a while. Fortunately, she remembered that at Hotel La Vega she could pay for a day pass to the pool and have lunch on the poolside terrace.

The bagnino handed her a white towel and had her settled within minutes on a sun lounger. He adjusted the sun umbrella to supply shade and brought her a large bottle of water.

Tara floated on her back in the cool, clean water of the pool, while waiting for the lunch she had ordered. The waiter, Agostino, was a sweetheart; he had suggested she take a dip while the chef prepared her meal: a whole local wild fish, *la pezzogna*, to be prepared *aqua pazza* style with a side dish of rucola.

As soon as she had toweled off, the waiter gestured for her to sit down at the restaurant table adjacent to the pool.

She ate the whole fabulous fish without a pause, scooping every bit of the delicious sauce with bread. Tara patted her belly.

Everything is going to be okay, she said quietly to her baby. She emptied her mind of any troubling thoughts of Max and offered a silent prayer of gratitude, then sauntered over to the lounger and pulled out her book. Tara hadn't even finished reading one page before she fell asleep under the umbrella.

The temperature was cooler and there was a slight breeze when Tara awoke from her nap. After paying her bill, she realized she was running out of cash and decided to look for an ATM.

Via Dalmazio Birago was quiet as Tara walked up the shaded footpath. Suddenly a skinny black cat jumped down from a high fence and landed at her feet; the cat had the longest tail of any cat she had ever seen. When the feline rubbed against Tara's legs, she couldn't resist and crouched down and caressed the cat's head.

Her thoughts went to Principessa. How she longed to pet her beloved cat and feel her rough tongue licking her forehead.

A woman's voice called out from behind the high fence next to Tara: "*Nedina, Nedina mia, addo staie?* (Nedina, where are you?)"

Tara realized the cat's name must be Nedina.

A gate opened, and an old woman with a stooped back peered out, leaning on a walker. Her hair was covered with a rose-colored cotton kerchief, and she had on a red plastic apron, and wore bright yellow crocs. Seeing Tara crouched down by the cat, tiny wrinkles spread out like a fan from the corners of her eyes.

After three cups of peppermint tea and homemade almond cookies, Tara and the tiny old woman called "Maria Carlotta" were best friends. They sat on a rusty swing in Maria Carlotta's garden of lemon and kumquat trees. Nedina lay purring on a blanket in Tara's lap, profiting fully from her newly acquired friendship.

Tara told Maria Carlotta about her work as a book illustrator and the story of how she became a yoga teacher. She told her all about Principessa, her precious cat, but she couldn't bring herself to mention Max or why she was on Capri.

"Why don't you stay on Capri and teach yoga here? You could also do your book covers and such. Capri is a good place to live, you know, and you could bring Principessa."

Maria Carlotta's proposal took Tara by surprise. "Maybe that isn't a bad idea? For a while anyway," she said with a smile.

Tara reflected quietly on her situation for a moment. Nothing was keeping her in San Francisco; she had her house, of course, but she could rent it out. It seemed unlikely she and Max would be together again. That had been wishful thinking. If she was going to raise a child alone, why not do it on Capri?

"Follow me," Maria Carlotta said, and shuffled with her walker towards a building at the end of the garden. Maria Carlotta was so short she just barely reached the rusted handle of the garden door; she pushed it open and pointed inside to the bare dusty room.

"Look, this room is empty. I don't use it for anything. I know it needs some repair and some paint, but I don't have the money to do it. There is a toilet and a sink behind that door in the back. Why don't you put a yoga studio in here?"

Maria Carlotta's generosity warmed Tara's heart. She was taken at once by the spacious room, about 3.5 meters[17] high, illuminated by natural light from tall double windows. Paint was peeling from the old wooden window frames, walls, and ceiling, but that could be fixed.

"Take your time, think it over. It may not look like it, but I'm not going anywhere soon, and you know, Capri is an excellent place for children—I mean, in case, you have any."

After embracing her new friend in a warm farewell, Tara found her way out of the garden and stepped through the gate back onto Via Dalmazio Birago. A few steps up the road, she stopped in front of a Madonnina, set into a niche in the wall, and pressed her closed palms to her heart. "Please help me do what is right for the baby," she prayed.

---

[17] 12 feet

CHAPTER 58 - CONSEQUENCES

THURSDAY, SEPTEMBER 9

M ax was passing the Campanile in the Piazzetta on the way to his appointment with Chief Inspector Monti at six o-clock when he heard someone call his name— "Max!

Max!" It was Graziella, standing by the newspaper kiosk. She rushed over and threw her arms affectionately around his neck, pressing her curvaceous body against him. Then she pulled his head down to hers and whispered into his ear, "I've been thinking of you."

She released his neck but kept her body close to his, wrapping a bare leg around him. Her long black hair cascaded down her arched back and her gray panther eyes looked teasingly up into Max's eyes:

"I know I said what we had was an adventure, but I didn't mean it could never be a repeat adventure. And it's not just because you're a local hero now that I want to see you again."

Max was at a loss for words; he had never received such a direct proposal from a woman, and a woman so sensual and so much younger than himself. He turned on his automatic response to trouble—escape.

With a sheepish smile, he untangled himself from her grasp and stepped back. "Great to see you!" Max looked up at the clock in the Campanile. "Oh, sorry, I've got to run to the police station; the chief inspector is waiting for me to sign a statement, I mustn't keep her waiting!"

After crossing the funicular square, he turned to look behind him and saw her standing in the same spot. He raised his arm and waved, and Graziella waved back; he felt like a fool. He walked briskly down Via Roma towards Due Golfi.

"Damn. Damn women!" He couldn't help smiling while he cursed them.

MAD JEALOUSY

Tara turned off Via Dalmazio Birago and walked along Via li Campi, continuing on Via Padre Cimino to reach the church square above the Piazzetta. Across from Santo Stefano, she climbed up the exterior staircase of Palazzo Cerio to reach the ATM between the balcony and the bank. She cashed out enough euros to get her through the next couple of days.

Back outside on the balcony, she rested against the balustrade to enjoy a view of the houses on the hillside and the clock tower in the Piazzetta below. Suddenly she heard a voice shouting. "Max, Max!"

It took Tara less than a second to realize the voice had come from the woman standing by the newspaper kiosk under the clock tower. She recognized her at once; it was the woman she had seen at the salon that morning, the exotic Graziella.

The scene below unfolded as if Tara had been given first-row balcony tickets to a show she had no desire to see. Max's figure came into view; Graziella ran over to him and the two of them embraced. Tara was not spared any visual details of the intimacy of the meeting: the woman's arms around Max's neck, his bending down to her face, her mouth touching his ear, her leg intertwined with his, the staring into each other's eyes. And then the coup de grace—after they parted, Max turned back to look at Graziella, both smiling and waving.

Tara felt faint . . . gasping for air, she staggered down the stairs and went into Santo Stefano. She collapsed in the first pew; her legs felt like lead, and she was trembling and cold with sweat.

A blast of raging jealousy tore through her. It was as if a heavy black smoldering fire was consuming her, obliterating every emotion except wild fury. How tormenting jealousy was, how raw the pain; she hadn't felt this awful since the night Max abandoned her on Capri. Waves of physical and emotional pain surged through her, crushing out the love in her heart—though Tara well knew that love was the very essence of survival.

Think about the baby, relax, breathe, she told herself. Breathe slowly . . . Just breathe . . . Count the in-breath: 1, 2, 3, 4. Count the out-breath: 1, 2, 3, 4. She repeated this until the fiery grip on her heart began to ease up.

How silly I was, Tara reasoned, to think it possible that a divorced couple could get back together. Her mind swiftly returned to that night three years earlier when Max had disappeared. Over time, she had managed to block the memory of those awful days, but now it all came flooding back in.

It was Max's betrayal that night that had caused her to want to end their marriage. He wrongly believed that Tara had left him for another man. It seemed less harsh to let him think that than telling him the truth: she'd left him because he'd destroyed her trust in him.

Tara had forgiven Max during her time in India. Now, in the midst of her jealousy attack, she learned that forgiving wasn't the same as forgetting; she cried bitterly, almost convulsing with pain.

Tara closed her painfully swollen eyes and Max's face appeared. He was looking up at her from the bench at Punta Tragara. To see him alive, right there in front of her eyes, was wonderful. Everything seemed possible at that moment, as if they were being given a second chance. Now one day later, she was in utter turmoil.

Tara began to question everything. She recalled that on the bench at Punta Tragara, she had an unsettling feeling—as if something was missing. Then she remembered that Max wasn't wearing the wedding day present from her, his *curniciello*. He had always worn it, even after the divorce was final. What had changed? she wondered. Was Max in love with someone else?

Folding her hands in prayer, she begged for strength. To quiet her mind, she slowed down her breathing until it was even and steady, inhaling up the front of the spine for seven counts, holding the breath for seven counts, and exhaling down the back of the spine for fourteen counts. She went into a deep meditation and lost track of time.

When she opened her eyes again, the early evening light was faintly streaming through the stained-glass windows of the church. She was calm now; she had found the strength to do what she had to do.

CHAPTER 59 - GOODBYES

THURSDAY, SEPTEMBER 9

After waving good-bye to Graziella, Max was hurrying down Via Roma when Katarina came into view in the arched passage of Via Castiglione. She was running at full speed, her golden curls bobbing.

"I'm glad to see I'm not the only one late for our meeting with our new friend Maria Maddalena Monti," Katarina joked as she joined Max.

Max smiled; he was a fast walker, but he practically had to jog to keep up with her. This Scandinavian girl knows how to move, he thought to himself.

Chief Inspector Monti was waiting for them. Montalbano lay faithfully under her desk. It took Katarina and Max all of four minutes to sign the written statements describing the dramatic events of the previous day. Max marveled that a few concise sentences could capture all of what had happened. The police and the law may not have much use for "nuances," Max thought, but the details of the events surrounding the investigation into Camilla's death would stay with him forever.

"Here are the belongings of Camilla Kallberg: the iPod, the Mikey, the cell phone, and the laptop. We have no need of them anymore; we copied the iPod recordings."

Monti got up from her desk and handed the items to Katarina, who put everything in her handbag.

"You may wish to get the recordings transcribed, Signora Kallberg, there are many hours of recordings, seemingly about her life. I understand they were to become a book. I can assure you I only listened to snippets. They are quite—how do you say it? — revealing." The chief inspector adjusted her tight grey-blue skirt.

Max thought he detected a tiny smile at the corner of her mouth before she glanced down at the papers on her desk.

"We searched Signor Vitale's hotel room and found three cell phones. One cell phone was registered to Signor Vitale, and the other two were registered to a person in Naples who was possibly a friend of Vitale. We know those two phones were used exclusively for communication between Camilla Kallberg and Ugo Vitale, as we have obtained transcripts of the phone records."

"Did you find Virgil's *Aeneid*—the book that was missing after the break-in at the villa?" Katarina asked.

"Yes, Signora Kallberg, we did. We conclude that Vitale was the one who searched your home. In his hotel room, we found three books with inscriptions from Ugo Vitale to Camilla Kallberg. Vitale wrote two of the books; the third book was indeed Virgil's *Aeneid*. He may have searched the home for the memoir Kallberg was writing, and when he did not find it, he may have thought to look for her iPod. The books will be returned to you, they are in our office in Naples."

"You didn't find a manuscript?" Katarina inquired.

"No, we didn't, but you will find several of Kallberg's recordings in the iTunes application on her laptop. I admit we were a bit sloppy—we didn't think about searching the recordings when we were looking for evidence."

"Were you able to analyze the so-called vitamin pills Ugo gave Beatrice?" Max asked.

"Your suspicions were right on target, De Angelis," Chief Inspector Monti said with an uncharacteristic tone of admiration. "We found a bottle half full of tablets identical to Signorina Beatrice's vitamin capsules in Signor Vitale's suitcase; the bottle was labelled as sleeping pills; we are waiting for confirmation from the lab. It does appear therefore that Signorina Beatrice was given drugs to put her to sleep so her father could skip in and out of the hotel undetected."

"So, the case is closed?" Max inquired.

"Yes, and we are glad it is all over. Thank you both. The Islanders and the tourists will sleep better knowing the murderer was a jilted lover who killed himself."

Monti bent down and picked up her dog before walking them to the door, "I wish you both safe trips."

"I may stick around on Capri," Max joked, "just in case you need my help again."

TWO CEMETERIES

"I'm going to say goodbye to Camilla," Katarina said as they came out of the police station.

"I'll come with you," Max said. "I'd like to visit my parents' gravesites."

They stopped at a flower shop near the entrance to the two cemeteries. Max chatted with the owner, his friend Antonio, while his son Leonardo helped Katarina choose a bouquet of white orchids to place on Camilla's grave.

Directly inside the entrance gate, they each took a different path. Max walked across the labyrinth of the Catholic cemetery grounds to reach his parents' resting place, while Katarina entered the non-Catholic cemetery.

The wild unkempt graveyard conveyed the impression of neglect, and yet Katarina felt the peace and stillness of this sacred place. Shaded by the tall cypress and pine trees weaving a latticed roof overhead, she walked past a row of headstones sheltered within the high stonewalls of the graveyard. She was surprised to see how many of the names carved on the stones were familiar to her. Without even realizing it, she had become quite familiar with the history of the foreigners who had come to Capri and ended up staying—just as her sister had. Many of them had been writers and painters; others were scientists or nature lovers—or just lovers and dreamers. Some had fled from oppression, and some came to escape from the cold. All had stayed because of their love of Capri.

The originality of the headstone designs impressed her. Some of the inscriptions were eccentric. One of them said: "There are no dead." On another, it said: "There is no Death."

When she reached her sister's bare gravesite at the far end of the graveyard, Katarina's heart sank; she wished there had been time for Camilla's headstone to be carved and placed at the site for the day of her memorial service and burial. She choked up at the memory of Camilla handing her the detailed instructions for her own funeral, including the inscription for her headstone: *Love is Infinite.*

Katarina didn't kneel on the ground, as she didn't want her ivory-colored dress to get soiled, so she bent over to gently place the white orchids on the grave. "I promise you, Camilla," she said, "I will try to be strong like you. I promise I will take care of everything you created here on Capri, and I will love and cherish the island and the people here. I promise to remember that love is infinite, and," she paused, "I promise we will meet here—again."

She realized at that moment that one of the reasons Camilla had chosen to be buried at this cemetery was so that she would keep returning to Capri to visit her.

Katarina pulled out a handkerchief to dab her eyes. She knew Camilla had always been crazy about white orchids, and felt pleased at how well they suited the somber atmosphere of the cemetery. Suddenly, she had the comforting sensation that Camilla was present and watching over her—as if she was standing there beside her.

"I think we will do a joint book project, what do you say?" Katarina said. "The first part of the book will be your transcribed recordings up to the day you died. The second part will be my story of how your murderer was brought to justice. What do you think Camilla, do you like the idea?"

Max knelt in front of his mother's simple tombstone and read the inscription chosen by her: *"Verità e Gratitudine"* (Truth and Gratitude).

"Is this message for me, Mama?" he whispered.

The image of his mother in the dream appeared to him once again, and Max remembered what she had said: *"A capa,'a capa Massimì, addo sta, che te si scurdato?* (Where is your head Massimì, what have you forgotten?)"

When he thought about it, he knew that he hadn't always been as grateful as he could have. But after his near-death experience, Max felt that he had changed—everything in life had become more precious. Truthfulness was another matter. Had he forgotten to be truthful?

Max pushed the question out of his head. No time for this now, he thought. He didn't want to be late for the appointment with Raffi and the Cortina brothers in the Piazzetta—but even more important, he couldn't be late for his meeting with Tara at eight o'clock.

Max kissed his mother's stone, "Thank you, Mammina," he said.

Walking down a flight of stone stairs to reach the non-Catholic cemetery, Max was struck by the contrast between the atmosphere of the two cemeteries. The large (for Capri) Catholic cemetery was sunny, with colorful fresh flowers on most of the graves; many of the more elaborate tombs were adorned with beautiful sculptures of angels. The small non-Catholic cemetery was dark and gloomy by comparison. Max didn't see a single flower on the graves—until he saw the white orchids on Camilla's fresh gravesite, with Katarina standing beside it.

At the sight of Katarina, he felt a kinship; he knew theirs was a friendship that would last for a lifetime. A miraculous joy spread through him. Thank God, I'm not one of the dead! How extraordinarily fantastic it feels to be alive! He could hardly wait to see Tara again.

"What do you say to a bottle of champagne to celebrate life?" he asked as he reached her side.

Katarina looked into Max's brown eyes, gleaming with tiny specks of gold. She nodded, and too overcome with emotion to talk, she took his arm and they walked out of the cemetery together.

CHAMPAGNE

Raffi was waiting at Gran Caffè R. Vuotto when Max and Katarina walked into the Piazzetta; a bottle of champagne was cooling in a bucket of ice on the table.

"You're a mind reader, you old rascal," Max said, glowing with happiness as he embraced his friend. "Welcome back. You wouldn't believe all that has happened since you left."

"I have heard a little—you know Capri—you know how fast news travels, but I am dying to hear every little detail. What a bummer I had to leave you guys to all the fun."

Raffi gestured to Mario to open the champagne bottle. The waiter smiled broadly as he expertly poured the champagne into the flutes.

"Congratulations, Max!" he said. "We are all so happy that you solved this mystery. I said all along that there was no way Camilla would have taken her own life."

Katarina and Max took turns completing each other's sentences as they told Raffi everything that had happened. Now and then,

369

Mario returned to their table, replacing the fast disappearing green olives, and refilling the champagne flutes, while getting snippets of the story.

"You scoundrels, champagne without the Scoiattoli," Paolo said, grinning, as he walked up to their table.

Mario added two chairs for the Cortina brothers and brought over another bottle of champagne.

Katarina's cell phone rang; she left the table to take the call, and came back with a radiant smile on her face.

"Good news?" Max asked.

"The best!" Katarina said, smiling as if she was hiding a delightful secret. When she saw Max's curious face, she whispered into his ear, "An old boyfriend from my high school days just called, we have a date when I get back to Norway."

Max raised his champagne flute to Katarina for a silent toast.

Soon they were discussing where to go for dinner to continue the celebration. "Sorry guys, count me out, I've got plans," Max announced.

"Really?" Raffi raised his camera to take a picture of the second-floor terrace of Piccolo Bar with its bright yellow awning.

"Yeah, would you believe that Tara is here on Capri? We're meeting tonight," Max said with a bright smile.

"Really."

Raffi's indifferent tone surprised Max. But then he realized that Raffi was busy adjusting the lens of his camera.

CHAPTER 60 - THE LAST BOAT

THURSDAY, SEPTEMBER 9

The receptionist at Villa Helios checked the boat schedule for Naples, and Tara made a quick decision to take the last boat, the fast ferry leaving at 8:15 pm. She had her bag packed and the bill paid in no time.

The rolling suitcase was small; she could easily roll it down to the funicular. She strapped her shoulder bag over the handle and hurried away. Going downhill on Via Croce from the hotel was challenging until she placed the suitcase handle under her butt, effectively breaking the speed of the bag.

The sun had set, turning the sky a luminous blue, but Tara didn't see it; she was wearing sunglasses and a hat, pulled low over her forehead. Now that she had decided it best for all concerned that she make an exit, she wasn't in the mood to be recognized.

As she walked through the arch from Via delle Botteghe into the Piazzetta, she saw Max sitting at a table at Gran Caffè. In a split second, she pivoted and walked back under the arch; she was convinced he hadn't seen her, as she had been that quick. What now? she thought. Luckily, Tara knew Capri well, but she didn't have much time left before her ferry departure.

She made a right turn, then a left down Via Vittorio Emanuele, and then a right up Via L'Oratorio behind the ex-cathedral Santo Stefano. She found herself back in the place where she had been just a little earlier that day, at the top of the flight of stairs to the church.

From this location above the Piazzetta, she could see Max's back. Raffi was sitting next to him. On the other side of Max was a blonde woman she had never seen before. Was this Katarina, the Norwegian woman who had told Sara she was in love with Max? Two fit and sun-bronzed men she didn't recognize were sitting next to Katarina. They all seemed very merry, laughing and toasting their champagne glasses.

Tara grabbed her bag by the carrying handle and, in less than a minute, was down the flight of steps and safely inside the entrance to the funicular. She congratulated herself on her decision to leave Capri. Feeling a twinge of guilt about not showing up for the appointment with Max, she reminded herself that Max had stood her up the previous night, and now, he seemed to be having the time of his life.

When she got back to San Francisco, she would call him.

CHAPTER 61 - DESPAIR AND BETRAYAL

THURSDAY, SEPTEMBER 9

Max paced back and forth in the Funicular Square between the campanile and the columns. It wasn't like Tara to be late, and he was getting increasingly worried. Did anything happen to her? he wondered. The bell in the clock tower rang ten times, eight long and two short rings; it was 8:30, half an hour past their agreed meeting time.

At a quarter of nine, he called Villa Helios.

"Signora De Angelis has checked out. She said she was taking the 8:15 ferry."

The receptionist's words cut like a dagger into Max. He swallowed twice. "Did she leave a message? Where was she going?" His voice was hoarse.

"No, she didn't leave any message, and I'm sorry, we have no information as to her destination."

The pain in his collarbone was nothing compared to the pain he felt shooting through his gut. Max fumed silently: How could you leave me, Tara? It's not fair. Why did you come to Capri if it was only to leave me, without even telling me why? How could you have the heart to do it?

Why the hell didn't I go to wait for her at hotel Helios? I should have gone there and rooted myself to the spot—like the giant Ficus Magnolia. Why didn't I think of getting a cell phone for her?

Max went on and on cursing himself for his stupidity. Now he had no way of finding her, no way of knowing where she had gone. He felt utterly lost without her.

It occurred to him that perhaps Tara hadn't left the island, that she had changed her mind and was waiting for him down in the port of Marina Grande. The gong in the Campanile tolled once; he had three minutes to make it to the 9 o'clock funicular departure. He ran into the funicular entrance, bought a ticket, bolted down the stairs and was the last passenger on the cable railway as the door slid shut behind him.

The ferry dock was almost deserted. He walked back and forth along the main drag of Marina Grande searching the restaurants and the cafés for Tara, and then he walked the long way to the end of the beach and back, cursing while slipping on the pebbles. She was nowhere to be found. Capri was suddenly the loneliest place on earth.

He walked slowly back up to town by way of the San Francesco steps, stopping halfway up to pull out his cell phone and make a call; the local time in San Francisco was 1:20 pm.

"Betty-Anne, this is Max." It was his last hope; that Tara might have called Betty-Anne.

"Hi, Max, it's good to hear your voice. You know that Tara called me from India? I told her you were on Capri. Is she with you now?"

"Eh, no—not yet."

"Is something wrong, Max? Your voice sounds strange."

Betty-Anne's friendly concern caused his vocal cords to tighten even more; he couldn't get a word out. "Anyway, Principessa is perfectly fine, she is right here next to me, purring, waiting for you and Tara . . ."

Back in the hotel, Max checked at the reception to see if there was a message for him. Nothing. He had already checked his cell messages and e-mail dozens of times; he checked again—nothing from Tara. He went up to his room and threw himself on the bed, utterly worn out. He closed his eyes, but no sleep came. The pressure behind his eyes increased, and his temples started to throb. He tried to think of an explanation for Tara's departure, but his mind was a mess. As if paralyzed, he just laid there on the big bed like a mummy, unable to move, unable to think.

Max didn't know how much time had passed when his cell phone rang; he sprang to his feet, hoping it was Tara.

"Hi Max, I hope I'm not disturbing you—just wondering if you want to get together tomorrow—that is, if you're not busy with anything, of course." Raffi sounded strangely embarrassed.

Max didn't have the strength to answer; he was too disappointed that it wasn't Tara on the phone.

"How did it go with Tara, is she with you?" Raffi asked.

"No. Are you up for a drink?" Max answered. "I could do with the company." Max knew he wouldn't be able to sleep.

"OK with me," Raffi answered, "shall we meet at the Quisisana bar?"

They ordered a couple of Hennessy cognacs from the barman and sat down at a table. Max hadn't eaten, but he wasn't at all hungry. Raffi nibbled on peanuts and chips while Max told him about Tara's disappearance. The posh bar of the Quisisana Hotel was almost empty; the bartender seemed surprised to see a couple of local chaps at that late hour.

Max looked around him— a long time ago he had learned to mix drinks at this hotel when he worked as a bartender. The elegant decor was black and white with chic magnolia-white leather furnishings. No one was playing the piano. Thomas, the talented musician who had played the piano in the Quisisana bar for more years than Max could remember, had called it a night.

"What went wrong, Raffi?" Max asked, after explaining that Tara had left Capri. "Do you think she left because I stood her up last night?"

Raffi crossed his right leg over the left; then he changed and crossed his left leg over the right, struggling to get comfortable.

"I haven't had a chance to tell you. I had just returned to Capri last night when I ran into Tara. It must have been after you didn't show up. In any case, she didn't tell me you were supposed to meet yesterday; she only asked me to call you, which I did, but you didn't answer. Then I called Hotel Gatto Bianco, and they said you weren't staying there. We were both hungry, so we grabbed a bite together."

Max was flabbergasted. What the hell, he thought angrily. Raffi and Tara went to dinner together last night?

"Where did you go?"

Raffi took a sip of the cognac; he didn't look at Max. "We went to Il Cucciolo."

"Are you kidding me? you dragged Tara into the boonies of Anacapri to one of the fanciest restaurants on the whole bloody island?"

Raffi didn't answer.

"To get a bite, you said."

Raffi still didn't answer; he was chewing peanuts.

"You've always liked Tara, haven't you?" Max's voice was sarcastic.

"So, what? I never fucked her if that's what you're thinking."

"Sure," Max said.

They sat in awkward silence for a while, not looking at each other.

"So, what did you talk about? Did she talk about me?" Max asked, in a cold clipped tone.

"Yes."

Max was furious. Why the hell was Raffi so quiet? he wondered. It wasn't like him at all. What the fuck was he hiding? Max's mouth was parched; he gestured to the waiter for two glasses of water and some more peanuts.

"And what did she say about me?"

Raffi waited until the waiter was out of earshot. "She asked me about the night when you went missing, that night three years ago when you said you went on a boat trip and couldn't get back until the next morning—remember?"

"And—"

"She remembered that you and I had gone to the night club together."

"So—"

"So, she asked me why I didn't go on that boat trip with you—"

"And—"

Raffi took another sip of the Hennessy and grabbed a few peanuts. Max's eyes narrowed to a slit while he looked at Raffi, who took his time chewing the peanuts before he answered.

"I told her I didn't remember why I didn't go with you on the bloody boat, but—"

"But what?" Max felt like a simmering volcano, ready to explode any minute.

"She said she knew it was a lie, the boat trip, she knew it all along. And she said—" Raffi paused again. He was driving Max insane.

"She said—that nobody—nobody should be required to lie for anybody—and especially a friend shouldn't be expected to lie because of their friendship."

The two Caprese friends sat in silence staring down into their oversized cognac glasses.

"Did you ever consider telling her the truth?" Raffi took a sip of water, "the truth about why you were gone that whole night—and morning? That is, of course—if you can remember what happened—"

Max had kept the lie alive for so long that he almost believed it himself. He had lied to protect their marriage, to protect their love—at least that's what he had told himself. Not trusting that Tara would be able to forgive him, he lied, and every question she asked led to another lie. Even when the lies didn't make sense, he kept to his story.

He remembered what Tara had said. *Our love cannot be based on a lie. If you lie about what happened, I have no way of forgiving you, because there is nothing to forgive.*

Still, he kept telling her the same stupid story. How angry he had been at Tara for not believing him.

◆ ◆ ◆

It happened three years ago, on the first night of his vacation on Capri with Tara. She didn't want to go out to a nightclub, so he went with Raffi. The moment he and Raffi entered Number Two, a beautiful girl turned her attention to him. The manager of the nightclub, a friend of Max, told him she was a celebrity, a famous Italian actress. He was flattered that she picked him; it reminded him of the old days when he had been working at that nightclub, and there was no limit to the number of girls interested in him. They ended up in her hotel room; he hadn't planned to stay the night, but due to the jet lag, the tiredness, and the sex, he had fallen asleep. When he woke up the next day, it was after noon.

On the fourth night of their vacation, he was feeling like shit from sleeping on his sister's couch after Tara kicked him out of their hotel room. He went back to the nightclub and ran into the actress again. When she invited him back to her hotel room, he went. It wasn't nice to turn her down, he reasoned; she would be offended if he treated her like a one-night stand. He convinced himself it was Tara's fault that he was going, and shut off his cell phone.

Tara had frantically tried to call him all night; she had even called his sister in her desperation to find him. She would later say that it was the second time he had abandoned her.

Three months later, Tara filed for divorce.

◆ ◆ ◆

Max and Raffi walked in silence out of the Quisisana bar and up Via Vittorio Emanuele. Max was bursting with anger at being betrayed by his best friend. Friendship was supposed to be sacred.

And friendship with the few who had left Capri was the most sacred of all.

On top of his anger at feeling betrayed, he now suspected that Raffi had always been attracted to Tara, and the jealousy was tearing at his guts.

There was an unwritten law against courting a friend's wife—had Raffi crossed that line? The fact that Tara was no longer his wife didn't make him any less angry at Raffi.

"You know I've always respected your marriage," Raffi said; he must have read Max's mind. "But let me be honest; you had your chance and you screwed up. You've been divorced for a long time now. I've waited all these years to see what would happen between you two, and I see you haven't really changed. You don't deserve her. I may not deserve her either, but I would move heaven and earth to have her. I can't let our friendship get in my way any longer. It's only fair that you know my intentions."

Max didn't utter a word as he turned his back to the man that he no longer thought of as a friend and walked into the arcade leading to Hotel Gatto Bianco. His anger was choking him so hard he nearly missed hearing Raffi's parting words:

"I respect Tara's right to choose; after all, it's only her choice that matters."

CHAPTER 62 - THE HERMITAGE

Max tossed and turned in bed for hours before he realized the futility of trying to sleep. As often happened when he was very troubled, he got a desperate urge to get away from it all and go climbing. He asked himself, as he had before, whether summiting a mountain was just a way to escape his problems, or if it also helped him to get a wider perspective on things. It didn't matter. He just knew he had to do it.

He got out of bed, pulled on a pair of jeans, sneakers, and a t-shirt and headed out of the hotel and up Via Vittorio Emanuele. It was still dark.

To get to the summit of Monte Solaro, he chose an infrequently travelled and overgrown path, the Passetiello, an old mule road connecting Capri and Anacapri.

From Due Golfi, he took Via Aiano di Sopra and walked quickly up the pedestrian alleyway past Capilupi, the local hospital.

Max continued up Via Torina, passing the cultivated fields and stone and stucco houses that clung to the hillside. Soon he was surrounded by the indigenous Mediterranean bushes and trees, steadily climbing higher and higher at a quick pace.

Sunrise was still more than an hour away. Max stopped for a moment to catch his breath and take in the view. The town of Capri in the predawn light was like a pastel painting with diffuse shades of gray, complemented by the faintest brush strokes of rose and peach in the sky. The aroma of algae rising from Marina Piccola far below mingled with the scent of pine trees and wild jasmine. The familiar smells from childhood calmed his frazzled mind.

Higher up on the path, the sensual pleasures vanished as Max was immersed in a thick foggy mist. The higher he climbed up the steep mountain trail, the denser the fog became.

Max knew that Monte Solaro was nicknamed Cloud Catcher, *Acchiappanuvole* in the native dialect, after the thick blanket of fog that forms at the summit, especially at dawn. The warm, damp sea air had condensed into a heavy mist on the ground, and when the temperature dropped during the night, the vapors rose to form the crown of clouds over Monte Solaro.

The clouds swirled around him, at times limiting his range of vision to a few meters. The humidity penetrated his clothes and he felt chilled and clammy; Max swore under his breath. Still, there was only one way for him, and that was up. He concentrated on his goal: to arrive at the top of Monte Solaro, while doing his best to block out the thoughts that continued to torment him.

He got to the critical point of the hike where he had to use both hands, grabbing onto rocks and tree roots to scale the rocky path cut into the mountainside. With his left arm still out of commission, the climbing was harder than usual. While reaching for a root with his right arm, it suddenly wriggled and came alive. He couldn't believe his eyes! He was face to face with a blackish snake about one and a half meters[18] long. His heart pounded, and he staggered backward, almost losing his footing; to support himself he grabbed onto a rock with his left hand.

"Mannaggia la miseria!" (Damn!) he yelled out. The pain shot through his left shoulder and broken collarbone with a vengeance.

The snake was a *bacchio*, common in Europe, similar to a western whip snake. He knew it was not venomous, as there were no poisonous snakes on Capri, but it was better not to risk being bitten. The snake must have been sleeping; it slithered away down the rocky path and into the mist.

The encounter with the snake had shaken him, and it had almost caused a nasty fall. Max vowed to be more careful, focusing his attention on the path directly in front of him.

The dense fog blocked the spectacular panorama otherwise accessible from that height. Max couldn't help thinking that the fog in his brain was just as thick. Do not think, he commanded himself, not now, just get to the top.

The path leveled off and opened onto the Valley of Cetrella; once the site, according to legend, of a pagan temple dedicated to the goddess Venus (Venere Citerea). The terrain was overgrown with bushes and grass wet with dew that brushed against his clothes, but Max barely noticed it, as he was already soaked through to the skin.

The aroma of mature fennel plants, with yellow flowers and feathery leaves, caught his attention. He pulled out his pocketknife and cut a bunch of the fragrant wild herb to make his favorite liquor, Finocchietto. Max thought about the times he had come there with his father to collect the precious aromatic herb at just the right time, when the grayish seeds were mature. The happy memory of his father was mixed with deep sadness. He missed his father. How stubborn Papa could be, and yet he was so wise about living life to the fullest with the little he had. There were times when he had little indeed, and even then, he had generously shared with others. Max missed not being able to share life's precious gifts, great and small, with his father.

---

[18] 4.9 feet

Just as he arrived at the end of the Cetrella Valley, the clouds started to drift away. A giant orange sun rose over the Amalfi Coast, burning through the last of the fog and illuminating the magical island of his birthplace. The panorama spanned the entire Bay of Naples, from Capo Misena to Punta Campanella, from Mount Vesuvius to the islands of Procida and Ischia. The two neighboring islands looked like floating rocks in the shimmering blue haze of the sea.

Max became aware of how cold and wet he was, and decided to go to the Hermitage of Santa Maria at Cetrella to see if it was by any chance open; he hoped to warm himself there before continuing to the summit of Monte Solaro.

If Max hadn't known exactly where the Franciscan hermitage was, from his many visits, he could easily have missed it—the ancient building was half hidden in a dense chestnut grove, and the monastery's stone fence was overgrown with weeds. Old pine trees reached to the sky on each side of the arched entry. Max walked into the cobblestone courtyard and placed the fennel branches on one of the white-painted stone benches flanking a small wooden door. Turning the handle, he found the door was unlocked. He stepped into the simple low-vaulted chapel dedicated to the Madonna Santa Maria, and walked up to the marble altar. In a niche above the altar was a statue of the Virgin and Child.

Max knelt on the floor in front of the altar.

In the past, Capri's coral fishermen would climb up to the chapel to pray to the sacred image of the Madonna before setting sail on their treacherous and often deadly pursuits at sea.

Max didn't believe in God, despite having been an altar boy—at least, that's what Max usually told people if anyone asked. He considered himself a man of science, and he didn't have much tolerance for religious practices. But at that moment, kneeling in soaking wet clothes on the cold floor of the chapel, he was on a pilgrimage.

This desolate and spartan chapel was the place that Max had chosen to ask God for help. He hadn't realized it until that moment: he had come to the hermitage to surrender to a higher power.

By some miracle, Tara had come back to him. By some miracle, Tara's gift of the red coral amulet had been returned to him. Why? he wondered. Tara had told him on the morning of their wedding day that the charm would bring him luck. What was the point of the amulet being miraculously returned, if Tara was only going to desert him?

Max pulled the chain with the *curniciello* over his head. He kissed the coral horn, and then reached up and carefully placed the necklace at the feet of the Madonna and child. The sacrifice of his most precious possession brought calm and peace to his troubled mind.

Kneeling on the cold stone floor, Max prayed for two more miracles—that Tara would forgive him, and that Tara would return to him.

CHAPTER 63 - ON THE TRAIN

FRIDAY, SEPTEMBER 10

T he hot Neapolitan sun was beating down on the windows
of the taxi that took Tara from the hotel on Via Partenope
to Napoli Centrale, the central train station of Naples. The

young taxi driver chatted nonstop, while turning his head to look at her or admiring her in his mirror—more often than watching the road, it seemed to Tara. She fumbled nervously for a seatbelt as they shot in and out of the traffic. Cars, mopeds, and pedestrians were fighting for the right-of-way. Luckily, they arrived at the station just as Tara's tummy (and the baby) started to object to the slalom course ride.

Napoli Centrale was bustling. Clutching the handle of her rolling bag with one hand, and holding her train ticket in the other, with her shoulder bag secured across her chest, she walked through the crowded railroad station that handled fifty million passengers a year. Underneath her dress below her pregnant belly, she kept her money belt with the passport and credit cards. Men ogled her as she hurried to catch her train.

The high-speed Frecciarossa train heading for Rome was nearing its top speed of 306 km/h (190 mph) when a merciless surge of nausea hit Tara, forcing her to bolt for the nearest toilet. She hurried along the corridor, holding onto every other seat for safety, but when the train swerved into a tunnel, she was overcome with nausea. Tara quickly brought her hand to her mouth to stop the vomit, causing her to stagger and lose her balance.

"I've got you!" exclaimed a woman standing behind her, who took Tara firmly by the shoulders and held her reassuringly. "Are you headed for the toilet?"

Tara nodded, and the woman guided her safely down the corridor. "I will wait outside, no need to lock the door; holler if you need help."

The noises coming from the toilet were unmistakable. Tara reappeared looking pale, and the woman steered Tara back to her seat, now with a lighter grip on her shoulders.

"I see that the seat next to you is empty, may I join you?" the woman said with a concerned look on her face. "I'll fetch my belongings first," she added.

Tara nodded and closed her eyes, sighing deeply. She had to learn to be more careful. It's not just about me, anymore, she reminded herself. Now she had her baby to consider. The wellbeing of her child mattered to her more than anything in the world. Tara's heart swelled with love for her unborn child, and she smiled softly.

The woman with the unusual accent sat down next to her. "Now, that is much better, isn't it?" she said.

When Tara opened her eyes, they were welcomed by a pair of smiling jade-green eyes. There was something familiar about this woman, Tara thought, although she was certain she had never met her before. For a moment, she wondered if she had known this woman in another life.

"I have one daughter," said the woman. "Is this your first child?"

Tara burst out laughing. "How did you guess?"

"I confess, I happened to be walking behind you on the platform towards the train, and the way you very cautiously stepped up that high step to get onto the train was familiar to me; it made me think you might be pregnant."

"Thank you for catching me in the corridor—I think I would have fallen," Tara said.

"Oh, it was no bother at all." The woman's soft melodious voice sounded like she was singing when she spoke, Tara thought.

For the next thirty minutes, they chatted about everything, and the two women soon found they had much in common. The woman joked light-heartedly about her divorce, raising her child, her work; almost making it sound as though everything had been a bed of roses. Her uninhibited laughter lifted Tara's spirit. Strangely, Tara suddenly felt as if she had found a lost sister, the sister she had always wanted.

"Where are my manners? I was having too much fun, and I forgot to introduce myself. My name is Katarina Kallberg, and I'm from Norway."

Upon hearing the words "Katarina" and "Norway," Tara's face paled.

"Are you getting sick again?" Katarina asked.

"No, no—I'm all right." Tara opened her purse and searched for a tissue, while trying to regain her composure.

So, this was Katarina! The woman who was in love with Max, according to the girl Sara. The sister of the murdered woman. Then Tara recognized her: Of course! This is the woman who was sitting in the Piazzetta next to Max and Raffi yesterday. Why, oh why, did she have to be so nice?

"My name is—Tamara, and I'm American. It's a pleasure to meet you. Have you been on vacation?" Tara asked, feeling ashamed about her deception. She felt even worse as she watched Katarina's eyes filling with tears.

"Well, I was on vacation on Capri to visit my sister, but—" Katarina hesitated, "well, I might as well say it—she was murdered."

"Oh, how horrible! I'm so sorry—" Tara squeezed Katarina's hand.

Katarina went on to confide in Tara what had happened and how she was forever indebted to the investigator who found the evidence to prove that it was murder and not suicide.

"So, who is this investigator?" Tara asked, feeling ashamed that she hadn't told Katarina that she was Max's ex-wife.

"Max De Angelis; he is originally from Capri but lives in San Francisco." Katarina's voice grew passionate as she continued: "He will be my hero forever."

"Thank God for this Max!" Tara said, sounding equally passionate.

"I'll tell you a secret," Katarina confided, "I fell in love with him."

"You did?" Tara couldn't help herself. She could hardly breathe. "And then?"

Katarina sighed deeply. "I fell in love with a divorced man who is still in love with his ex-wife."

"He is? I mean, uh—you believed him?"

"Yeh, unfortunately for me. I was very much in love—and I was hoping he was, too. But no—he didn't even try to have sex with me. I should have known from the very beginning—his voice and his face when he was talking about his ex-wife said it all. I guess I thought I could change that, but I learned I couldn't."

"Oh, I'm so sorry—" Tara's words didn't match her feelings; inwardly she was jubilant.

"It's OK—it wasn't meant to be. It was my fault, I guess. I was in a way looking for love in the wrong man. But, you know, he's not only handsome and smart—and sexy, he's also kind. I can't be blamed for trying, can I?"

Tara didn't blame her at all, not at all. She couldn't stop herself from digging for more information and risked another question. "A man like that—didn't he have other women?"

"It's possible. There was another woman he was seeing; I met her—once, a local girl, she was gorgeous."

Tara's heart sank.

Katarina continued, "I was jealous at the time, but I saw his face when he looked at her. He looked sheepish—not like a man in love. I had my hopes up and—well, I think he did like me."

Tara couldn't blame Max; Katarina was not only exceptionally beautiful, she was intelligent and delightful to be with—full of life.

"I am sorry—" Tara repeated.

"Oh, please, don't be. I'm usually not a person to force things; they will unfold as they are meant to be. Now I want to tell you a funny story, but I must be quick, as I think we have only ten minutes before we get to Rome."

Katarina was filled with amusement as she told Tara about her experience signing up for an Internet dating service. She said that the men had described themselves as princes, but proved to be toads when she met them; kissing them had been out of the question.

"Camilla, my sister, was very much against Internet dating, but in the end, it seems it was an excellent idea after all." Katarina lowered her voice to a whisper. "There was one exception to the toads."

Katarina told Tara her story. One man had stood out among her suitors, not by his looks, because he never submitted a photo, but by his fascinating emails. They started corresponding. After a while, it became clear that the mystery man knew her, but he refused to reveal his identity and insisted they learn about each other through correspondence before meeting. Katarina had been intrigued; she wondered who he could be.

After the man learned from watching the news channel in Norway that Katarina was suspected of murdering her sister, she received an e-mail from him saying he knew she could never have done it.

"Guess what?" Katarina said with a radiant smile. "The mystery man finally called me—yesterday."

"And who is he?" asked Tara

"His name is Bjørn."

The train pulled into Roma Termine and they got up from their seats to collect their belongings. Tara guessed Bjørn must be someone incredibly special, judging from Katarina's excitement.

"Can you believe we went to the same school and hung out together in our early teens? We were good friends, but we drifted apart. Then I met my future husband Petter, and we had our daughter Anna. Now and then I would read about Bjørn in the local paper; he is an athlete in Norway competing in sailing and cycling, but we haven't seen each other since high school."

Katarina went ahead of Tara down the train steps to the platform, so Tara could pass her their rolling bags.

"Last night, when Bjørn called me, he said that he always knew we were meant for each other."

The smile that lit up Katarina's face was so bright, there was not a doubt in Tara's mind about her feelings. "I'm happy for you," Tara said.

"And Bjørn said that he would never let me get away from him again!"

"And you won't," Tara said, hugging Katarina.

"Here is my card, please do keep in touch—of course, only if you feel like it. I have a feeling we were destined to meet and that we are soul sisters. One day you will visit me, either in Norway or on Capri. And good luck to you!" Katarina smiled as she gently touched Tara's belly.

Tara's hand closed tightly over the card. "I will, I promise."

They parted ways. Katarina headed for the connecting train to the Leonardo da Vinci airport. Tara walked over to the railroad ticket booth.

CHAPTER 64 - LOOK THE LIE IN THE EYE

"*H*a na' faccià conosciùt. (He looks familiar.)"
"*Si, ma chi è?* (Yes, but who is he?)"
"*Fors iss sap iucar a scopòn.* (Maybe he knows how to play cards.)"

Max did not know if he was awake or asleep—Were the voices of the three men speaking in local dialect coming from a dream? All he knew for sure was that the bed he was lying on felt awfully hard.

The first voice spoke again: "Look at what I found lying on the floor, a *curniciello*! I wonder if someone lost it?"

On hearing those words, Max opened his eyes and leaped to his feet. "It's mine!" he cried. His amulet must have slid from the altar to the floor, he thought. He had placed it at the feet of the statue of the Madonna and Child before falling asleep in the little church of the hermitage, utterly exhausted from his predawn hike up the mountainside.

"We were not going to steal it." The offended sounding voice belonged to an old man with a long white beard. Max realized he was the one who had spoken first while he was laying half-awake on the church bench. The old man was of medium height with an ample waist; he was bald, with pale blue eyes set in a round pinkish face. His clothes and shoes were typical of a workman—maybe a mason, Max thought.

"Here." The old man passed the chain with a horn made of red coral to Max.

"Thank you," Max mumbled, embarrassed that his outburst was interpreted as an accusation. How strange, he thought—for some mysterious reason, the *curniciello* seemed destined to be returned to him. He looped the chain around his neck.

"So, what are you doing here, anyway? Your own bed too comfortable for you? Or did your wife throw you out?"

This was the second man's voice; it belonged to a tall skinny man wearing an apron and a checkered shirt with rolled up sleeves, shorts, and track shoes with high white socks. He looked even older than the first man, with a mop of uncombed wild gray hair. His eyes were bright blue, set in a pale, angular face; his large smiling mouth was missing a few teeth.

Max ignored the teasing. "I came up for a cup of coffee," he joked.

"Ha ha, that's a good one," said the skinny man in the apron. "In that case, I'll go put on the *cuccumella* (espresso maker) and we'll meet on the terrace."

"That's Davide, he's a cook—no one better anywhere," the man with the white beard volunteered. "I'm Maestro Gianni, and this little devil is only known by his nickname Volpetto (little fox)." He pointed to the third man. "Our friend Beppe was supposed to be the fourth for our Friday card game, but he had to visit his mother who is 104 years old today. Beppe's mother still takes the stairs two at a time, can you believe it?"

"*Guagliò,*" Volpetto said (using the local expression for "young man"), "Do you know how to play *Scopone?*[19] We play for one euro each game. If you don't have any money, I'll lend you some—unless you insist on putting up your *curniciello.*"

Volpetto was younger than the others, suntanned with olive skin and brown eyes. He was wearing long slacks, a t-shirt, and track shoes. He looked familiar to Max.

"Of course, I play. Do you know any Caprese who don't?" Max grinned. "I'm Max," he added.

They walked out onto the small terrace past the refectory. Max marveled at the setting for their game of cards: on a mountain precipice that dropped straight down to the valley. The fog had evaporated; in front of him lay the splendor of Capri with the Faraglioni rocks and the shimmering azure sea all around. Under the shade of a pergola covered in wisteria vines, there was a long wooden table and two benches.

Max felt like a bird perched in a nest high above the world. He sighed with contentment and settled onto a bench after taking off his t-shirt to dry it in the sun, as did Volpetto, who showed off a leathery sun-bronzed chest and muscular arms.

The bearded Maestro Gianni placed a plastic cloth with a blue floral pattern on the table, and Volpetto brought out a bowl of sugar,

---

[19] Scopa is an Italian card game, and one of the two major national card games in Italy. The name is an Italian noun meaning "broom", since taking a scopa means "to sweep" all the cards from the table. Watching a game of scopa can be a highly entertaining activity, since games traditionally involve lively, colorful, and somewhat strong-worded banter in between hands.

spoons, and four cups, each a different color. Max was given a hand-painted blue and yellow ceramic cup; he turned it over to see the name of the artisan.

"Yes," said Volpetto, "it's Sergio Rubino. Impressed eh?" He laughed, delighted that Max had noticed.

Max was honored. The work of Sergio Rubino, the ceramic artist from Anacapri, was known all over the world.

Davide, the chef, carried out an old-fashioned Neapolitan flip coffee pot, the *cuccumella*. He flipped the pot, and they waited patiently while the hot water dripped through a dark, finely ground espresso roast.

Nobody talked while they savored the precious, strong coffee.

Maestro Gianni brought out the Scopone 40-card picture deck, a pencil, and paper for score keeping.

When Max said he knew the game, he wasn't exaggerating. His skills as a mathematician coupled with his extraordinary memory made him a formidable player. As a boy, he had honed his knowledge of the strategy of the game by playing with grownups. It didn't take him long to realize that these old boys were no pushovers. He and Davide teamed up against Maestro Gianni and Volpetto, who showed himself to be an old fox indeed. After a couple of hours with much banter and laughter and lots of name calling, the teams were even, and they called it quits.

"It's time for cooking," Davide said.

Max laughed, "Where?" he asked.

The old boys, it turned out, were members of a charitable group called *Amici di Cetrella* (Friends of Cetrella). The members were mostly from Anacapri; many were retired, and some of them, these old boys included, were part of a group restoring and taking care of a building in the Cetrella Valley that was once home to the British writer Compton Mackenzie. The Friends of Cetrella had also volunteered to restore an old storage house across from the hermitage. Every week, weather allowing, they came to work, cook, and eat lunch together.

Davide had the fire blazing within minutes in the wood-burning pizza oven in the kitchen of the old storage house. His hand-rolled mini pizzas, *le pizzette*, with delicious fresh tomato sauce and mozzarella cheese were placed on a long stake and stuck in the oven.

On the wood-burning stove, the pasta water came to a rapid boil while Davide stirred another pot with a sauce of chopped fresh vegetables, garlic, and herbs from his garden.

Max learned that Davide was originally from the Monte Fusco area on the mainland and had worked as a chef in several of the most renowned restaurants on the island. Maestro Gianni, who was an expert master mason and had built the pizza oven, opened a bottle of red wine made with grapes from his vines.

Meanwhile, Volpetto set the table, conveniently using paper cups and plates. Now Max recognized Volpetto. Before his retirement, he had been a taxi driver famous for having owned one of the most admired of the old antique cabriolet cars once used as taxis on Capri.

The four men sat down on benches at a long farm table in the storage house, and they ate and drank like kings.

"Would you like to try my *Finocchietto*?" Volpetto had brought four small glasses and a bottle with a green-colored liquid. "Made with fennel picked here, of course," he winked at Max. He must have guessed that it was Max who had left a bunch of fennel herbs on the bench outside the hermitage door.

"*Salute.*" They toasted. Max didn't think he had ever tasted a better fennel liqueur, except for his father's.

Maestro Gianni put his glass down. "So, what's up, Max? Tell us why we found you sleeping on a bench in the church this morning."

"Yeh, what's your story, Max?" asked Volpetto.

"My story is—ha, ha—" Max broke into a bitter laugh, "I'm the biggest fool in history."

"We are all fools at times," said Davide, as he untied his apron, folded it neatly, and put it in his rucksack.

Max gave them a condensed version of what had happened to his marriage while they cleared the table and washed the pots.

"Not only was I unfaithful, but I blamed my wife for ruining our marriage," said Max, concluding his story.

"You aren't the only fool to have tried that old trick," Volpetto chimed in.

"The problem is I didn't only lie to her, I lied to myself." Max's voice was quiet and sad. "I couldn't face myself for having ruined the most beautiful thing in my life. My whole life I have tried to be perfect and do the right thing, the moral thing."

"So many of us believe we are incapable of doing such damage to ourselves," Maestro Gianni said, "and we can't live with ourselves when we screw up. If we admit we have been lying to ourselves, it's as if the very ground we stand on crumbles away. We're afraid we might just disappear into the void if we admitted that we, knowingly and willingly, did something that had terrible consequences. That's like facing death itself, isn't it?"

Volpetto shivered at hearing the word death and crossed himself.

"Once a wise friend told me that if you base your life on a lie, your life force will become weak," Maestro Gianni said, placing his hands on Max's shoulders. "That's a serious matter."

"So, what must I do?" asked Max, the weight of Maestro Gianni's hands was heavy. He stood up and walked towards the pizza oven. The fire had died out and the embers glowed.

The three old men watched Max's slumped defeated back. They looked at each other and shrugged their shoulders, then held up their palms to the sky.

"So, it's hopeless for me, then?" Max turned around to face them; he looked ashen.

"Nah," said Maestro Gianni, "there is always hope, don't despair. Now I remember—my good friend once told me about a secret remedy."

"What is it? *Please tell me.*" The desperation in Max's voice was heart wrenching.

"It's quite simple, but you will need courage, and—" Maestro Gianni paused; his eyes were gleaming. "My friend said it's a three-step process."

Max tried to control his impatience. "So, are you going to tell me what it is or not?"

"Sure, sure, take it easy." Maestro Gianni stood up and moved to the head of the table. He placed his fists at his stout waist, with his wrinkled elbows sticking straight out, and stared into Max's eyes.

"First you need to look the lie squarely in the eye and acknowledge the existence of the lie. You created it, and now it exists, thanks to you. Imagine the lie being a snake, if you like, as my friend once suggested."

Max had no trouble imagining a snake after his recent encounter with *il bacchio,* the snake; he asked himself, was his lie just as real?

"Yeh, I got it; I can see that my lie is as real as a snake, and I created it, all right. What's next?"

"Now comes the second part. You have seen the snake, and you know it exists. Then the snake sneaks out of sight, and you don't know where it is; it continues with its life. It might even bite someone someday."

"So?"

Maestro Gianni continued, "And so, your lie takes on a life outside of your imagination, and you cannot control it anymore. You have to accept that you are responsible for the consequences of the lie since you yourself created it—"

Volpetto interrupted, "So that means, anything that happens because of a lie, you have to look squarely in the eye and take ownership of it?"

Maestro Gianni nodded. "Yes, and depending on the circumstances, that can be the hard part. Lucky is the one who ruins only his own life, my friend said."

"And the third part?" Max was glum; he remembered looking the snake in the eye, and he hadn't enjoyed it.

"My friend said the third and final part of the remedy was the simplest—but maybe the most difficult to do."

Maestro Gianni fell silent for a moment, while Max and the others waited in suspense. Then he spread his arms wide and said, "All that is left is for you to forgive yourself!"

CHAPTER 65 - COMING HOME

T he funicular was packed with excited weekend visitors chatting and looking out the panoramic windows; most of them were Neapolitans. Tara was squeezed into the last compartment, supporting her tired body by holding onto the handrail, as the little cable railway slowly and silently climbed the hill from Marina Grande to the town of Capri.

Tara had fallen in love with the island during her very first ride on the funicular. Somehow, on Capri, she felt secluded and protected amidst the grandeur of nature. The rocky cliffs of the island, with the shores and the sea all around, were like a mystical ring encircling her in a passionate embrace.

The ride took only a few minutes. She waited patiently for the crowds to disperse and was the last person to ascend the broad flight of stairs to the terrace outside the funicular station.

Tara took a deep breath. Every time she arrived at this spot, she stopped to marvel at the spectacular scenery. She had always loved that first magical moment whenever she returned to Capri. But this time something felt different. What was it? she asked herself. Then it hit her—she was *home*. How strange to have this feeling; she couldn't remember having ever felt quite like that before, not even in San Francisco when she and Max were still together.

Without thinking, Tara walked past the entrance to Bar Funicolare and around the corner to the little terrace where she found Raffi sitting at a table with his face bent over his iPad.

"Raffi, you don't know how glad I'm to see you!" she said.

Raffi sprang up from his chair. "Tara, you're back! I'm so happy to see you," he exclaimed with a delighted grin. "Where have you been?"

Tara placed her rolling bag against the wall and dropped down into a chair. "I wanted to travel to San Francisco, but I only got as far as Rome, before I decided to return," she said. "I'm exhausted. I desperately need a cup of tea and a bite to eat."

Raffi flagged down a waiter.

After finishing a pot of tisane, Tara pushed her half-eaten sandwich to the side and turned to face Raffi.

"I've been stupid," she said.

"I doubt you're ever stupid, Tara."

"Have you seen Max?" she asked. "Do you know where he is?"

The smile on Raffi's face vanished. "Yes, I saw him last night." His voice sounded sad. "He's staying at Hotel Gatto Bianco."

A feeling of guilt came over Tara; she hadn't been fair to Raffi. Had she used him? she asked herself. She knew that Raffi liked her, and she liked him very much, too—but as a friend. Now she wondered if Raffi had deeper feelings for her.

"Oh Raffi, you've always been there for me. You cannot imagine how much your support and friendship has meant to me." She touched his hand, silently hoping he would forgive her selfishness.

"Let's go, I will take you to Max."

Raffi managed a bittersweet smile as he swung his camera around his neck, packed his iPad in his backpack, and walked into the bar to pay the bill.

Tara was thankful that Raffi was the perfect gentleman. He insisted on rolling her bag, and even slung her not-so-light handbag over his shoulder. Arm in arm, they walked across the Piazzetta and down Via Vittorio Emanuele to Hotel Gatto Bianco, while Raffi made pleasant small talk. Good old faithful Raffi, Tara thought. She was immensely grateful to him, as she was too tired and too embarrassed at her selfishness to talk.

Renato was stroking Matisse's neck when Tara and Raffi walked into the reception.

"Nice to see you, Raffaele," Renato said. "What can I do for you?"

"Is Max De Angelis in? This is Signora Tara De Angelis; she is here to see him." Raffi hoped Renato would understand that she was Max's ex-wife.

"Of course, I understand." Renato eyed her rolling bag. "Signor Max De Angelis is staying with us, but he is out at the moment. Does the Signora wish to wait in the lobby or in the garden?"

Tara was utterly worn out from her day of travel to Rome and back. "Do you have any place where I could lie down for a bit?" she asked. "I'm not feeling very well, and I'm very tired."

Raffi became alarmed, suddenly aware that she didn't look quite like herself. He looked at Renato with raised eyebrows, "You don't suppose that—"

"Of course," Renato said, "If Signora De Angelis wishes to wait in Signor De Angelis's suite, that can be arranged."

CHAPTER 66 - FORGIVENESS

"Here, why don't you take this?" Max handed the bunch of fennel branches to Volpetto. "You make the best Finocchietto, why compete with perfection?"

Volpetto grinned, he was flattered. "Thanks, I accept, but only if you promise you will come back to play Scopone with us again."

Max promised.

Davide and Volpetto headed up to the summit of Monte Solaro to take the chairlift down to the town of Anacapri. Max and Maestro Gianni decided to walk down to town.

All that is left now is for you to forgive yourself—that was what Maestro Gianni had said, but Max was still confused.

"Tell me, Maestro Gianni, why can't I forgive myself?"

"My friend says it is because of the ego."

"But the ego isn't a bad thing, is it?"

"Not at all, we need the ego for all kinds of things to live in this world," Maestro Gianni explained, "but it is when you identify yourself with your ego that the trouble begins. Like when you confuse what you do for a living with who you are. For instance, if you as a soccer player win, you think you are a success, and if you as a soccer player lose, you think you are a failure. That kind of thinking is wrong thinking."

"I don't think I do that Maestro Gianni."

"OK, so let's have a conversation about it."

With his thick sturdy legs, Maestro Gianni treaded nimbly on the loose gravel of the steep downhill trail. He was so quick and so light on his feet, they barely touched the ground, and he had a technique of spreading out his arms to counterbalance his weight.

"First, Max, let me ask you this. Do you think you could forgive somebody who has lied to you?"

"I think so."

"Second, do you think that somebody could forgive you for lying to them?"

"I hope so." Max's voice was serious. He kept his eyes on the path; he had already skidded on the loose gravel a couple of times.

"Third, can you forgive yourself for willingly lying and screwing up your life?"

"It depends," Max answered.

"Depends on what?" Maestro Gianni asked Max. "What makes the third scenario different from the other two scenarios?"

Max tried to think of an answer, but he had difficulty concentrating; the magnificent birdsong from the nearby bird sanctuary was interfering with his thoughts.

"If I could forgive someone for lying, and someone could forgive me for lying, why can't I forgive myself?"

"Is it because you are holding yourself to a higher standard than everybody else?" Maestro Gianni asked.

"Yes, I guess I am. I feel I should know better."

Maestro Gianni pressed on relentlessly: "But the fact is, you did screw up, didn't you? And what you did had consequences."

"Yes, guilty as charged." Max felt terrible.

"So that means you are neither better—nor worse than anybody else. You made a mistake because it's human to make mistakes; in fact, that's how we learn. There is nothing unusual about it. Yes, you are unique, as is every one of us humans, but you are capable of all the same vices as everyone else, because we are all the same."

"What do you mean when you say, we are all the same, Maestro Gianni?"

"Ok, let's think about snow, shall we? It will do us good in this heat. Each snowflake is different from every other snowflake, but it's all snow, right? The snowflake can turn into ice, or steam, or a drop of water, and it will eventually become part of the ocean. It's the same with us humans, each one of us is unique, but we are all part of the sea of humanity. Every single one of us has the potential to screw up, and every one of us has the potential to forgive."

"Mm, I guess so," Max mumbled; he knew he had the potential for screwing up.

"The confusion starts when we start to identify with being special or better than others, or the opposite side of the coin—worthless or bad. When our pride and our attachment to results and material goods make us think we are a success, or when our fears, mistakes, and faults make us believe we are a failure, that is the ego trying to control our life. These are some of the ego traits that get in the way of living our lives to the fullest potential."

The descent ended at a flat paved footpath, Viale Axel Munthe. Max stopped outside a large gray building on his left with an inscription above the entrance: I.I.S.S. AXEL MUNTHE.

"Can you believe it? I'm returning to my old school, Maestro Gianni. I'm going to be the new mathematics teacher in the science department in just a few days. It's hard to believe. Between us, I admit I'm quite nervous. It's my first teaching job."

"Just be yourself, Max." Maestro Gianni shifted the focus back to their topic. Indeed, he kept his attention razor sharp, as sharp as when he played Scopone. "The fact is, you did lie, didn't you?"

"Yes, I did lie," Max said quietly, almost under his breath.

"So, we are right back at the beginning of our conversation. You asked why you can't forgive yourself. Here are some answers:

Your pride is stopping you from forgiving yourself because you cannot admit to yourself you are not better than anybody else.

Your fear of the consequences of admitting you lied is stopping you.

Your anger at yourself for screwing up is stopping you.

Take your pick Max: pride, fear, or anger—what is your preference?"

"You may be right, Maestro Gianni, maybe all of the above." Max's voice was barely audible.

"You see, Max, these traits, we all have them in our personality, every one of us. We have pride, anger, fear, jealousy, greed, revenge, guilt, shame and so on. These traits are not bad in themselves; it is only when we mistake these traits for being who we are that we ruin our life. We are, in truth, much, much more. We also have kindness, compassion, hope, and forgiveness—and most important, love in our hearts."

Maestro Gianni looked at Max to see if he understood what he had been saying before he continued. "When we recognize and accept these traits in ourselves, we begin to understand humanity, and then we can have compassion for all, even for ourselves, and indeed we can forgive."

Max didn't say anything; he was reflecting on what Maestro Gianni had said.

"The worst of it, Max, is that when you are not able to admit that you lied, you cannot begin to forgive yourself, as there is nothing to forgive, thereby you defeat yourself. By harboring the lie deep in your heart, you are never free, are you? Every year the burden of the lie becomes heavier and heavier to carry, even if you are unaware of it."

"Maestro Gianni stopped to wipe the sweat from his forehead with the sleeve of his shirt. "What do you say we get something cold to drink, Max?"

They stopped at a bar on the pedestrian street of Via Capodimonte and ordered two freshly squeezed lemonades at the counter.

"When you understand that your pride is preventing you from living life to its fullest and that it is preventing you from loving or being loved, then you will be able to forgive yourself. And then—only then—will you be able to ask forgiveness of the person you lied to."

Maestro Gianni and Max hugged each other, and the master mason pulled on a helmet and jumped on his dilapidated scooter parked by the gas station just past Piazzetta Vittoria in Anacapri.

Max had to admit it, Maestro Gianni's parting words rang true. He remembered every word that Maestro Gianni had uttered, and he felt lighter already, having finally admitted he lied.

Suddenly he remembered the dream of his mother, and the inscription on her tombstone: *Verità e Gratitudine* (Truth and Gratitude). So that was what his dear mother had wanted to remind him of; that he had forgotten to be truthful!

Max was waiting in line for the bus down to the town Capri, when his cell phone rang.

"Max, old rascal, where the hell are you? I've been trying to reach you."

Max was glad to hear Raffi's voice. He realized that his anger at Raffi had evaporated like the clouds.

"I'm at the bus stop in Anacapri. I was up on Monte Solaro; you know there's no cell coverage up there. I've been an idiot, Raffi. I need to buy a ticket to San Francisco to find Tara and be back here in a week's time to start work—"

Max was talking so fast, he had to take a breath of air before he continued. "Raffi— ahem—I am sorry about last night, I was an ass. You were right of course about Tara's right to choose—"

"Relax, Max! I've got something for you—a present, a very special present—"

"A present?" Max sighed. What the heck? was Raffi trying to make him feel like even more of a jerk?

"Yeah, I delivered the present to your hotel. It's waiting for you in your suite. You'd better go and claim it." Raffi laughed.

"And by the way, the present is perishable, so don't wait too long." Raffi was still laughing when he hung up.

CHAPTER 67 - HARVEST MOON

FRIDAY, SEPTEMBER 10

Max and Tara walked down the paved footpath of Via Krupp in the twilight. The sky and sea had merged into a brilliant cobalt blue, gradually darkening into shades of ultramarine. The dramatic path leading from the Gardens of Augustus to Marina Piccola had often been called a work of art. The eight hairpin bends carved into the rock harmonized perfectly with the cliff-face; each turn brought a different breathtaking view. Despite the many times Max had walked this path, today it seemed as if he was seeing everything for the first time.

Now and then Max glanced sideways at Tara. God, how beautiful she was! She looked the same as on the first day he met her, the day he fell in love with her. Well, almost. Now that he looked more closely, he wondered if she had gained a couple of pounds; it suited her, giving a rosy glow to her cheeks.

There was so much he wanted to ask her, and so much he wanted to tell her, but all that could wait. Everything that had happened in recent weeks now seemed of little importance. Only this time together right now mattered.

Max smiled to himself, recalling the unforgettable moment when he returned to the hotel after his adventure on Monte Solaro and found Raffi's "present." He searched for it in the suite's living room and then in his bedroom without finding anything. Then he went to look for it in the second bedroom. The sight of Tara laying on top of the bedcovers in a sweet summery dress, sound asleep, made his heart jump for joy.

He wrote her a note and placed it on the nightstand beside her bed:

My darling most precious treasure,
I am out buying a picnic to enjoy in Marina Piccola tonight,
if you are up for it.
Please rest in our suite. I will come for you around 7 o'clock.
Your Max

The sun had long since disappeared behind Monte Solaro when Max and Tara walked into the little square of Marina Piccola. From San Andrea, the fishermen's church in the square, a dozen or so stairs led down to two public beaches and several private beach establishments; the lidos.

The local fishermen who lived in Marina Piccola were few. They still practiced the ancient ways of their forefathers, pushing their small craft out to sea at four o'clock in the morning, and laboriously pulling them up on the pebbled beach of Marina di Mulo at the end of their day.

A couple of fishermen were sitting in front of *i munazzeri*, the storage rooms for their fishing equipment. Max knew them, they were brothers, Sergio and Aldo; their proud angular faces were marked by years of sun, sea, and salt.

"*Uè, guagliò, aro' vai?* (Hey kid, where are you going?)" Sergio winked at Max, while sliding his thumb down his cheek, the symbolic gesture for "that's a smart thing to do."

Max grinned; he knew what the fisherman was referring to. They both looked at Tara, and she smiled.

"*Fatti e' fatti tuoi. Piens a pescàr. Eh, quantì anni ci vogliò ppe sposàrt?* (Mind your own business. Concentrate on the fishing. How many years before you get married?)" Max joked. He knew that Sergio had been engaged to his beloved fiancée for more years than anybody could remember.

"*Vai a chillu pais, va.* (Get lost)." Sergio smiled as he raised his hand in greeting.

Max and Tara climbed up the stone stairs between the two small public beaches to reach a rocky promontory, a lido named Lo Scoglio delle Sirene (Rock of the Sirens). They were all alone. Having found a perfect spot for a picnic, Max opened the bag he was carrying and spread out a delectable feast on a paper tablecloth.

"You are wearing your coral amulet, the *curniciello*, again." Tara reached out to touch it. The sensation of the light pressure of the coral and two of her fingers against his chest gave him immense pleasure. How long had it been since he had felt her touch?

"I have always worn it—except on two occasions," he said. "First, the necklace broke and got lost in my near fatal fall, but it was found and returned to me. The second time, I offered it in a church, praying that you would come back to me. Miraculously, both you and the amulet have returned to me."

Max brought the *curniciello* to his lips, and then pointed to the rocky coastline beyond Marina di Mulo. "Remember when we met for the first time, over there on the small hidden beach among the boulders? We named it 'My Heart's Desire Beach.'"

Tara's blue eyes darkened as they filled with tears.

"Oh Tara, please don't cry!"

"The memory is too beautiful—"

"Look!" Max cried in excitement; he was pointing in the opposite direction, towards the far end of the bay of Marina Piccola.

An enormous saffron-colored moon appeared between two of the Faraglioni Rocks. Max and Tara sat side by side in awed silence as they watched the full harvest moon continue its ascent above the rocky icons, slowly changing from orange to brilliant white, transforming the sea into ripples of shimmering crystals.

They took their time savoring the delicacies Max had bought. Max drank the red wine and Tara chose mineral water. Laying on their backs, they watched the bright stars and listened to the gentle lapping of the waves.

"Tara, will you forgive me?" Max asked in a muffled voice, breaking the silence. "I've been a fool. I lied to you. Please believe me when I tell you that I'll never lie to you again—and I'll never be unfaithful again."

Max didn't look at Tara, fixing his eyes instead on the bright star of Venus. He swallowed hard before continuing.

"I understand how difficult it must have been to live with me. I've changed Tara—I've grown. From here on, I'll do whatever is necessary for us to be happy together." Max sat up, looking expectantly down at Tara before he summoned all his courage.

"I want you to think about this—and take all the time you need—to decide whether—you want to—Tara, will you marry me—again?"

Tara remained motionless on her back, gazing up at the stars; her skin was luminous in the moonlight. Max wasn't sure that she had heard his words.

"Before you answer, there is something you need to know," Max continued.

Tara sat up.

"I've accepted a job here on Capri teaching mathematics; the offer is initially for six months, but after that, I will go and live with you anywhere in the world you like. It is up to you, you decide."

Tara tilted her head back, still gazing at the sky, as if searching for the right words in the stars. "I've forgiven you—it took me a long time—it wasn't until I was in India, and—well—I realized I had been stupid. I'm sorry, too, I made mistakes." She looked at Max. "And—there is something I need to tell you as well."

Max's face turned to stone. Did she love someone else?

"I'm expecting a baby, Max—I'm pregnant."

Max was astonished. A baby? So, there was another man after all. He needed to think. Why was Tara here? Why was she telling him this?

Tara watched the changing emotions on Max's face; it seemed ages before he responded.

"Tara, I'm happy for you. If you love the father of the baby, I can live with that. If you don't love anyone else, then—maybe you can love me again—someday. I will love and raise your child as my own—that is—if you will have me."

"You silly idiot!" Tara cried.

Max looked away. "I understand," he muttered.

"No, no, you understand nothing!" Her voice was jubilant. "It's your child I'm expecting!"

His child? Max was confused. How? Then he remembered the passionate night in front of his fireplace in San Francisco, the night she dropped off their cat Principessa before leaving for India. A light flared up inside his heart, a light so warm and bright it spread across his face in a brilliant smile.

"I love you, my wonderful idiot," Tara said, as tears of happiness filled her eyes. "I have always loved you—and only you. What do you think, shall we raise our child here on Capri? I can do my book cover designs anywhere. Luckily, I have a little money saved up, and I want to teach yoga as well. I have found a perfect place to fix up as a small yoga studio. We will have to bring Principessa to Capri, of course. Shall we call Betty-Anne and tell her?"

Max got up on his knees and fished out a small velvet box from the zippered pocket of his jeans. A picnic wasn't the only thing he had planned for that afternoon. He opened the box, pulled out a ring, and threaded it onto Tara's finger.

When she brought her hand up to her shining eyes, the sapphire ring sparkled in the moonlight.

"Will you—"

Max didn't finish his question before Tara's lips were on his.

EPILOGUE - SIMPLICITY

WEDNESDAY SEPTEMBER 15

A young American couple, Susan and John, are on their honeymoon. They are sitting on the terrace of La Tortuga, a snack bar overlooking the entrance to the Blue Grotto. On the table are two plates of Insalata Caprese; fresh mozzarella di bufala slices cover big crunchy red and green-veined tomatoes topped with fragrant leaves of locally grown basil. Cold pressed olive oil from Massa di Lubrense is drizzled on top. A bottle of Falanghina white wine is in an ice bucket.

John pushes his sunglasses onto the top of his head and lifts his wine glass: "Here's looking at you kid, and what great looking it is!"

Susan raises her wine glass to toast John's. "Not bad looking yourself. Here's to us!"

The couple is wearing white and beige linen, Capri style, just bought in the local shops. Susan is wearing handmade Capri sandals with glittering stones, and John is wearing blue suede loafers. Both have Borsalino Panama hats and black sunglasses. On an extra chair, several shopping bags are piled up.

Susan lifts her wrist to admire her new bejeweled Capri watch.

"Susan, my dearest," John says, "if you hadn't insisted on doing all that shopping on the way to the Blue Grotto, we might have managed to see the famous grotto before it closed. We just missed it; too bad it's our last day on Capri."

"You're right, darling," Susan replies, peering over her sunglasses at John, her voice as sweet as honey, "but this island, my handsome husband, is divine. You couldn't have picked a better place for our honeymoon than Hotel Caesar Augustus. This is the best trip of my life. Now we have an excellent reason to return—to see the Blue Grotto."

The waiter expertly navigates around the chair loaded with packages; the narrow terrace ledge doesn't leave much room for passing. He lifts the bottle out of the bucket and pours a small amount of the chilled wine into their glasses. "Is everything OK?" he asks.

The waiter, Mario, is also the proprietor; he is middle-aged, tall, thin, and still handsome. His large brown eyes have kept their warm sparkle; his hospitality is legendary. Mario's Capri ancestry goes back hundreds of years. His father Gabriele, together with his partner nicknamed Riccio, started the restaurant and bathing establishment once called 'Add'o Riccio e Gabriele', just a stone's throw away from La Tortuga. It has new ownership and is now named 'Il Riccio.'

"Yes, everything is just perfect, thank you," John answers. "Out of curiosity, when I was preparing our trip here, I read in the newspaper that there was a mysterious death under investigation on the island. Did they find out if it was a murder?"

"Ah, yes," says Mario, raising his forehead. "That case has been closed."

"And what was the verdict? Was it murder, suicide, or an accident?" John asks.

Mario's mouth opens in a wide grin and there's a glint of mischief in his eyes as he says, "All three."

John stares in disbelief at Mario.

"It's true, it all happened. A murder, an accident, and a suicide— all at the same location, all within a month this summer." Mario throws his hands in the air.

"Whoa!" says John, "unbelievable things happen on this island." Mario only smiles and nods.

"What is that activity down at the entrance to the Blue Grotto?" Susan asks, peering over the railing. "We were told the grotto is closed now."

"Well, there is a wedding today—inside the Blue Grotto, and yes, it is past the usual opening hours."

"You've got to be kidding, a wedding in the grotto?" John sounds skeptical.

"I'm not kidding you." Looking at John and Susan's doubtful faces, Mario's grin grows wider. "You don't believe me? Yeah, well, trust me —everything is possible here on Capri." Mario laughs.

"Ah, here they come," Mario says, as he leans over the railing.

A tiny rowboat comes into view outside the entrance to the Blue Grotto. A couple stands up in the boat and embraces in a passionate kiss. The boat rocks precariously from side to side. The handsome bronzed barcaiolo stops rowing and starts clapping. One by one, six more little rowboats, each with its boatman and three or four people inside, emerge from the narrow grotto opening and encircle the first boat. The barcaioli break into a Neapolitan song. The groom is wearing black shorts and a white shirt with the sleeves rolled up to his biceps. The bride is wearing a long white fishnet dress over a strapless white bathing suit. White camellias crown her long blond hair.

Mario sees the couple's bare feet rubbing against each other in the bottom of the boat, and his eyes get misty.

"I guess everything is possible on Capri," Susan says as she turns to Mario. "What is the name of the song they're singing?"

"Semplicità," Mario smiles, "it simply means—simplicity. It is about love—or as we say here on Capri—*ammore.*"

414

O sole t'ha pittato sti capille,
'o cielo ha ricaato st'uocchie belle.
Quanno mme guarde tu lùceno 'e stelle
e 'a primmavera ride attuorno a me.
Semplicitá
tu tiene dint''o core.
e a 'o munno, nu tesoro,
cchiù bello nun ce sta . . .
Vicino a te,
mme scordo 'e tutt''e ppene
e cchiù te voglio bene
pe' 'sta semplicitá.
I' campo sulamente pe' st'ammore,
ca fa felice 'o core
e cchiù mm'attacca a te.
No, nun ce sta
n'ammore cchiù 'nnucente
cchiù semplice cchiù ardente:
Tu si' 'a semplicitá.
Bona e sincera comm'a mamma mia,
tu si' ll'ammore ca nun more maje.
Si pure tu mme dice na buscía
è ingenua e santa comm''a veritá.
I' campo sulamente pe' st'ammore.
Ca fa felice 'o core
e cchiù mm'attacca a te.
No, nun ce sta
n'ammore cchiù 'nnucente,
cchiù semplice, cchiù ardente:
Tu si' 'a semplicitá.

Murolo—Mazzocco

THE END

CPSIA information can be obtained
at www.ICGtesting.com
Printed in the USA
FSHW012105280620
71641FS